INFLAMED BY AN INCUBUS
ETERNAL MATES BOOK 19

FELICITY HEATON

THE ETERNAL MATES SERIES

Discover more available paranormal romance books at:
http://www.felicityheaton.com

Or sign up to my mailing list to receive a FREE vampire romance ebook, learn about new titles, be eligible for special subscriber-only giveaways, and read exclusive content including short stories:
http://ml.felicityheaton.com/mailinglist

PROLOGUE

Aderyn grunted as she hauled Fenix into a deep, dank area that came and went, flowing in and out of focus as he struggled to remain awake. Her fear seeped into him through their bond, a tangible thing that drove him to reassure her, to steal that emotion away by somehow healing the gaping hole in his side that was leaking blood.

Probably leaving a trail of it for someone to follow.

His beautiful mate adjusted her grip on his shoulders, fisting the black leather jerkin he wore, her claws piercing the material. "Stay with me, Fenix."

She sounded desperate, her usually light voice strained with fatigue and fear, and he reached for the connection that linked them, needing to soothe her.

"That trick is not going to work this time." She huffed and grunted as she dragged him into a large cavern and paused to look around. He stared up at her and wanted to curse when she kept wavering in and out of focus, a blur of spun gold and violet one moment and clear the next. She glanced down at him, worry in her pale eyes that almost matched the colour of her hair as it swayed away from her purple leather corset. "This will do."

She eased him down onto his back and he grimaced as his side blazed. He needed to get a look at the wound because it felt as if someone had punched a hole clean through him. The surrounding area felt cold, the chilly air in the cavern sucking the heat from the blood that continued to pump from him. He was losing too much.

Aderyn eased to her knees beside him and looked him over, the worry in her golden eyes growing as her fine eyebrows furrowed. Those eyes darted to meet his. "We need to help this close."

Fenix swallowed hard and shook his head, because if she did what he thought she was going to do, then he would pass out and he needed to remain awake. He needed to be here for her, in case the mage came after them again.

"Should not... have... killed her." Every word was a struggle as he pushed them from his lips and he hated the way her expression shifted, her emotions changing with it.

He didn't want to hurt her, but it had been a mistake to kill the wife of the mage, a female Aderyn had befriended and believed able to help her find a way to reopen the gateway between this world and the one of her phoenix kin—a portal that had been sealed shut for centuries. He could understand the betrayal had wounded her and part of him couldn't blame her for how she had reacted. He had felt how crushed she had been when they had discovered the female had wanted to lure Aderyn into a trap, gifting her husband with the power contained in Aderyn's phoenix blood.

But killing her hadn't been the answer.

The mage had come after them because of what Aderyn had done.

Fenix gazed up at her, seeing how much she still hurt because of the betrayal, that pain hidden beneath the worry she felt for him. He cursed the mage's wife, the less reasonable part of him—the part ruled by his instincts as her fated mate—wishing he had been the one to make her pay for how she had treated Aderyn.

His kind, beautiful Aderyn.

If his female had one flaw, it was that she always saw the good in people and never the bad.

He supposed his flaw was that he too often saw the bad in people and not the good.

The corners of his lips twitched at that.

Fate truly had made them for each other.

Aderyn leaned over him and claimed his lips, tearing a low groan from him as hunger surged and he felt her strength pouring into him. He greedily devoured what she offered to him, savouring her kiss as he fed upon it, part of him trying to hold back his own needs so he didn't hurt her while the rest of him craved more, demanded he take everything from her. She tasted of heat and spice, a hint of smoke and love. He wanted her to break this kiss while at the same time he never wanted it to end.

A warm haze rolled through him, fogging his mind as his incubus nature rose to the fore and attempted to steal control. He relished the feel of her lips upon his and how strong she was—strong enough to withstand him even when he was starved, maddened by a need to feed. A weaker female would have been killed by him in the throes of his hunger, when he was mindless and vicious in his pursuit of the pleasure that would feed him. Not his Aderyn.

His mate had brought him back from the brink more than once, feeding him well enough to leave him sated for weeks, surrendering herself to him and giving him more than sustenance. She gave him pleasure too. Something he had never truly felt with anyone other than her.

She drew back and feathered her fingers down his cheek, concern shimmering in her eyes as they shone with flecks of amber fire and her brow furrowed. He mourned the loss of the feel of her touch as she sat back and glanced down at his side, her expression growing sombre.

"I am sorry." She gave him that look, the one that said this was killing her but she was going to do it anyway, was going to go against his wishes and deal with the wound. "I cannot let you bleed out."

Was it that bad?

He moaned and grimaced, his lips pulling taut as he tried to sit up and get a look at the wound the mage had dealt him when he had struck him with a glowing orb of blue magic that had poured lightning through Fenix's veins. Pain blazed through him, stole his breath and ripped an agonised bellow from him that echoed around the cavern as he sank back against the damp stone ground. He struggled for air, his heart labouring as he fought to remain conscious.

Aderyn pressed her right hand to his shoulder and leaned over him, and he had the feeling she was doing it to keep him in place. She smiled softly.

"Look at me, Fenix."

He shifted his gaze to lock with hers, cursed her in his mind when he saw the apology in her pale golden eyes and knew in his heart it wasn't only because she was about to hurt him.

"Do not," he croaked, desperation flooding him, making him restless as a need to stop her from doing something so reckless and dangerous seized him.

Her smile wobbled.

Heat blazed across his side, the firelight chasing over the sculpted planes of her face as she gazed down at him, as tears lined her eyelashes.

Fenix tipped his head back and screamed as the scent of burning flesh reached his nostrils, choking him. Every inch of him was on fire, on the verge of turning to ashes.

Darkness rolled up on him and he fought it, desperately clung to consciousness, aware that if he passed out then no one would be here to stop Aderyn from doing something foolish.

But he wasn't strong enough to hold back the rising inky tide and it swallowed him.

The sound of water dripping in the distance roused him from the dark embrace of sleep.

Fenix groaned as awareness slowly returned, his senses gradually coming back online. His side throbbed at the same tempo as his heartbeat and he swallowed thickly, his mouth as dry as ash.

"Aderyn?" he husked, willing her to respond as the haze of pain and sleep cleared from his mind and he remembered what had happened.

Only the plip-plip-plip of water answered him.

He gritted his teeth and rolled to his right, away from his injured side, and opened his eyes. Everything was blurred. He rubbed at his eyes, clearing the salty grit from them, and tried again. A cave greeted him. Dark. Damp.

Empty, save for him.

"Aderyn?" He tried again, louder this time, hoping she was somewhere nearby and would hear him.

Only he couldn't sense her.

His connection to her was weak, like a fragile strand of spider silk that could snap with the gentlest of touches.

Fenix got onto his knees, grimacing as small chips of basalt bit into them through his black leathers and jabbed his palms. He scanned the cavern again, aching to see Aderyn, to know that she was safe and hadn't done something reckless.

Even when he knew in his heart that she had.

She had gone after the mage, still believed he knew the way to open the gateway, that he was the key to succeeding where she had failed so many times before.

He needed to get to her.

He needed to stop her before it was too late.

He pressed his hand to his left side, the hole in his black jerkin so large that he could fit his entire hand in it. The skin beneath his palm was puckered and sore, tender to the touch, but it was healed.

She had saved him.

Now he would save her.

His beautiful mate was headstrong and obsessed, driven by her desire to reunite with her people, and while he couldn't understand that, he could understand the need that blazed within him—a desire to reunite with her.

He pushed onto his feet, collapsed back to his knees as his legs gave out, and then tried again, refusing to give up. He was healed and that meant he was moving, going after his female. There was no way in this world or the mortal one that he was going to let her face the mage alone.

Drystan would kill her.

Or worse.

He would use her as a source of power, slowly destroying her by stealing her blood to fuel his magic and his immortality.

Fenix couldn't let that happen.

He made it onto his feet and turned slowly, not trusting his legs. His senses reached out around him but he still felt nothing—no trace of Aderyn—so he focused on himself instead, summoning his strength.

And teleported.

His knees buckled as his boots hit the uneven black ground and his head spun as he tried to look around him, the strange dead garden of the obsidian stone house wobbling in and out of focus.

A scream blasted through the air.

His heart squeezed.

"Aderyn."

His head whipped to his left, towards the small two-storey house and he teleported inside, stumbled and slammed into a wall. The scent of sulphur and smoke hit him, laced with the tinny smell of magic, and he pushed off, staggering along a wide hallway towards his mate. He could feel her there, ahead of him somewhere. He clenched his jaw as his head turned again, gripped his side and pushed onwards, refusing to let the weakness invading him stop him from reaching her.

His mate needed him.

Another scream cut him to his soul.

"Aderyn!" he bellowed and teleported again, grimaced as he landed on his hands and knees this time and his vision tunnelled.

He was pushing his luck.

He sucked down a breath.

Froze as the scent of blood hit him.

"Aderyn," he whispered and lifted his head, wanted to roar in fury as he spotted her.

The white-haired mage held her by her throat, colourful glyphs swirling around his hand and her head as she struggled against him, her legs flailing a few feet off the ground. Her boots caught the flowing hem of the black robes the mage wore, each frantic kick knocking the material away from his leathers.

Panic seized Fenix's lungs as he sensed her weakening. His gaze darted over her and stopped when he found the cut on her neck.

Crimson dripped from it, but rather than flowing down her chest to seep into her violet leather corset, those droplets rose into the air, slowly lifting upwards until they reached a point just above her head, where they gathered into a rippling sphere.

"Let her go." Fenix pushed onto his feet and grimaced as his right leg gave out and he staggered sideways. He grunted as he hit a heavy wooden bench table and sagged against it. His side blazed as the mage turned cold red eyes on him.

Malice filled them, fury so dark and deep that Fenix swore he could feel the male's rage.

Drystan slid Aderyn a look.

She screamed, throwing her head back as her body contorted, as another cut appeared on her chest and began to spill more crimson.

"No." Fenix lunged for her, desperate now. "Let her go. She—"

"She killed my wife," Drystan snarled, his face blackening as he angled it towards Fenix again. "And now she wishes to kill me."

Fenix shook his head. "She only wants to open the gateway."

The mage spat, "Lies. She wants me dead. All her kind do. I lived a peaceful life. I had all I needed... meant to live with my mortal wife for the rest of our days and then pass on as she did."

His face twisted in vicious lines as he cast a black look at Aderyn where she struggled in his grip, her movements weaker now.

"And she took that life from me."

Fenix gritted his teeth, anger surging through him too now. "Your wife was luring her into a trap. She meant to gift you with Aderyn's blood to make you live longer!"

"I will not hear your lies. My sweet Cyra wanted to do no such thing. She was happy as we were."

Fenix didn't think she had been. Drystan's *sweet Cyra* had spoken of immortality, had seemed desperate and wild when Aderyn had realised what she had intended to do to her and had turned on her.

"Cyra wanted her blood. She wanted to be immortal and she thought you could make it happen." Fenix growled those words, feeling as desperate and wild as Cyra had been as he looked at Aderyn and saw her fading. She was losing too much blood. If the mage stole much more of it, she wouldn't be able to resurrect. "Let her go."

Drystan opened his hand and dropped her.

She hit the ground hard, slumped onto her side and didn't move. Fenix hurried to her, his heart lodged in his throat as his senses locked onto her. She had to be all right. He couldn't live without her. Didn't want to.

He sank to his knees beside her and pulled her onto her back, so she was resting with her head on his thighs. "Wake up, Aderyn."

The mage stared down at them and Fenix struggled to keep his focus on her as her eyelids fluttered. Her pale golden eyes opened, a glassy quality to them that he didn't like as she struggled to lift them to meet his. He stroked her cheek, wishing he could give her strength as she could give it to him. If he could, he would drain himself to the brink of death to save her from it.

His eyes misted as he gazed down at her, as he fought to believe that she would make it through this death and that the mage hadn't taken too much precious blood from her. Her power was in that blood and if the mage had stolen too much of it and she died—

"She will die," Drystan said. "There is no way of stopping that now."

"Shut up." Fenix kept his focus on his mate. "Come on now, sweetheart. Do not do this to me."

Her eyes slipped shut and his chest constricted.

But then they fluttered open again.

"I loved as deeply as you do, and that love was ripped from me." The mage came to loom over him and Fenix looked up at him, that tight feeling growing in his chest again as he saw the darkness in the male's red eyes.

The need for revenge.

Fenix shook his head, silently imploring the male to leave her alone, to leave them both alone.

"I will ensure she does not come after you again. Please. Let her live." Fenix's brow furrowed as he gathered Aderyn closer and crossed his arms over her chest in a protective gesture that he knew was futile. If the mage wanted to get to her, he would. Fenix wasn't strong enough to stop him.

"Oh, she will live. As will you." The white-haired male raised his hand and closed his eyes, muttered words in a foreign tongue that had the hairs on Fenix's nape rising and charged the air around him.

Tiny sparks of electricity skittered over his arms and he shook his head as Aderyn moaned and tried to curl up into a ball.

The mage crouched and reached for her.

Fenix batted his hand away and glared at him.

Locked up tight as the male's crimson eyes collided with his.

Fenix unleashed a frustrated snarl when he tried to move and found he couldn't. Damn this mage. He tried to yell at the male, to make him leave her alone, but his mouth wouldn't cooperate.

All he could do was watch as the mage pressed his palm to her chest and continued to mutter something over and over again.

The mage's red gaze lifted to meet his.

Blazed like fire as the static charge in the air grew stronger.

Aderyn disappeared.

The mage rose to stand before Fenix, his gaze never straying from him, burning like an inferno but as cold as ice.

"I condemn you both. Her to die and forget you if she ever recalls her love for you. You to forever chase her ghost, desperate to make her love you again."

Drystan turned his back on him and strode away. He disappeared before he reached the door of the room, but his words lingered in the icy air.

"Enjoy your eternity."

CHAPTER 1

EIGHT DEATHS LATER

It had been that dream again. Fire. Shadowy figures. The feeling that she was burning up and about to explode into flames.

Evelyn tried to shake it off as she sipped water from her violet bottle, each cool drop of it quenching her thirst and feeling as if it was lowering her temperature. She nodded to a few of the men and women she passed in the bright corridor on the third floor of the sprawling building in the heart of London, not stopping to talk to the ones she had worked with in the past.

She was on a mission.

Her black T-shirt stuck to her back as she hurried towards her destination and she grimaced as she tugged at it. Maybe she should have let herself cool down after her training session and the shower that had followed it before pulling all her clothes on, but she had overheard one of the other women in the changing room mention that the alpha team was finally back from their latest trip to Hell.

Evelyn hadn't seen Archer in close to six months, not since she had been forced to rest up following the incident in the Fifth Realm of the demons. The doctors had refused to sign her off for duty, had kept her locked inside headquarters, stopping her from heading into Hell with one of the teams working there to chart the realm. She had tried petitioning the higher-ups but had met with the same result.

Boring rest.

She wasn't even supposed to be training, but Rob, the man in charge of the gym and practice rooms, was sweet on her and had turned a blind eye.

For the first time in weeks, the cream corridors didn't look dreary and dull, and she wasn't desperate to get out on patrol.

Well, maybe she was a little desperate.

Might be thinking up ways to bend her partner around her little finger and make him agree to take her out. No one would argue with her heading out if her partner was with her. Surely?

Evelyn reached the end of the corridor and glanced at the sign above the twin doors. The Central Archive. He was bound to be here. Her partner was nothing if not predictable. She pulled the door on the left open and smiled as she spotted him sitting at one of the computers spaced along the double row of desks that ran down the centre of the room, his back to the wall of black cases that contained the servers. The screen reflected off his black-rimmed glasses as he leaned on his elbow, his chin propped up on his palm as he worked the mouse with his other hand.

"Couldn't have guessed I would find you here." She let the door swing close behind her and ignored the looks the other hunters in the room gave her, ones that told her to be quiet. It wasn't a library. She was allowed to speak here.

Archer glanced up from the screen, his dark eyes dropping to it again before he lifted them once more and sat up this time. He rubbed his left shoulder through his tight black Henley, his lips quirking towards that side as he massaged it, and then sank against the back of the chair and pushed his glasses up his nose with his index finger.

He pulled off the handsome geek look, had half the women in HQ panting after him and envious of her for being assigned to him as his partner. She'd had more than one run-in with a jealous woman in her time here, something that wasn't helped by how close she was to Archer. There had been a few times when she had thought about them romantically, but she had never acted on it. It wasn't that the timing had never been right. It was just a feeling she had that they weren't right for each other and making the shift from partners to lovers would only ruin this good thing they had going on.

Archer was absolutely her only friend in Archangel, had had her back more times than she could count and was the reason she was here working for them, had joined their mission to protect people from dangerous non-humans.

Because he had saved her from one of them.

She didn't want to mess up their friendship.

So she had never acted on the occasional spark of desire she felt for him.

Archer ran a hand over his dark brown hair, mussing the longer lengths, and stretched, clasping his hands together as he raised his arms above his head. When he was done, he sank deeper into the chair and placed both hands behind his head, supporting it as he looked at her and drawing the gazes of the other women in the archive.

Those women would probably claw her eyes out if they knew she had seen him naked once, had witnessed him in all his glory, could have drunk her fill of his honed muscles and maybe done more than that if she had accepted his offer to skinny-dip in the lake with him.

The thought of swimming in pitch-black water under a moonless sky and not knowing what else was in there with her had been enough to keep her on the shore.

Archer raked his dark eyes over her, a flicker of a frown dancing on his brow before he relaxed again. "How are you doing? Cleared for action?"

Evelyn touched her side through her black T-shirt and grimaced. "Still a little sore. I'm not sure why I'm taking so long to heal. It's not like me."

The doctors had always been fascinated by how quickly she could heal any wound she picked up in the field, and sometimes they had looks in their eyes that unnerved her and made her wary of them. The sort of looks they gave the guests held in the pens downstairs.

So she was worried that it was taking her months to heal, even when the doctors she had seen at her regular check-ups had assured her that it was normal to take a long time to fully recover from a wound like this. The wound was in a spot that was easily aggravated by her moving and there had been extensive tissue damage. Enough that the surgeons who had patched her up had told her countless times she was lucky to be alive.

She wouldn't have been if not for Archer.

Archer sat up and brushed her hand away from her right side, lifted her T-shirt and didn't hesitate to sweep his fingers over the still-pink scar on her skin just above the waist of her trousers. That earned him a few gasps from their audience and her a few death looks.

It wasn't her fault that Archer didn't operate in the same way most men did. He had never been backwards about doing this sort of thing. It didn't even seem to register that it wasn't the done thing for a man to just bare a woman's skin and touch her. Sometimes, she had the feeling he was nothing like other men.

His fingers were warm against her flesh and seemed to grow hotter as they paused over the scar.

"You need at least a few more days rest. Maybe a couple of weeks. This should be healed by now." His hand dropped from her side and he sat back in his chair again and tossed her an unimpressed look. "You've been ignoring the docs again when they tell you to relax and take it easy, haven't you?"

11

She tensed.

Rumbled.

Archer had caught her fair and square, and the edge his dark eyes gained said he wasn't happy about it. He sighed.

"It doesn't take a genius to see you've been hitting the gym, Evelyn. Water bottle. Damp T-shirt. Flushed skin. You're only hindering your recovery." He glanced at the mouse and looked as if he wanted to take hold of it and continue his work, a few tense seconds passing before he looked back at her. "I'm worried you're pushing yourself too hard. Take the time to heal."

"It's been months already," she snapped, the frustration of being stuck inside HQ for all that time getting to her. She didn't like being short with Archer, but the inaction grated on her, had her going out of her mind. "I'm ready to get back out there."

"It wouldn't have been months if you had followed doctors' orders and rested until you had completely recovered." Archer looked at the screen and grabbed the mouse, scrolled down a little.

"I have been resting!" She glared at him, her hackles rising as she tugged her T-shirt down to cover the scar. "It was just a little gym time. I didn't want to get out of shape."

He lifted his gaze back to her.

There was an accusation in that look—a look that set her on edge and had her easing back a little.

"What?" she murmured, a feeling that he knew more than he was letting on rolling through her.

Archer shifted his gaze back to the screen. "Marty snitched on you."

"Son of a bitch!" she barked and then scowled at the other occupants of the room when they all glared at her.

She turned her frown on Archer.

He smiled easily. "Do you really think I don't have spies everywhere?"

Evelyn huffed, planted her backside against the edge of the desk beside him and pouted at the servers. "I should've known he would tell on me. Fine, I did go out. I was going crazy being stuck inside and I needed some air. Marty swore he wouldn't tell anyone if I went on one patrol with him."

Archer rapped a knuckle against the screen, his gaze fixed on her face. "You knew he would have to file a report the moment you got into it with that vampire."

"The vampire had it coming." She pulled a face at him, could practically see her shot at getting out of this damned building slipping through her grasp as Archer's unimpressed look shifted towards anger.

"And some might say you had it coming too." He jerked his head towards her side, his eyes darkening. "You opened it up pretty good according to Marty."

Evelyn folded her arms across her chest and made a mental note to make Marty pay for including everything in his damned report. Marty knew how protective Archer was of her and that he would find that report and come down hard on her about this. It was the reason she had wanted to keep it secret from him.

But apparently Archer was right and nothing got past him.

"If Marty had been more help, maybe I wouldn't have reopened the wound." Did she look as pouty as she sounded? She mentally waved goodbye to all thoughts of hitting the streets, her hope dying a swift death as Archer gave her that look.

The one that said she wasn't going to be bending him around her little finger this time.

He patted the seat beside him. "Come do some research with me."

Evelyn let her head fall back on an exasperated groan. "Not research. Anything but research!"

She let her head fall forwards again and slumped over, her arms dropping to dangle between her thighs and her will to live bleeding from her as she thought about sitting in front of a computer screen, poring over boring documents and sifting through reports. She curled her lip and looked over her shoulder at his screen.

It was filled with a long list of reports.

"Ugh. No thanks. What are you researching anyway?" She scanned the titles of the reports, trying to figure it out before he could answer.

"Witches. Magic." He casually pushed his glasses up with his index finger as his dark gaze drifted over the screen.

The same thing he was always researching.

Evelyn sighed and nudged his shoulder. "Come on patrol. Getting some fresh air and stretching your legs will be good for you. You'll only get a flat butt if you insist on sitting around all the time."

He scowled at her, the black slashes of his eyebrows meeting hard. "I have to remind you I only just got back from Hell? I've not been sitting on my backside. You have."

She grumbled about that.

Archer shook his head and went back to his reports. "Not going to happen. You need to rest."

"No." She snatched the mouse from him and refused to give it back even when he levelled a black look on her. She smiled sweetly. "I haven't seen you in forever. I thought maybe we could catch up while we patrolled."

His dark eyes narrowed, his broad mouth flattening as the corners turned downwards. She tensed as seconds trickled past, the way he scrutinised her making her painfully aware of him and that he was on to her.

He huffed, gripped her hand and pulled the mouse free of it. "You just want to question me."

He glared at the computer screen.

"You don't believe me."

Evelyn grimaced and pressed a hand to her side, feeling awful as it burned and she saw the anger in Archer's eyes, together with hurt. The wound blazed as hotly as it had that day as she thought about what had happened in that dreadful demon castle, her awareness of the other occupants of the archive room fading away as she stared at Archer.

"It just seems so…" Her brow furrowed as she replayed everything and her voice dropped to a whisper. "I swore I was dead."

"You would have been if it hadn't been for me." Archer positively growled those words, anger rolling off him as his handsome features pinched tightly. "I saved your life."

"I know that." She reached for him and flinched when he leaned away and glared at her, stopping her from touching his arm. She sighed, eased back again, and looked down at her hands as she twisted them in front of her hips.

Archer had led the team that had slipped into Hell ahead of the one Sable, another hunter for Archangel, had been preparing to lead to the Third Realm of the demons to aid King Thorne in his war against the Fifth Realm. Evelyn had been part of his team, together with a dozen other hunters. Their mission had been to document as much about the Fifth Realm as they could, a covert operation approved by those in command and kept secret from Sable.

One of the scientists had identified a non-human in the pens who had sworn they could teleport their team into the Fifth Realm and had done so in order to gain their freedom.

The operation should have been simple—scout the terrain and gather as much information as possible about the demons of that realm, the army Sable's side might be up against, and anything else that would help them and return to Archangel headquarters in London to deliver it to command.

Only they had been discovered by a group of demons and brought before their king, and he had declared they were spies and ordered their executions.

"I told you, Evelyn. I saw a chance and I took it. When you were stabbed, I made my move. It was risky, but it worked. I managed to catch them off guard and took out a few of the demons with tranq darts and in the ruckus my attack caused, I got you away from them. I carried you to a place nearby where we would be safe and patched you up. You were out for a few days before you came around." He leaned back in his chair, his face remaining etched in hard lines that spoke of irritation. His deep voice took on a hard edge as he continued, "You passed out again and I carried you to the nearest town over the border and found someone who helped us get back here. What about that is so difficult to believe? Or perhaps you don't trust a word I say?"

She leaned back and frowned at him, unable to hide her hurt as those words hit her.

"I do trust you." She reached for him again and he glared at her hand, stopping her. A sigh leaked from her lips as she thought about what she was doing, as that acid feeling scoured her insides again and an urge to apologise rose within her. She scrubbed a hand over her damp blonde hair instead, feeling awful as he continued to scowl at her.

"You said yourself in your report that everything had been a blur. The pain of your wound and fear combined with adrenaline made it impossible for you to grasp what was happening, and you were unconscious for a good part of it too." He whipped his glasses off and pinched the bridge of his nose, his broad chest heaving in a deep sigh as he sank against the back of his chair. When he lowered his glasses and hand and looked at her, a hurt edge to his dark eyes, that feeling in her gut worsened. "What do I have to do to make you believe me?"

She shook her head and wanted to tell him she was sorry but she couldn't find her voice.

Everything *had* been a blur, and even now, it was still a little hazy. Whenever she sat down and tried to remember what had happened, things slipped through her fingers like smoke. Not just the finer details of what had gone down in the Fifth Realm either. Pieces were missing. Big pieces. Like some of the events that led up to them being in the castle, and some of the things that had happened when they had been held captive. Other things were hazy, like she could remember something but she could never pull it into focus to see what it was.

And she hated it.

"You've not seen me in weeks and the first thing you do is question me." He put his glasses back on and began scrolling through the reports.

Giving her the cold shoulder.

She deserved it.

He was right and it was wrong of her to question him like this. It was hard for her though. He put it down to fear and adrenaline severely affecting her at the time, but something deep inside her said it had been more than that. She pulled down a breath and tried to calm her mind, told herself that he was right and she hadn't been able to cope with everything that had been happening. She had blanked. It had been too much for her and fear had made her numb, had messed with her head somehow. That was why she didn't remember what had happened. That was why there was a gap in her memories between the cold kiss of steel in her side and her life draining before her eyes and waking back in the med bay in Archangel.

But it didn't explain why her memories of the time before they had been captured were patchy.

"If you want, I'll tell you everything all over again, but it isn't going to change." Archer clicked on one of the documents and glared as he viciously scrolled through it.

Evelyn placed her hand on his, stopping him. "I'm sorry. It just… You know how difficult it is for me when I don't remember things. I hate it. Sometimes I wonder if what those non-humans did to me all those years ago is still affecting me."

He stilled and looked up at her, his expression instantly softening. His hand slipped from beneath hers as he stood and moved closer to her, raised his other hand and brushed her hair from her face.

"You're free of that place now, Evelyn," he whispered. "You're free of that part of your past. It was just the stress of the moment that made you forget a few details."

He heaved another sigh and his fingers lingered on her cheek.

"I'm sorry too. I've been under a lot of pressure recently and I'm tired. Maybe I need a break." He smiled softly and shrugged. "Or a drink. I could buy you a drink as an apology."

"Cafeteria beer? I'll pass." She gazed at the servers, seeing beyond the array of blinking red, green and orange lights in her mind, to the world out there. "I just want to be back on the streets. I want to leap back into my work and forget about what happened… which is ironic since I hate forgetting."

She chuckled.

Archer's steady gaze drilled into the side of her face.

She kept hers locked on the servers, a heavy feeling settling inside her again. She hated being inactive. It gave her too much time to think and she kept finding herself mulling over all the times she had felt there was something wrong with her.

That she wasn't right.

"How about we get some decent beer then?" Archer's hand dropped to his side and he gave her a stern look. "I'm not taking you on patrol, but we could gather some intelligence... something not dangerous... like a trip to Switch or Underworld."

Two nightclubs run by non-humans.

She gave him a sly smile. "I could use a cold beer."

He smiled right back at her, shook his head and then nodded towards the door. "Come on then. We can walk. Fix this *flat butt* of mine."

Evelyn slid a sidelong look at it as he walked past her, rounding the end of the row of desks. It wasn't flat at all. She wasn't sure how he did it, but he could sit in a chair most of the day and not ruin one hell of a fantastic backside. She wasn't the only one who stole a peek at it either. Several of the women in the room also tiptoed to see past the monitors to him as he strode towards the door, a sensual shift to his movements that made him look like a panther on the prowl.

On a satisfied sigh, she pushed to her feet and followed him, resisting the temptation to continue admiring the view.

"Swing by my quarters first? I need to grab some things." By *things*, she meant her favourite tranquiliser gun, just in case things got a little wild.

Archer nodded as she fell into step beside him, and she led the way to her quarters in the dormitory wing of the enormous building. She ditched her water bottle and grabbed her holster, wrangling her arms into it so her pistol sat snug against her ribs, and then turned back towards Archer where he waited in the doorway.

He reached around to his left, unhooked her black leather jacket and tossed it at her. "Might want to cover that piece."

She slipped her arms into the worn leather and smoothed it over her ribs so it concealed her weapon and then grabbed the pack of darts from the side table near him. He waited for her to pocket them and then turned around and stepped back into the cream hallway. She closed the door behind her and followed him down through the building, across the large bright foyer and out into the night.

The air was cool against her damp hair and she breathed deep of it, savouring it as if it was a fine wine, not thick with the scents of London. She glanced back at the elegant sandstone building as they left it behind, a place that had been her home for years now, since Archer had saved her life the first time.

"Let's cut through here." Archer pointed to the park and she immediately went on high alert, her focus narrowing to the shadows that clung to the trees.

If Archer switched his focus to looking for danger, he didn't show it. He casually jammed his hands into the pockets of his black combat trousers and tipped his head back to gaze at the night sky.

"I'm not sure how you can be so calm about walking through a pitch-black park." Evelyn scanned the darkness, her cheeks warming a little as she tried to pick out whether anyone was lurking in the patches of black beneath the trees. She absently touched her face when it grew hotter and her head felt a little foggy.

What was wrong with her these days?

She kept feeling flushed, hot all over, and she was starting to worry that her wound was infected even though the doctor at her latest check-up said she wasn't showing any signs of infection.

"You all right?" Archer stopped and caught her arm. He pulled her around to face him, a soft look of concern etched on his face as he studied her. When he lifted his hand and touched her cheek, she almost gasped. It was so cool against her flesh, a blissful relief from the heat that scalded her cheeks. "Maybe we should forget about getting a beer and head back. You don't look so good."

"I'm fine."

She locked up tight, her muscles clamping down on her bones as movement just beyond him caught her eye and she looked there. Her gaze collided with that of a man who was running right at Archer's back and she couldn't tear her eyes away from him.

He was handsome.

Gorgeous even.

And strangely familiar.

Evelyn frowned at him, trying to place him as heat bloomed in her veins and she fought the sudden wave of desire that threatened to steal her breath.

She saw a flash of him in the courtyard of a dark grey stone castle.

Felt the cold bite of steel in her side again.

He had been there.

His gaze shifted to Archer and narrowed, and panic lanced her, the haze of desire swift to dissipate as she realised he meant to attack her friend.

She barked, "Stop right there."

And drew her gun.

CHAPTER 2

Guilt gnawed at Fenix's stomach as he stepped out of the teleport into the grand entrance hall of his home in the heart of the Scottish Highlands.

Would the little witch be all right with the mad elf prince? Maybe taking Rosalind with him instead would have been the wiser move, but stealing her away from her mate would have been a death sentence. The last thing Fenix needed after spending months locked in a cell in that dank demon castle in the Fifth Realm was a powerful and dangerous male hunting him down to slaughter him.

Although Fenix suspected that Vail would draw out his death, savouring it and ensuring it was as painful as possible.

And not because he was insane.

Fenix wasn't a stranger to the crazy things being mated made a male do.

Case in point, he had been so caught up in tailing his own mate that he had ended up captured by the same demons who had cornered and overwhelmed her team of mortals. Frayne, the king of the Fifth Realm at that time, had ordered their deaths and forced Fenix to watch as he had skewered his mate through the side with a sword.

Fenix relived that moment every time he tried to sleep.

Had spent countless hours deliberating the things he could have done differently and how they might have affected the outcome, fully aware that he couldn't change the past.

His mate was dead.

Stolen from him before he could even accidentally make her fall in love with him this time.

The end result would be the same—her body teleporting to somewhere far from him, her rebirth happening, and her not remembering anything. By now, she could be anywhere, adjusted to her missing memories and living a new life without him.

And while part of him wanted to leave her to that life and wished her all the happiness in the world, the rest of him had been restless and eager to find her from the moment he had felt her vanish from the courtyard of the demon king.

He wasn't sure whether he felt a powerful urge to find her because he loved her and couldn't live without her or because of the curse.

Maybe it was a mix of both of those things.

But as always, he was back to square one. He had no lead on her new location, no clue as to how to find her, and still didn't feel any closer to tracking down the mage who had done this to them, condemning them both to a miserable eternity.

Fenix felt sure the bastard was still alive—that he had chosen the path of immortality like all blood mages now. Or at least he hoped that was the case. Drystan had to be alive. It felt as if all of Fenix's hope hinged on it. He needed a reason to keep going, to keep searching, something more than potentially finding a cure for this curse in the research of other mages.

One of his small clan came out from the drawing room to his right, took one look at him and turned around and walked away.

Fenix cast a grim look down at himself, not blaming the young incubus for making a fast exit. He was a mess, every inch of his bare chest covered in grime and his low-slung black jeans caked with dirt and other unmentionable things. His hair was long and shaggy, his nails needed a damned good clipping, and his beard was irritating. He probably looked like a homeless person who had wandered into the mansion.

Months in a damp cell in the basement of a castle would do that to you.

"Tiny," Fenix hollered, sensing the male just beyond the dark wooden door. "I hope you've been keeping the house in order."

Tiny peeked around the doorframe and blinked wide blue eyes at him, his sandy hair scruffier than the last time Fenix had seen the incubus-in-training. "Oh my gods! We all thought you were dead… this time."

Fenix scowled at him for that. So he had a bad habit of disappearing for months at a time, leaving the running of his mansion in the hands of his subordinates. It wasn't as if they needed him here.

"Any trouble?" By trouble, Fenix meant in-fighting, attacks from rival incubi clans, and general calls by the police about missing females.

Tiny shook his head, frowned when a thick hank of his wild hair fell down over the left side of his brow and blew it back out of his eyes. "Des has been taking care of everything in your absence. Rane and Mort have been busy."

Fenix huffed. "By busy, you mean ferrying females to and from the local fae town for *visits*?"

Visits being a nice way of saying raunchy, week-long, no-holes-barred parties with the two older incubi.

Tiny grimaced.

Rane and Mort knew that he didn't like them hosting groups of females under his roof, that his drawing rooms weren't there to be used in ways that meant they had to be sanitised every time he came home and wanted to relax. He had taken the males into his home to give them shelter, but they had grown into, well, mature incubi.

With the hunger of an average adult of his breed.

"I told them to keep their parties to the fae towns." Fenix undid his ruined jeans and headed for the left side of the grand twin wooden staircases that curved upwards to meet at a landing that overlooked the entrance hall and a chandelier that really needed a good dusting. He made a mental note to talk to Des about that. Or maybe he would make Rane and Mort tidy the entire house as punishment. A grin curled his lips and he paused halfway up the steps and looked back at Tiny. "Are they in?"

The scrawny youth shook his head. "Des is around though."

Fenix shrugged off his irritation and made a mental note to talk to Rane and Mort next time he was home at the same time they were.

"Just tell them no more parties or they'll have no more roof over their heads." He had been intending to relax in his home for a few days, fighting the need to find his mate. Now, he just wanted to get clean and get back out there. He paused again at the top of the stairs and grimaced, and then cast another look down at Tiny. "And sanitise every inch of the house while I'm gone."

"Where are you going?" Tiny called up to him as Fenix turned away from the banisters.

"Where do you think?" He tossed that over his shoulder and headed along the wood-panelled corridor to his right, moving swiftly towards his apartments.

At least they were firmly off-limits and so far Rane and Mort hadn't dared break that rule.

Relief swept through him when he opened the door to find everything as he had left it and sniffed the air, catching only a faint musty scent that told him no one had been in his room for weeks at least. He strode to the right window of the two that flanked his enormous four-poster mahogany bed and lifted the sash to let some fresh air in, and paused.

The grounds were beautiful, bathed in golden evening light, the sprawling lawn perfectly tended and the low hedges that formed intricate patterns in the formal garden neatly clipped. Tiny and Des had been busy. The older incubus liked to spend a lot of the warmer days in the extensive grounds, taking care of it, and the last time Fenix had been home, Des had told him that he had been training Tiny in the art of gardening too. It was good for the young incubus to have a hobby. All incubi needed ways to keep their minds occupied, otherwise their nature steadily took over, luring them into spending more and more time pursuing females and pleasure.

Until it became an addiction.

Fenix sighed as he stared at the towering dark pines and firs that formed a thick forest around the grounds, stretching between the lawn and the distant mountains that enclosed the house on three sides.

He feared Rane and Mort were heading towards addiction.

He didn't want to see either male sliding down the slippery slope towards being more incubus than human. Millennia ago, incubi had been more like the demons that history books and dictionaries portrayed them to be—dangerous, unscrupulous, and liable to force liaisons with females, taking them against their will. Incubi had slowly embraced their more human side though, learning to balance their needs so they could live among humans, enjoying everything the world had to offer together with other benefits that came from tempering their hunger.

Such as not transforming into murderous psychopaths in the throes of passion.

Of course, starvation could also turn an incubus dangerous.

Fenix raised his right arm and brought his fist up to his shoulder. He stared at the fae markings that tracked in a line up the underside of his forearm. The swirls, dots and slashes churned with blue and gold, a sign of his hunger. If he didn't feed soon, he would start losing his mind.

He dropped his hand to his side and went to his dresser, slid the top right drawer open and grabbed the small gold and blue enamel pill box there. He flicked the lid open and froze when a solitary yellow pill stared back at him from its bed of black velvet. Not good. He popped it into his mouth and hunted through every drawer in the dresser, looking for more. When he didn't find any there, he went to the nightstand and frantically pulled the drawer open. Pill bottles rolled back and forth, rocking to a halt. He checked every one of them and grimaced when he found pills in only one of them.

And even then it was only four.

Fenix hesitated and then swallowed two of them, reserving the rest for later. He needed to get more.

The three pills would take the edge off for a few hours at least, long enough for him to do his usual dance against his need to feed. He wanted no other female, craved only his Aderyn, and didn't want to be disloyal to her, even when she had always told him he could feed on females as long as it never went further than kissing them.

Kissing another female felt good for a few seconds, while his hunger was being sated, but the moment what he had done sank in, he always felt dreadful.

Which is why he had sought out a powerful witch in the fae town in Geneva. All the rumours about Hella had been true. She had been able to create a pill for him, one that would keep his hunger at bay, giving him more time between needing to feed.

The pill usually worked wonders, but in his haste to follow Evelyn into Hell when she had been sent there with Archangel, he had forgotten to top-up his supply and had gone after her with a half-empty travel pillbox in his pocket. Not that it would have mattered. The demons had taken it from him when he had been captured.

It had now been months since he had fed, possibly half a year, and that wasn't good. He could take all the pills he wanted, but they wouldn't have the desired effect when he was this hungry. Whether he liked it or not, he was going to have to find a suitable host or he was going to start sliding down into that dark place where his incubus nature would dictate his actions.

Losing his mind and turning into a demonic bastard who would murder his host to drain every last drop of energy from them had never been appealing to him.

So, he would find someone to kiss for a while.

As much as it sickened him.

His gut clenched at the thought of soft lips beneath his as he stripped off and headed for the bathroom, the thought of betraying Aderyn—Evelyn—whatever she was called now—sitting heavily in it. But then his head grew hazy and those lips became her lips, yielding to his as he tugged her close to him, bending her to his will. He groaned as he turned the shower on and stepped under the spray, tried to keep his thoughts on track and what he needed to do next as he thoroughly scrubbed every inch of himself twice over, but she was there in his mind whenever he closed his eyes. Smiling at him. Throwing her head back as he touched her. Crying his name as she came undone.

Fenix pressed his left hand to the wet tiles, hung his head under the jet of the shower, and firmly gripped his aching shaft in his right hand. He groaned as he fisted himself, his knees weakening as he imagined Aderyn on hers before him, her mouth on his length, sucking and teasing him. Release roared up on him and he grunted as he spilled, every throb and pulse of his shaft sweet agony.

He blew out his breath as he twisted and sagged back against the tiles, letting the water cascade over him.

Tipped his head back.

Opened his eyes and stared at the ceiling.

Where was his sweet Aderyn now?

Gods, he needed her.

He needed to see her.

No. He shook his head, lifted his hands and ran them over his wet hair, slicking the long tawny lengths back. He couldn't see her. It was better that way. It was better he suffer this pain and torment, this madness that afflicted him whenever they were apart, than put her through the hell she always experienced whenever they came together.

He didn't want her to die again.

But gods, he couldn't live without her.

He dug his fingertips into his scalp, gritted his teeth, and unleashed a feral growling sound as frustration got the better of him. If he could just see her, maybe that would be enough to tide him over. He could keep his distance this time.

"I won't make contact with her." He whispered those words to the heavens beyond the layers of the building above him, making it a vow. "I just want to see her."

He would find her and then he would continue his mission to locate the mage who had cursed them and free them both of it.

No.

He couldn't let his need to see her control him like that. He didn't even know where to start looking. If he went after her now, it could be months before he found her. Months in which he would be forced to feed on other females and wouldn't be any closer to finding a way to break the curse.

It was better he focused on taking care of himself first. He needed more pills. Those pills would keep the hunger at bay enough that he could retain the clarity of mind that was necessary when searching for Aderyn. If he popped enough of them, he might not even have to feed.

Besides, Hella might have a tonic ready for him, something he rarely accepted from her because of the source of it. But he needed it now, and it was better than being with another woman.

Plus, the witch might have information for him. Hella always kept her ear to the ground, had young witches spying for her across fae towns in several locations, listening in on conversations and reporting any mention of blood mages back to her. She had given him the lead that had brought him to Evelyn. She might have one that would bring him to Aderyn's latest incarnation.

And if she didn't, she might have leads on mages, something to keep him busy and keep his hope alive, and maybe even bring him the results he desired.

A way to break the curse.

Fenix shut the water off, stepped out of the cubicle and grabbed a towel. He dried himself off, slung the towel around his waist and found his shaver and scissors. His mind ran over everything he had felt all those months ago when Frayne had killed Evelyn and then ordered him taken to the cells, and then drifted further back as he cut his hair as neatly as he could manage alone, taking some of the length off it, and trimmed his beard back to stubble.

He tossed the scissors and shaver into the sink, and then ran a hand over his now shoulder-length tawny hair and tied it at the nape of his neck with a leather thong as he stared into his eyes in the mirror. His body ached from the fight to escape the castle in the Fifth Realm of the demons, and from the drain of teleporting so frequently to reach the nearest portal and travel back to the mortal world, but he couldn't rest.

Geneva.

He would head to Geneva to see Hella and get more pills and any information she might have for him. If she didn't have a lead on the location of Aderyn, he would go to another source that had helped him in the past. He would go to London to hit up the jaguar shifter he had been building a rapport with over the last few years. The male knew a lot of immortals and Fenix had asked him to keep an eye open for his mate. Maybe she would end up back there. It was a long shot, but he had to begin somewhere. He had to hold on to hope that he could find her quickly this time, using it as a shield to shut out the part of him that was already convinced that it was going to be one of those times where he didn't find her for years, ending up travelling around the world and Hell on repeat until he finally crossed paths with her.

Fenix cast the towel aside and padded naked into his bedroom, breathing deeply of the cool, clean air that swept in through the window. It was nice being away from Hell again, out of that damp, dirty cell that had been his home for far too long.

He caught his reflection in a full-length mirror and paused. He ran his hands down his lean torso, hardly recognising himself as he took in every inch of his body, warning bells ringing in his mind as he saw how much muscle he had lost. He couldn't put off feeding. He was too close to starvation.

The line of fae markings that continued up from his forearms to snake over his biceps and curl around his shoulders churned gold and blue, constantly shifting colour. If he could feed, he would regain his strength in hours, together with his physique. The muscles that had wasted away during his captivity would return. He stroked the faint ridge over his hips, not liking how scrawny he looked right now.

He looked like Tiny.

Weak.

Fenix grabbed the top of the mirror and tipped it downwards, spinning it to face the wall. He wasn't weak. He clenched his fists and strode to his dresser. He just needed to feed and then he would be strong again, back to his old self.

Capable of taking on anyone who stood between him and his mate.

Between him and his forever.

He opened a drawer on his mahogany dresser and plucked out a pair of black trunks and some socks, and tugged them on, and then crossed the wooden floor to his matching wardrobes and picked out a fresh pair of black jeans and a black dress shirt, and found his favourite Chelsea boots. Once dressed, he closed the window and thought about going to talk with Tiny, but took another pill instead.

And teleported.

CHAPTER 3

Fenix stared at the scrap of paper he clutched and then at the buildings surrounding him. They had seen better days and were far from the witches' district in the more upmarket end of the fae town in Geneva. He hadn't even realised it had an area like this. He had thought the whole of the sprawling town, one that occupied a cavern beneath a mountain, looked like the areas he had visited—elegant and refined, with beautiful pastel European townhouses sporting very Parisian lead roofs, or pretty terracotta-roofed cream cottages like the one Hella had lived in the last time he had visited her.

What had made her move to an area like this one? He tensed as he sensed eyes on him and glanced at the shadows between two of the run-down two-storey houses. Crimson eyes glared back at him. Vampire. If the warning bell clanging in his head was anything to go by, this vampire was hungry too. Fenix had no intention of becoming lunch for someone else, so he picked up the pace, heading at speed along the cobbled road.

He checked the address someone had given him again and looked at a building to his left, one that had flaking pale blue paint and a door that looked ready to fall off its hinges. Judging by the number scrawled on the stonework that looked an awful lot like it had been done in blood, he was close to his destination.

Fenix checked every door from that point onwards, and paused when he found the one he was looking for. He shoved the piece of paper into his jeans' pocket and rapped his knuckles on the wooden door of the white house. When no one answered, he reached out with his senses, trying to see if anyone was home.

Maybe the witch he had spoken to had been playing a trick on him, had thought he meant Hella harm and had sent him on a wild goose chase.

He detected a faint signature on the other side of the door but it was hazy, as if something was blocking him. He drew down a deep breath, attempting to catch Hella's scent. Only he smelled nothing but the rank odour of urine and old blood.

Fenix huffed and turned away, stopped himself from leaving and looked back at the door. He studied it with his eyes and his senses, trying to detect whether someone had placed a spell on the building, one designed to hide whoever was inside.

Was Hella in trouble?

The witch he had spoken to had looked worried when he had shown up at Hella's place to find the little brunette hastily tidying up what had been one hell of a mess. She had been quick to shove the piece of paper at him and shoo him away. Maybe she hadn't done it to protect Hella by sending him on a fruitless hunt for this building. Maybe she had done it because someone was after Hella and she hadn't wanted him hanging around for that someone to spot and follow him.

Fenix faced the door and knocked again. "Hella, it's me. It's Fenix. Are you in there?"

The door cracked open an inch, not even enough for him to see who was on the other side in the dark. A slender hand shot out and gripped his wrist, and he grunted as it yanked him inside, bashing him into the door.

The little blue-haired witch shoved both hands to his chest, planting his spine against the wall near the door, and cast a fearful look into the street. "Were you followed?"

Fenix shook his head. "I don't think so. What's this all about, Hella? I came to see you and I'm told you've moved and—"

"I had to," she interjected, released him and shut the door, sliding several locks into place, some of which his senses told him were magically reinforced. "I had a pest problem."

She sounded as breezy as ever as she bustled away from him, but he knew her well enough to see her pest problem had shaken her.

"It's not like you to be scared of anything. What's this pest problem you have?" And how could he help her deal with it? He owed Hella a lot. His debts to her were endless, infinite, and he would do anything she asked, if it would go some way towards repaying her for all her kindness and help over the years.

She shrugged and hefted a carpet bag onto a thick bench table in the middle of the dimly-lit cramped room. "It's nothing. Really. I've not seen you in months, and I really don't want to talk about me. Let's talk about you. What happened to you?"

She was deflecting, which meant she was in serious trouble. The only time he had seen Hella act like this, a group of witches from the local male coven had been after her because she had put a potion in their water supply that had made it impossible for them to get hard.

Repayment for them coming on too strong to one of the young witches she had taken under her wing.

"This and that. Got caught in the Fifth Realm and thrown in the cells. Lost Aderyn again." He cleared his throat as it tightened, failing in his attempt to be as glib as Hella could be when he felt the pain of his mate being torn from him all over again, experiencing the stretch and snap of their connection as if it had happened only hours ago, not months.

"Oh, Fenix." Hella turned to face him, hurried to him and wrapped her arms around his waist. She buried her head against his chest, froze and gripped his hips to push him back. She patted him down and her emerald gaze grew worried as she looked up at him. "You've lost so much weight. Hang on… I have just the thing. I've been saving it for you."

She rushed away from him again and dug through her carpet bag, doing a marvellous impression of Mary Poppins as she pulled one thing after another out of it, and set them down on the tabletop.

"It's here somewhere." She dug deeper, stretching her arm inside the bag, and then pulled something out and twisted towards him with a triumphant look on her face. "It survived!"

She motioned to the only armchair in the room, one that looked as if something had chewed its way into the cracked brown leather.

"I'll stand, thanks." He closed the distance between them though, curious about what she was doing as she shrugged it off and went to work.

"I knew you'd be back, so I continued our work." She didn't lift her eyes from her hands as she set out a row of different coloured vials and pulled a glass flask out of her bag. She placed that in front of her and uncorked the vials one by one, adding a dash of each to the flask. "I have a whole bunch of leads for you. Several locations of mages I think you should definitely check out. I'll dig them out of the bag when I'm done with this."

"That's the best news I've had in a long time." He watched as she uncorked the vial she had been excited about finding and poured the entire contents into the flask.

She swirled it around and the liquid turned a pale shade of pink.

Hella offered it to him and he stared at it.

"Still seeing the nymph?" He took the flask from her and sniffed it, shivered as heat rolled down his spine. It was potent stuff.

"No." She turned back to the vials and corked them all, her actions sharp and rough. "He got too clingy."

And judging by the shift he felt in her mood, the breakup had been rough.

He took in the room again. Old furnishings. Musty air. This place hadn't been lived in for a long time before Hella had come here to hide, and he had the feeling he knew who she was hiding from now.

"He the reason you're in some back-alley squat?" Fenix braced himself as she turned on him with a glare, stars sparkling in her green irises, and her mood shifted course again, veering sharply towards anger.

"Change the subject," she snapped and shoved the vials back into her bag, filling the tense air with the sound of glass clinking. "I am so over him already."

She muttered something else beneath her breath, but he didn't catch it.

"If he's giving you trouble, Hella, you're welcome to stay with me for a while." Fenix lowered the flask and held his hand out to her, and all her fight left her, her shoulders sagging.

"Things would have to be dire for me to throw myself into the lion's den." She sighed and brushed a hand through her hair, pushing the wavy blue lengths from her face. "I think I have this under control."

The fact that she didn't sound confident set him on edge. He couldn't remember the last time he had heard Hella sounding unsure about anything. In fact, he couldn't remember her ever sounding like this.

"You know they'd behave themselves. You know you're welcome in my house." He lowered his hand to his side.

She glanced at it and heaved another long sigh. "I know, Fenix. It's just… things are complicated. Now drink up before it spoils."

Fenix didn't want her efforts to go to waste, so he lifted the tonic to his lips and swallowed it down in one go. Heat swept through him the moment the pink liquid hit his tongue and he held back a groan as his eyes slipped shut. His hand drooped, his muscles going lax as intense pleasure rolled through him, energy coursing through every tired cell in his body to rejuvenate them.

"Like it? It's pure, unfiltered passion. I distilled it myself." Hella's light voice wobbled in his ears as he wavered on the spot, swept up in the taste of the tonic and how hazy it made him feel.

How strong.

He didn't want to think about the fact it was her passion—satisfaction—captured from the air by a spell and distilled into liquid form. It was what he needed and that was all that mattered.

And gods, it was good.

Chased the hunger from his veins and more than took the edge off.

"You need more pills too?" She moved around the small room.

"Uh-huh," he mumbled, drifting in the haze, savouring it and his returning strength. He could practically feel his body putting on muscle in response to the hit of sustenance, devouring the energy to push him back towards his physical peak.

She took the flask from him and he opened his eyes, tracked her as she moved back to the bench and set it down next to an array of colourful bottles and her pill press. She went back to work, humming to herself as she mixed powders together in a silver dish.

"So you broke up with the nymph?" Fenix wanted more information about what had happened and why she was now on the run from the male, because the last time he had seen her, she had been practically going steady with him.

Something which had surprised him given the fact that nymphs weren't known for their fidelity.

"And he wants me back. Let's leave it at that." She slid him a look, one that asked him to do that much for her.

He tamped down his desire to question her and changed the subject instead, because he could see how much she didn't want to talk about him.

"So who's warming your bed these days then?" He moved to the bench, coming to stand opposite her, and leaned over, resting his elbows on the rough wooden top and watching her work. He had never asked what she put in the pills. She had told him they would work and not to ask questions because he might not like the answers. Fenix figured it was her passion, mixed with other ingredients that were most likely vile and questionable.

Her green gaze lifted to meet his and she smiled saucily. "It's not a single who. I've decided to dabble in everything the town has to offer. I've even been mixing my flavours."

The wicked sparkle in her eyes said that she had been enjoying it too.

He groaned at the mental image of her with multiple partners at once. It had been a very long time since he had indulged in such a thing himself, but as good as they had been, he didn't want to go back to those days.

"Just keep away from my breed." He pushed a purple glass pot towards her when she reached for it.

She plucked the lid off it and scooped out some of the green powder with a small spoon. Fenix pretended not to see the sliver of bone poking out of the surface.

"You don't need to warn me." She lightly tapped the spoon, dislodging the powder onto the pile she was building in the dish. "I like my magic. Although, I've been hearing rumours that demon seed doesn't exactly do what we were told by our elders. Whispers say a witch in England has an incubus mate and still has her magic, but bears a sort of scarlet letter in the form of silver hair. I admit it's intriguing. Can a witch take demon seed into her without losing her powers? I'd be interested to find out... but... I'm not one to take unnecessary risks, so demon breeds are strictly off the menu. I'm on a diet of shifters and vampires, with the odd fae thrown in. Just the other day, I had two lion shifter brothers, and oh boy did I make them roar."

She flashed him a wink when he groaned and pushed his hands against the counter, straightening to stand again. She was doing it on purpose, tormenting him with the imagery, something she loved doing whenever he was hungry. Apparently, it amused her.

"Stop torturing me. I'm starving." He rubbed his stomach through his shirt, glad to feel more muscle there now. He lowered his hand to his left and felt the arch of muscle that ran over his hip. It was more pronounced now. At least her tonic had worked.

She pulled the handle down on the press and lifted it, popped the pill from the mould and flicked it at him. "Here, take the edge off. I'd thought the tonic would be enough. You know, there was at least half a dozen sexual encounters in that dose."

He groaned again as he caught the pill and sagged against the wall behind him. "It's been months. I mean it when I say I'm starving. Was starving. The demons didn't exactly give a damn about my condition. Left me to rot in that cell."

She stilled and looked at him, concern flickering across her pretty face. "How did you get out?"

He popped the pill into his mouth, swallowed it and sighed.

"Teamed up with an elf prince and a witch." He shook his head as he thought about Rosalind. "Not sure I made the right decision in leaving her with him. They're fated but... he has this whole bunch of issues when it comes to witches."

"You worry he'll hurt her." She stroked the handle of the pill press.

He nodded. "If anything happens to her—I'm not sure what I'll do. It'll be my fault. I trusted him with her, and I don't want to find out I've made a mistake and got her killed."

It would haunt him forever.

"Is she strong?" Hella lowered her gaze to the dish again and went back to work.

"As strong as you are. She has powerful light magic inside her and a spirit that isn't easily broken."

She popped a pill out and set it on another dish as she smiled. "Sounds like she can handle herself, but if you give me her name, I can have my spies keep an ear open for news about her."

"I'd appreciate that. Her name is Rosalind."

Hella paused. "Rosalind. British. Blonde. About this tall?"

She held her hand a few inches lower than the top of her own head.

He nodded.

Hella grinned. "Believe me. If this is the same Rosalind I've heard about, you should be worrying about the elf and not her."

That was reassuring.

"Here. Leaf through these while I finish these pills for you." She rifled around in her carpet bag again and produced a stack of papers of all different sizes, set them on the counter and slid them over to him.

Fenix took them and scanned each page, the tiny seed of hope inside him growing as he read report after report about blood mages. Hella had been busy in their time apart. Some of them had updates declaring the target had apparently moved on, but others indicated places that sounded a lot like permanent homes of mages. He kept the pages about those and pushed aside the dead ends, and read them again.

"The ones in England and America sound most promising." Hella placed the last pill in the dish, picked up a metal bottle and carefully tipped them into it. She held it out to him.

And something banged upstairs.

Fenix looked up at the wooden ceiling as the sound came again, a harsh thud that had dust raining down and sounded a lot like someone had just kicked the floor.

Hella put the bottle down, hurried to a broom, grabbed it and smacked the tip of the handle against the ceiling. "Keep it down. I'm doing business here."

A muffled voice responded and more bangs came, these ones so hard and heavy that he feared the ceiling would come crashing down on his head.

Fenix arched an eyebrow at Hella.

She grumbled, "Don't ask."

He looked at the ceiling again when a decidedly masculine voice bellowed an obscenity aimed at her.

"He was asking for it," Hella muttered, issuing him a look that told him not to say a word or attempt to interfere.

Fenix took his pills and his leads and held his hands up, because he didn't want to know.

Her expression softened and she lowered her broom, that look enough to stop him from teleporting and leaving her to her business.

"Don't lose heart, Fenix." She came around the bench and squeezed him in a bear hug before releasing him and stepping back. Her gaze lifted to lock with his again. "Fate made you for each other. Destiny will bring you together again."

It lightened his heart, chasing some of the shadows of despair from it as he clung to those words and made himself believe them.

He had always found Aderyn, no matter how far the curse had placed her from him, and this time would be no different. He looked at the stack of papers in his hand, leads that could bring him to the cure he desperately wanted, and nodded.

Fenix teleported, landing back in his rooms. He wondered what fate had in store for Hella and whether it was destiny that was responsible for the male he had sensed in her home. If it was, Hella would fight it. She wasn't one to be tied down.

He placed the papers on his nightstand and refilled his pillbox, and then went to the mirror. He swung it back over to face him and took a good look at himself. He was looking better already. A little more juice in his tank and he would be back to full strength and able to follow up the leads Hella had given him.

Fenix focused again, picturing London this time.

He could visit the nightclub owned by the jaguar and get a hit of energy from the crowd while discovering whether or not Kyter had any leads for him too.

He teleported.

Meant to go straight to Underworld but found himself standing in a park.

Staring at the old sandstone building that was the London headquarters of the hunter organisation Archangel.

CHAPTER 4

Fenix stared at the illuminated façade, an ache forming in his breast that throbbed stronger and stronger as he lingered in the dark park, thinking about his mate. She had worked there, and he had found a thousand excuses to sit in this park to watch her come and go with her partner or a group of fellow hunters.

He still couldn't believe his mate had become a member of Archangel, had actively participated in missions that pitted her against immortals. Over the year or so that he had known her as Evelyn, he had wanted to approach her countless times to tell her she was working against her own kind, that she wasn't human, and that by working for Archangel she was placing herself in grave danger.

If they discovered what she was… gods, it didn't bear thinking about.

They wouldn't just study her. They would vivisect her.

That throbbing, pounding sensation inside him grew stronger still, had his heart racing before he knew it. He frowned as he caught the light scent of rose with an undernote of sweet smoke on the still night air. He had to be imagining it.

And then a voice.

"I'm not sure how you can be so calm about walking through a pitch-black park."

That sultry sing-song drew his focus to a point just forty feet off to his right, closer to the building. He narrowed his gaze on that spot, his senses sharpening as he tried to make out the couple heading towards him, because he had to be going crazy.

It couldn't be her.

"You all right?" A male voice answered, and Fenix wanted to growl as he instantly recognised that regal accent that was more country house than London town and the familiar scent he associated with someone he wanted to butcher hit him. The lighting in the park was non-existent, but Fenix could see well enough to experience one hell of a spike in his anger when the male stopped and caught her arm, pulling her around to face him.

To face Fenix too.

He stared at her. Aderyn. How?

He had seen the demon king stab her with his own eyes, had watched her fall as he had been dragged away and had felt her disappear. He didn't understand. He had seen her die. Had felt her die. She should have been reborn, the cycle beginning again.

Only it was definitely Aderyn—Evelyn—standing before him with her cursed partner.

Fenix tried to content himself with just knowing she had somehow survived and was safe, and how the sound of her voice calmed him, warmed him and gave him the strength to keep going.

Only the way she smiled at her partner and the way that male lifted his hand and touched her face had a vicious hiss filling his head and had his fingers curling into fists as rage poured through his veins like molten lava.

And the way her eyes slipped shut briefly and she leaned into his caress pulled a fierce reaction from him.

"Maybe we should forget about getting a beer and head back. You don't look so good," the male said, his voice distant in Fenix's ears as he kicked off.

She murmured, "I'm fine."

And then tensed and her gaze whipped towards Fenix, her golden eyes widening as they collided with his. Heat rolled through him, sparked to an inferno by their gazes colliding, as if it had been the match that had lit the tinder of his passion. He couldn't breathe as he stared into her eyes, at flecks of gold so familiar and warming, comforting even.

But then awareness of the male and the memory of how she had leaned into his touch had the flare of white-hot jealousy returning, and he couldn't stop himself from sliding a black look at her partner.

She barked, "Stop right there."

And drew her gun.

Fenix launched at Archer's back, nimbly dodging the small dart that flew at him as she depressed the trigger. He slammed into the male, grappled with him and managed to get his arm around his neck from behind. He might not be at full strength again yet, but he didn't need to be in order to teach the human a lesson he would never forget, ensuring he kept his filthy paws to himself.

Archer seized his left forearm and twisted with him, tossing him off him, and Evelyn fired again.

Missed again.

She bit out a ripe curse and reloaded.

Fenix rolled to his feet, pivoted on the grass and kicked off again, pure unadulterated fury at the helm as he glared at Archer. How dare he touch Fenix's mate. How dare he seek to take what was his. Aderyn—Evelyn—belonged to him, now and forever. No male would take her from him. She was his.

Archer was ready for him again, moved inhumanly fast as Fenix dropped his shoulder to plough it into his gut, grabbed him by the back of his shirt with both hands and surprised Fenix by managing to seize his left wrist. Fenix bellowed in agony as the male twisted his arm up his back, had his elbow burning white-hot and panic setting in as it felt as if it might snap. He arched forwards and cried out again as Archer shoved his hand further up his spine.

He had been mistaken. He wasn't strong enough yet. But he would be.

His head fogged as the pain became too much and he tried to shake it off, focused on the male behind him and somehow managed to bring his right elbow up. Aimed it at the male's pretty face. Archer easily blocked it and shoved a knee into his back, knocking him down onto the grass. The hunter's full weight came down on him, pinning him to the damp ground, and Fenix struggled, refusing to give up.

Even when he knew it was over.

Attacking the hunter had been a mistake.

Not because he was weak from hunger.

But because Archer was incredibly strong.

Far stronger than Fenix had thought, and far stronger than was humanly possible for a male of his size.

He slid Archer a look out of the corner of his eye, met his gaze and held it, drawing on what strength he had and summoning a gift that always came in handy at times like this. Archer's pupils slowly dilated as Fenix turned on the charm, his grip growing weaker. Fenix grinned inside and kept up his assault, getting into the male's head and stirring passion in him, a desire to do whatever Fenix wanted.

Which boiled down to letting him go.

The hunter's gaze suddenly sharpened, his eyes narrowing as his dark eyebrows knitted hard and he dug his knee harder into Fenix's spine. The male leaned over him, shoving him into the dirt, and Fenix couldn't believe it. He wasn't at full strength yet, but he should have been able to charm the hunter. That ability grew stronger as he grew weaker, was always on hand when he needed it. Archer should have been putty in his hands, aching for him and willing to do whatever he wanted.

Archer brought his mouth close to Fenix's ear.

"Not going to work, incubus," Archer hissed. "You should have stayed away."

Fenix jerked back against him and summoned another ability, because he was damned if he was going to let the hunter win.

Only when he tried to teleport, nothing happened.

He stared at Archer out of the corner of his eye, shock rolling through him as the male slowly smiled at him, his smug look telling Fenix that he knew what he had just tried and failed to do. Fenix glared at him, silently letting the hunter know that he was on to him too. His inability to teleport wasn't because he was weak still and had tapped himself out by teleporting from Geneva to Scotland and then on to London. Something was different about Archer.

Archer sneered at him and reached into the thigh pocket of his black fatigues, pulling out a small radio device.

Evelyn came to tower over them both, her golden eyes cold as she stared down at him, her gun aimed at his shoulder. Maybe he could work with this. Every instinct he possessed screamed at him that he could. His mate was right there and that look in her eyes said she wasn't going to let him go. This was an opportunity—a chance to get through to her and make her see that she wasn't human and didn't belong at Archangel. He relaxed beneath Archer, his struggles ceasing as he accepted his fate, determined to make it work in his favour.

He would convince Evelyn to leave Archangel and her partner and together they could find the mage who had cursed them. They could have that forever they had always wanted with each other.

The rose-hued image in his mind of a happily forever after got a huge crack in it that bled oily black all over it as he met Evelyn's gaze and the more sensible part of him, the one not swept up in seeing his mate again, whispered that it wasn't going to be that easy.

Fenix realised with sickening dread that his rash actions had landed him in a whole lot of trouble—the sort that involved vivisection—when she took the radio from her partner and brought it to her rosy full lips.

"Prepare a pen for a new guest."

CHAPTER 5

Evelyn looked at the blood smeared over the side of Archer's throat and frowned as a thin rivulet trickled down towards his collarbone. "You should get that looked at."

He shrugged his wide shoulders, rolling them beneath his tight black Henley. "After we get him to the cells."

The him in question was the incubus who hadn't stopped staring at her since Archer had hauled him off the ground and they had marched him into headquarters through the parking garage entrance. Evelyn kept her eyes off him, the whole of her focus remaining locked on Archer as he touched the wound on his neck. It was only a shallow gash, but it hadn't stopped bleeding.

"I can handle him." She touched Archer's forearm, her brow furrowing as she gazed up into his dark eyes. "You get that looked at."

The incubus bared his teeth at Archer.

She still wasn't sure why the non-human hadn't teleported out of Archer's grip, something he could have easily done at any point during their walk to the building and the check-in station just beyond the car park entrance, where Archer had cuffed him with restraints designed to inhibit his powers.

And had been clocked pretty hard by the incubus.

Archer hadn't retaliated, had taken the hit on the side of his face without even grunting, and had only glared at the incubus when he had realised the male had cut his neck with the steel shackles.

"Seriously. Go to med bay. I have this." Evelyn gently nudged Archer on his shoulder, pushing him towards the corridor that led to the hospital area of the building. "Got my escort and it's hardly a long walk to the pens. What could happen?"

Archer pushed his glasses up his nose and gave her a look that said a lot could happen even in such a short space of time. He looked at the incubus, who narrowed his swirling cerulean and gold eyes on Archer and sneered.

Either the incubus had a real problem with her partner or he was angry with the world after being detained and processed. Water dripped from the ends of his long hair, rolling down his bare chest to soak into the black cotton trousers he had been issued after being stripped naked and hosed down.

Evelyn tried not to notice how his lean muscles flexed beneath his pale skin as he curled his hands into fists, or how flushed she felt as his gaze edged towards her. He was tall for his breed, stood an inch taller than Archer's six-four, and had a slender build, with square shoulders that tapered into a trim waist. There wasn't an ounce of fat on him either. Every muscle on his torso was pronounced, there for everyone to see.

A wicked feast for her eyes.

She shook her head, trying to dislodge that thought. No. Not for her eyes. He was charming her somehow, tricking her into wanting him. She didn't want him. So why couldn't she pull her eyes away from him?

Why did she feel so drawn to him?

He edged around to face her, his gaze scalding her as she found herself tracing the ridge of muscle that arched over his hip with her eyes. She tried to look away, but was powerless to resist following it down to the low waist of his cotton trousers.

And lower still.

Her cheeks flushed and her temperature soared, and she dragged her gaze away from him as Archer moved a step closer to her. She glanced at him, catching the concern in his dark eyes before she looked away and touched her cheek. It was burning up. It burned even hotter as shame swept through her. What was wrong with her? She shouldn't be looking at a non-human in the way she had been, entertaining thoughts that were dangerous and more than a little wicked.

Evelyn pulled down a breath and straightened her spine, and purged all the feelings the incubus had stirred in her, shutting down those unruly emotions and leaving herself cold and empty. Exactly how a hunter like her should be in this situation.

She risked another glance at Archer. He looked as if he wanted to say something, and she willed him not to, because she didn't need him bringing up her reaction to the incubus in front of the male and the guards. It had been a momentary slip.

It wouldn't happen again.

"Move it. Play nice for the lady." Archer grabbed the incubus by his left upper arm and shoved him forwards, and then slid another worried glance at her.

"I'll be fine." She patted his shoulder and jerked her head towards the two guards who had been assigned to her. "Cell twenty-seven-D is our destination, lads. Keep an eye on him."

She took the lead, aware of the incubus's gaze on her back as he followed her along the pale corridor. Heat stirred in her veins again and she denied it this time, focused her mind and put a lid on her feelings. She glanced over her shoulder, surprised to find him walking without the guards forcing him. She couldn't remember the last time she had brought in a non-human who was so calm and almost compliant. Most of them kicked up a fuss and did a lot more damage than a graze to those who had captured them.

Evelyn glanced back at him again and found him staring at her, his eyes swirling in that strange way an incubus's did and the markings that tracked over his biceps and shoulders shimmering with the same gold and blue. Their eyes locked and she shivered as intense heat rolled through her, shut it down and steeled herself. Apparently, he didn't need access to his powers in order to be charming. She was sure he was using that ability on her. He was trying to make her desire him. It wasn't going to work.

She faced forwards again, keeping her focus on her destination and off the male.

When she took the first turn in the maze of corridors that would lead her to the cellblock, the incubus finally broke his spell of silence.

"You shouldn't be here. It's dangerous."

Her spine stiffened.

"Dangerous? Are you threatening Archangel?" She looked back at him again. "I saw you in that demon realm… in that castle. You're working for them, aren't you?"

His dark eyebrows met hard above his swirling eyes. "No. I don't work for demons. I don't work for anyone."

She scoffed. "It was definitely you I saw."

"I was a captive of theirs too." His voice took on a hard edge, and she had the feeling she had irritated him. Because she wouldn't believe him? Or because she had all but accused him of working for her enemy? He didn't give her a chance to ask, continued before she could decide which question to pick. "The reason I was in Hell and ended up in that castle is standing right in front of me."

She tensed again and tossed him another glance, this one curious. There wasn't a hint of a lie in his eyes as he gazed at her. His face was sinful perfection, had her lingering and her step slowing. The feel of the guards behind him looking at her had her snapping out of it and she wanted to curse the incubus for using his charms on her, attempting to weaken her.

He wasn't going to escape her.

Although, he could have if he had wanted to.

She faced forwards as she thought about that again, mulled over all the chances he'd had to teleport away from them. Why hadn't he taken them?

Because he had wanted the opportunity to talk to her? To feed her lies designed to sway her? Was she just a part of a plan he had? The more she thought about it, the more she felt sure this wasn't a coincidence. She had seen him in the Fifth Realm—he had confirmed that—and now he was here and he had let her capture him. He was up to something.

She just wasn't sure what it was.

He moved closer to her back and whispered, "I needed to stop you from dying."

She tensed as those words rolled over her, the earnest way he spoke them rattling her. There was so much pain in his deep voice, so much need that she swore she could feel the depth of it and how badly he wanted to protect her.

Not wanting him to know he had shaken her, she looked over her shoulder at him and rolled her eyes. "You expect me to believe that?"

His expression was deadly serious as he said, "You were dead. I felt you die."

A chill swept through her, had her step faltering as she struggled against it, trying not to let him shake her further. She couldn't believe him. Her hand drifted to her side and she pressed her palm to the wound, felt it burn as she saw a flash of the blade piercing her and her life flowing from her.

"I didn't die," she murmured, her voice distant to her own ears. "I survived... with Archer."

The incubus growled, "I'm not sure about your *partner*. Something is off about him."

"Are you getting a rise out of this?" She scowled at the corridor ahead of her and several of the hunters walking along it gave her a wide berth. The incubus was just trying to rattle her and she was letting him succeed.

Sure, Archer had been acting a little strange over the last year, but this incubus seemed to be making out he wasn't human.

And she was done with him.

She mentally zipped her lips and shut him out.

Thankfully, he remained silent for the rest of the walk to the cellblocks.

Although that didn't stop her from feeling unsettled. The way he stared at her back had her on edge, flushed with heat at times, and deeply aware of him. She glanced back at him as she led him along the corridor between two rows of cells, catching his reflection and hers in the thick glass that formed one wall of each cell and served as the door. He continued to stare at her, his intense gaze warming her right down to her bones, making her heart flutter despite her best efforts to not let him affect her.

As she led him deeper into block D, his gaze drifted away from her from time to time, darting briefly to the white-walled cells and their occupants. The facility was high tech, had everything necessary for containing non-humans, including the ability to gas the occupants of each cell with a drug designed to knock them out and a handy device created by a witch long ago that dampened their abilities. That same tech was woven into his restraints, but apparently it didn't work against his power to charm females.

Or at least she really hoped it didn't and that was the reason she felt so flushed around him, her head a little hazy whenever he gazed at her.

Evelyn touched her cheek. It was overheating.

"Are you ill?" His deep voice rolled over her, cranking her temperature up a few more degrees.

"None of your business," she snapped and dropped her hand to her side.

Evelyn stopped in front of the empty cell and the thick glass panel whooshed into the ceiling.

She scowled at the incubus. "In you go."

He didn't move, just glanced at the featureless white room and then back at her, levelling her with a look that said he wasn't going to make this that easy on her. He opened his mouth to speak but she nodded to the guards and they shoved him forwards, pushing him towards the cell. He stepped over the gully in the floor where the glass would meet it and then stopped in the middle of the cell.

The incubus turned around to face her as the men backed off, joining her in the corridor, and the glass dropped to settle in the gully. The shackles he wore beeped and fell open, dropping to the ground at his bare feet, and then a panel in the ceiling swished open and a humming sound vibrated in the air. The incubus stepped back as the shackles shot up into the opening, pulled there by the magnet.

He peered at the ceiling as the opening closed and then dropped his gaze back to her.

The guards walked away from her and she turned to follow them.

"Evelyn."

Her gaze whipped to the incubus, her eyes wide as she stared at him, the desperation that had laced her name drawing her back to him.

Green emerged in his irises, like tiny emeralds nestled among the gold and cerulean, and he stepped towards the glass panel that separated them. He pressed his palms to it as his brow furrowed, a hint of worry in his eyes now as he gazed down at her, and his voice was soft as he spoke two words.

"Be careful."

Evelyn wasn't sure what to make of that or of him.

She forced herself to leave and ended up heading to her quarters rather than the infirmary to see Archer. She slumped onto her small beige couch in the living area of the open-plan room, her thoughts weighing her down as she ran over everything that had happened in the Fifth Realm and the things the incubus had said.

When she started getting sleepy, she stood and stripped off, shedding her clothes on the way to her bedroom. She sank onto the double mattress face-first and rolled, pulling the covers over her, and curled into a ball. Sleep was quick to take her, the darkness comforting as it enveloped her.

And then flames roared to life all around her.

She squinted and covered her mouth, flinched away from the heat that seared her as she peered through the flickering wall of flames, trying to make out the shape that loomed on the other side of them.

Voices swirled around her and the flames guttered and swept away from her on her left side, and she shrieked as a huge bare-chested demon lunged at her, appearing human for the most part. His horns flared from behind the tops of his pointed ears to curl around to his lobes and grew as he came at her, his leathery wings beating the hot air towards her.

Her eyes widened as pain bloomed above her hip and she looked there, saw the silver blade protruding from her side and blood rolling down her thigh.

Everything whirled again, a blur of orange and black, and then Archer was there, looming over her with a worried edge to his rich brown eyes. She clung to his shoulders, desperate for him to stay with her.

Or desperate to stay with him?

"That was a close call." His voice warbled as if the heat was affecting it as the air shimmered around him and the temperature rose again. "You really need to be more careful."

Evelyn glanced around her. She didn't remember being moved, but the castle was gone and a basic room surrounded her, the only furniture in it a rickety-looking wooden bed with a sunken mattress.

"What happened?" she breathed, swallowed to wet her dry mouth and flinched as the air grew hotter still.

Tiny sparks of gold and red chased in the air beyond Archer, dancing and mesmerising her.

Archer looked away from her, casting his grave gaze at the wooden floorboards.

Dread pooled in her stomach. "The others didn't make it."

He shook his head and paced away from her, moving to the window. "We'll move soon. Once it's safe."

Those embers grew brighter, little flames leaping from some of them that caught on the bed and the walls and began to spread hungry fire around her.

"Archer?" she whispered, afraid of the flames for some reason.

He looked back at her.

She gasped.

Seven shimmering colourful bands of symbols appeared on his bare forearms, from his wrists to his elbows, each thicker than the last.

And the whole of his eyes turned inky black.

And then the fire engulfed her.

CHAPTER 6

Fenix sat in the corner of his white cell, his forearms resting on his bent knees as he glared at the glass. Captive again. This hadn't been the plan. He chastised himself for what felt like the millionth time, anger at himself curling through him to keep his mood dark. He had been an idiot, should have been stronger and not reacted the way he had.

But he hadn't been able to stop himself.

He still seethed with a need to find the hunter called Archer and put him in his place.

"Not going to happen," he muttered and the black-haired male in the cell across from him cast him a wary look.

Fenix clenched his fingers to resist the urge to flip him off. He wasn't a threat to the male, but he kept looking at Fenix as if he was.

Or maybe he thought him mad.

He couldn't really blame him if he did.

He had spent most of the night talking to himself after all.

Ironic that he was now the one acting crazy while another male looked at him as if he was mad. Maybe it was punishment for the way he had reacted to the elf prince during their captivity in Hell. He sighed as he thought about Vail and Rosalind again, his heart filling with hope that the little witch was doing okay. Hella was right. Rosalind was strong and the elf was probably in more danger than she was. Besides, he had seen the way Vail had reacted to her, how he had distanced himself whenever he had grown dangerous and dark. He doubted the elf could lift a finger to hurt her. The male would probably sooner die.

He huffed as he took in his surroundings. He had swapped one prison for another, and he wasn't sure how he was going to get out of this one.

His topic of one-sided conversation that had gotten him through the night had revolved around planning that escape. Sure, it was dangerous to talk aloud about his plans, but it was better than sitting in silence, watching the hunters and the white-coats coming and going along the corridor, aware it was only a matter of time before they stopped in front of his cell and it was his turn to be *studied*.

They used that word as if it were harmless, fooled far too many immortals with it too. Even the fae across the way had relaxed when he had been told they only wanted to *study* him. He hadn't looked so relaxed when they had brought the poor bastard back with a nice fresh set of stitches across his bare stomach.

"Wouldn't do that, mate," Fenix said in the fae tongue as the male absently scratched at the black stitches. "Will only make them worse."

The fae's fingers paused and he looked down at the reddened skin, dropped his hand to his side and deflated, his shoulders slumping as he leaned against the wall.

Poor wanker couldn't even sit down without hurting himself, had been on his feet for hours.

"How long have you been here?" Fenix moved to the glass panel, ensuring he had the male's attention.

"A lunar cycle." The male had to be one of the Hell brand of fae, evidently didn't get out of that realm much given he was talking about months in terms of lunar cycles. He cast a wide-eyed look of almost-wonder at his cell and edged towards Fenix. "You speak my tongue."

Fenix flashed the undersides of his forearms, revealing the markings that depicted his incubus lineage. "Because I'm fae and my dad didn't do everything wrong. He taught me how to speak the tongue."

And then when Fenix had been barely Tiny's age, not even mature, his father had run off and Fenix had never seen him again. No great loss. He had stuck around longer than most incubi did when they sired a kid.

"They catch you in Hell?" Fenix looked him over, unsure what he was. There were a lot of different breeds of fae, some more myth than reality. This male could be anything from a nymph to one of the seelie.

Or worse, an unseelie.

Fenix had made damned sure he had never crossed paths with an unseelie.

They were vicious and often quite demented, and driven by an insatiable urge to bring down the seelie. Which Fenix couldn't really hold against them since the Seelie Court wanted to destroy their darker counterparts too. Something about a prophecy.

It sounded a little like the relationship between incubi and succubi, a war that had been raging for millennia. Although, the war between his breed and their female counterparts normally played out in the odd scuffle and some vicious rounds of taunting each other. It was rare for them to go as far as killing each other. Mostly, incubi and succubi avoided each other.

If anyone asked Fenix, he would say that the succubi had a bigger problem with his species than his had with them, but then it had been a long time since he had bothered to spend much time in a fae town, where the outbreaks of violence between the two breeds were most frequent. In fact, it had been a long time since he had met a succubus.

Long enough that he might have shaken the hatred of them that had been bred into him from the moment he had been born.

"I must leave this place. They swore if I helped them through the portals that I would be set free." The fae gazed longingly at the floor.

Fenix guessed he was thinking about Hell. Although it existed on another plane and not below their feet, even immortals thought about it being there beneath the crust of the planet because of how it looked—all black cragged lands that were still forming in places, gigantic volcanoes spewing lava to increase the landmass into the unending darkness.

"Yeah, well, they're a bunch of liars." Fenix glared at a passing hunter as he said that and for a moment the female looked as if she was considering giving him an earful but then she tipped her chin up and strode out of view. He slid a look at the fae.

The male was picking at his stitches again.

Fenix clucked his tongue, stopping him, and the fae looked at him. "How many did you ferry through a portal?"

The fae's expression turned pensive. "Twelve perhaps. I do not remember the precise number. They tell me now that if I reveal the locations of another three portals that I can leave."

"You going to?"

The male gestured to his stitches, sweeping his long fingers downwards in front of them. "I no longer feel inclined to do so."

That was good, because Fenix didn't like the sound of Archangel wanting to know the locations of the portals between Hell and this world. It unsettled him for some reason, made him feel the organisation was up to something and whatever it was, it was going to be bad.

Fenix snapped his mouth closed when two hunters marched a poor female of some kind past him, heading deeper into the cellblock. Hunger licked through him as he watched her, the bruises and welts she bore on her bare skin doing nothing to dampen the desire that rolled through him. He fought to tamp it down, swore he could feel his markings churning with the blue and gold of hunger as he tracked her with his gaze until she disappeared from view.

Gods, he was starving.

Hella's tonic and the pills he had taken apparently hadn't been enough to satisfy his hunger. He still wanted more. Ached to gorge himself on a female or two. He clenched his jaw and pushed back against that desire, because it wasn't going to happen. He absently touched the spot below his hip where his pillbox would have been if he hadn't been stripped of his clothing and forced to wear plain black cotton trousers.

A pill could have taken the edge off, but there was no chance of him getting one in this place. He doubted the hunters would reunite him with his pillbox if he asked it of them. Which meant it was only a matter of time before his incubus nature began to slowly steal control, his hunger bringing it to the fore to give it power over him and rob him of his humanity.

When he finally wrestled his hunger back under control, he returned his focus to the fae. The black-haired male was watching him closely again, that wary look back in his silver eyes. Fenix wanted to tell him not to worry about him, that he wasn't a threat to any male in the area, but he didn't get the chance.

Two white-coats stopped in front of his cell, one male and one female.

Together with Evelyn.

Fenix kept his eyes away from her, afraid of what might happen if he looked at her. The hunger was still riding him hard, filled his head with images of her beneath him, yielding to him and crying his name as she broke apart. If the white-coats saw the effect she had on him, it would place her in danger.

The female checked her clipboard. "An incubus. Raise your arms."

She glanced at him, her grey eyes cold.

"Fuck off," he spat and placed them behind his back instead, stoked the anger that was quick to come as he thought about what these nefarious humans probably wanted to do to him.

A nice round of studying.

"Black and red. Make a note of that." She angled her head towards her male partner and he scribbled on his own clipboard. "They were a different colour when we arrived. Incubus gold and blue. The subject is hungry."

"And now the subject is angry." Fenix growled those words at the brunette and glared at her for good measure when she arched an eyebrow at him.

"The subject is mouthy," she said and her thin lips curled into a vicious smile. "Perhaps the subject wants a dose of gas?"

"There's no need for such extreme tactics," Evelyn put in and he almost looked at her as she stepped forwards, emerging from between the two white-coats, her black uniform of a T-shirt and fatigues a stark contrast to them. "The incubus might be more inclined to assist us if we don't go gassing him over the slightest thing."

"The incubus is never going to be inclined to help you. I see what you people do to immortals like me. *Studying.* Nice way of saying slicing and dicing and seeing how we tick. I don't remember being a danger to any humans so I'm not sure why I'm here." He squared up to the front of his cell, still keeping his eyes off Evelyn, holding on to the anger he felt burning in his blood as he clenched his fists behind his back.

"Not a danger to any humans?" Evelyn frowned at him. He could feel her surprise and fury as her gaze seared him, as her emotions trickled into him through their bond. Could she feel his rage too? She should be aware of it, but maybe she had misinterpreted it as her own anger. "You attacked my partner."

He shrugged. "Like I said. I wasn't a danger to a human."

She huffed and he could easily picture her rolling her eyes. "This again? Fine, have at him."

She turned away from him and he wanted to lunge for her, to tell her to stay close to him, to roar at her that she was in danger here, surrounded by humans. She didn't belong in this place.

"Tell us about your lineage," the male said, his gaze on his clipboard and pen poised to write down the information.

"Dead, I'm afraid." Fenix lied through his teeth, something he had become good at over the years. An incubus quickly learned to protect himself and his kin upon maturing, when his need to feed came to the fore and he found himself caught up in fights over whether or not he had stuck to the code of honour.

Which was utter bullshit some incubi had come up with before Fenix had been born, declaring they would never feed from an unwilling host or use their powers to persuade one who didn't want to be seduced. It had probably sounded like a fantastic way of avoiding conflict when the males had come up with it, stopping the wars against the incubi that had broken out over the centuries. Most modern incubi felt neutered by it, driven to conduct their seductions in private in order to avoid revealing that none of them upheld that code.

Well, none of them except Fenix and maybe a few other mated males.

"Where are your family from?" The male gave him an exasperated look that revealed he already knew what Fenix's answer would be.

"Here, there… around." Fenix shrugged his bare shoulders.

"Perhaps we need to try a different tactic." The male looked at the brunette, his brown eyes sharp with frustration.

"You are not our first incubus guest, but there is something different about you that warrants further study." The female ran an assessing gaze over him from head to toe and back again and he bared his teeth at her.

"The word *guest* implies I'm free to come and go as I please," Fenix spat. "So how about you lift this barrier and I walk out of here? I've done nothing to warrant being your prisoner."

Evelyn's soft voice had the rage blazing in his blood dropping to a simmer and then spiking again as her words registered. "He attacked my partner without provocation."

He slid a glare at her. "Not without provocation."

She frowned at him and stepped towards the glass, her golden eyes scrutinising him as her lips compressed and her eyebrows knitted. He didn't like that look. He felt as if she was peeling back his layers, stripping away his defences in her quest to seek the answer to the question that gently rolled from her delectable lips.

"Not without provocation?"

Fenix refused to say any more than what he had. It had been a mistake to answer her but part of him had felt compelled to make her see that her partner had had it coming and that he wasn't some mindless, brutal immortal out to hurt the innocent.

"What is your name?" the male said, his tone dull as he moved to the next question on what had to be a standard list of them that he knew Fenix wouldn't answer given how bored he sounded.

He stoked his rage again, ensuring his markings churned with obsidian and crimson, and growled at the white-coats. "Go to hell."

The brunette smiled coldly as she closed the distance between them.

"Hell is where you're going." She glanced at the man beside her. "Order a full suite of tests."

Sickness swelled inside Fenix and he cast a panicked look at Evelyn, soul-deep aware of what the white-coat meant by that.

Evelyn stared at the brunette and he wanted to believe he hadn't imagined that sudden spark of shock and fear in her eyes. He reached with his senses against his better judgement, fixing them on Evelyn, needing to discern what she was feeling.

"What do you plan to do with him?" Evelyn pivoted to face the white-coat, a flicker of panic trickling through their bond to reach him.

Brunette waved her away. "You may leave now. We'll take it from here."

She looked as if she didn't want to, but then she stepped back and turned away, and glanced back at him with a solemn look in her eyes before she disappeared from view.

The male brought a small radio device to his mouth. "Request subject from twenty-seven-D be transported to room eight-C."

Fenix's pulse spiked, panic swift to flood his veins as his eyes darted between the two humans.

Before he could form a protest, vents opened in the ceiling and mist poured into his cell. His vision wobbled as he breathed it in, his strength leaving him in a rush, and he collapsed into the darkness.

When that darkness receded, his faculties came back online in an instant, the fog in his head lifting swiftly. He blinked at his new surroundings, went to lift his arm to rub at his eyes and frowned down at his right one when he could only move it a short distance.

The panic returned as he stared at the metal cuff locked tightly around his wrist and the chain that attached it to a clinical steel board behind him. He tugged at the chain several times, each jerk of his arm more frantic than the last as his heart raced and fear crowded his mind. Not good.

He looked down at his body.

His very naked body.

Not good at all.

His breathing trembled as he kept yanking on the chain, as panic really set in to have him shaking as he desperately fought his bonds.

Something made a crackling, buzzing noise.

And then a familiar female voice echoed around him.

"Approach him."

Fenix sought the owner of that voice, wanting to give the white-coat hell. His gaze landed on a nude female standing at the other end of the featureless room, her arms folded over her stomach and her green eyes holding a fearful edge as she stared at him.

He shook his head as hunger roared to life inside him, warning her to keep away from him. She was pretty, got his incubus side going, but she did nothing for him. He didn't want her—his instincts did. They clamoured in his mind, screaming at him that she was a willing host, that he could feed on her and regain his strength, that he needed to taste her lips and take her body.

Fenix gritted his teeth and unleashed a long growl of frustration as he waged a war against his own body.

Sometimes it felt as if there were two sides of him—two people trapped inside this one body.

When his incubus side came to the fore like this, he found it hard to control himself, did things he didn't like.

Things he didn't want to do.

"Approach him," the white-coat said more sternly and the female in the room with him tensed and swallowed hard.

She cast him a look that was somewhere between an apology and desperation, and shuffled towards him.

Fenix shook his head and wrestled harder against his shackles. When he still didn't break free, he bared his teeth at her. "Stay away from me."

She didn't want to do this. He could see it in her eyes. He didn't want to do this either.

She halted before him, nervously hooked her long dark hair behind her ears and flicked a glance at the wall to his left.

"Continue." That word fell heavily upon him.

And upon the female too, judging by how she hesitated and had to suck down another breath. Her hands fell to her sides and she didn't look at him as she stepped up to him, as she pressed her palms to his chest and tiptoed. He bit back a groan as the feel of her hands against his flesh had his hunger spiralling out of control, had his markings churning with gold and cerulean, and a haze sweeping through him to blur his thoughts.

"I'm sorry," she whispered. "They said they'd let me go if I did this."

He didn't get a chance to beg her not to do it, wasn't sure he could have found his voice even if he had. His incubus nature was in control now, had him focused on her, slowly manipulating her feelings, bending them towards desire as he gazed down at her. Heat flushed her cheeks, passion darkened her eyes, and her breath hitched as she pressed against him. She shifted her body restlessly against his.

Her lips opened, begging for a kiss.

Fenix resisted and growled silently as he felt trapped inside his own body, a slave to his hunger and need.

She kissed him instead, moaned as she claimed his lips and worked her body against his, her hard nipples brushing his chest, rousing his hunger to the point where he lifted his hands towards her, eager to seize hold of her and take her. She was willing. Wanted him.

He didn't want her.

He screamed that in his mind.

Even as he stole energy from her kiss, he resisted the clamour in his mind that compelled him to either take her or let her take him. He couldn't do that to Aderyn—Evelyn. He wouldn't.

When her hands dropped to his hips, her mouth froze against his and she pulled back, a hazy quality to her heavy-lidded gaze as she looked at his flaccid penis.

"Interesting." The haughty female voice rolled over the sound system again. "This warrants further investigation. We've never had an incubus refuse a female before."

"Let her go!" Fenix looked off to his left, guessing they were there somewhere, in the direction the female with him had looked before she had obeyed them. "Let her go!"

It was like shouting into a void.

No one answered him.

Fenix struggled against his bonds, fear at the helm again as the nude female stepped back from him and looked in the direction he was, as if she was awaiting instruction.

"Again," the voice said.

Fenix bared his teeth at her as she approached him, yanked at the chains that held him and fought the hunger that rose within him. He wasn't sure how much more he would be able to take before he cracked, feared he wouldn't be able to hold out and would eventually take her.

He would hate himself for it too.

The only female he wanted in this world was the one he couldn't have.

And he intended to keep his vow.

He would remain faithful to her.

Even if he had to die to achieve that.

CHAPTER 7

Not without provocation.

Those words had been spinning around Evelyn's mind for the last few days, keeping her preoccupied as she had tried to figure out what the incubus had meant by them and had found herself avoiding Archer.

She had dreamed of fire again too, and this time the incubus had been there, or at least some part of her felt sure it had been him. She hadn't seen him. In the dream, he had been like a ghost—a shadow within the white-hot heart of the flames. She had felt him there. Felt him. As if he was a presence inside her. No. A part of her. Joined to her somehow.

She wasn't sure what that meant.

Evelyn sighed as she looked at the piece of paper she clutched in her left hand, wondering if she was losing her mind. Maybe she needed another session with one of the staff psychiatrists. She hadn't been to see them in a long time now, not since she had managed to overcome the panic attacks that had set in whenever she had forgotten something or done something strange. Even the most basic of things. Like, being sleepy and accidentally putting the milk in the cupboard and the jar of coffee in the fridge or misplacing her keys. The slightest thing had triggered her back then, but she had learned to deal with it and in the end had emerged the victor. No more panic attacks.

The nice doctors could probably help her with this feeling she had that something was wrong with her too, but for some reason she couldn't bring herself to speak with them about it.

Was afraid of them on some level.

And now the incubus was filling her head with rogue thoughts that backed up that feeling that she was different to the hunters she passed in the hallways as she made her way down to the pens.

Evelyn shook it off, focusing on the list of questions printed on the paper. One of the scientists had delivered them to her in a manilla envelope this morning and issued an order that came from Annette, the woman in charge of learning more about the incubus. Annette wanted her to go to see him again.

This was the third time Annette had sent her to the incubus, but the first time she had been issued a standard set of questions to ask him. The other two times, the scientist had told her to make conversation with him, and she hadn't really known what to say. When she had overcome how awkward it was to stand there in the corridor being watched by not only him but by the fae in the cell opposite his, her attempts to strike up a conversation had always ended in failure.

The incubus had refused to look at her, let alone speak with her.

It had been two days since she had last been sent to him. She wasn't sure why Annette had left a gap between her visits. She put it down to the scientist declaring her a failure and wanting to try a different tack. Whatever the reason, she was back to visiting him again, and she doubted the list of questions they had provided her with were going to get him to talk.

Evelyn ignored the harsh words and threats the occupants of the cells in block D hurled at her as she passed them, heading for one near the far end of the corridor. Nerves rose. She tamped them down and told herself she had no reason to be afraid of seeing him. He was beyond a wall of glass, unable to reach her.

That wasn't true.

He could reach her.

He could say things like he had before, things that had shaken her and still rattled her now, had her unable to focus on anything other than unravelling what he had meant.

Maybe she could start by asking him about that.

She stopped in front of his cell, checked her list of questions and then lifted her head. Her eyes widened as they landed on him where he sat in the corner of the white cell, his green eyes glassy as he stared at the wall opposite him, his face gaunt and skin sallow. Was he sick?

The thought that he might be evoked a strong reaction in her, had her taking a step towards him and pressing her free hand to the glass before she had realised what she was doing. She froze as she glanced at her hand, as it struck her that she had wanted to touch him and not the cold barrier that separated them, had been driven to reach him.

Evelyn flicked a glance at the CCTV camera mounted on the wall above the cell behind her, pointed at her back and his cell. They were watching and she hoped to God they hadn't noticed her reaction to him, because the last thing she needed was them questioning her about something she didn't understand herself.

She cleared her throat and read the notes at the top of the page. Annette had been trying to coax him into feeding so they could study him. So far, he had resisted their attempts. She glanced at him, noting how pale he was and how worn down he looked. Would he die if he didn't feed?

She eased down into a crouch, bringing her eyes level with his, but he still refused to look at her.

"What's your name?" she murmured, just loud enough that he would hear her through the five inches of toughened glass.

He slid her a disinterested look and then fixed his green eyes back on the wall, but his markings shifted with colour, hues of deepest pink and gold with streaks of blue. She studied them, fascinated by every swirl, dot and slash that ran in a line up the underside of his forearms and snaked over his biceps and across the back of his shoulders. They were beautiful in a way. In all her years working for Archangel, she had never seen anything quite like him.

"You know my name already. I think it's only fair you tell me yours."

His dark eyebrows lowered and the corners of his lips turned downwards, and yes, it was mean of her to guilt him into telling her his name. She knew that. He didn't need to show her how much he didn't like what she was doing.

She sighed and looked at the sheet, scanning it for the next question.

"Fenix."

His deep voice rolled over her like a powerful wave, but one that warmed her and eased the tension from her muscles, as if it calmed her. The power of an incubus? One that even the cell's tech couldn't strip from him? Or just an effect he had on her?

She didn't want to peer too closely at how she reacted to him to discover the answer to those questions.

"Fenix." She didn't bother to jot it down on the paper. "And what's your real name, Fenix?"

He scowled at her, worsening that feeling that churned her stomach to acid and making her regret asking. Some fae breeds had an unusual affliction, what most might consider a curse. Their true name was power and it gave anyone who knew it the ability to control them. Incubi and succubi were two such breeds.

"That isn't something I'm willing to give you as you are now." He looked away from her, turning his cheek to her and revealing his profile again. Even that was sinful perfection. Straight nose and angular jaw, lips that looked kissable even from the side.

She shook off the wave of heat that swept through her and focused on what he had said. She frowned as she realised he was at it again, playing with her.

"As I am now?" She wasn't sure she should play along with his fun, but she couldn't stop herself from asking that question, from being curious about what he had meant.

He slid her another sidelong look. "You used to be different."

Evelyn frowned at him, not really following him.

And then it hit her.

She pressed her hand to the glass again as a desperate sort of feeling surged through her. "Did you know me before the fae stole my memories? Before I was taken captive by them?"

Although she wasn't sure why she would have known an incubus.

He scoffed. "Is that what Archangel told you?"

She eased back. "No, that's what Archer—"

Evelyn cut herself off as it hit her that he was probably playing her, that this was all a game to him, and for some reason he wanted to make her question everything, including her partner. She narrowed her eyes on him. Incubi were fae.

"Did you take me captive and steal my memories?" That question leaked from her lips, spoken too quietly for her liking, lacking strength and echoing how she felt as she stared at him, fearing his answer.

"No." He scowled at her, his eyebrows meeting hard as his green eyes gained a dark edge and his markings shifted colour, veering towards ashy black and blood red again. "I would never—"

"But you know my name and you followed me to Hell," she interjected, unwilling to let him keep spinning lies meant to soften her, to weaken her for his entertainment or whatever this sick dance he was playing with her was meant to be. "And now you're here and you know about my missing memories. Don't you?"

He didn't deny it.

In one far-too-sexy and fluid move, he rose onto his feet and strode towards her, looking like a panther, or perhaps just the predator he was.

He stopped on the other side of the glass, the five inches it occupied now the only distance between them, and gazed down at her, an almost earnest edge to his expression as it softened and his markings settled. The colours dancing across them changed again as he fidgeted with something, the red transforming into shades of purple and blue that drifted among the black.

She wasn't familiar with those colours, or the ones he had displayed when he had first seen her.

Evelyn stared up into his eyes, deeply aware of the eight inches he had on her, of the way his muscles shifted beneath his pale skin with each breath he drew as he gazed at her. She swallowed hard and told herself to look away from him, but God, she didn't want to stop looking into his eyes. They bewitched her as spots of gold and blue danced against an emerald backdrop and she found herself pressing closer to the glass that separated them, aching to get to him.

She tried and failed to convince herself he had a power over her, to label the feelings he stirred in her as the product of his ability as an incubus to charm females, denying they were real. They felt real as she stood in silence with him, her breaths coming faster and her heart racing as her blood heated.

A voice from deep within her whispered this was real. It was real and a little frightening. She had never felt like this with any other man. She had never been this attracted to someone.

Never burned for them so fiercely.

His left shoulder flexed, his arm moving slightly, and she dropped her gaze to his hand, curiosity tugging it there as a need to know what he was doing filled her.

A flicker of a frown danced on her brow as she noticed the gold band he wore on the ring finger of his left hand—a ring he was now spinning slowly with his thumb.

He was married?

She had never heard of a non-human marrying someone before.

Evelyn ignored the jab of white-hot fire that stung her heart as she gazed at the ring and thought about the fact that somewhere out there, there was a woman waiting for him—a woman he loved. She shook it off and cursed herself for getting too caught up in him. She shouldn't have allowed herself to be drawn to him, should have resisted his attempts to talk to her and not let anything he had said affect her.

But it was easier said than done.

She lifted her eyes to his face again.

Met his sombre gaze.

Felt soul-deep aware of him as he stared at her in silence that felt far too comfortable, that began to tilt her world off-kilter as she fell into his eyes and again found she didn't want to look away. She tried again to blame his incubus power, but the flimsy attempt failed as her heart supplied that was impossible. She had checked the archive records, looking into how the cells worked and discovering that incubi were like any other species of non-human. The cell stripped him of the ability to charm and seduce her.

Although he did still have his sinful good looks to fall back on and use to his advantage.

He heaved a sigh that shifted his bare shoulders, tempting her to glance at his body. She denied it, aware that if she even so much as flicked a split-second look at the sculpted perfection of his chest that she would end up gawping at him for hours.

"Evelyn," he whispered and pressed his hand to the glass that separated them, his green eyes taking on a desperate look as he glanced at his hand and then at her, and she swore she could feel how deeply he needed to touch her.

A stray thought shook her to her core.

Or maybe she was the one desperate for him to touch her.

She went to turn away.

He stopped her in her tracks.

"I'm not a threat to you, Evelyn. I never am. It's rare for you to see it that way though." He smiled slightly when she looked back at him. "I shouldn't tell you any of this. It never ends well when I tell you things."

He chuckled mirthlessly.

Or perhaps maniacally judging by the glint in his eyes.

"It never ends well regardless."

Evelyn swallowed hard and told herself that he was only trying to rattle her, was probably enjoying watching the conflict that was no doubt playing out in her eyes as she stared at him, as his words sank in and her mind raced, trying to make sense of them and the apprehension she felt.

She turned her cheek to him, hesitated and glanced back at him, unable to bring herself to leave without another glimpse of him, and then forced herself to go. She marched along the corridor, picking up speed as everything he had told her whirled around her mind, as she tried to purge it and deny it.

He was trying to shake her, probably acted like this around everyone who came to him.

But the thought that he didn't, the notion that he might be different around her, plagued her and filled her mind and her heart with a question she tried to ignore.

Had he known her before she had lost her memories?

CHAPTER 8

Evelyn had dreamed of fire. Again. She had woken in a cold sweat, her heart racing and head spinning, and an urge had shot through her.

A need to see the incubus.

Instead of heading to his pen, she had hit the gym, had worked out until she had dropped and then returned to her quarters. Archer had left a note under her door. He was worried about her and had the feeling she was avoiding him.

She finished drying her hair off and groaned into the towel, pressing it to her face. She wasn't sure why she felt the need to stay away from Archer. No. She was. It was the incubus. He had put it in her head that something wasn't right about Archer and that she couldn't trust him. The incubus had succeeded in driving a wedge between them.

Well, she was going to remove it.

She would track Archer down and make things right between them again and apologise for being so distant.

But first, there was something else she needed to do.

She had to know whether the incubus's behaviour around her was different to how he acted around others.

She clung to the idea that it wasn't. He didn't treat her differently. He didn't act differently when he was alone with her.

To prove that to herself, she pulled her uniform on and jammed her feet into her boots, and left her quarters behind to wind her way down through the building. When she reached cellblock D, she didn't head for him. She went straight to the observation room at the start of the cellblock and grabbed a mug of coffee from the machine at the back of the darkened room before nodding a greeting to the man overseeing the wall of monitors that covered every angle and cell in the block. He dipped his head and went back to his work, and she settled herself in front of one of the monitors reserved for watching footage. She knew a lot of hunters who liked to be an active part of what happened to their detainees, but that had never been her style.

In fact, she could count the number of times she had checked out the CCTV feeds on one hand.

Evelyn tied her damp blonde hair up into a high ponytail, put the headphones on and sipped her coffee. She scrolled through the list of recordings and frowned as she spotted other recordings on the same dates put together with them, only they weren't of his cell. She clicked on one of them, curiosity moving her finger before she could get the better of herself and stay focused on viewing the footage of his cell.

Her stomach twisted slightly as the image came up on screen and she made sense of what she was seeing. The incubus was naked in it, strapped to a metal board that had been tilted at an angle so he was standing upright, and he wasn't the only one in the room. There was a nude female too.

Evelyn set her mug down as that female approached him, anger spiking in her blood for some reason as she watched her rubbing herself all over the incubus and kissing him. Her fingers tightened against the mug until she had a white-knuckle grip on it, her temperature soared and her jaw clenched as she closed the recording and tried another one, and found it was the same scenario.

But a different female.

She clicked the next one, and then the next, moving faster and faster through close to a dozen recordings that each showed the same thing.

A woman trying to force herself on the incubus.

And the incubus resisting.

Evelyn closed the recording and looked at the one dated today, resisted the urge to click on it and stared at the list, her pulse pounding in her ears as she fought to make sense of what she had seen and the fierce reaction it had tugged from her, how angry she felt as she rolled through everything in her mind, replaying woman after woman throwing herself at him.

A desire to storm to his cell and yell at him, to open it and strike him pounded inside her, unsettling her.

She stilled as something struck her.

He hadn't kissed most of them.

Some of them he had kissed, but it had been brief and he had looked angry when he had made the female leave him alone, his face as dark as midnight and markings churning with obsidian and crimson.

Why hadn't he seduced them? It was clear to her that the scientists wanted to record an incubus seduction and study it. Was he resisting because he didn't want to go along with their plans and was trying to anger them?

Or was it because of that gold band that encircled his finger?

Evelyn breathed slowly and deeply to calm her racing heart, giving herself a moment to banish the unruly emotions that had her head spinning. When she was settled again, back in control, she switched to watching the footage of his cell, studying how he was around others.

She noticed something as she fast-forwarded through hours of video, pausing only to watch the times someone stopped in front of his cell, or he was talking to the male in the cell opposite him.

She jotted down timeframes on a piece of paper someone had left near the monitor and flicked between them, making sure she hadn't just imagined it.

And then sank back in her chair and stared at the incubus paused on the screen.

His markings were different whenever she was the one standing before him.

He reacted to her in a way he didn't with any other.

"There you are."

Evelyn jumped out of her skin and spun on the chair to face Annette as the brunette entered the room. She quickly forced herself to relax at the same time, not wanting the scientist to see how rattled she was. Her heart kept pounding a fast rhythm though, wouldn't settle, no matter how many times she told herself it was fine that she had been watching footage of the incubus. She felt as if she had been caught doing something she shouldn't be though.

She felt guilty.

When Annette glanced at the screen behind Evelyn, she realised it wasn't guilt she was feeling.

It was nerves.

She had discovered something about the incubus and the look slowly settling on Annette's face left her in no doubt the woman was going to demand to know what it was that had her so jumpy. Her first instinct was to lie, and she caught herself before one could leave her lips. She had no reason to lie to her colleagues. She had no reason to protect the incubus.

Evelyn looked over her shoulder at the screen, unable to shake the strange feeling that she did.

She had a reason, only she couldn't remember it.

"What have you noticed about him?" Annette came to stand beside her.

Evelyn cleared her throat. "I was just studying the shifts in his behaviour. He seems comfortable with the male in the cell across from his. They talk quite frequently. Seems to be the fae language."

Not a dialect Evelyn was familiar with though. She knew a little of the common fae tongue, enough to get her by, but was far from fluent.

Annette's lip curled. "That can't be a good thing. Anything else?"

"His…" She forced herself to say it, because she didn't know the incubus, and she owed everything to Archangel. "His markings are different at times. I noticed it yesterday when I was speaking to him."

"They change colour frequently, although he seems intent on remaining angry towards us."

She shook her head and frowned. "No. I mean, I know that. His markings were gold and blue, but there was dark pink in them too."

Annette looked intrigued now and Evelyn didn't like the way she eyed the screen, staring at the incubus. "We've not seen those colours before. And you say it was when you were speaking to him?"

She nodded.

"I need to know what they mean. This is new information and I would like to see it for myself." Annette gave her an expectant look.

Part of Evelyn wanted to refuse the silent order to help her and the rest nodded in agreement. Archangel had been good to her. This was her home. Her people. The incubus had filled her head with doubts, probably in an attempt to turn her against Archangel. She had no reason to trust him or protect him.

She stood and followed Annette from the room.

The nerves she had felt upon Annette discovering her watching the footage only grew as they made their way through the cellblock, as she looked in on several of the detainees and began to feel differently towards them. A few of them cast her bleak looks, their brows furrowing as they held her gaze until she was out of sight. She steeled herself, tried to tell herself that she had only been doing her job by bringing in the incubus, and that her fellow hunters had only been doing their jobs when they had brought in every miserable non-human she passed.

Only it was hard to make herself believe it as she thought about the incubus. He had attacked Archer, but he had hardly been a threat to regular humans, and he had told her that her partner had provoked him. How had Archer provoked him?

She looked into a cell at a female. What had she done to warrant being caged? Or the male who occupied the cell opposite her? What had any of these non-humans done to deserve being captured?

To deserve being strapped to a metal board and forced to endure an attempt at seduction?

She stopped in front of Fenix's cell and every inch of her froze as she stared at him.

At the raw, red marks on his wrists together with mottled bruises that tracked up his arm and gave her the impression someone had restrained him with enough force to leave those marks.

"What did you do to him?" She turned to Annette, sure she was to blame for how pale Fenix looked and how he remained with his head bent, muttering things in the fae tongue as he rubbed his chafed wrists.

"I'm sorry," Annette said.

And for a heartbeat, Evelyn was sure the woman hadn't heard her and was asking her to repeat herself.

But then the brunette grabbed Evelyn by her hair and dragged her head back hard enough to make her cry out.

Fenix launched to his feet on an inhuman snarl, his eyes transformed to pure swirling gold and blue, and his markings writhing with the colours of rage. He smashed his fists against the glass that separated them, his eyes narrowing on Annette as he fought to break through the barrier.

"Get your fucking hands off her." His voice was a vicious black growl as he glared at Annette.

"I had suspected as much," she whispered and tightened her grip on Evelyn's hair, pulled it so hard that Evelyn's hands flew to seize her wrists, fear screaming at her that the bitch meant to pull her hair out. "But I've never seen an incubus display such possessive—no, protective—behaviour."

Evelyn had been about to introduce Annette's ankle to her boot, but she froze as those words hit her and several pieces of the puzzle fell into place.

Archer had provoked him.

Her eyes slowly widened.

It made sense now in a terrible, unsettling way.

The incubus had been talking about her. He had witnessed her partner touching her and being friendly and concerned towards her, and it had provoked him into attacking Archer.

To keep him away from her.

Fenix tore himself away from the glass and began to pace, his steps clipped and his gaze fierce as he kept it locked on Annette, glittering with malevolence and darkness. With a hunger for violence.

And for some reason, he felt more familiar than ever.

As she watched him restlessly moving back and forth in his cramped cell, visibly itching with a need to attack, she felt sure that she knew him, but that feeling was intangible in a way—like a hazy dream.

Or the shadow of a memory.

"Unhand the female," he growled and pivoted, his eyes narrowing on Annette and his markings veering closer to all-black. "I won't ask again."

"How do you intend to carry out that threat?"

"I would do what the incubus is asking, Annette. Release Evelyn." That male voice held a note of authority, had Evelyn tearing her gaze away from Fenix to look to her right.

Mark's clear grey eyes remained fixed on Annette, and the two hunters that stood behind him looked ready to leap the moment he issued an order. He folded his arms across his chest, causing his tailored dark grey suit to stretch tight over his shoulders and biceps, and stared the scientist down.

"Release her."

Annette obeyed this time, loosened her hold enough that Evelyn could wrench free of her grip. Evelyn fought the urge to lash out at her, to hurt her as repayment for what she had done, aware that Mark was watching both of them. He signalled his men and the two hunters were quick to rush forwards and seize hold of Annette to drag her away.

"I'm right," Annette yelled, her voice growing quieter as the hunters pulled her towards the entrance of the cellblock. "He's exhibiting behaviour we know nothing about. It's my job to document…"

Mark heaved a deep sigh and looked Evelyn over, a flicker of concern in his gaze as he checked her from head to toe. "Are you hurt?"

She shook her head.

Fenix rammed the glass with his shoulder, landed a punch on it that left a bloody smear, and then paced away from her, luring her gaze with him. He turned his back to the white wall and slid down it to his backside, rested his arms on his bent knees and hung his head between them. He muttered in the fae tongue, and the only words she caught weren't good ones. It sounded a lot like he was planning all the ways he wanted to kill Annette for hurting her.

Evelyn looked at his reddened wrists and shifted to face him, barely leashing the urge to press her palm to the glass and tell him that she was fine, that she hadn't really been hurt. His markings swirled with vivid colour, violently churning, but they slowly settled as she gazed at him, as if her eyes on him was enough to calm him.

She lingered, some part of her wanting to offer him this comfort and make him see that she hadn't courted Mark's concern, that she hadn't asked for it, and that she wasn't interested in him. The need to show him all those things was strong, like an instinct, one she didn't understand but one that controlled her all the same.

Her gaze slid to the ring on his finger.

What was she to him?

What was he to her?

She had read about mates in the world of the non-humans, how the males of some species grew violent if they felt another male was making moves to take their mate from them. Fenix's behaviour had all the hallmarks of a mated male.

"I'm sorry," Mark sighed those words. She glanced at him and found his grey eyes fixed on the incubus. The hard edge to his expression as he ran a hand over his sandy hair and his gaze drifted back to her told her that he wasn't happy about what had just happened, but she didn't care about what Annette had done to her.

She only cared about what Archangel had done to Fenix.

"Did you sanction whatever they did to him?" she bit out, refusing to back down when the sensible part of her warned her that talking to her superior—to one of the senior commanders in Archangel—in that way wasn't going to get her what she wanted—it was going to get her fired and kicked out of her home.

But her blood was running too hot now, the sight of Fenix in pain and how Annette had thrown woman after woman at him seared on her mind to keep her anger at boiling point.

"I've been away, dealing with business at one of the satellite offices. I came back to find a report on my desk that someone had witnessed the subject restrained and screaming in one of the labs. I tried to locate Annette to question her about it and received word she had been seen heading towards this cell block. I came here directly." Mark slid her a look that had her shoulders locking up tight and her gaze darting away from him before he could see in her eyes just how upset she was by how Annette had treated the incubus.

Her gaze landed on Fenix.

Screaming. Restrained.

She swallowed hard. She didn't have the stomach to ask for more information and was glad she hadn't looked at the recording from today now.

She wasn't sure what she might have done if she had seen how terribly Annette had treated Fenix.

Regret washed through her as she looked at him, and for the first time since joining Archangel, she felt terrible about something she had done. It was her fault that he was in this condition. It was her fault that he had been subjected to awful things, to what amounted to torture. She felt sick as she crouched at the glass of his cell and pressed her hand to it, no longer sure this was the place for her.

How many other non-humans had been treated like him?

She glanced over her shoulder into the cell behind her, where a tall, handsome man stood with his silver eyes locked on her, throwing off a dangerous vibe that had her wanting to keep her distance from him. That gnawing feeling of guilt in her gut only grew worse as she looked at his stomach and saw the healing stitches there. Had he deserved to be cut open like that?

Did any of them?

"Evelyn," Mark murmured and moved a step closer to her. "What Annette did was inexcusable. It is not how we work."

It was. It was exactly how Archangel operated. They brought in non-humans and ran tests on them, studying them and calling it vital research that was necessary in order to protect innocent humans.

But what about the innocent non-humans that had no doubt been captured in raids or while they were out living their life? She was sure plenty of them were captured too and treated abominably by Archangel.

Possibly even killed.

Mark sighed softly. "I need to speak with Annette… but… I would like to speak with you too when you have a moment. I want to hear from you what happened."

She nodded, but didn't take her eyes off Fenix, not even when Mark walked away, leaving her alone in the corridor between the cells.

Fenix lifted his head, his eyebrows furrowing as he gazed across the cell to her, a hell of a lot of worry in his eyes that made her feel he could sense how she was spiralling, her thoughts dragging her down, and how the questions rolling through her mind, multiplying rapidly, were shaking her to her soul, leaving her feeling off-balance and as if everything she had believed in was a lie.

The line of swirls, dots and slashes that tracked up his arms changed colours again, shimmering with deep pink, gold and sapphire.

"What do those colours mean?" She couldn't get her voice above a whisper as she asked that, as a need to know flooded her and made her lean towards him, desperate to make him answer her because she knew that whatever feeling caused those colours, it was about her.

And only her.

He looked away and covered his arms as best he could, concealing the markings, as if he didn't want her to see them.

"Fenix," she said.

And his eyes locked with hers.

That fire she kept seeing filled her mind and she could almost feel the heat of it as she stared into his eyes, could feel the flames licking her skin and making her burn.

It was him.

He was the fire.

He made her burn like no other.

And one touch from him was all it would take to burn her will to resist to ashes.

CHAPTER 9

Fenix was slowly wasting away. He knew it, could feel it as a sort of gnawing sensation inside him, as if his body was eating itself. He pressed a hand to his bare stomach above the waist of his black cotton trousers and stared at the glass front of his cell, his thoughts far away.

Wherever Evelyn was.

Where was she?

Since the white-coat had attacked her, provoking him into revealing that he cared about her, and she had confronted the other male who had reeked of a leader, she hadn't come to see him.

In fact, no one had come to his cell.

Whenever someone approached it, he expected them to stop before him, but they moved past without paying him any heed, without slowing in the slightest. Every hour that trickled by was torture, had his mind conjuring vile images of Evelyn with that—whatever Archer was. Not human, that was for sure.

He needed to see her again.

He needed to know she was all right.

But more than that, he needed to see that look in her golden eyes again, the one that had left him feeling sure that he was getting through to her, and had made him feel as if he was treading a dangerously thin line. There had been warmth in her gaze and her actions, and it unsettled him.

He couldn't let her fall for him. Not this time.

It had been a mistake to get caught by Archer and brought here by her. It had been a mistake to lower his guard and be gentle towards her, revealing that he cared about her. He should have remained hard and cold towards her, keeping her at arm's length and giving her reason to not hate him, but not begin to like him either.

Gods, he didn't want her to hate him.

That was always the crux of his failings with her.

He could never bring himself to be cruel and callous enough towards her to stop her from falling for him.

One time, he had felt sure they had been close to unravelling the curse and finding a way to break it. The belief that they were going to succeed had made him lower his guard and he had screwed everything up.

Aderyn had fallen for him again.

She had ended up killed by a mage, ripped from Fenix to reincarnate somewhere far from him with her memories missing.

The lights suddenly dropped, blanketing everything in darkness.

Fenix tensed and immediately went on high alert, cocked his head and listened as the occupants of the cells around him grew restless and wary, all of them as on edge as he was.

"What is happening?" the fae across the corridor asked.

"Don't know." Fenix listened harder as a siren wailed, trying to hear over the infernal shrieking sound, and flinched as a red flashing light punched back the darkness.

Revealing glimpses of the black-haired male across from him.

The fae covered his ears with his hands and glared at the ceiling, the red lights that chased over him catching on his silver irises and making them look crimson.

Fenix arched an eyebrow as he covered his own ears to protect his sensitive hearing.

Or perhaps his eyes were now crimson.

He moved closer to the glass of his cell, narrowing the gap between him and the fae, curious as to what the male was. His irises weren't entirely crimson. They were jagged silver in the centres around his now-elliptical pupils.

The fae bared his teeth at the wailing siren.

Or more accurately, bared fangs.

A whole set of them. His canines were the longest, but the incisors next to them were sharper and longer too.

Not a vampire. Not an elf. This male was something else. Something Fenix had never seen before.

His skin paled, the tips of his ears growing pointed, and his lips darkened towards black.

In the flickering crimson light, inky markings curled around his biceps to sweep around his shoulders and trace the line of his pectorals from his armpits around the square slabs of them and up to his collarbones where they curved around and faded into a point. These markings weren't the fae tongue people spoke these days, the language of Fenix's own markings.

This male's markings were ancient fae. A dialect lost in time.

Although Fenix would bet his left nut that the male spoke that tongue too.

Fenix had seen it once, in a tome owned by a witch in the fae town near where he lived. Abigail treasured that book as if it was special, even though she couldn't read the damned thing. He shook his head. She would love to get her hands on this male and convince him to translate it for her.

The male slid him a look, his voice a black snarl. "I want out."

Fenix bet he did.

He didn't only want out either. He wanted out and he wanted to rip into every hunter who came to an abrupt halt to cast a fearful glance at him before hurrying off to wherever they were heading.

The fae pressed his ghost-white palms to the glass. The top thirds of each finger were as black as night and the lower parts were marked with another line of inky symbols that tracked downwards to the edge of his palm.

Son of a bitch had black nails that were an inch long and as sharp as claws too.

"We must leave this place."

Fenix wanted to ask whether the male was talking about *we* as in Fenix and him leaving together, or whether he was talking about the nice friendly guy he had been a few minutes ago and this darker version of himself.

He kept his mouth shut though.

Mostly because the alarm fell silent.

"What is happening now?" the fae growled, flashing those killer teeth of his.

"Not sure." Fenix pressed his cheek to the glass and tried to see along the corridor. He couldn't see shit though. Nothing past the cell next to the fae's one. "Something is happening. Just be ready to move if these cells open. Not liking our chances here."

His gut twisted, a need pouring through him, one that said he was going to have to take his chances with all the armed hunters if he did get the opportunity to escape. He couldn't leave Evelyn here. He needed to find her and take her with him. He tried to battle that urge, fought a war with himself that he knew he would lose the moment the glass lifted. No matter what decision he made while trapped in this cell, it was going to change the second he was free.

His instincts as her mate wouldn't let him leave her behind.

More armed hunters rushed past the cell.

The alarms started again, the flashing lights stinging his eyes as he pressed closer to the glass, desperately trying to see something, anything that might tell him what was happening.

A shriek pierced the wailing noise, had the fae across the corridor growling low, and Fenix knew why. He smelled blood too.

Archangel was under attack.

The metallic clash of weapons rang along the hallway and Fenix breathed harder, mentally preparing himself for a fight he was sure was coming, rolling his way. He strained to hear who was attacking Archangel, reached out with his dampened senses and cursed the cell that surrounded him. He could feel someone out there. Someone powerful. But he couldn't tell what breed that person was with the magical-whatever-it-was hindering his powers.

The siren ceased and the lights stopped flashing, and the fae bit out a ripe curse in his native tongue as white lights burst back to life. They blinded Fenix too and he flinched away from the glass.

He sensed that the powerful person he had detected was closer now, strained to listen in on murmured voices that were still at a distance.

Grimaced and grunted as a loud bang echoed along the corridor and the floor bucked, knocking him to his backside. A deep fracture snaked like a jagged bolt of lightning across the thick glass barrier of his cell. Hope bloomed inside him. He looked at the fae. The male was on his knees now, flashing fangs and digging the points of his claws into the glass as he slid a black, vicious look towards the direction the shockwave had come from. Pieces of glass bounced past Fenix's cell and he banged on the fractured barrier, trying to get the attention of whoever was blasting people out of their cells.

He saw a sliver of a leg clad in skin-tight black armour consisting of tiny scales.

An elf.

"Hey! Mate! Let us out," he hollered and the blue-black-haired male reared back and glanced at him.

"Desist!" That deep, commanding snarl had the elf's head snapping towards the far end of the corridor and his violet eyes widening.

A wave of power washed over Fenix and he banged his fists against the glass, didn't want to be stuck in here with whoever had just shown up because they were strong, far stronger than he was, and his gut said they weren't on good terms with the elf in the corridor.

That elf was quick to disappear, and Fenix sensed two others vanish with him.

"Fuck," he bit out and eyed the glass barrier, checking every inch of it, desperately trying to find a way to make it open.

The newcomer he had felt drew closer and Fenix heard voices again, too quiet for him to make out what they were saying. He couldn't see the owner of that deep voice either. He looked at the fae, wanting to know if he could. The fae shook his head and returned to stroking his fingers over the glass, his crimson-to-silver eyes roaming over it as he muttered things to himself beneath his breath.

Long seconds ticked past as Fenix banged his fist against the cell door, haemorrhaging hope at a rapid pace. Any second now, the person in the corridor would do as the elf had done. They would have broken out whoever they were here to save and they would be gone, and every soul in the block would pay for what had happened. The hunters were bound to punish those left behind.

He stepped back from the glass and assessed it again. If he rammed it hard enough, would the faults in it widen? Could he keep beating it until it gave and shattered?

He wasn't sure he had the strength to do it, but he was going to try.

Fenix mustered his strength, pulled down a breath and blew it out, and ran at the glass, dropping his shoulder as he neared it.

The barrier whooshed upwards and glass bit into his bare feet as he crossed the corridor at speed and collided with the fae, who was staring in shock at the ceiling.

The male grunted as Fenix accidentally took him down, landing on top of him.

"Sorry, mate." Fenix pushed himself up, leaped off him and to a distance when the fae growled and tossed him a black look, and he felt just how powerful the male was.

Whoever had been in the corridor had nothing on this fae.

A sense of darkness and danger buffeted Fenix in powerful waves that had him easing another step back, moving to what felt like a safer distance. If there was such a thing. The male's power continued to press down on him, thickening the air as he picked himself up and dusted off his black trousers, and shock trickled through Fenix as he swore the sensation was growing stronger.

Darker.

Fenix clung to the belief that the male wouldn't harm him, replayed all the hours they had passed in idle conversation, when he had begun to feel the fae liked him.

He glanced into the hallway as half-dressed males and females hurried past. Someone must have opened the barriers in the entire block. He tested his abilities and managed to teleport a few feet to the other side of the fae's cell. Not everyone running past them had the ability to teleport. They would have to escape by making it past the hunters. Maybe it would provide a big enough distraction that he could reach Evelyn.

"Come on." Fenix held a hand out to the fae, unsure whether he was a breed that could teleport.

Unsure what the hell he was.

The fae gripped his wrist. "We must leave."

Fenix looked at his hand and then into his eyes, and knew in his gut that the male was right, but heard himself saying, "I can't. I have to get Evelyn out of this place."

"The huntress?" The fae released him when Fenix nodded, his words a black snarl and his expression letting Fenix know exactly what he thought about Evelyn. "That is madness. Do not sacrifice yourself for someone so unworthy."

"She's my fated mate. I can't just leave her."

The fae glanced at the corridor as shouts broke out, as screams followed and the scent of blood grew heavier in the air. The male looked reluctant when his eyes met Fenix's again.

"I will go with you."

Fenix shook his head, changing his mind in a flash as he took a good look at the fae.

As much as he could use the male's help, he had been through enough already. Fenix wasn't sure he could live with himself if the male was caught again. This was his chance at freedom, and Fenix couldn't be selfish and jeopardise it, not now the male had revealed this side of himself. He glanced at the small camera mounted above his own cell, pointed into this one. Archangel would have witnessed the change the male had undergone and he would be at the top of the list for studying if he was caught again.

"Can you teleport?" Fenix glanced at the corridor again as a human sailed past, screaming at the top of their lungs.

The fae nodded.

Fenix hesitated for a heartbeat, the power he could sense in the male tempting him to take him up on his offer of help. He shook it off.

"Then go. Get out of here." He stepped back from the fae and smiled softly as he realised something. "I never introduced myself. Fenix. My name is Fenix. If you ever need help, just head to the fae town in Scotland, find a witch called Abigail or her sister Agatha, and they'll direct you to me."

"Fenix." The male stepped forwards and held his hand out to him. When Fenix went to take it, the male moved his arm forwards and gripped him by his elbow, and Fenix mirrored him, so their forearms pressed together. The fae looked deep into Fenix's eyes, his voice earnest as he spoke. "Prince Oberon owes you a debt, Fenix of the Incubi, one you can claim at your leisure."

Fenix was too rattled by the name he had spoken to pay much attention to the rest.

Prince Oberon.

Prince bloody Oberon.

Fenix had always thought of the male as a story—a legend—or perhaps a myth, but he was flesh and blood.

Fire seared his arm where Prince Oberon gripped it and then the male turned to black mist that sparkled with gold flecks and was gone.

Fenix twisted his right arm away from himself and stared at the patch of skin just below his elbow as orange embers swirled around it, forming a circular design that had a stag and dragon in the centre of it and ancient fae symbols that followed the curve.

A brand to mark him with the prince's name for any of his breed to see or a promise that Fenix could cash in to remove it from his skin?

He swallowed hard. Either way, he wasn't sure he had ever experienced a day as crazy as this one was turning out to be. He stared at the mark.

Unable to believe that a prince of the Unseelie Court owed him a favour.

A huntress went flying past the front of the cell and a female wearing the standard black tank and trousers of the prisoners gave chase. Fenix shook himself back to his task and hurried from his cell, banking right and teleporting past a group that was fighting. He landed at the far end of the corridor and hurried around the bend, his senses stretching outwards, seeking Evelyn.

He sensed her ahead of him, gritted his teeth and forced another teleport, one that had him shaky and breathing hard as he landed right in front of her.

She back-peddled hard, her golden eyes widening as they landed on him.

"We have to go. You can't stay here. It's not safe for you." He lunged for her and realised his mistake too late.

She wasn't alone.

Archer seized his wrist and twisted his arm so viciously that Fenix's shoulder screamed in pain, and he was forced to drop to his knees to avoid having his arm broken. His gaze leaped up to the dark-haired male, colliding with Archer's as he loomed over him, a malevolent look in his dark eyes that had all of Fenix's senses sharpening as best they could while he was hungry.

Because Archer wanted to kill him.

Fenix bellowed as Archer slammed a fist into his face and followed it with a swift knee to his sternum. The bastard hit like a truck. Fenix summoned a teleport, one that carried him only a few feet from the male, and did his best not to sag into the wall as his strength bled from him and hunger roared up on him, had his head pounding and his incubus nature stealing control.

Whatever Archer was, he definitely wasn't human.

Fenix flicked a look at Evelyn where she lingered behind her partner, her eyes still wide and her face pale as she stared at him. His brow furrowed and he couldn't resist the urge to reach for her, his need of her flowing too strongly in his blood to deny it. Her golden gaze lowered to his hand and for a heartbeat, he swore she wanted to reach for him too.

And then Archer came at him.

Fenix bared his teeth at the male and dodged the heavy blow Archer aimed at his face, ducked beneath it and leaped backwards, his gaze darting to Evelyn again as he landed.

And realised that he couldn't get to her.

Archer wasn't going to allow it. The male was hellbent on protecting her, and Fenix seethed with a need to take him down, to remove him from the equation so he couldn't steal his mate. Only the sensible part of him won for once. He listened to it as it screamed in his mind, telling him that if he tried to get to her, that Archer would be the one killing him. He wasn't strong enough to fight this male, not right now.

But that didn't mean their war was over.

As soon as Fenix was strong enough, he was going to return for a rematch and he would be the victor.

His eyes locked with Evelyn's again.

He cursed.

"I'll get you out of here. Whatever it takes." He took one last look at her, making his words a vow so she would know he meant them. "I'll set you free."

And teleported just as Archer threw another punch at him.

One that made the air smell like the tinny scent of magic.

CHAPTER 10

More than a week had passed since the break-in at Archangel HQ in London, and Evelyn still couldn't shake the way the incubus had looked at her, or what he had said.

He had wanted to take her away from Archangel.

Had looked desperate to make that happen.

Why?

Was it purely because he wanted her for himself?

Or was the growing feeling she had—the one that said she knew him— right, and he honestly believed she was in danger among the hunters and scientists?

She didn't feel as if she was in danger as she sat on the roof of the building, gazing out at the skyline of London, her eyes roaming over the hotchpotch roofs and the striking BT Tower that punched high into the air to loom over them.

Evening was approaching, the fingers of clouds in the sky already threaded with pink as the sun sank lower. It was beautiful up here. Quiet. She had been coming here more and more frequently, compelled to find a space where she could breathe.

Where she could think.

She relaxed and sank into her growing habit of mulling over everything she knew about Fenix. Didn't notice Archer pushing the roof access door open and striding towards her until he was right next to her. That wasn't good. She was too swept up in the incubus, should have been aware that someone else was up here with her. It worried her.

The look on Archer's face as she glanced up at him said it worried him too.

She was distracted, and distracted hunters got themselves killed. There were countless non-humans out there who were looking for hunters to take out, wanting to weaken Archangel and claim themselves a trophy. She didn't want to become a trophy, but she couldn't purge the incubus from her mind and was finding it harder and harder to stop thinking about him.

"Needed some air," she murmured and returned her gaze to the sunset.

Archer sat beside her on the black rectangular protrusion that had a vent on the rear side of it and acted as the perfect bench. Judging by the cigarette butts littering the area around it, people used it frequently. When Archer reached into his back pocket and withdrew his own pack of smokes, she arched an eyebrow at him. He sighed and put them away.

Instead of lighting a cigarette as he had clearly wanted, he leaned forwards, resting his elbows on his knees, his noble profile to her as he studied the city in silence. A black Henley covered him to his wrists, hugged his biceps and shoulders, and the first few buttons had been undone to reveal a strip of his toned chest. For once, he wasn't wearing his standard-issue fatigues, had donned a pair of black jeans that rode up a little around his ankles to reveal Chelsea boots. He looked like he was going out for a night on the town rather than a patrol, and she wanted to ask if he had plans.

A date maybe.

She almost scoffed at that.

Archer didn't date.

He could have his pick of the women working in HQ, but he kept to himself, and the one time she had asked if his tastes ran a different course, he had been quick to shoot her down and declare he was straight as an arrow.

He just wasn't interested in mixing business with pleasure.

Whatever that meant.

Archer casually pushed the black frame of his glasses up his nose with his index finger.

Evelyn waited, aware it was only a matter of time before he picked her up on the fact he kept finding her here.

When he said nothing, she couldn't hold her tongue, failed to deny the question that bubbled up from her soul and had her aching with a need to know the answer to it.

"Do you think I knew him before?" She risked a glance at Archer and dropped her gaze to her knees when he frowned and slid her a look that said he was more than worried about her now. She sighed. "I think I've seen him before. He was there in the Fifth Realm, but I'm sure that's not the first time I've seen him. He's so familiar... and the things he said."

"He's an incubus and he was being held captive." Archer's deep voice rolled over her, no hint of malice in it or any emotion at all. He sounded as if he was stating facts, repeating lines he had practiced to perfection in his head, but then his tone softened and warmed, and concern lit his dark eyes. "You can't trust him. He was playing you, Evelyn."

Something flickered in his gaze before he averted it, his shoulders shifting on a long sigh. If she had been forced to name that emotion, she would have called it guilt. Why?

"You'd be better off not trusting anyone," he muttered, his expression darkening.

What had him so moody today?

He idly picked at the left wrist of his top, his jaw flexed and he husked, "You shouldn't go trusting non-humans. It's not the Archangel way."

Evelyn frowned at that. "It might not have been once, but things are different now. There are a few tentative truces between us and the immortals... Prince Loren and the demon king Thorne—"

"That demon king just caused a fight in the cafeteria that put a dozen hunters in the infirmary, and reports place the elf in the cellblock a week ago, soon after the attack started," he snapped and his dark eyebrows knitted hard as he narrowed his gaze on her. "I don't think there's a truce between Archangel and the two you mentioned. Not only that, but do I really have to remind you that you were almost killed by a demon king? None of them are to be trusted. You need to remain loyal to Archangel and not let the non-humans sway you."

Evelyn leaned away from him slightly and didn't stop frowning at him even when his look softened, an apology entering his eyes. It wasn't like him to be this snappish with her. Sure, he sometimes had a hard edge to his tone or said things that cut her, and she did the same when frustration or something was getting the better of her, but the look in his eyes screamed that he wanted to have a full-blown argument with her over this and she wasn't sure why. Because she kept thinking about the incubus? Was he jealous? Or was his anger just his worry coming out in a bad way?

He blew out his breath and lifted his glasses, rubbing the bridge of his nose as his eyes closed.

She really didn't get Archer at times.

She had seen him avoid conflict with the non-humans.

He didn't know that she had, but she had witnessed it when she was off duty. She had gone for a walk and he had been participating in a nightly patrol with three other hunters. When she had spotted him among them, she had changed course to intercept them and say hello, but two vampires had appeared.

Archer had avoided participating in taking them down.

He had intentionally distanced himself when the team had moved in on them, and she had the feeling it hadn't been the first time he had avoided conflict with immortals either.

That feeling had only grown when the demon king had shown up in the cafeteria. Archer hadn't attempted to help the hunters who had gone there to take down Thorne when he had been trying to whisk Sable away to Hell.

She shoved that thought aside, trying not to let it colour her opinion of him. A lot of hunters had avoided the brawl that had broken out, not wanting to get between a demon king and Sable. Sable didn't tend to react well to people interfering in her business. When the elves had broken into the cell block before that, Archer had come to her to check she was safe, and he had ended up teaming up with her. He had stopped Fenix from taking her, and she was grateful to him for that.

"Sorry," he muttered. "Long day. Should've taken a break from the screen a lot earlier."

Evelyn gazed at his arms as he knitted his hands together above his knees, his eyes on the sunset as a comfortable silence fell between them, the tension that had filled the air only seconds ago swift to fade.

She shifted her focus to the sunset too, but her gaze strayed back to his forearms and she couldn't convince herself to look away.

Archer's head slowly swivelled towards her, his voice a low whisper. "What is it?"

She shook her head, feeling like a fool for wanting to ask him something she already knew the answer to, but her dreams always seemed so real, left her wondering if maybe she had imagined his arms didn't have markings on them.

He rarely showed them off after all.

Long sleeves had been standard-issue for him from the moment she had met him. It was rare for him to wear short sleeves.

"You've been on edge recently… since we brought that incubus in. You can talk to me, Evelyn. I promise I won't judge you." He heaved a sigh that stretched his Henley across his back and sat up, resting his hands on his thighs as he twisted towards her. His smile was soft, teasing. "I won't even judge him. I just want to know what's going on with you."

"I—" She sucked down a breath and blew it out, told herself that he wouldn't think she was crazy if she asked him, if she explained everything. Talking to him about it all would probably make her feel better. She glanced up into his eyes and then back at his forearms. "I've been dreaming weird things... and I think they mean something."

"What kind of weird things? You always tell me you're not the superstitious type."

"I'm not." She shook her head, tilted it back and stared at the sky. It was getting dark now, the temperature dropping as the sun disappeared below the horizon. Soon, the first faint stars would be visible. She focused on the sky, watching for them, using the task to distract her from how stupid this was going to sound. "You don't have any tattoos, do you?"

She risked a glance at him, sure he would be looking at her as if she had lost her mind.

He looked tense, his shoulders rigid as he stared at her, his expression slowly darkening. "You know I don't. What's this all about?"

She shook her head again. "You'll think I'm crazy."

"Try me." He placed his hand on her thigh, the hard edge to his features smoothing to reveal a hint of concern again.

"I dream of fire... and sometimes you're there... and you have these tattoos on your forearms. Like bands made up of lines and symbols, thinnest near your wrist and thickest near your elbows. Seven of them. And—"

The intensity of his gaze increased with each word that left her lips, his features pinching again, etching his face with darkness that had her wary of him for some reason.

"And?" he prompted, frowning at her now.

She loosed a sigh and pushed the words out. "And your eyes go all-black. Like... totally black. Even the whites."

He took his hand back and looked as if he wasn't sure what to say or maybe he wasn't sure what to make of the way she had seen him in her dream.

She rubbed a hand over her face, dragging it down, and shrugged it off. "It's probably just that incubus getting to me and putting ideas in my head. He kept telling me you weren't human and now I'm dreaming of you as a non-human and... It's probably just stress."

But it didn't feel like stress to her.

It had felt real. Right. She glanced at his forearms. It felt as if she had seen him with those markings on his skin and his eyes fathomless black, had witnessed it first-hand but hadn't remembered it until the dreams had started.

Archer pulled his sleeves up, revealing his toned forearms.

"No markings here." He flashed them at her, turning them so she could see as much of his skin as possible, and then lifted his left hand and pressed his palm to her forehead. A wealth of concern filled his dark eyes as his brow furrowed. "I think you're right and it's stress. Maybe you need to take a couple of days off... or get your mind off this incubus. This all started with him."

It hadn't. It had started before she had met him. Or maybe not. She frowned at her knees, trying to seize hold of her smoke-like memories and pull them into focus as a feeling stirred inside her. She had met the incubus before she had gone to the Fifth Realm. She had known him, and some part of her was sure he had been telling her the truth. He had been there at the castle because of her. Her memories of what had come before her close call were a little hazy and elusive, but the more she thought about it, the stronger another feeling inside her grew.

The constant sense that something was wrong with her and the dreams that had her waking in a cold sweat had all started when the demon king had tried to kill her and Archer had saved her.

What was that supposed to mean?

She stared at Archer's forearms, at unmarked skin. God, maybe he was right and she needed some time off or a visit to the staff shrink. She definitely needed to get her mind off Fenix.

He had put too many ideas in her head and her imagination was running with them, making Archer out to be something other than human.

"Stay away from the incubus," Archer said, each word hard and clipped, sounding like an order.

She lifted her gaze to meet his. His look was serious, sober, and as hard as his tone had been.

"If you see him, you stay away from him." He took hold of her hand, his gaze holding hers. "Promise me that you will."

She looked at his hand and then back into his eyes, frowned a little at how deadly serious he was, and then said, "I will."

A new question drifted through her mind.

Why was Archer so insistent about it?

She dropped her gaze to his arms again.

And saw a flash of the markings that had been in her dream.

CHAPTER 11

Fenix had lost track of how many weeks it had been since he had escaped Archangel. He idly scratched the point where Oberon's mark sat on his skin, the lines and symbols slightly raised, enough that he could feel it through the black material of his shirt. The heels of his boots were a steady tap against the black cobblestones that lined the main thoroughfare in the sprawling town in the free realm of Hell where he had exited the portal. This had to be the right place.

In between attempting to resist the urge to see Evelyn, and failing dismally at least once or twice a week, he had busied himself with following up the leads Hella had given him, and had been tracking down a lead on something else.

Something vital.

A way back into Archangel.

Whenever the need to see Evelyn had become too much for him to bear, Fenix had ended up stalking her, watching her from a distance for the most part. There had been three, possibly ten, times where he had approached her though, and every time he had tried to make contact with her again, her damned partner had been quick to shut him down and drive him away.

The last time he had tried to talk with her, she had been the one to tell him to leave her alone, or she would capture him and put him back in the cells.

As much as he wanted to be close to her, to have the opportunity to work on convincing her that she wasn't human and that her partner was a liar—and an immortal—he hadn't fancied being experimented upon, studied and possibly vivisected, so he had left.

Since that encounter, she had been spending all her time inside the Archangel building, beyond his reach. The need to see her again was building to an unbearable degree, had him restless and unable to sleep, and he couldn't focus for shit.

He needed his mate.

But what could he do?

Sure, he could teleport to a place he had been before, but that left him with some poor options. The only places he had been inside the building were the cell blocks, the rooms where the white-coats took pleasure in torturing immortals, and the corridor on the lower level that had always been busy with hunters.

To stand a chance of not being taken captive on the spot, he would have to charm a male hunter out on patrol, convincing him to hand over his uniform so he could use it as a disguise. And then what? He wandered the halls searching for Evelyn? He walked around asking after her?

He could charm anyone who grew suspicious, but it was too dangerous.

If he ran into Archer, he was screwed. If he ran into Evelyn when she wasn't alone, he was probably screwed too. Hell, if he ran into Evelyn when she was alone he was probably also screwed, unless he could snatch her before she tranquilised him, cuffed him and tossed him back in a cell.

So going in solo wasn't an option. He was damned if he was going to end up back in a cell again. He needed to take every possible precaution.

Which meant he needed someone who knew the building better than he did or who was powerful enough to create a diversion without endangering themselves while he searched for her.

Or both.

So Fenix had hit upon an idea.

Which hadn't panned out.

It turned out that finding the Unseelie Court wasn't as easy as it had sounded.

In fact, finding an unseelie or a seelie to speak to had proven impossible. Most people he had asked had spoken of the breeds as if they were just a fairy tale, something wild and fanciful told to young and impressionable fae to make them want to grow up big and strong, honest and judicious, or terrified of the things that went bump in the night. They had given him looks that had questioned his sanity.

One or two of them had spoken of them living in another realm, one that was so dangerous that few non-fae who entered it returned.

That realm was Lucia.

As far as Fenix knew, Lucia was where nymphs and sirens lived, not seelie and unseelie, so he had discounted those rumours and had given up on tracking down Oberon.

Instead, he had switched to hunting for the people who had been responsible for the break-in at Archangel. Two elves and a silver-haired shifter. Asking around in Hell this time had proven more fruitful. Apparently, the elves had a big reputation that also had many people terrified of the things that went bump in the night—things in this case being the two elves themselves.

They were assassins.

Ran the top guild in Hell.

And one of them was a tainted mad bastard.

The jury was out on the other one.

Fenix's steps slowed as he approached the end of the shopping street, where stores in the Tudor-style buildings all in black were making a fast trade in everything from meat and vegetables to the finest jewellery and rare silks, and weapons.

He had noticed a lot of stores selling weapons.

Which made a dreadful kind of sense as he stared at the imposing three-storey black building that loomed in the square ahead of him, resembling a gothic cathedral with its wings that made it form the shape of a cross. Two towers that soared to five-storeys tall flanked the wing to the right from his angle, the one he imagined was the front of the guild. Their conical tiled roofs pierced the dark sky of Hell, leading his eyes back down to the steeply pitched roof of the main building that formed the third floor. Windows were set into it at intervals, and between them were sharp railings.

Someone call the Addams family because Fenix had just found them their next home.

He slowly, cautiously, stepped out into the square and rounded the building, heading to the right of it, his eyes scanning it as a heavy feeling settled in his gut. Possibly dread.

Whoever had built it had done a good job of striking the right image. It was perfect for a dark guild of assassins, probably inspired this feeling growing inside him in all who looked at it.

This had to be the place.

He reached the main façade of the building and his gaze tracked up to the point where the straight sides changed into a steep angle to form a triangle. He stared at the large circular stained-glass window that occupied a lot of that space and lowered his gaze to the arched doorway below it.

Both of the heavy and ancient-looking wooden doors were open.

It did nothing to make the place look more welcoming.

Fenix swallowed hard and strode forwards, his step confident despite the fear that trickled through him. That fear fell away as he thought about the reason he was here, as he followed the arched entrance hall to a large reception room that was as black as the building was on the outside. These elves could help him reach Evelyn. He needed to have a way to get to her once he was ready and everything was in place.

This time, he would save her.

A huge black-haired male with bright cerulean eyes shoved a door near the right corner of the wall opposite Fenix open and stormed across the polished onyx flagstones towards him. The male clenched his fists so hard his arms bulged, tightening his black T-shirt across his biceps and chest, and Fenix readied himself for a fight when the big male's glowing blue gaze slid to him.

The shifter bared short fangs at him as the distance between them narrowed down to only a few inches, and then huffed and changed course, heading for the exit instead.

Either the guy was a monumental dick with a bad attitude, or his meeting hadn't gone well.

Fenix looked towards the door he had entered the reception room through and then around him, and his gaze snagged on the horseshoe of black couches around a monstrosity of a marble fireplace off to his left. Two males lounged there.

"I need to meet with someone," he hollered and took a step towards them, and froze when he felt the same powerful presence he had that night in Archangel.

His gaze slid to his right, to the door, as two elves exited it, one dressed in form-fitting black armour made up of tiny impenetrable scales, and the other a black knee-length tunic, tight trousers and riding boots.

Both males regarded him with curious violet eyes, but the one with the longer hair, wearing the armour, had a dark edge to his that warned Fenix he wasn't happy about the intrusion.

The elf growled and bared fangs at him.

"You the boss?" Fenix jerked his chin towards him, part of him hoping that he wasn't, because the elf looked as if he wanted to gut him rather than help him.

Fenix was oddly familiar with elves looking at him like that after his time in the cells of the Fifth Realm's castle.

The elf with the shorter blue-black hair stepped forwards and moved in front of the other one, as if he was trying to block Fenix's path to him, a feeling that only grew when he folded his arms across his chest, causing his black knee-length tunic to tighten across his shoulders and over his arms.

"I would be the male in charge here." The male's deep baritone had Fenix fixing his focus on him, but he still kept tabs on the other one with his senses, not trusting him.

Relief began as a slow trickle in his blood as he walked towards them, their familiar scents setting him at ease and taking some of the weight from his shoulders as he finally felt as if he could dare to hope that they could and would help him.

That he was one step closer to saving Evelyn.

As he neared them, their expressions shifted, their eyes widening slightly as recognition dawned in them.

"I know you," the leader said as he regarded Fenix with a frown now. "You were there the night we broke Harbin out of the hunter facility."

Fenix guessed Harbin was the silver-haired shifter he had seen. He looked between the two elves, not missing how the one that felt more dangerous to him had a distant look in his violet eyes now, as if he was miles away. Probably a good thing. Something about him set Fenix on edge, and he wanted to ask the leader if they could speak alone, but his gut said that the other male wouldn't allow that.

They both seemed very protective of each other.

"I need your help. I'll pay whatever it takes, and I know the job I'm offering is dangerous, but you're the only ones who can help me." Fenix tried to tamp down the need that roared in his blood, that rose to the fore to flood him with a desperate desire to make them help him, to force them using his charms and to leave for Evelyn now.

He sucked down a steadying breath. Pushing the elves to help him would most likely backfire on him, and he couldn't rush this either. As much as he wanted Evelyn away from Archangel, he needed to stick to the plan this time.

"Who do you need us to kill?" The leader ran a hand over his wild hair, tousling it and drawing Fenix's hand to the shorter, choppy lengths of his own hair.

He rubbed the back of it, just above his nape, still finding it strange. He had cut it more than a fortnight ago, after another failed attempt to reach Evelyn. He had been angry with himself, and with her rejection, and some part of him had been convinced that if he changed some things about himself that she would be more inclined to listen to him.

Or maybe he had been pathetically hoping that she would find him attractive.

It was only after he had cut his hair that he had realised it matched Archer's style.

"I don't need anyone killed." Not true. He wanted that male dead and buried, but killing her partner wouldn't exactly make Evelyn like him, so he bit his tongue. "I need to break into somewhere."

The elf's eyes darkened. "Break into somewhere?"

"Archangel," Fenix whispered, his brow furrowing as he thought about Evelyn. What was she doing right that second? Did she ever think about him? Did she feel anything for him? He shut that down, not wanting her to soften towards him. She couldn't. Not yet. It was too dangerous. If she felt something for him, she would end up dead and this whole, horrible cycle would start over again. "My mate now works for them... and I need to get her away from that wretched place. It's poisoning her mind and making it impossible for me to make her see the truth."

"The truth?" The male frowned.

"That she isn't mortal." Fenix raked fingers through his scruffy hair, still hating the style and the male he had copied it from. "I just need to get her away from them, but her partner has too tight a hold on her... the whole damned organisation has brainwashed her on top of the spell she's already under."

The other elf tuned back into their conversation and slid his partner a look that was equal parts wariness and concern.

"Your name?" the leader said and took a step towards Fenix.

"Fenix." He offered his hand.

The elf took it and gave it a hard shake. "We will help you, Fenix."

The second elf curled his lip and lost himself in thought again, drawing a worried glance from the leader.

"My name is Hartt. We can discuss terms in my office." He swept his free hand out towards the door.

Fenix shook his head. "Later. I have a few things I need to finalise before I can move ahead with this. I'll return once everything is in place... and as I said, whatever it costs... I don't care. I just need to get her out of Archangel undetected."

Hartt nodded. "Very well. We shall discuss terms upon your return."

Fenix released his hand and stepped back, satisfied that at least one part of his plan was in place.

Now he just had to do the hard part.

CHAPTER 12

Fenix's first port of call upon leaving Hell via a portal to the fae town in Scotland was to teleport to the outskirts of a small town in rural England. He landed in the forest of a country estate, a quiet and secluded spot he had found after driving to this location, and got his bearings, giving himself a moment to steel his mind and his heart. As much as he despised having to be near mages after what they had done to him and Aderyn, he needed to question as many of them as he could in order to discover the whereabouts of the one who had cursed them.

During his travels over the last few months, he had worked his way through Hella's leads and others he had found while looking into them. It had turned out more than half of them were no longer home to blood mages, a breed of witch who preyed upon phoenix shifters, capturing them and using the power contained in their blood for everything from spellcasting to keeping themselves young.

Now, he had four places where he knew mages lived still. He had visited them all, travelling by conventional means to places close to them so he could then teleport freely to the locations once he was ready to take a closer look. A few days ago, he had scouted the first of them from a safe distance, cataloguing the faces of everyone who had come and gone, glancing between them and the small portrait that was burning a hole in the pocket of his black jeans.

Fenix pulled out the oval silver case and opened it. He peered down at the painting it contained, one he had done himself, and sneered at it. He had gotten pretty good at sketching the bastard who had cursed him and Aderyn, had honed his skills over the years, refining this image of the mage. It wasn't to remind him of what he looked like, because the male's face was seared on his mind. He had painted it so he could show it to other mages when he was asking them about the one he was looking for.

He walked until he was at the edge of the forest, where it thinned to reveal a palatial sandstone mansion that would have been at home in any period drama. It put his own mansion in Scotland to shame and made him seriously consider hiring someone to sandblast the stone to give it a good clean, although it wouldn't stop his house from looking grey in comparison. The local granite he had built it from was closer to dove-grey than golden like the blocks used to make this one.

Fenix shrugged it off.

His home looked moodier in shades of grey, fitted into the wild heather-strewn mountains and dense pine forest.

He liked it.

When he was as close as he dared to get, he hunkered down and studied the building with his senses. Hunger had them sharp and eager to detect a female within the elegant walls of the house, made it easier for him to pick out how many people currently occupied it—a lot—and something else too.

His eyebrows drew down as he felt the familiar power in the air.

Phoenix shifters.

The mages here had captives.

An urge to break cover and help them speared him, had him rising to stand again, but he tamped it down and forced himself to count how many other people were in the building, and how many of those were mages.

More than a dozen if his senses were right.

He was no match for two mages, let alone six times that number. Blood mages had a power, one that had made life difficult for him more than once when he had decided to take a mage he had encountered out for good, removing one of their vile kind from the world.

They could create copies of themselves, magical clones that they controlled like marionettes, pulling their strings to make them fight for them. One powerful mage could create dozens of these milky-eyed clones that resembled zombies and were as relentless as one too. During fights against them, he had stabbed and even dismembered them, and it hadn't stopped them at all. It had only slowed them down.

But gods, the urge to help the phoenixes they were holding was strong. The thought of the mages tormenting them and stealing their blood, even going as far as killing them to drain every last drop of their power, sat heavily in his chest, weighing his heart down as his mind filled with his mate.

She had spent so long believing herself the only phoenix shifter in this world, that she was alone in this place, and he ached with the need to show her that she wasn't. There were others like her here in the mortal realm and in Hell, and he had helped them whenever he could, had set many of them free in the past.

Just as he wanted to free these phoenixes too.

But attempting it would get him killed.

He hated himself for it, but he had to think of his mate. She needed him. He needed to focus on helping her. Once he had done that, he would rally some troops and come back for these phoenixes, and he was sure she would want to help.

He forced himself to watch the building instead, studying the mages that moved past the windows or passed time in the formal gardens, hoping to spot the one he was looking for. Hours ticked past as he put the faces of the mages he saw to memory and counted them in his head, and it was growing dark by the time he realised he had seen every male witch in the building, and none of them were the one he was looking for.

Fenix eased back into the woods, moving to a safe distance where the mages wouldn't be able to sense him before he teleported to his next location.

It was still light on the east coast of the USA when he landed on a densely forested island in the middle of a large lake. His senses immediately stretched around him, charting everything nearby. There were some humans at a distance, and an animal or two, but nothing for him to be concerned about.

He gave himself a moment to recover from the teleport before following the trail that would lead him to a large wooden lake house that had been painted in shades of white and grey. If he kept teleporting, he would have to feed again sooner rather than later, and the last time he had been forced to feed had left a bad taste in his mouth.

Fenix rubbed his hand down his face.

Gods, he needed his mate.

He couldn't go on like this, stealing energy from kisses that were never quite enough to top his tank up all the way, always had him skirting the edge of hunger.

Even his pills weren't helping.

Resisting the allure of Evelyn was steadily growing more difficult, his incubus nature becoming a restless beast inside him as he forced himself to live on stolen kisses and pills, unwilling to do anything else with the females he encountered. As it was, kissing them turned his stomach, had him wanting to find his mate and apologise to her for what he had done.

He felt dangerously close to screwing everything up in the same way he always did.

His need for Evelyn was intense, and the more he denied himself what he really needed to keep him strong and keep the hunger at bay, the more that need grew.

Until he reached breaking point and found himself seducing his mate.

Which, in turn, always made her fall in love with him again.

And got her killed.

Not this time. This time Fenix would live with the guilt of kissing other females, would continue to feed as best he could without crossing the line he had drawn for himself, and he would stay the hell away from Evelyn until he knew where the mage was.

As soon as he had the male's location, he would go to her and free her of Archer's grasp, and would take her to the mage and force the bastard to undo his curse.

Fenix reached the lake house and studied it in silence, covering every inch of it with his senses.

It was empty.

Again.

He stretched his senses out around him. Nothing as far as they reached. He was alone.

Not the best result, since he was yet to see the mage who lived here, but also not a total loss because he had resolved to do a little snooping if the house was empty this time. Maybe this mage would have some scrolls or whatnot that were about curses.

He peered through a window and teleported inside, landing in the main living area of the house, and turned in a slow circle, his gaze sweeping over the mundane furniture that made it look like something out of a magazine. He bet none of the humans who happened to visit the mage who lived here had a clue what he was—that he wasn't human. It all looked so normal.

So normal that Fenix started to worry that Hella had been mistaken about this place and it wasn't the home of a blood mage at all.

He prowled through the large house, covering every inch of the ground floor and noting that there wasn't a basement. When he reached the main staircase again, he headed upstairs and found three very normal looking bedrooms that cemented the feeling he had been wrong about this house.

Fenix considered teleporting to his next location and then glanced at the two doors he hadn't checked yet. He might as well check them out. The first door was a bathroom.

He approached the second.

And froze mid-stride as the hairs on his nape rose on end and he caught the faintest whiff of magic.

He hurried to the door, shoved it open, and frowned at the room on the other side, unable to believe his eyes.

Well, the neighbours would certainly worry about whoever lived here if they saw this room. There wasn't anything normal about it.

On the wooden floor, someone had scrawled symbols, some of them carved into the planks and some of them painted. Fenix wasn't sure what kind of spell it was, but considering he hadn't smelled or sensed magic until he had been on top of this room, he figured it was a cloaking spell.

He hesitated, his eyes on the markings, apprehension pouring through him as he debated whether he really wanted to risk stepping into the room to sift through its contents. For all he knew, the spell could be a trap for intruders.

Fenix eyed all the ancient books that filled the shelves lining two of the walls and the stacks of parchments and scrolls that littered an old oak desk in front of him, and all the glass bottles and canisters of every shape, colour and size that occupied another bookshelf off to his left. Somewhere in here could be the answer to undoing the curse the mage had placed on him and his beloved.

He sucked down a breath.

So he was doing this.

If he got trapped, he got trapped.

He stepped into the room, tensed and braced himself as he waited to feel something. Only he felt the same as he had on the other side of the edge of the spell. He grinned and headed for the desk, and sifted through hand-written parchments that dated back decades. Most of them were spells and elixirs involving phoenix blood. None of them looked like a curse. Not that he really knew what a curse looked like.

But he knew someone who might.

He just needed to get all these documents to her.

Fenix turned to look for a box.

Froze as the hairs on his nape rose and the air shimmered in front of him.

"Bollocks," he muttered as a tall blond male materialised.

The mage's dark blue eyes widened as they landed on him and his lips parted, and the sound of glass smashing drew Fenix's gaze down to the male's polished black boots. Pieces of a crimson bottle swam in a glowing golden liquid that gradually faded before his eyes. An elixir.

Fenix tensed when the mage swiftly raised his right hand and a single clone appeared between them and launched at him on a strange hissing sound. He grunted as he ducked beneath a blow the milky-eyed doppelganger aimed at him, twisted and swept his leg out, catching its ankles. The clone stumbled but didn't fall, and Fenix shoved off, rolling and coming up onto his feet in the far corner of the room.

He twisted and braced.

And frowned when he saw there was still only a single clone.

His gaze darted to the liquid on the floor and then to the mage. Sweat beaded the young male's brow. It seemed Fenix wasn't the only one not at full strength. The elixir must have been made with phoenix blood, designed to give the mage a much-needed boost.

"How about we just talk?" Fenix knew it was a long shot as he grabbed a sturdy leather document tube as the clone came at him, swung hard and smacked it in the face, knocking it back into the desk.

It stumbled and landed awkwardly, knocking over several jars and spilling their contents. Smoke billowed and Fenix choked on the acrid air that swirled around him, struggling to get enough oxygen into his lungs as they burned. What the hell had been in those jars?

The mage came at him while the clone was recovering, and it had been a long time since Fenix had seen one actively participate in a fight. They usually let their clones do the dirty work. It reinforced the feeling Fenix had that this mage wasn't at his physical peak.

All the more reason for the male to take him up on his offer of talking rather than fighting.

The blond didn't seem to see things his way as he swung at Fenix, a wild haymaker that had no chance of making contact. Fenix ducked and twisted, brought his right fist up and hit the male hard in his kidney.

Knocking the wind from him.

Or at least that had been the plan.

His knuckles struck something that was as solid as steel rather than soft and fleshy and a pained grunt burst from his lips as fire ricocheted up his arm. He staggered back a step, gaining some room to manoeuvre, and wanted to growl when he spotted the blue glyphs that shimmered over the front of the mage's black coat.

"I have no quarrel with you, mate," Fenix said as he teleported to the other side of the room. He reached for the portrait in his pocket but didn't get a chance to pull it out and explain himself. The clone grabbed him from behind, hooking his arms around Fenix's elbows and yanking them back, restraining him. He struggled against the clone's hold as its fetid cold breath skated over his nape and stared the mage down. "Let's be reasonable. I have a portrait in my pocket. I'm looking for a mage called Drystan. He cursed me and my fated one, and I just want to end that curse."

The mage's blue eyes narrowed on him. "Why did he curse you?"

Fenix grimaced. "No reason in particular."

"Sounds a lot like you crossed him somehow… and now you expect me to help you? I don't know a Drystan, but I am sure the leaders at the New York coven would be interested in speaking with you."

Fenix had the feeling by 'speaking with you' the mage meant holding him in a cell, a feeling the male reinforced by waving his hand through the air and producing a set of rusty steel manacles that had faint glowing runic symbols on their pitted surface.

Nope.

Fenix lunged back against the clone as his heart shot into overdrive, as the thought of being placed into yet another cell and kept from his mate tore down his sanity and burned all reason to ashes. He cracked the back of his head against the clone's face, ripping a howl from him, and then teleported.

The world disappeared and when it came back, he was standing behind the mage.

The mage turned towards him and Fenix held it together, denying the urge to rip him to shreds that surged through him. He turned on the charm instead, staring into the male's blue eyes and slowly manipulating him, nudging his feelings in the right direction. As much as he wanted to wipe this mage from the face of the planet, eradicating another threat to the phoenixes, he needed to make sure the male knew nothing of value and the easiest way to do that was to ask him.

Since the bastard wasn't inclined to do this the easy way, Fenix would do things the harder way.

The young male's gaze grew hooded, his pupils dilating as he stared into Fenix's eyes. His lips parted as his cheeks flushed, and Fenix smiled slowly as his aura shifted towards desire, with a touch of confusion and conflict. That happened a lot when Fenix charmed males who didn't feel the slightest attraction towards their own gender. He worked through it, holding the male under his spell, slowly stirring feelings that weren't his own until they were strong enough to drown out the ones that were.

The mage slowly relaxed, and beyond him, the clone did the same. Weird. Fenix had never charmed a blood mage before and hadn't realised that whatever they felt was echoed inside their clones. Having the milky-eyed doppelganger gazing adoringly at him was beyond disturbing.

Fenix shuddered.

"You want to help me with this little problem I have," he murmured and inched towards the mage, closely monitoring him and applying just the right amount of charm to make him compliant but not horny as hell. The last thing he needed was a horny mage and his clone hurling themselves at him. "Help me and I'll help you with that."

He pointed to the hard-on that was tenting the mage's black slacks.

He wouldn't help the mage with it, but it was better than telling the truth and letting the male know he was gone as soon as the curse was or the mage had proven himself a dead end.

The mage moaned and palmed himself, a desperate look on his face as his brow furrowed. The clone did the same. Gross.

A wave of nausea rolled through Fenix.

Not disgust.

His shoulders tensed and he held it together as he realised how low on energy he was. Not good. If he ended up tapped out, his incubus nature would steal full control of him and before he knew it, he would be the one all over the mage, stealing his energy in a kiss. From there, it was a short hop to seducing every human on the island until he was sated and then he would come around in a few days to find himself in the middle of a sea of naked people, confused as to how he had gotten there and sore in ways that left far too many questions in his head.

It had happened before, a very long time ago.

Fenix didn't want it to happen again.

So he needed to move faster and wrap this up before he spent the last of his energy.

He looked from the clone to the mage.

Who was looking down at his hand in horror.

"Bollocks," Fenix muttered again as green orbs swirled around the mage's hand and he raised it.

So much for charming the male into helping him.

He swept his hand out and grabbed one of the heavy glass jars on the desk, brought it up and threw it in the mage's face. Powder exploded from the jar, showering the male and blinding him. The mage coughed and spluttered as he stepped backwards, the twin orbs of green that had been spinning around his hand shooting towards the ceiling as he lifted it towards his face. They struck the ceiling, blasting a hole in it. Splinters of wood and plaster rained down on the mage. Fenix didn't give him a chance to retreat.

He kicked off and closed the distance between them, seized the front of the mage's coat in his left fist and slammed his right one into his jaw, knocking his head to one side. Blood burst from the mage's lips, stark against the pale powder that covered him. The clone came at him, shrieking as it slashed at him with sharp claws. A water pipe burst in the attic, pouring like rain into the room, saturating the mage and the clone.

Fenix gritted his teeth as fire blazed in two lines down his left shoulder as the clone sliced through his shirt and twisted at the waist to bash the mage against him.

It screamed as some of the powder on the mage's face landed on its damp papery skin.

Fenix grimaced as smoke curled from the clone's cheek, as the skin burned away to reveal pink flesh and tendons, and then teeth. What the hell had been in that bottle?

He froze.

Oh gods.

His gaze leaped to the mage, his eyes widening as he saw the blisters on his face and another grimace tugging at his lips as one of them burst, spilling liquid that cut through his skin as the mage howled in agony. Fenix was quick to release him, stumbled back a step and checked his hands, panic at the helm as the mage and the clone continued to bellow and shriek. Pale residue coated his knuckles and he pivoted, his gaze seeking something dry to wipe it on.

When he spotted a robe hanging on the wall, he teleported there, avoiding the water. He hurriedly wiped his hand on the soft black material, ridding himself of every last speck of the powder and not stopping until the room fell quiet and his senses said that his shot at getting information had just died.

Fenix breathed hard, turned and slumped against the wall as he checked his knuckles. Relief poured through him as he stared at them, his hands shaking as his mind raced, conjuring images of how badly things might have gone for him too if the water had mixed with the powder.

All of his focus remained on his hand, part of him waiting for his skin to start blistering, as he stared at the dead mage. Water poured down on the male where he lay in a ball on the floor, the flesh of his face and his hands melted, leaving only bone behind.

Fenix twisted to his right and vomited.

Grimaced and spat when his stomach was empty, and heaved a sigh as he sagged into the wall again.

He grabbed the robe and tossed it over the body, and made a mental note not to go around throwing any ingredient owned by a mage in the future. He surveyed the room. A lot of it had survived. He wasn't sure how long he had to clear the place out before the authorities arrived though.

He was going to need help.

CHAPTER 13

Fenix edged out of the room, avoiding the dead mage, and found two filing boxes in another room. He placed them by the entrance to the mage's study and went downstairs, found the water shut-off valve and twisted it. He headed back upstairs, grabbed the boxes and went to the first bookcase. He popped two pills as he loaded the boxes up with the scrolls, tomes and scraps of paper, aware he was going to need more energy in order to clear out the room and put his plan into action. Once the boxes were full, he stacked them on top of each other and bundled them into his arms.

He teleported to the main entrance hall of his home in Scotland.

And almost ran straight into Tiny, who was tidying the evidence of what looked suspiciously like a party.

Tiny locked up tight, his grip on the broom handle tightening so fiercely his knuckles burned white and Fenix was surprised he didn't crush the wooden pole.

"Don't tell me," Fenix huffed, already able to imagine who had caused the sea of panties, plastic cups and bras that were draped over all his antique furniture and littered the floor. "I don't want to know. Here, take the top one."

Before he dropped both of them.

Teleporting so many times had left him depleted again, despite his pills. Maybe Hella would have another tonic for him, because he really needed a hit of energy, and he didn't have the time or inclination to find a female to kiss. His mood soured at just the thought, until Evelyn danced into his head, making it foggy as heat rolled through him in response and his cock ached in his jeans.

Tiny was swift to drop his broom and reach for the box. The broom clattered as it hit the tiled floor, startling Fenix out of his daydream about his mate, and a male voice echoed along the corridor at the top of the stairs.

"Gods, Tiny, you scared me half to death. You need to work on your coordination. Dropping shit like that. I thought Fe—" Rane came to an abrupt halt at the top of the right wooden staircase that swept up to the first floor, his swirling blue-gold eyes impossibly wide. The enormous male swallowed hard, cleared his throat and nervously said, "Fenix. You're back. Look at the mess Mort made. I told him that—"

"Spare me the bullshit and put some clothes on. I'm not talking to you while you're standing there stark bollock naked and reeking of sex." Fenix set the box he held down on the floor and glared up at the younger incubus.

Rane cast a glance down at his bare body and awkwardly scrubbed a hand over his dark hair. "Uh... forgot to get dressed."

Fenix narrowed his eyes and advanced on him, stoked his anger so the male would feel it and know he was in deep shit. "You want to leave my house, then you're going about it the right way. No more parties. No more guests. My house isn't a bordello. It's not a sex den. You want to live that kind of life, you do it elsewhere."

He never had been interested in treating a home as if it was just there to house extravagant orgies like many incubi, and he wouldn't tolerate another incubus treating his home in that manner either.

He reached the top of the stairs and squared up to Rane, glaring right into his eyes as they settled, turning brown again.

"Last warning, Rane. I scent even a whiff of sex in this place, I hear a female has set foot on this property without my consent, and you and Mort are out on your arses... no more protection." Fenix pressed his chest to Rane's and smiled slowly as the colour drained from his face. "I'm not sure how long you'd last out there on your own."

Rane's throat worked on a hard swallow as his brow furrowed. "Fenix... please... she'll kill me."

Fenix shrugged and pivoted away from him, heading back down the stairs. "Not my problem if you keep on the way you've been keeping on... You should have thought about the consequences of messing with a witch. You know we classify as demons in their world."

And no witch could accept the seed of a demon in her body without it deeply affecting her connection to the earth and her magic.

And marking her like a scarlet letter for all witches to see.

Fenix looked up at Rane and couldn't miss how shaken he was by the thought of an angry witch discovering where he was hiding, something she could do if he left the grounds of this house for more than a few hours. The only reason she hadn't tracked him down yet was the spell Abigail and Agatha had kindly done for him, one that concealed this place and everyone in it, and provided them with a twelve-hour period in which they remained concealed if they travelled outside it.

As soon as Rane remained beyond the boundary of the spell for longer than that, the witch would be onto him. It would only be a matter of time before she found him.

"Get dressed. Get Mort." He turned away from Rane again. "We have a lake house to raid."

He was going to read every document, every scrap of paper in that house, was going to strip it bare in the hope he could learn something, even if it was only more locations of other mages. He had to do something.

Maybe he would get lucky.

He huffed and watched Rane trudge back towards his room.

He had never been lucky.

Outside, lightning split the sky and shook the earth.

Rain hammered the windows.

The scent of magic laced the air.

Fenix had the feeling that Rane's luck was about to run out too.

Rane hurried back to the landing, his brown eyes wide and his skin paling as he stared at the windows that flanked the main entrance behind Fenix and Tiny.

As angry as the incubus made him at times, as furious as he was right that second because of the way Rane and Mort insisted on treating his home, Fenix couldn't stop himself from going to the male and placing his hand on his shoulder. He squeezed it gently but Rane didn't look at him. His eyes remained locked on the front of the house.

"It'll be okay. The mansion is well protected. The witch can't get in," he said and tensed as thunder shook the ground again, rattling the windows.

Although she could unleash hell on them from a distance apparently.

He palmed Rane's shoulder, massaging his tense muscles. "Go get dressed. I'll take you, Tiny and Mort to the lake house and you can oversee their work until the place is empty or the authorities arrive."

Which wouldn't take very long, but Rane looked as if he needed a moment to pull himself together, one away from the witch currently trying to break her way into the mansion grounds using brute force.

Rane nodded weakly as another peal of thunder echoed around them.

When the incubus still didn't move, Fenix sighed.

"I could go and talk with her."

Rane flicked him a look that asked if he was mad and quickly shook his head. "She doesn't really know I'm in here, right? The spell… it conceals us. You said that once. She just knows there's incubi here and she's presuming one of them might be me. Right?"

His dark eyes leaped between Fenix's and Fenix nodded, not because he was obeying his need to reassure a male who was like family to him, one he had taken under his wing decades ago, but because Rane was right. The witch was just trying her luck.

"Maybe she'll be gone by the time we get back." Rane backed away from him, the haunted look in his eyes telling Fenix he didn't believe that, even when he desperately wanted to.

"Maybe." Fenix watched him go, worry arrowing through him as another lightning bolt struck nearby.

Rane deserved the witch's wrath, but he was damned if he would let her hurt any member of his makeshift family. Whether Rane liked it or not, if she crossed a line, Fenix was going to deal with her. For now, he would let her rattle the windows. He had more important matters to attend to.

Mort came jogging down the hall, his short blond hair damp and dripping water onto his open dark blue shirt. Droplets clung to the strip of chest and stomach it revealed. Mort must have been in the shower when the witch had shown up.

The incubus hastily buttoned the lower half of his shirt and tucked it into his black jeans, his blond eyebrows quirking as another rumble shook the building and his hazel eyes seeking Fenix. "What the fuck is going on? Are we under attack?"

Fenix shook his head. "Just an angry witch. Nothing to worry about. Nothing the spell can't handle."

"Rane," Mort muttered, as if it was a curse word. "I warned him not to mess with her. Idiot couldn't resist the challenge though."

Rane and Mort had become fast friends when Fenix had picked Mort up in a fae town near London. He had met Mort on the streets, penniless and exiled from his clan for reasons Mort had never shared, but Fenix suspected it involved the pretty little succubus he had spotted watching Mort from a distance with a worried look in her dark eyes. Mort had been quick to take him up on his offer of a new home—a new family. Rane had brought the male out of his shell and Fenix had been grateful for his help, until the parties had started.

So many parties.

Rane returned, dressed in a black T-shirt that hugged his broad chest like a second skin and tight black jeans and heavy boots. Fenix grabbed him as soon as he was within reach and teleported with him to the lake house.

"Don't touch that." He pointed to the covered corpse and then the desk. "Or anything over there. Forget those papers. Whatever is in those jars is dangerous and you do not want to end up like this mage."

Rane cast a curious look at the heap in the middle of the room. "What happened to him?"

Fenix swallowed the bile that rose into his throat. "Think end of *Raiders of the Lost Ark*."

Rane blanched and nodded vigorously. "Noted. Not going to set foot in that part of the room, and I'll warn the other two."

Fenix released him and stepped back. "I need to ask a favour of Hella. Have you got this?"

The brunet's eyes darkened at the mention of a witch, but he nodded. Fenix teleported, landing outside the last place he had seen Hella—the run-down white shack in the middle of the bad part of the Geneva fae town. Rather than knocking this time, he pushed the wooden door open.

And got an eyeful of Hella bent over the heavy wooden bench.

The big, mean-looking son of a bitch who towered behind her, fisting her blue hair in one hand as he pounded into her, settled glowing golden eyes on Fenix. Hella moaned and cried out as the male took her harder, their combined pleasure hitting Fenix with enough force to make his head hazy and take the edge off his hunger.

The dark-haired wolf shifter growled and bared huge fangs at him.

Fenix took the hint and backed out of the door, closed it behind him and turned his back to it.

Although even outside he couldn't escape the guttural grunts or how they were shaking the whole building.

He willed them to hurry up while at the same time hoping they would keep going, a battle erupting inside him between the part of him that wanted to get on with his plan and the part that was hungry as hell. Each cry that Hella loosed had heat rippling through Fenix's blood, their combined pleasure seeping into him as he stood sentinel outside the door.

A passing old woman arched an eyebrow at him.

Fenix held his hands up. "Nothing to do with me."

She wasn't the only one who stared at him as he waited for Hella to finish, settling on willing her to hurry up as the noises coming from the building behind him grew louder, drawing everyone's attention, including several of the people living in the ones opposite him. He smiled awkwardly as he fielded disgusted looks, curious glances, heated stares and accusatory glares.

Eventually, the wolf howled to the rafters, loud enough Fenix was sure the entire bloody town had heard him, accompanied by noises from Hella that couldn't be mistaken for anything other than a female climaxing.

A few minutes later, the door opened and Hella limped out, fighting her messy blue hair, a hazy edge to her green eyes. He arched an eyebrow at the way she was walking as she came to him and she blushed harder, her cheeks turning deep red.

"Things seem… *different*… between you and your captive." Fenix edged his gaze towards the door, his senses pinpointing the wolf with ease. The male wasn't moving. Fenix wasn't surprised. The hit of energy he had received upon the wolf howling had been incredible after all. Hella probably wasn't the only one walking funnily now. In fact, he doubted the wolf would be able to use his legs for a while.

Hella's blush somehow deepened further as she muttered, "Don't judge me. It was a pity fuck."

Good gods, if that was a pity fuck, Fenix didn't want to be around for when the two of them decided to give the real deal a go. Hella's passion had been off the charts for someone who was apparently just there as a way for a male to get off.

She rubbed her right arm and diligently kept her eyes off the people who still lined the fronts of the buildings opposite hers, staring at her.

"The wolf was going out of his head. Some witch cursed him to think I'm his…" She swallowed hard and he sensed the shift in her emotions as they veered towards uncertainty mixed with nerves, or possibly fear. She kept her eyes on his belt as she blurted, "He thinks I'm his mate… and he was coming on a bit too strong, which is why I chained him. I've been trying to break the spell. He's doomed to slowly waste away and die if he doesn't bed me and it wasn't looking good for him."

Her pace picked up as she explained herself, something she didn't have to do for his sake. He didn't care why she was bedding the wolf. He only cared that she didn't end up getting hurt in the process.

"You okay?" He angled his head when she continued to stare at his waist, dipping it so he could see her face.

When he reached for her, an unholy growl rumbled from inside the building and she tensed, her fingers flexing against her arm.

Fenix knew possessive when he heard it, and gave the wolf a break, lowering his hand to his side again. He had hated it when Archer had touched his female, so he could understand why the wolf didn't want him laying his hands on Hella. Even if it was just a spell as Hella claimed, it probably felt real to the bloke.

Now Fenix was the one pitying him.

"Look, I need your help… in Scotland." Fenix glanced at the street and the neighbours who were still watching them. "Might be nice for you to get away from this place for a while."

She sighed, a flicker of uncertainty crossing her face as she glanced over her shoulder at the door.

Or maybe reluctance.

"You can bring your pet," he said, holding back his smile so she wouldn't realise that he was on to her and beat the living daylights out of him.

"He's not my pet." She scowled at him, silver and gold stars sparkling in her eyes as the scent of magic charged the air around her.

"So what is he?" He held her gaze, already aware of the answer to that question but curious as to whether she knew it. How deep did her denial run? Could she see that she more than liked the wolf?

She grumbled, "I'm no longer sure."

She was sure. She just didn't want to admit it. She didn't want the wolf to know he was coming to mean something to her.

Fenix could understand that. Being fated was complicated enough. Feeling as if you were fated for each other and being unsure whether it was real or whether everything you felt was a manipulation caused by magic sounded like a head fuck.

"I have lots of nice documents I know I won't understand. Might be a few new spells in there. Might be a way to break my curse… or his." Fenix slid a look at the door as the big wolf filled the space there, his steel-grey eyes fixed on the back of Hella's head.

She tensed and fidgeted, and then tipped her chin up and flicked her blue hair over her shoulder. "Fine. I'll help, but if one of your boys steps out of line—"

"They won't." Fenix grabbed her before she could utter another word and she seized hold of the wolf.

By his hand.

Interesting.

The wolf stared wide-eyed at her hand, where it tightly gripped his.

Fenix knew that look.

Spell or no spell, the wolf was done for.

Hella owned him, whether she wanted him or not.

CHAPTER 14

Fenix teleported with Hella and her wolf, landing in a guest room in the mansion, one that smelled a little musty and needed a bit of sprucing up. The wolf slid Hella a heated look as Fenix released her and she continued to hold his hand.

"Get settled in and then come down to the library." Fenix made a fast exit, was out of the door in under a second and charging down the hallway, because he didn't need to be the audience for a repeat performance of what he had witnessed in the fae town.

He took the stairs down to the ground floor and went to the library, where Mort, Rane and Tiny were waiting for him. Tiny looked up from arranging the papers, rolls of parchment, and books spread across the long wooden table in the centre of the room.

"Des headed out for the night." Tiny went back to his work.

Fenix knew why the older incubus had decided to hit the fae town. It had been a while since the male had fed and having Hella around would wreak havoc with him. He glanced at Mort where he stood at the end of the table with his back to the roaring fire and then at Rane, who was propped up against the wall near a window, looking for all the world as if he wasn't at all tempted to look out of it or bothered by the storm that was still shaking the mansion. At least they had both fed recently. Although, that didn't mean they would be on their best behaviour around Hella.

"You brought a female into the house. I thought that was a no-no?" Mort drawled as he sifted through a stack of papers, his hazel eyes fixed on them.

"My house. My rules." Fenix strode towards Tiny, grabbed the final box and tipped the contents out onto the table. "Besides, she isn't alone. I'm only going to warn you once that there'll be no flirting, no attempted seductions, not even *innocent* looks at her. Break the rules and the wolf with her will probably break every bone in your body."

The door opened and Hella strolled in, her blue hair twisted into a knot at the back of her head and a corseted black thigh-length dress accentuating her curves. Mort tensed, locked his eyes on the table and glared at it like he was trying to set it on fire with his mind. Rane flicked her a disinterested look.

Tiny blushed when he caught sight of her stripy black and white stockings.

Hella stopped beside Mort, leaned in close and sultrily breathed, "Oh, he'll rip you apart like a chew toy, incubus."

Mort swallowed hard.

"Hella," Fenix chided and she sashayed her way along the length of the table on the opposite side to him. It was bad enough she had chosen to change her clothes for the occasion, picking something far too revealing. He didn't need her provoking Mort and the others. He had the feeling she was trying to rebel, was punishing the wolf for something, but he was damned if his family were getting caught in the crossfire. "I have rules for you too. No teasing my family."

Lightning shook the building, making the lights flicker, and Hella cast him a questioning look.

"Pest problem," he muttered, using her words against her, and pushed a stack of books towards her. Papers stuck out of the yellowing pages of the leather-bound tomes, bowing their covers with the added thickness. "Anything you think might be useful, flag it for us. We can all speak fae and Mort knows his way around runes."

Mort scrubbed the back of his blond hair when Hella looked at him, her eyebrows pinned high on her forehead and surprise glinting in her green eyes. It was unusual for incubi to know such a language, something normally reserved for those who could access magic. Fenix had never been able to get the reason why Mort knew runes out of him, and he doubted Hella would be able to succeed where he had failed. Mort had a tendency to play his cards close to his chest.

Fenix rolled the sleeves of his shirt up and felt Hella's gaze on his right forearm. Without looking at her, he muttered, "Don't ask. Unless you know ancient fae?"

When he glanced at her, she shook her head.

"There are probably a few in Lucia you could ask about that mark though." She leafed through the first book, tossing some of the loose pages into an empty box and reserving others in a pile beside her. She also dog-eared pages in the book.

"Lucia? That where your nymph boyfriend is? Does he know the language?" He weathered her mock-scowl and held back his smile as she rolled her eyes when he added, "Oops, forgot you traded up. Furry is more your thing now."

"MacKinnon isn't my boyfriend, and neither is the nymph." She moved to the next book, continuing before he could mention the fact MacKinnon was a local wolf pack from a small area near Glen Coe and now that he knew the male's name, he suspected he was their alpha. "And nymphs aren't the only breed in Lucia."

"I know. Sirens live there too." He set aside a stack of pages that only had diagrams scribbled on them.

Hella rocked his world on its axis.

"Sirens won't be able to help with translating that mark, but the seelie might."

"The seelie?" His gaze snapped to her and he bit out a ripe curse. "I've been trying to track an unseelie. I didn't go to Lucia because I thought it was only home to—damn it."

"Why do you think few people who go there come back?" She scoffed. "It's not the nymphs and the sirens killing or capturing them." Her voice lowered to a faint mutter. "Although the bastard nymphs do love taking captives."

Another piece of Hella's pest problem puzzle fell into place. Her nymph ex had come after her and taken her captive, and that was why she had resorted to hiding out in a hovel with a cursed wolf for company.

"You're staying here until some of the heat you're feeling in that fae town dies down, got it?" Fenix stared across the table at her, leaning on the polished top with his right hand. Her lips flattened, her green eyes brightening as her mood shifted, taking a sharp, dark turn. She never had liked taking orders from anyone. She glared at him for a full minute before she huffed and looked back at her book, and nodded. He added, "Your boyfriend can stay too."

That earned him another glare.

And a bolt of electricity that shot across the table to zap his hand as she pressed hers to the other side of it.

She smiled wickedly as he glared at her now and went back to her work. Silence fell as everyone set to it, broken only whenever someone found something of interest, and the minutes rolled into hours. Fenix stretched, pressing his hand into his lower back, as he reached for another stack of books. What time was it?

He glanced at the clock on the mantel, but his gaze landed on Hella where she sat sideways on one of the leather wingback armchairs by the fire, her legs bent over one of the arms and her booted feet bobbing up and down as she flicked through a huge book. She looked tired. He was surprised her wolf hadn't come down to protest about the fact she had been away from him for too long or to join her in going through the documents. Had she done something to him to keep him in their room?

Fenix walked around the end of the table furthest from her and Mort and went to the other side to check out the papers and books she had reserved.

And noticed Rane had drifted to the sash window at some point.

The brunet stared out of it, his brown eyes fixed on the dark world outside as rain streaked down the pane. Lightning struck, illuminating the grounds and Rane's face, casting shadows around his eyes and in the hollows of his cheeks. He looked tired too.

"No point standing there staring out of the window," Fenix said and rounded the table again, heading back towards the younger incubus.

Rane glanced at him as if he hadn't noticed he was there and his voice lacked his usual confidence as he quietly asked, "Will the barrier hold?"

It was Hella who answered that question.

"It will hold." She looked up from her book, her gaze settling on Rane's back.

Rane tensed, his dark gaze sliding towards his left before it darted back to the world beyond the window. Fenix couldn't blame him for being on his guard around Hella, but he wanted the male to see she wasn't a threat to him, that he could trust this witch.

Mort cast her a heated glance and then abandoned his work to casually lean against the armchair opposite her, his left elbow resting on top of the tall back. "I bet you could reinforce it for us. You look as if you could cast spells that would make the witch who had cast this one look like an amateur."

Hella rolled her green eyes and went back to her book as she sighed. "Shoo. You can't charm your way into my panties."

Mort shot him a worried look and Fenix knew why.

He feared that the reason he couldn't charm Hella was because she was his fated one.

Fenix shook his head. "It's not that. She takes precautions. A spell that makes her impervious to our powers."

Mort had never looked so relieved as he raked long fingers through his blond hair.

Until Hella raked a slow, leisurely look over him from head to toe, and purred, "It is a shame you're an incubus and off the menu. You're almost as handsome as Fenix." She looked at Rane and then Fenix, and finally settled her gaze on Tiny. "This would have been a dream come true once if you all weren't incubi."

Fenix rolled his eyes now, because he knew she was just teasing as she lounged in his favourite armchair, her ruffled black skirt riding up to show a strip of bare thigh between the hem of it and her stockings. Mort and Tiny tensed, their eyes gaining gold and blue swirling flakes as they stared at her. Tiny's cheeks heated and he quickly sat down, covering his lap with a book.

Rane just sighed and stared out of the window as rain hammered it.

Until a feral, booming howl of rage shook the house, causing all three incubi to tense and look at the door.

Fenix flicked Hella an unimpressed look and muttered, "I think he heard you."

She tried to shrug it off, but Fenix could see in her aura that she was rattled by the whole thing with the wolf—a male he was beginning to suspect she had growing feelings for that scared her. He got that. Curses were powerful things and she feared everything she was feeling was a lie, a product of a spell. He looked into her eyes, silently telling her that she wasn't alone, that he was there for her if she needed anything.

Although, right now, he was the one who needed something from her.

Banging and creaking came from upstairs, and it sounded an awful lot like the wolf was going on a rampage, destroying every bit of furniture he could see.

Fenix gave her a pointed look, one that ordered her to go and see to her male, because he didn't need an angry alpha wolf wrecking his home.

Hella hurriedly stood and put her book on the seat of her armchair, fidgeted with smoothing her skirt down and waggled her finger towards the door. "I'll... um... I'll just go and calm him down."

She practically sprinted out of the door.

Mort turned to him. "Is she going to fuck him? Because you said no sex in the den."

Fenix sighed and looked at his ragtag clan, a family he had tried to make for himself after the decades of being alone had begun to get to him, wearing him down. He had needed company, and had found himself turning back to his incubus brethren for it, ending up giving a home to those who were like him and didn't have one.

Mort looked ready to go spy on Hella and MacKinnon. Tiny was blushing like a beetroot and staring hard at the same page he had been looking at for ten minutes. Des had done the honourable thing and excused himself so he didn't offend Hella. Rane was still staring out of the window.

For all their faults, they were his family, one he had chosen but one that meant everything to him, and he wouldn't swap any of them for anything in the world.

Another lightning bolt shook the mansion.

Fenix slid a look at Rane.

Or maybe he would swap one of them.

"You're going to have to face her sooner or later," he said.

Rane gave him a look in return.

One that said it was going to be later—much later.

CHAPTER 15

The team had gone dark.

Evelyn tried not to worry about that as she trekked beside Archer across a black wasteland dangerously close to the area Archangel had discovered was home to dragon shifters. Tried and failed. The images those five words conjured as they ran around her head in Mark's clipped voice weren't easy to stomach, had adrenaline constantly simmering in her veins, and made her twitchy. The slightest noise or shift in air currents had her locking up and scanning the bleak landscape that looked the same in all directions—a broad flat valley basin surrounded by towering cragged onyx peaks that put Everest to shame—and then the dull grey sky that glowed orange off to her right.

Archer had picked her up on her nerves and had subtly suggested another reason for them.

The incubus.

Some part of her was soul-deep aware that her team of twenty weren't the only ones who had passed through the portal a fae captive had opened for them, one that had brought them to Hell around a five-mile trek from the last known location of the group that had suddenly gone quiet.

Fenix had tailed her through it.

Her heart drummed a rapid beat against her ribs as she thought about him, heat quick to bloom in her veins as his handsome face filled her mind, and sparked flashes of the dreams she'd been having.

Dreams that had starred the incubus.

Dreams she definitely wasn't going to tell Archer or anyone about.

She fanned her face with her hand as her cheeks burned, her temperature soaring at just the memory of how wicked those dreams had been and how she would wake up grinning like the cat that got the cream until reality caught up with her, bringing her back down to earth with a harsh bump.

Dreaming of the incubus was dangerous. Sure, it was incredibly satisfying for some reason too, left her feeling better than most men had—or possibly all men since she couldn't recall ever sleeping with one—but it was dangerous. She was letting him get under her skin, and the last few days had revealed that was a bad thing.

Because she had begun wondering why he hadn't come to see her recently.

And she had discovered she was angry about his prolonged absence.

Evelyn switched from fanning her face to rubbing a hand down it and suppressing a groan. She felt Archer's gaze on her and ignored him, couldn't bring herself to look at him while she was mentally chastising herself for getting caught up in Fenix. For all she knew, this was all part of his plan. She wasn't sure how she would feel if it turned out that Archer was right about him and he was playing her, using her for some nefarious purpose.

She let her hand drop to her side and took in the grim valley again, that part of her she couldn't quite tame wondering where Fenix was. She was sure that he was here somewhere, although she hadn't seen him. She had felt his gaze on her though, like a caress. Knew it was him.

Was he here to gather intelligence on the operation, spying on Archangel?

Or just spying on her?

One of the scouts in the team, a blond man named Tim, lowered his binoculars from his face and cast a glance over his shoulder at Archer.

"Got eyes on something here."

Archer strode towards him, narrowing the gap in only a handful of steps, cutting an imposing figure in his black combat trousers that had been tucked into his boots and an equally dark T-shirt that hugged every muscle on his torso. She hadn't missed that he had been wearing more T-shirts recently, and she didn't think it was because their latest adventure had brought them into a realm most referred to as Hell. He was trying to prove to her that her dreams of him were wrong and he didn't have tattoos.

But it hadn't stopped her from seeing them every time he appeared in her dreams.

He tugged a rag from his back pocket and patted his nape with it, and watching him do that made her feel even hotter, made her more aware of how stifling the air was.

The temperature in this part of the sprawling, enormous plane of Hell was on the high end in their current location, had sweat trickling down her spine and the rest of the team looking as uncomfortable as she felt.

While Archer borrowed Tim's binoculars to check out what he had seen, the group took a break, and she reached for the canister hanging from her hip. Just the thought of a sip of water was enough to make her want to moan and when she unscrewed the cap and lifted it to her mouth, and cool liquid splashed across her tongue, she almost did just that.

"How much further?" Sally, one of Archangel's newest recruits, a wet-behind-the-ears brunette who had a death grip on her rifle, cast a glance around the bleak valley.

"I'd say less than a mile." Archer handed the binoculars back to the scout and joined the group, his expression grave and dark eyes troubled.

"What is it?" Evelyn went on high alert, her gaze leaping around the valley before it locked on to the direction Archer had been looking. "Dragons?"

Everyone tensed.

Archer gave her an unimpressed look and she frowned right back at him, because she hadn't meant to make everyone more jittery than they already were.

"I don't think so. Lights around the encampment are dark. Power is out. Can't see much else from this distance, but… it doesn't look good." Archer looked at the whole team—his team—appearing every bit the commander Mark had made him for this operation. "We should move quietly from here on in. Weapons ready. Not sure what we're going to find there."

If it was a dragon, they were all fucked.

Evelyn kept that to herself, but the look Archer gave her, his gaze lingering on her the longest, said he was worried about it being one of that breed too. Some of the smaller species in Hell they could handle, but men and women who could shift into a sixty-foot winged reptile with fangs as long as her arms and toughened scales protecting their vital organs were way beyond the level of firepower the team were packing. Their bullets, even the ones specially designed to deliver a nasty dose of toxin or tranquiliser upon impact, were only going to aggravate a dragon and make it kill them faster.

Archer signalled the direction they were going to take and everyone drew a collective breath and readied their weapons before following him. He cast another look at Evelyn and she read the silent order in it, moved through the team to come up beside him. Before they had left, he had told her repeatedly to stay close to him, and she had seen the concern in his eyes. He was worried that being back in Hell would be too much for her.

After all, the last time she had been here, she had almost died.

The walk to the camp was a twitchy one, with several of the team looking ready to shoot at invisible foes. Evelyn held her nerve, mentally preparing herself for what lay ahead, sure that the reason the team had gone dark was because they had been massacred. Venturing this close to the dragons and the realm that glowed orange in the distance had been a mistake, but according to the report Archer had shown her, Archangel had sent them here for a reason.

They had been looking for something.

The list of the team's members backed that up. Most of them had been from the sciences division. Researchers mainly, and a couple of technicians for some reason. The team had been assigned less than a dozen hunters to protect them. Archer suspected it had been done to keep their profile as low as possible, stopping the locals from noticing them.

Unfortunately, it looked as if it had failed to do that.

The gloom slowly took on shapes ahead of her, and the dead lights weren't the first thing she noticed.

The dead hunters were.

Behind her, Sally retched.

"Shit," one of the men muttered. "You think they're all dead?"

"Keep it down," Archer growled and motioned towards the mountains.

Evelyn looked there and spotted what he had. Halfway up the cragged basalt peak there was a cave and ropes hung from the ledge at the mouth of it. Hell of a way to get up there. She frowned at the mouth of the cave, staring into the shadows, and then slid a look at Archer.

"I don't like it."

He shrugged.

"I don't like it either." He cast her a glance, his dark eyebrows knitting hard, and nodded to her handgun as she drew it. "Keep that at the ready. Not sure what we're walking into here."

Evelyn nodded and sucked down a breath, hoping to steady her nerves.

Archer looked at the rest of the team. "Everyone with a rifle is on lookout. I want you forming a perimeter around the camp, close to the mountain. The rest of you split into groups. Gather as much research and equipment you can get your hands on. We're in and out, people. I'm not hanging around here."

He glanced at her and then three of the men, singling out the biggest in the team.

"You four come with me. We're going up."

She swallowed hard and followed him towards the mountain, doing her best not to look at the pieces of bodies that littered the black ground. When the scent of decay hit her, she covered her mouth and gagged, barely stopping herself from vomiting. Archer gave her a worried look and reached into his pocket, pulled out a clean white handkerchief and held it out to her. She nodded her thanks and took it, using it to cover her mouth and nose. It smelled like him, and faintly of some kind of herb.

Covered the disgusting scent of death quite nicely.

It was a struggle to ascend the mountain using the climbing ropes, one that had the back of her T-shirt soaked with sweat and everyone out of breath by the time they made it up to the ledge. Archer got there first, reached over and held a hand out to her. She grabbed it and thanked him with a smile as he hauled her up and set her down.

The three men clicked their flashlights on and checked out the cave, covering every inch of it.

He looked between everyone. "Gather what you can. Keep your voices down. We're not sure if there are tunnels running off this cave or if it's home to something. Group up and stick together. You're with me."

Evelyn had expected that. For some reason, Archer had gone into crazy protective mode the moment they had been issued the order to take a team to Hell. She figured it was just because of her previous experience of this realm, but sometimes she had the feeling it was more than that. He was worried about her being here.

She was strong, capable, and could handle this. He didn't have to worry.

Evelyn turned on her own light and immediately grimaced, came close to gagging again as it revealed the interior of the cave. It had been a massacre. Everywhere she looked, there were dead hunters and researchers, all of them ripped to shreds. The researchers were hardest to look at, their white coats stained crimson with their own blood.

"You seeing this?" One of the men swung his flashlight towards a dead hunter.

She frowned. Someone had taken their clothes. What kind of sick bastards killed someone and then took their clothes?

"What do you make of this?" Lance, the smallest of the three hunters and one she had worked with before, looked back at Archer.

Evelyn closed the distance between her and Lance and frowned at the sheets of paper spread across the floor. They didn't look like something the researchers had done. They looked like a puzzle. Her eyes widened as she caught a few words on one sheet that would link up with the ones on another.

"It's a message." She dropped to her knees beside Archer and gathered all the pieces before her and slowly placed them in order so she could read them. "Brink. Her name is Aryanna. She's your fated one. Archangel might have her. Take this note to King Thorne of the Third Realm. I owe you and I'll help you get her back. Grey."

"Who's Brink and who's Grey?" Lance said.

Evelyn was more concerned about the demon king's involvement in it all. Archer remained silent.

Evelyn looked up at him and found him staring at one piece of paper in particular, his dark eyes wide and his gaze distant. "What is it?"

He tensed and shook his head. "Nothing."

It was something, and he didn't want to tell her. His gaze grew unfocused again as it drifted back to the paper and she tried to make out which one had his attention. It was a toss-up between the one that said 'Brink' and the one that said 'her name is Aryanna' or it might have been the one that mentioned Archangel.

She stood to get a better angle, one more like his, and he moved before she could chart the trajectory of his gaze.

"Photograph it for analysis." He swept past Lance, but she didn't miss how his gaze darted back to the message before he had his back to it.

Something about it had unsettled Archer.

"Are you worried there's a plot against Archangel in motion?" She came up beside him as he was checking another area of the cave. "Maybe that break-in that happened recently was about this. King Thorne was part of it and we don't know if this message predates that break-in or not. Do you know of any detainee called Aryanna?"

He quickly shook his head and refused to meet her gaze. He was lying. He knew that name.

Archer nodded towards the back of the long cave. "Let's move."

She kept pace with him as he picked his way over the carnage and pressed his handkerchief harder against her face as the smell of rotting meat grew stronger where the air didn't move as freely. She was going to vomit. She kept her light at chest height and her eyes on the walls, not daring to look at all the dead.

"Tunnel here." The biggest of the men flashed his light towards it.

"Follow it." Archer cast her another worried glance.

She scowled at him. She was fine. He didn't need to coddle her. He arched an eyebrow at her and turned his cheek to her, locking his focus back on their surroundings as they entered a tunnel that led downwards. The path split into three where the air grew hotter, but thankfully smelled less disgusting.

"Follow the lights." Archer pointed them out with the beam of his torch.

Evelyn hadn't noticed them before, probably because she had been doing her best not to look at the mutilated bodies. There were no bodies here though, just rough rock walls and lights spaced at intervals. They were dead too. She figured the generators had run out of fuel a long time ago, or someone had switched them off.

When the path narrowed further, the rock protruding into the tunnel to make it harder to navigate, the men were forced to turn sideways. The three of them squeezed through the fissure in the black rock ahead of her and Archer moved behind her. She cast a look at him and he nodded, silently telling her to go ahead of him.

Protecting her again.

Evelyn holstered her weapon and inched through the gap, shuffling sideways and trying not to catch herself on the more jagged sections of the rockface.

It opened out into an enormous cavern and she lifted her flashlight and stared in stunned silence at one wall of it. Archer came out of the fissure behind her, almost colliding with her.

"What is it?" His deep voice echoed around the cavern.

And then the beam of his torch joined hers in roaming over the wall in front of her.

On it was a detailed carving around four metres wide by three metres in height, one that must have taken the artist years to create. The black stone had been chipped away to reveal an incredible amount of detail and two figures.

A dragon on the right and a female in human form on the left.

They stood on the precipice of a mountain, valleys stretching beyond her, and the sun rose above a lake in the distance, its rays filling the sky.

"The sun." Lance pointed his flashlight at it and looked back over his shoulder at Archer. "That means this is based on our world, right?"

Archer nodded and eased a step forwards, his dark eyes fixed on the woman.

Her long robes flowed behind her together with her wavy hair as she held her hand out to the dragon looming above her. It stood with its huge wings spread and one paw lifted from the rock, and as Evelyn looked at it, she couldn't shake the feeling that it was reaching for her too.

There was a strange sort of melancholy about the carving.

One that she guessed Archer felt too because he looked sad as he gazed at it.

Symbols ran beneath the relief, written in a language she didn't recognise. Some kind of fae? The dragon tongue? They twined and flowed like a ribbon around the dragon and the woman too, as if they were linking them.

On the black sandy floor of the cavern, several drawing pads had been discarded. She squatted and touched one, turning it over. Had the researchers tossed them aside in the panicked rush that had seen them ending up in the cave where everyone had been killed?

She pulled another one towards her. On it was a sketch of the female. She checked the other three. They had drawings of the symbols and notes scrawled around them.

"It looks like the researchers were trying to decipher the language." She glanced up at Archer.

He continued to stare at the woman as he drifted towards the carving, his gaze growing distant again.

"Archer?" She pushed to her feet.

The flashlight dropped from his right hand as his fingers relaxed and he reached his left hand out towards the figure of the woman. He brushed unsteady fingertips over the symbols that flowed beneath her bare feet, intricate swirls and spots, dashes and sharp angles.

She opened her mouth to say his name again in the hope he would shake himself out of whatever spell he was under.

"Aryanna," he murmured quietly, his fingers pausing on one of the symbols, his eyes never straying from the woman.

Impossible.

"You can read that?" Evelyn took a step towards him and he shook his head. "Then how do you know it's her?"

If it was Aryanna, did that make the dragon in the carving Brink? The message had said that Aryanna was Brink's fated one and that Archangel had her.

Evelyn took a step back this time, and then another one, until she could see the whole of the carving. A chill tumbled down her spine as she looked at the sun that told her this scene had taken place in the mortal world—her world— and a feeling stirred inside her as she considered the fact the one she believed to be Brink was in his dragon form there.

Her gaze leaped to the woman.

According to the intel Archangel had recently gathered, dragon shifters couldn't live in the mortal world. The moment they crossed into it, their powers were stripped from them and they suffered a slow, agonising drain on their strength that would eventually result in their death if they remained there. Everyone believed it was because the dragons had been cursed by a powerful sorceress.

This woman?

The one Archer believed was Aryanna?

Good God, if he was right… then she wasn't sure what to feel—felt as if she might be losing her mind as she considered that Archangel potentially had the sorceress who had been able to banish an entire species to Hell and curse them to a painful death.

Archer looked as if he was already one step ahead of her as he stared at the woman with a crazed edge to his wide dark eyes and whispered, "They do have you."

"Archer?" She moved a step closer to him and his gaze snapped to her, darkened in a way it did in her dreams, and she braced herself, waiting for his eyes to go all-black.

He shook his head, shattering whatever spell he was under. She studied him closely, wary of him as he closed his eyes and lifted his glasses to rub the bridge of his nose.

"Grab everything you can," he muttered and kept rubbing his eyes, his shoulders stiff and his actions jerky. "Take it to the front cave. We'll bring it all down and haul it back to the portal. Tell the others we can rest a mile south of here."

When no one moved, he dropped his hand and glared at everyone.

"Go!" he barked and fished his phone out of his pocket. "I'll document this carving."

Evelyn had the sneaking suspicion he didn't really want to document it. It was just an excuse to remain here alone while she and the three men carted everything out of the cavern.

She grabbed the sketchpads and everything else she could carry, and followed Lance to the fissure.

Stopped and looked over her shoulder at Archer's back as he stared at the carving.

She had the feeling that Archangel weren't the only ones who were up to something.

Archer lifted his left hand, pressed his palm to the female, and whispered something she couldn't make out.

That bad feeling she had grew worse.

What did Archangel want with a powerful sorceress?

She stared at Archer.

What did he want with one?

CHAPTER 16

Fenix kept low, crouching behind a large basalt boulder across the valley from the Archangel soldiers. And they were soldiers. There was no way he was going to call the groups he had come across in Hell over the last few weeks anything other than that. They weren't hunters when they were in this realm, weren't protecting their breed from others they viewed as a threat to them. Hell, they didn't even really do that in the mortal world. The organisation had been slowly settling back into its old ways, taking down any non-human they could get their hands on rather than singling out those who were a known danger to mortals.

But no, the ones he had seen in the towns he had passed through, all of them pretending to be part of the general population in the free realm of Hell, weren't there as hunters. They were up to something. Their disguises might fool some species, but not him. His senses were so attuned to the different species in this world and the mortal one that he could detect a human among a sea of fae, had easily spotted every single one of them in the towns he had passed through. Where there was one, there was always a dozen more too, strategically positioned around the busy streets. He had started observing them, and had noticed something.

They were observing everyone else.

Cataloguing everything.

In secret.

If Fenix had been in the mood to bet, he would have placed it all on Archangel being up to something and that it wasn't a mission of peace by a long shot. They were scouting towns and other locations. Charting Hell? For what purpose?

He adjusted the dial on the binoculars he had borrowed from Rane. He didn't want to know why the incubus owned a pair of high-end binoculars that were more like a damned telescope than the kind Fenix remembered using years ago. Rane had looked as if he had wanted to explain himself and Fenix had made a fast exit. What the incubus got up to when he wasn't within the grounds of the mansion was none of his business.

Although, Fenix suspected that Rane had acquired the binoculars recently, after a witch had rattled their den with a thunderstorm. Fenix had reassured Rane that the witch couldn't cross the boundary of the property thanks to the spells Agatha and Abigail had put in place, but it hadn't been a comfort to the male. Rane had been looking more and more haggard over the days since the witch had come knocking, was jittery and pale, and Fenix had the feeling he was going to have to lift his ban on females entering the house so the male could feed.

Not that Rane showed any inclination to do that.

According to Tiny, Rane spent most of his days skulking around the house, casting fearful glances at the windows. Windows that Fenix suspected the male used together with the binoculars in an attempt to spot the witch and see if he was safe from her wrath.

The most worrying report was one Des had delivered when Fenix had returned to the mansion to borrow the binoculars. The older incubus had taken him aside and told him that he had overheard Rane muttering to Mort about how he couldn't face the female because he couldn't use his charms to make her leave.

Immunity to an incubus's charms was a sign that she was his fated mate.

If Rane's mutterings were true, then the male was in a world of trouble. Not only were the old stories about how a witch lost her powers when she took demon seed into her body a lie, something the female had proven by rattling the mansion with a thunderstorm that had lasted five days and had only been present over the house and grounds, but Rane had gone and angered his fated female to the point where she more than likely wanted him dead.

It was one mess that Fenix wasn't getting involved in.

He had his own problems with his fated female to iron out.

Fenix adjusted the dial again, bringing the humans across the valley into focus. He scanned them for Evelyn, and when he couldn't spot her among the mortals that were poring over the bodies and equipment spread around the dusty black bowl of the valley, he looked for Archer instead. No sign of him either.

He spotted the ropes that pooled on the ground near the side of the mountain and tracked them upwards to a cave. More movement there. He tried to zoom in and ended up making everything go out of focus, huffed and brought the binoculars away from his eyes to figure out what he had done wrong. He fiddled with a few things, shrugged and lifted them back to his eyes.

Frowned.

Evelyn. She was standing at the edge of the ledge of the cave now, talking to two males he didn't recognise. He wished he could hear what she was saying, because she looked worried. The two males nodded and she walked away from them, heading towards the back of the cave and disappearing from view.

Fenix watched the men as they worked with a team on the ground to set up what looked a lot like a zipline, and then hooked up a large black case to the wire and attached a rope to it. One of the men kept hold of the rope, controlling the ascent of the case.

He had seen cases like that before, back at the portal where Evelyn's team had entered Hell. Her group weren't the only ones who had been there. There had been other ones, some of them waiting for a captive to open it so they could leave, while others had been arriving and checking over the contents of some seriously large black plastic cases.

The kind people in movies shipped weapons and other seriously destructive and dangerous things in.

Fenix studied the humans as they stacked up the cases and packed away the equipment, his mind on the ones he had seen arriving. Those cases had been bigger than the ones the soldiers were placing lighting and other innocent things in. He tried to shake off the bad feeling he'd had upon seeing groups of men struggling to lift just one of the cases, and how cautious and on edge everyone had been, but it had been plaguing him every second of every day.

Steadily growing stronger.

He spotted Evelyn again and stared at her, the need to go to her almost overpowering him. He needed to get her away from Archangel, because he had the sinking feeling shit was about to go down and he didn't want her caught in the crossfire.

Fenix kept track of her, following her as she went about her business, keeping the binoculars trained on her even as Archer joined her and the whole team moved off.

He lowered the binoculars, stared at the cave, and teleported.

Covered his mouth and nose the moment he landed and the vile scent of rotten meat hit him.

He kept it covered as he checked out the cave, his gaze scanning everything for a sign of what Archangel had been up to this close to the Devil's domain. Fenix had never met the fallen angel, but he had a reputation for not liking people encroaching on his territory. He glanced at the mutilated bodies, at the long gashes in their clothes and the flesh and bone beneath. It fitted the modus operandi of a fallen angel, although Fenix doubted the Devil himself had done this.

A short way into the cave, he found something.

Stopped dead as he read the note someone had scrawled in huge letters across several pieces of paper on the ground.

He recognised two names.

King Thorne.

And Grey.

Fenix looked back over his shoulder at the mouth of the cave, making sure he was still alone, and then eased into a crouch and stared at the note. Grey. The same Grey he knew? But what would the tiger shifter have been doing here in Hell?

Unless…

Talon, Grey's twin brother, had recently been held in Archangel headquarters in London. He had managed to escape and apparently must have lost his mind because he had wanted back in. King Thorne had helped him with that, causing a diversion while two elves, one of which was the mate of Kyter, the owner of Underworld, helped Talon break out people he had been held with in the facility. Talon now worked as a bartender for Kyter.

Fenix owed the tiger. One of the people he had gone back in to save had been Agatha, and she had nothing but good things to say about the male and the others who had been taken from the fae town with her.

Although, her emotions always subtly shifted course whenever she mentioned a demon male, something Fenix's incubus abilities allowed him to detect. If Fenix pressed her to talk more about him, she clammed up and changed the subject.

He looked back over his shoulder again, his senses stretching outwards as a need to feel Evelyn rolled through him.

He didn't want to leave her, but that feeling that something was going down was growing stronger by the second now, and he needed answers.

Fenix teleported to the nearest portal that would take him to the mortal realm and used it to reach a side street in the heart of London, not far from the nightclub where he hoped he could find those answers. The Grey in the note had to be the brother of Talon, and hopefully Talon would know why he had been in Hell and what Archangel were doing.

There was a line a mile long outside the old redbrick warehouse that was now Underworld, and Fenix strolled past all the humans and immortals, heading straight for the main entrance. A few of the immortals cast him looks that silently told him to get to the back of the queue, but for once, Fenix wasn't in the mood to be British about things. He made a beeline for the huge shaven-headed male who guarded the door beneath the neon sign, his dark gaze fixed on the clipboard he clutched.

A vampire judging by his scent.

The heavy beat of the rock music made the cooling night air vibrate as Fenix walked right up to the male, and he got a direct blast of it in his right ear when the other male on the door, this one a violet-haired human, opened it to allow two women to enter. Fenix curled a lip at the same time as the vampire. While his own hearing was delicate enough, the vampire's was a good three times more acute and sensitive. He couldn't imagine what had possessed the male to take a job guarding the entrance of a nightclub.

"Fenix. Here to speak with Talon and Kyter." Fenix didn't bother to look at the clipboard as the male checked it.

The vampire grunted, "You're not on the list."

"I know. Maybe just call it in? I need to speak with them about a delicate matter involving…" He leaned towards the vampire and cast a wary look at the humans, making sure none of them were listening. "Archangel."

The vampire really curled his lip now, flashing a hint of fang as a faint crimson glow lit his irises.

He grabbed the walkie-talkie from his belt and brought it to his mouth, and growled, "Boss man? Got a Fenix here wanting to speak with you and Talon."

Fenix waited, aware of the stream of humans and immortals all watching him, the tension he had felt back in Hell increasing one-hundred-fold as he waited to see whether the jaguar shifter would turn him away or invite him in. He didn't want to wait at the back of the queue. The night was wearing on already, and chances were high that he wouldn't reach the entrance before the club closed.

The radio crackled.

"Let him in."

The vampire shrugged and jerked his chin towards the violet-haired human, who opened the door for him.

Fenix braced himself as the music hit him, the pounding beat of it reverberating through him, and strode through the door into a packed wide entrance hall. Some of the patrons were dropping off items at a desk to his left, while the rest were grouping up or waiting for friends to get in. He wove through them all, heading deeper into the heaving nightclub.

Hunger rolled through him as the scent of so many females swirled around him, hitting him hard. He clenched his jaw and ignored the desire to look at some of them, to charm them a little in order to steal a kiss here and there, feeding on the sexual energy it would stir in them.

When the urge became too great, he filled his mind with Evelyn.

His beautiful mate.

She was there in Hell, vulnerable and exposed, and he didn't trust Archer to protect her well enough to keep her alive should the dragons, or worse, the demons of the Devil's domain come across them. He needed to focus on his business here and get back to her as quickly as possible so he could watch over her and keep her safe.

He made it to the point where the corridor met the cavernous main room of the nightclub. The black wall to his right continued as it was, only extending upwards to three times its height, but to his left the entire room opened up. The dance floor there was packed, the energy the males and females gave off as they writhed and grinded enough to give Fenix a hit. It was part of the reason he had grown to love this club. He could come here and soak up some sexual energy without having to lift a finger, or betray his mate.

It wasn't only the dance floor that supplied him with fuel to keep him going. Surrounding the expansive space were two tiers of booths, and a lot of the ones on the upper floor that were set back from a balcony had the heavy black curtains drawn across them to give the people occupying them some privacy.

All kinds of wicked things were happening up there, charging the air around him.

The music changed and flashing coloured lights chased the beat as a cheer went up and the dancers began bouncing and waving their arms.

Fenix squeezed his way through the crowd around the long bar that hugged the right wall of the club. The lights that illuminated this part of Underworld rotated lazily, gently shifting between colours. He wriggled his way to the front, and had to smile to disarm a female as she scowled at him and looked ready to scold him for jumping the queue. She instantly fluttered her black lashes and gave him a come-fuck-me smile instead.

He ignored her and scanned the people working behind the bar tonight. To his right, a female and male he didn't recognise were putting together drinks, pressing glasses to the optics of the colourful array of illuminated bottles mounted on the mirrored wall. Beyond them, the big silver-haired male he knew to be Cavanaugh, a snow leopard shifter, poured two pints, his standard-issue white shirt stretching tight over his muscles as he worked the pumps.

Fenix leaned forwards and looked to his left.

Relief poured through him.

Talon, a big black-haired bastard who rivalled Fenix's six-five height but had a good hundred pounds on him in muscle, leaned against the cabinets that lined the space below the bottles. He clutched a phone to his ear in his right hand and had the index finger of his left pressed into his other ear to block out the noise, the rolled-up sleeves of his white shirt revealing the tattoo that started at his left wrist.

Fenix leaned over the bar and waved his arm, catching the tiger shifter's attention. Talon's amber gaze slid to him and his black eyebrows pinched hard, and then his features relaxed and he jerked his head to his right.

The crowd were more than happy to let Fenix out of the crush, were swift to squabble over the gap he had left at the front of the queue. He made his way towards the far end of the bar and around the side of it, and waited next to the plain door that had a keypad beside it.

Talon finished his call and ignored the dozen patrons who suddenly shouted for his attention. The big tiger shifter lifted the section of bar at the end nearest Fenix, stepped through and lowered it again. He prowled towards Fenix, standing a good head taller than most of the patrons, and stopped close to him.

"What is it? We're busy tonight." Talon cast a glance towards the crowd, as if Fenix needed the male to point out that they were at capacity.

"Your brother been to Hell recently?" Fenix held his amber gaze.

It widened and then Talon frowned and leaned closer still, bringing his mouth to Fenix's ear. "What do you know about that?"

"I saw the message he left in a cave," Fenix said into his ear over the thumping beat of the music and the tiger pulled back, frowned at him and then looked over his shoulder and signalled Cavanaugh.

Cavanaugh glanced his way and nodded when Talon motioned that he was going out back, gesturing to the door beside Fenix.

Fenix waited while the male punched a number into the keypad and opened the door. He followed Talon through it and breathed a sigh of relief as it slammed closed behind him, blocking out most of the noise.

Kyter stepped out from a door off to Fenix's right in the double-height room, his long fingers tousling his thick sandy hair as he muttered about something. He paused and glanced up, frowned as he noticed Fenix, and crossed the room to him.

"What's this about?" The jaguar shifter's golden eyes brightened as he caught the serious look on both Fenix and Talon's faces. "Fucking Archangel. I'm right, aren't I?"

He growled, the strange sound echoing around the room.

"They're up to something in Hell." Fenix looked from Kyter to Talon. "I followed a team of soldiers into a wasteland and found a note in a cave there, one where Archangel had been doing something. I was hoping the Grey who left the note was your brother, and I'm guessing it is."

"He went there for me. I needed information and he went to Hell to find it, and uncovered a massacre. A fallen angel tore through the whole team." Talon's amber gaze hardened. "Bastard almost killed my twin too."

A chill skated down Fenix's spine and a need to return to Evelyn right that second blasted through him. "Is the angel dead?"

Thankfully, Talon nodded.

Fenix blew out his breath, some of his tension fading. "The team I followed were gathering everything from the camp. They would have seen this note too. It mentioned someone called… Aryanna… and Brink."

"Aryanna," Kyter growled. "We found information in documents that Sherry and Emelia managed to download from Archangel's Central Archive when we were breaking Talon's buddies out. Something about Aryanna and Abaddon. We're still not sure what Project Abaddon is, but we know it relates to this Aryanna and that can't be a good thing."

The bad feeling that had set up a permanent home inside Fenix grew stronger still. "Why? Who's Aryanna?"

Talon worried the hair above his nape, his amber eyes gaining a flicker of concern. "A sorceress. She's the one who banished the dragons to Hell. She cursed them."

"Fuck," Fenix muttered and the gravity of what he had stumbled across hit him hard and solidified that feeling that shit was about to go down.

"Our thoughts exactly. What does Archangel want with a witch who had enough power to banish an entire species to another realm and make it so that if they set foot in this one they're powerless and die a slow death?" Kyter's handsome face blackened. "Our guess is they want to use her to do the same thing to every one of us."

Fenix didn't like the sound of that. If Archangel managed to convince Aryanna to do as they wanted, then every immortal living in the mortal world would either die or be forced to live in Hell for the rest of their lives. Not everyone could use the portal pathways without assistance either. Incubi and succubi, in particular, needed help from witches, regularly buying bespelled goods that granted them the power to use the portals so many times before they needed a magical recharge.

Gods, just the thought of Evelyn being stripped of her power and subjected to a slow death had him wanting to rage and tear down the hunter organisation.

They had firmly crossed a line.

Immortals had peacefully co-existed with mortals since time immemorial. They had lived in this world for thousands of years, evolving alongside their mortal neighbours. They weren't the threat Archangel thought they were.

"Why hasn't Archangel tried to go this route before? If they have Aryanna... What made them suddenly want to remove immortals from this world?" Fenix looked from Talon to Kyter.

A beautiful, tall female clad in black leather trousers and a boned corset appeared next to him, her long inky blue-black hair caressing her slender bare shoulders and parted to reveal the pointed tips of her ears.

An elf.

Her violet eyes were bright with anger as she snarled, "They learned of the existence of Hell, thanks to one of my own breed. The mad elf prince—"

"Hey now, sweetheart," Fenix interjected. "Let's not go tossing insults around like that. Vail might be a little... *unhinged...* but he's a good bloke at heart."

Her right eyebrow arched. "You know of him?"

Fenix shrugged. "Met him in the cells of the castle of the Fifth Realm a while back. Me and the future-missus-Vail were being held there for different reasons and the demons captured him and brought him down to the cell opposite mine. The rest is history. Rosalind must have tamed Vail by now, or at least hauled him a little closer to sane."

"I do not think he will ever be sane," she muttered, ignoring Fenix's glare.

Kyter patted her shoulder. "Your opinion is just being coloured by your brother. Bleu hates the guy with a passion and it's rubbed off on you."

She scowled at him too, and if her mate didn't watch his step, he was going to be sleeping on the couch tonight. "That prince is tainted."

Apparently, Iolanthe was one of those elves who despised those of her breed who had allowed the darkness that lived within them all to take the reins a little too much. Elves called them tainted, because of the black that coloured their violet irises, and wanted them all eradicated to remove the stain on their good name.

So, Fenix wasn't going to mention he had cut a deal with one, possibly two, tainted elves who were going to help him save his mate.

"I know who this Aryanna is now and what Archangel want with her, but who's Brink?" Fenix shifted his focus back to Kyter.

It was Talon who answered.

"Brink is a dragon and the mate of the sorceress. The cave was his home once and he lives near there in a village now. He doesn't remember his mate. He forgets her whenever he manages to recall her."

That struck a chord in Fenix that had him feeling a strange sort of connection to the dragon, because the curses that afflicted them were similar in a way, only his mate was the greatest victim and she forgot him whenever she fell for him. If this Aryanna was still alive, could she help him lift the curse? It was worth a shot.

"Grey left him the note because Brink remembered her and went after her. My twin was worried that Brink wouldn't forget her until he had passed through a portal to this world, and then he had felt bad that he was going to forget her period." Talon folded his arms across his chest, causing his white shirt to stretch tight over his muscles. "He wants to help Brink, and that's why he pointed the dragon to King Thorne."

"Any word from King Thorne about this?" Fenix caught the grave look in Talon's eyes.

"None. Grey is heading back to the dragon village to see if Brink is there." Talon looked worried about his brother now, his dark eyebrows furrowing slightly as he glanced at Kyter.

The jaguar shifter sighed and placed a hand on his shoulder. "Grey will be fine. Lyra is with him. Nothing bad will happen to him, but… he had to go. I'm not sure what he'll do if he finds that Brink never returned to the village though."

If that were the case, there probably wasn't much the tiger shifter could do. It would mean Brink was probably in this world already, somewhere unknown to them, dying a slow death and not even sure why he was here if he had forgotten his mate again.

Fenix thought about his own mate, back in Hell, exposed to all the dangers of that realm. He wasn't sure what was a bigger threat to her—travelling through Hell or working for Archangel. He was sure of one thing though.

Archangel were up to something nefarious.

And it was time he got his mate out of there.

CHAPTER 17

Evelyn couldn't shake the feeling that had been plaguing her from the moment she had seen that carving in Hell. Something was coming. Something bad. It had her on edge, had brought her to the Central Archive every day since she had returned from the dark and shadowy realm. She couldn't remember ever spending this much time in front of the computers. She couldn't remember ever being this interested in research reports either.

So far, she had pored over hundreds of documents in the database, seeking the answer to the question ringing in her mind—what was Archangel doing?

She had never doubted the hunter organisation before, but ever since that incubus had come into her life, ever since she had almost been killed in the Fifth Realm, her faith in them had been steadily chipped away, until she had started to doubt them.

Now, she saw everything in a different light. A cold light. Things that would have seemed normal to her before, completely innocent even, now took on a dark edge that had her looking closer for the first time.

The number of fae Archangel were capturing was on the rise, and during a walk through the pens, several of those fae had been muttering to themselves. For once, she had listened to their ramblings, tuning in to them, and all of them spoke of the same thing.

Portals.

Some of the hunter teams who were bringing the fae in had been demanding the non-humans give up the locations of portals in this country and also places where there were portals in Hell too. Other teams had even gone as far as making their fae detainees take them through portals. Evelyn had looked up their reports and had been stunned by the sheer number of these gateways Archangel had uncovered so far. The list of GPS coordinates had been mind-blowing, with at least thirty documented in the United Kingdom and a dozen in France and Ireland, and close to one hundred in Hell.

Why did Archangel need to know the locations of so many portals?

What had they been doing in that cave in Hell?

She clicked on the next document and sipped her cold coffee, on a mission to unearth the answer to that question in the research her team had brought back from Hell. The researchers had meticulously typed it all up and added it to the database. Or at least, they had typed up some of it. Things she had seen with her own eyes were missing—like the note that had been left for Brink.

Evelyn scrolled through the report and moved to the next one, hunting for answers, hoping she would find something that would set her mind at ease. She didn't like feeling unsettled, and she really didn't like the fact she couldn't put her finger on why she felt this way.

That report was a dead end too.

Instead of clicking on the next one, she ran a search.

It returned a long list of results. She sighed and set to work, reading each document. A few locations popped up, most of them in Europe, and more than one mention of warlocks—a generic term that Archangel applied to all male witches.

Two locations in particular mentioned Aryanna.

One of them was in New Hampshire in the States. It had been investigated recently by a local Archangel team, but it had been empty. Stripped bare. As if someone had gotten there before them.

The other location was a place in Norway. The remoteness of the building was causing a problem. Archangel hadn't managed to get a team out there yet, but it was high on the places of interest due to recent satellite imagery.

Evelyn clicked on the first of the attached images.

Her eyes slowly widened.

It was an aerial photograph of endless white valleys and huge mountain ranges, and in the centre of it was a dark patch.

She went back and clicked the next image. This one was zoomed in on the patch, revealing a huge area of scarring in the snow that looked recent to her. It reached from one end of the valley to close to the other, where a building stood. She leaned forwards, peering closer at it, amazed by how even the trees had been affected, the snow blasted off them. Some of the trees had even been... burned?

Evelyn closed the image, just the thought of fire had her cheeks heating, and opened one of the reports, focusing on it to take her mind off the sudden spike in her body temperature. It marked the area as a potential battle site. Who had been fighting there to cause such devastation?

The report went on to mention how the trees in the area looked as if they had been subjected to a high-heat fire.

She reeled back in her chair as an inferno flashed across her eyes and her hand flew to her chest as it tightened, a strange stabbing pain stealing her breath as her body heated to an unbearable degree.

"Are you sick?" Archer's deep voice rolling over her startled her back to the room and she jerked her head up and to her left, her gaze colliding with his.

"What makes you say that?" Panic lit her veins. Was she sick? She rubbed her chest, desperate to soothe that twinge now as fear that it might be something dangerous swept through her. "Maybe I should talk to the docs."

The light that had been in his eyes faded, his handsome face shifting towards serious. "I meant you were sick because you're in the Central Archive... somewhere you never like to be. It was a joke. Are you sick though? Is something wrong?"

A thousand needles prickled her skin and she tried to shake off the fear it might be. She turned towards Archer, needing him to reassure her that she was fine.

"You look flushed." He frowned at her now, a wealth of worry in his dark eyes.

She touched her cheek. He reached for her other one and brushed the backs of his fingers down it in a gentle caress.

"I think I might be coming down with something. I've been getting terrible sleep... and I'm having the strangest dreams... and I keep feeling hot and there's this tightness in my chest. It only lasts for a few minutes and then I feel fine... but... maybe it's an infection? Something from the wound?" She searched his eyes, desperate to hear him say that she was overreacting and panicking about nothing.

Archer shifted his hand to her forehead and pressed his palm to it as he stared down into her eyes. The coolness of his touch was bliss, had her eyelids falling to half-mast as she savoured it and a sigh escaping her as the heat abated and she felt normal again.

His hand dropped from her forehead. "You feel fine to me. Nothing to worry about. Might be hormonal."

She scowled at him for that and ignored the heat that flushed her cheeks because it wasn't a fever this time—it was embarrassment.

"I jest." He leaned his backside against the desk and folded his arms across his chest, and she didn't miss the fact he was back to wearing dark Henleys again. He glanced at her screen. "So what are you looking into that has you here all hours of the day and night? Don't think I haven't noticed you stealing my haunt."

She sighed and leaned back in her chair. It squeaked as she twisted towards the screen again and idly scrolled down the page.

"Nothing really. I was just curious about the things we saw in Hell and was looking for some answers about the mysterious Aryanna." She lightly tapped on the curve of the mouse, nerves rising as she waited to see how Archer would react to that.

He had been acting strange in that cave, hadn't been his usual self.

"Find anything?" He sounded curious. Hopeful even.

She glanced at him, meeting his gaze. "The name comes up in a few places, relating to a Project Aryanna and a Project Abaddon. I can't access the files on Project Abaddon, so I've been chasing the information trail on Aryanna. A team in the States were sent to investigate a location with ties to her, or warlocks or something. Her name popped up."

"Anything there?"

She shook her head. "It had been emptied. Only other place mentioning Aryanna is one in Norway."

She showed Archer the photographs and his face darkened by degrees as he stared at them, his lips compressing as the corners of them turned downwards. That feeling ran through her again and had her gaze falling to his covered arms. Were there bands of glyphs inked on his skin beneath the black material?

Archer folded his arms across his chest and huffed. "Still on that?"

She was quick to shake her head and smile. "Sorry. It just felt so real."

He looked as if he wanted to say something and then his expression softened and he tilted his head towards the screen. "Want me to see if I can access the Abaddon files?"

Being elevated to a commander would have increased his clearance, meaning there was a chance he could access them. She scooted aside, trying to keep her hopes down as Archer pulled up a chair and rolled into the spot where she had been. He pushed his glasses up his nose and leaned over the keyboard, his fingers moving swiftly over it, and she waited as tense seconds rolled into long minutes.

And his expression darkened more and more with each one that ticked past.

On a deep huff and with a black scowl aimed at the monitor, he shoved his palms against the edge of the desk and rolled backwards. He pushed to his feet and glared at the access denied message on the screen, and when his fingers curled into tight fists, Evelyn eased backwards. For a heartbeat, he had that crazed look in his eyes again, and she felt sure he was going to unleash hell on the computer.

But then he pivoted away from it.

"I need some air," he growled.

"I'll go with you." She rose to her feet.

He stopped her with a dark look over his shoulder and she tensed. She waited for his eyes to go all-black as a feeling struck her, a sensation that the air was growing thicker around her, harder to breathe, and the hairs on her nape and forearms rose.

"Or not," she muttered.

And remained where she was as he stormed away from her.

The moment the twin doors swung closed behind him, the air in the room seemed to lighten again, the oppressive feeling that had been building in it fading away. Evelyn glanced at the other occupants in the room, sure they would be looking at her as if she were crazy, or maybe she just felt that way for thinking she had sensed some kind of malevolent power coming off Archer.

Only the man and woman working at the other end of the line of desks both looked as pale as ghosts and were staring wide-eyed at the spot where Archer had been.

Fenix's words rang in her mind, clanging like an alarm bell.

She tried to ignore them, told herself that Archer was human, just like her, but this time that feeling that Fenix was telling the truth refused to leave.

So she followed Archer.

Evelyn shoved the doors open and spotted him at the far end of the corridor. She kept pace with him, moving swiftly down through the building and out into the night. He picked up the pace, his long legs carrying him away from her, and she had to jog to keep up. Rather than cutting through the park, he took one of the side streets, heading between the old white townhouses to the main road.

When he turned the corner, she moved faster, not wanting to lose sight of him.

She rounded the corner.

And ran straight into him.

Archer seized her by her arms and glared down at her, his eyes darker than she had ever seen them. "Tailing me now?"

"I was worried about you." She swallowed to wet her suddenly parched throat as her heart hammered a staccato rhythm against her ribs. "I just wanted to check you were okay."

His grip on her loosened and he pushed her away. "Go back."

She shook her head. "We can get some air together."

He stepped up to her, his voice a black commanding snarl. "I said go back. That's an order, Evelyn."

"You're not out for air, are you? You're up to something. I want to know what it is." She stood her ground, denying the part of her that wanted to back off because he was scaring her.

He backed off instead, the hardness leaving his eyes. "I can't tell you that. I'm on a mission and you're not on the list of those I can speak to about it."

That hurt.

"We're not partners anymore, Archer?" She wrapped her arms around herself as a cold gulf opened inside her and backed away from him when his expression softened and he reached for her.

On a long sigh, he closed the distance between them and touched her arm, his caress light this time. "We are. I would tell you if I could, Evelyn. You know that. This... it's a paygrade thing."

She could understand that, but it did nothing to soothe the hurt. Archer was her only friend at Archangel, had been there for her for a long time, and now she had the terrible feeling she was about to lose him and she would be alone.

She didn't want to be alone.

He nudged her arm, his tone gentle. "Go back. Get some rest. I'll swing by in the morning and we can have coffee on the roof. Sound good?"

She forced herself to nod. "Sounds good."

He gave her a little smile and then turned away, and Evelyn watched him go, that heavy feeling in her chest growing worse with each step he took.

With every moment she tried to make herself believe what he had said and found she couldn't.

Because she knew him, better than he thought she did, and she had developed a talent for telling when he was holding something back.

He was lying to her.

He wasn't on a mission for Archangel.

He was on a mission for himself.

And she was going to find out what it was.

CHAPTER 18

Fenix blanked the trio of males clad in black who sat up and took notice of him as he entered the enormous onyx reception room of the assassin's guild. Their gazes tracked him as he crossed the polished obsidian floor and he kept his locked on the door in the far-right corner of the room, making a beeline for it. Not one of them tried to stop him as he had anticipated.

He pushed the door open and strode along the corridor on the other side, an equally black affair that had several doors leading off it to his left and right. The smell of the oil lamps that illuminated it was strong as he sharpened his senses, trying to figure out which door led to the office of the male he had met.

When he spotted the one at the far end, it hit him that he didn't need to check every room with his senses.

The elf would be there.

If he had been the boss of an assassin's guild, he would have chosen the office at the far end of the corridor too, ensuring he looked powerful and in command.

The door opened just as he reached it and the same violet-eyed male he had met locked gazes with him. Only now the elf looked tired and a little worse for wear. A cut darted over his left cheekbone, slicing towards his dishevelled blue-black hair. His eyes held a dark edge that slowly dissipated as he stared at Fenix.

"It's you." Hartt's deep voice rolled with authority along the corridor and Fenix sensed movement in the office beyond him.

The other male he had met, the one who was clearly tainted, appeared in view just behind Hartt. Fenix expected to see the same dark, hungry intent to kill in his eyes as he had last time. Only when he flicked a glance at the male, he looked relieved and muttered something in a lyrical language Fenix didn't know.

"We've been looking for you." Hartt stepped back into his office and gestured for Fenix to enter, waving his right arm out at his side.

"I should have left my details. I would have come sooner, but I still don't have everything in place. I don't have time to get everything in place now." Fenix stepped into the room and the male closed the door behind him. "I don't like it, but I need my mate away from Archangel as soon as possible. Some kind of shit is going down and I think it's going to affect all of us. And I mean all of us. Everyone in Hell and the mortal realm. I was hoping you would know some of the people in charge of the realms here... so you could warn them."

"Warn them?" Hartt frowned at him, a flicker of concern lighting his violet eyes. "About what?"

"I'm not really sure yet. I saw some stuff here in Hell, close to the dragon realm... research Archangel was doing before a fallen angel slaughtered them all." Fenix worried his lower lip with his thumb as he thought about Evelyn. He told himself that she was back in London now, but it didn't give him the relief he needed. She was in as much danger there as she had been in Hell. "I spoke to Talon and Kyter... they work at this nightclub in London called—"

"Underworld," Hartt growled and his eyes darkened again. "I know of it."

Judging by that look in his eyes, the elf knew of it and didn't like it one bit.

The other elf muttered black-sounding things now and began pacing, his fingers twitching with each long stride that carried him back and forth across the office.

"Fuery," Hartt murmured, his tone softer now, and the male stopped and glanced at him, his brow furrowing as his corrupted violet eyes sought Hartt. "All is well. We have no need to go there."

Fenix guessed something bad had happened to the elves at Underworld and the experience had been traumatic enough that Fuery couldn't even handle remembering it. The door behind him opened and a female with long blue-black hair wearing an ankle-length dark violet dress hurried into the room and crossed it to Fuery.

The male's face crumpled as she opened her arms to him and he swept her into his, buried his face in her neck and held her close as she softly whispered things to him in the same language he had been speaking before.

The sight of them reminded him of Rosalind and Vail, and filled him with a need to track them down and warn them about what Archangel might be up to so they weren't caught up in it.

"What were you speaking about with the males you mentioned?" Hartt pulled Fenix's focus back to the room.

Fenix looked him in the eye. "There's this sorceress called Aryanna—"

Hartt lunged for him and seized his left arm, gripping it tightly as his eyes widened. "You can tell me the rest when we reach our allies. We need you to help us and it all has to do with this Aryanna. Fuery, remain here."

Fuery nodded and Fenix didn't have a chance to ask what this was all about.

Chilling darkness engulfed him, had a shudder rolling down his spine as the inky black seemed to close in on him from all sides.

And then he was standing before a beautiful sun-soaked English thatched cottage in the middle of a colourful garden full of blooms and buzzing with life.

Fenix slowly took in his surroundings as Hartt released him and strode towards the worn wooden door, a black shadow that was out of place among the bright hollyhocks and cornflowers and the lush red roses that clambered over the stone walls of the cottage.

He breathed deep of the warm, clean air and stilled as he caught the smell of magic among the scent of all the flowers.

They were here to see a witch?

His eyes widened as the door opened.

"I thought we agreed no pop-ins? You know what—" Rosalind cut herself off as her large sapphire eyes landed on him.

Shoved Hartt aside so hard he stumbled and fell into a cluster of bright orange crocosmia.

She grinned as she hurried towards Fenix, her wavy ash-blonde hair bouncing against the shoulders of her drab knee-length black dress, the traditional garb of a witch on duty. Her pace picked up as her face lit up and he grunted as she hurled herself at him and looped her arms around his neck.

"Fenix!" She squeezed him so hard he choked.

Fenix risked it and wrapped his arms around her, his senses on high alert, scouring the area for her mate because if Vail saw him touching her, the elf would kill him. He couldn't stop himself from holding her and squeezing her tightly as relief poured through him though, as he told himself that she was alive and safe.

She released him and pushed his shoulders, and he dropped her to her feet. She clutched his shoulders through his black shirt as she leaned back.

"Let me get a good look at you. Oh, you look tired. You haven't been getting enough sleep. Hartt told me about your problem." She frowned and pouted a little, framed his face with her palms and fussed over him like a mother would.

Or how he imagined a mother would.

He had never known his.

"It's good to see you, Rosalind." He smiled at her, those words coming straight from his heart as it warmed. It was better than good to see her. He had been worried about her from the moment they had parted ways, had cursed himself a thousand times over for not getting her address so he could visit her and make sure she had escaped Hell without the demons, or possibly her mate, killing her. He flicked a wary look at the one-and-a-half-storey cottage. "I've been checking fae towns trying to find you. Didn't figure you for a country girl."

She beamed at him. "My own little slice of heaven. I might have been a town gal once, but the country is where it's at. I get all the space and sunshine, no bother from demons, and I can grow my own food and potter about the garden all I like. Speaking of pottering about the garden."

She grabbed his hand in a firm grip and tugged him along the path to his right, one that looked as if it led around to the back of the house.

Fenix tensed the moment he sensed it.

Rosalind noticed of course and flicked a mischievous look over her shoulder. "You know… he still isn't happy that you dumped me with him… or that you tricked me with your powers, making me compliant so you could escape alone."

"I wasn't trying to escape alone." He frowned at her now. She was only teasing and stirring the pot, but he hated the thought she might believe he had ditched her so his chances of survival had increased. "We all agreed we should split up."

"We didn't all agree. I didn't want to split up, and you men grouped together to overrule me." She huffed and glowered at him. "Bros before hoes, right?"

Fenix sighed. "It wasn't like that, and you know it. It was safest for you to go with your mate. I was only thinking of you, sweetheart. I hope… He wasn't too… Did he—never mind."

Rosalind paused at the side of the building and sighed as she turned to face him. "It was rough there for a while, but we worked things out. Maybe you're right. It was better I went with him. It allowed us the time we needed to get to know each other and… I totally made him fall in love with me."

Fenix could easily believe that. "And how is your husband? Is he housebroken yet?"

She grinned at that.

"Nearly. He's getting there." Her smile faltered. "And your mate? Vail told me what you said about her."

Fenix exhaled hard as all the light and warmth that had been filling him faded away. "I need to see her every second of every damned hour and I can't, because if she sees me too much there's a chance she'll fall for me… and then it starts all over again. It's tearing me apart, Rosalind. I need her so damned much."

Her fair eyebrows furrowed and she stroked his arm. "We'll help in whatever way we can."

He appreciated that.

Wanted to tell her as much but a feral growl shattered the pleasant day, rolling across the land like a thunderstorm.

Fenix lifted his gaze, looking over Rosalind's head towards the rear garden of the cottage, and braced for impact as he spotted Vail storming towards him.

Rosalind spun away from him.

Vail disappeared, leaving only a faint shimmering outline of himself behind, and Fenix's pulse jacked up as he tensed and sent up a prayer to any god that was listening, sure his life was about to come to an end.

The elf reappeared right in front of him, not an inch separating them, and grabbed hold of him.

Not to kill him, but to hug him tightly.

Fenix stood as still as a statue, unsure what to make of the elf prince's reaction or what to do in response to it. Rosalind gave him a pointed look when he glanced her way and nodded with her chin towards her mate. Fenix followed her silent order and embraced the male, awkwardly patting him on his back.

And realised Vail wasn't wearing his armour.

The male drew back, his tainted violet eyes bright as they locked with his, and it was strange seeing the elf smiling when the one he had left in Hell had spent every second looking homicidal or smitten.

"It is good to see you." Vail cupped Fenix's nape and drew him closer, pressed their foreheads together and murmured something in the elf tongue. He released Fenix and glanced down at his petite mate.

While Vail had an inch on Fenix, he had twelve of them on Rosalind. She barely reached his chest. It didn't stop her from snuggling up to him with a big smile on her face as her blue eyes lifted to lock with his. They sparkled with silver stars.

With happiness.

Vail growled and swooped on her lips, swept her up into his arms and pulled a giggle from her as he dropped his mouth to her neck and peppered it with kisses.

Fenix couldn't hold back his smile. It was good to see them getting along. When he had left them in Hell, they hadn't exactly been on the best of terms with each other, but now looking at them made Fenix yearn for Evelyn, for his mate, all the more.

Rosalind caught his look and pushed against her mate's shoulders, her fingers rucking up his black T-shirt. "We have guests."

Vail scowled at him, a look Fenix was more used to seeing on his face and one that said the elf wanted to eviscerate him so he no longer had a guest and could focus on doting on his mate. When Rosalind clucked her tongue, Vail reluctantly set her down and eased her away from him. The two of them looked as if they really did belong together, with Rosalind in her black dress and Vail clad in black jeans and a matching T-shirt.

Fenix suspected that Rosalind was responsible for his wardrobe. Vail had the air of an elf who would have dressed in the more traditional black knee-length tunic jacket, tight trousers, and leather riding boots that Hartt wore if left to his own devices. The sort of clothing that would have made him stand out in the mortal world.

"I tried to heal the flowers you pushed me into but today is not a day where nature likes me." Hartt huffed as he rounded the corner behind them and exchanged a look and a nod with Vail before looking at Fenix. "Have you filled them in on why I brought you here?"

Fenix shook his head and felt the weight of Vail and Rosalind's gazes on him as the air surrounding them grew tense. "I'm not really sure myself. I mentioned my suspicions that Archangel are up to some dark shit and finding information on a sorceress called Aryanna, and next thing I know I'm here."

"Aryanna," Rosalind murmured. "What do you know about her?"

"I know Archangel have her according to a note someone left for a dragon called Brink, and I spoke with Talon and Kyter about her at Underworld. Talon's brother left the note. Went to Hell for Talon after he dug up info on her from a covert mission they performed at Archangel HQ in London." Fenix followed as Rosalind gestured at him and started towards the rear garden.

Vail trailed after her, his gaze constantly locked on her, as if he couldn't bear to look away from her for a second. Fenix knew how that felt. Gods, he needed to see his mate again.

And he would.

As soon as he was done here, he would check in on her and make sure she was safe.

Someone had set up a circular wooden table on the patio near the cottage and four matching chairs encircled it beneath the shade of a large cream cantilever parasol. Rosalind picked a chair with its back to the garden and Vail slid into the seat beside her. Fenix took the one opposite her and Hartt sat to his right.

"I need to get my mate away from Archangel as soon as possible." Fenix leaned forwards and rested his elbows on the teak table. "Aryanna was the sorceress responsible for cursing the dragons and banishing them to Hell. If Archangel do have her—"

"They have her." Rosalind's words hit him hard, had him leaning back in his chair. "Our intel says they have her, but we don't think they can reach her or access her or something like it. It gets sketchy there. We only know a mage we fought wanted access to her, and he believes someone else is going to beat him to her now."

That didn't sound good.

"Someone not Archangel?" He glanced at Vail and then Hartt.

Both elves shook their heads.

"We think someone is working on the inside to reach her. We're not sure why they want her, but... it can't be good... just like it isn't good that Archangel have her." Rosalind cast everyone a worried look and then settled her gaze back on him. "It's why we wanted to get in touch with you. Hartt told us that your mate works for Archangel now."

"She does." He nodded and then it hit him. "You want me to convince her to find out where they're holding Aryanna. Rosalind... it's too dangerous. I'll get in there. Hartt can help me. I'll go and I'll find her, but I'm not getting Evelyn involved."

"Evelyn?" Vail frowned at him and sat up straighter. "You said she had called herself Evelyn before her latest death."

"Latest death?" Hartt's brow crinkled as he looked between Vail and Fenix.

"Apparently, she didn't die. She survived, but I was sure that she had died." Fenix was still convinced he had felt it happen.

"How much did you see?" Vail said and held his hand up when Hartt went to speak, silencing the male.

"I followed her and her group across the Fifth Realm, observing them from a distance. Didn't want to get too close. It looked like they were scouting the land, charting it before the other team joined up with King Thorne for the battle against the forces of the Fifth Realm. King Frayne hadn't left yet. Part of me felt maybe they wanted to take him out and end the war before it really kicked off." Fenix shrugged and shook his head, no longer feeling that had been the case. Archangel had started documenting Hell the moment they had learned of its existence. Evelyn's team had been there to do just that. "When they were caught by the demons, I got myself caught too. I had to protect her. I thought I would have a chance to get her away via a teleport, but the shackles they placed on me... well, you know."

Rosalind glowered at him. "I do know. I can't stand that my powers were taken from me like that."

Her mate cast her a sheepish look and then lowered his gaze to his knees, and her features softened as she noticed. She reached over and patted his knee.

"I'm not angry with you, silly. You did what you had to do and it probably kept me safe." She smiled for Vail when he finally looked at her and his face crumpled, his brow furrowing, and he seized her and pulled her onto his lap.

Rosalind didn't fight him as he petted her hair, as he kissed her cheek and murmured things to her with an earnest edge to his expression and a lot of love in his eyes. She wrapped her arms around him and got herself settled, shifting to face Fenix and Hartt, as if it was perfectly normal to hold an intense conversation while being fussed over.

The gods knew it probably was for her.

Vail was ridiculously protective of her after all, probably didn't let her out of his sight around males, was driven to stamp his claim on her and ensure everyone knew she belonged to him.

Fenix fought the smile that wanted to curl his lips, one that lightened the weight on his heart for a moment, because it was nice they were happy. There was a marked difference between the Vail he had known in the cells of that dungeon and the one sitting beside him now. It was good to see Rosalind had been working her magic on him, coaxing him back from the darkness.

An ache formed in his breast and he rubbed his sternum through his black shirt, trying to soothe it. He would have his mate at his side again soon enough.

He looked at the trio around him, a small group of warriors who had all been tested in battle.

This time, he wasn't alone.

This time, he was going to succeed.

CHAPTER 19

Fenix thought about what to tell Rosalind, Vail and Hartt as the sun beat down on the canopy of the parasol, the warmth of it reaching him.

"Frayne killed the hunters right in front of me. Cut them down one by one and when they got to Evelyn, I tried to stop him, but it only made things worse. The wanker had his soldiers take me away and I couldn't stop them. I felt the connection between me and Evelyn fading and I was distraught." His throat closed as he relived that moment, how he had sat in that dank, dark cell desperately reaching for their connection and feeling it disappearing. He had never been so aware of her dying as he had been then, alone in that cell, feeling her slipping away from him and knowing there was nothing he could do to stop it. "I waited for the bond we share to black out for a moment like it always did and then come back when she was reborn, but—"

"Reborn?" Hartt interjected, his violet eyes wide. "Wait. Your mate is a phoenix too?"

Shock rolled through Fenix, what he had been saying falling away as his mind blanked and he stared at Hartt.

"She is," he muttered, unable to believe what he was hearing. "I didn't think you were mated."

"I wasn't... not when you first came to me." Hartt shuffled to the edge of his seat. "I met Mackenzie after that. We were contracted to eliminate the same target. Turned out it was all a ruse to get the three of us to kill each other. A blood mage had a vendetta against myself, Mackenzie and Grave Van der Garde of the Preux Chevaliers."

The King of Death.

Someone had been crazy enough to take on a contract to kill the most dangerous vampire in Hell. Fenix frowned. Not just one someone either. Both

Hartt and Mackenzie must have been desperate for coin, or to prove something, to take on that contract.

"What happened with the blood mage? One of those wankers cursed me and Aderyn... or Evelyn as you all know her now." Fenix gave the elf the whole of his attention, not wanting to miss a thing, because the feeling that this male could help him had just increased a hundredfold.

"We tracked him to Norway," Rosalind put in.

"Norway?" Fenix's gaze snapped to her as that feeling grew stronger still. "What happened there? Whereabouts in Norway? Did any of them look like this?"

He leaned back and reached into the pocket of his black jeans, pulled out the silver portrait frame and opened it. He showed it to Hartt and then Rosalind and Vail. They all shook their heads.

He wasn't sure whether to be relieved or frustrated that they hadn't seen the mage he was after. Relieved seemed more appropriate, because he had seen Vail fight. The male probably hadn't left anyone alive.

And Fenix needed the mage alive to break the curse.

He wasn't going to bet everything he had on Aryanna being able to help.

"We wiped out a few of them, but none looked like that." Hartt peered at the portrait again. "No. He definitely wasn't there."

Fenix pocketed the frame. "I've been following leads, trying to find the mage who cursed us so I can free her. One of those leads pointed to Norway, but I haven't been there yet. I've checked out others. One in New Hampshire that has turned up nothing so far, but I have Hella and my clan looking through what we took from the house. There's another place in England. I only scouted that one from a distance. Too many mages there at present. Norway. Maybe he's there. Did you go inside the building?"

Rosalind shook her head. "We left it standing."

She said that as if it was an accomplishment.

Fenix eyed the trio. It probably had been.

"I need to check out that building. Even if the mage isn't there, there could be research that might help me or a clue that will lead me to him." Denying his need to get Evelyn away from Archangel while he investigated the building in Norway was going to prove hard though. It was going to take all of his will to stop himself from going to her, but he needed to find a way to break the curse. He couldn't risk taking her captive when there was a danger she might fall for him. He thought about the other place the mage might be, one that was looking more accessible now he wasn't alone. "The mansion in England had several mages living in it... and I sensed phoenixes there too."

Hartt growled, his top lip curling back off his emerging fangs. "I need that location. I need you to take me there."

"I will." Because Fenix could see how much the elf needed to know where it was and he knew the reason why. He wanted to give his mate, Mackenzie, the location so she could help her kin. "I'd like Evelyn to meet your mate. She always thought she was alone in this world, trapped here away from her kin. We travelled across Hell, finding information on the spell the mages had used to seal the gateway between that realm and the phoenix world, and we came close. The mage who cursed us is the closest we came to finding out how to open it. He knows. I'm sure of it."

"Mackenzie will definitely want to speak with her... when the curse is broken and she can remember who she is." Hartt half-smiled at him, a sympathetic one that told Fenix he had his doubts that would ever happen.

It would.

Fenix wasn't going to fail this time.

Although he wasn't one hundred percent certain she would ever remember who she had been before or the things she had done.

"So... did you sense her disappear or not? Because this is like an awful cliff-hanger at the end of a series that got cancelled, and I'm bloody damned if I'm going to wait much longer to find out whether I'll ever discover what happened. I'll make up my own ending." Rosalind shifted on Vail's lap.

The elf's eyes darkened, glittering with hunger that rolled off him in powerful waves as she wriggled on him.

Fenix levelled her with a black look. "Stop teasing your mate. I'm hungry enough as it is."

Her look was all innocence. "I wasn't."

Vail growled and flashed fangs at him, and Fenix waved the gold band that encircled his finger at the male.

"I told you I'm mated. I'm not interested in her." Fenix didn't wait for the apologetic look he knew would be coming. He couldn't really blame the male for turning aggressive towards him, after all. If it had been Evelyn wriggling on his own lap and firing him up, he would have been angry at any male in the vicinity too, the thought that they might try to steal her from him pushing him to threaten them. "She did disappear as I expected, but now I'm thinking about it... she wasn't the only one who disappeared."

"Colour me curious." Rosalind leaned forwards, pressed her left elbow to her knee as she crossed her legs and planted her chin on her upturned palm. "Do tell me more."

Vail wrapped his arms around her waist, keeping her in place on his lap, his gaze unfocused as he trailed it down her golden hair to her back and lower.

Fenix cleared his throat and scowled at the elf when he glanced his way, trying to hammer home the message to dial it back. Vail looked unrepentant. Instead of helping Fenix out by banishing his wicked thoughts about his mate, Vail loosened his grip on her and skimmed his hands over the curve of her waist, bringing out the silver stars in her blue eyes.

So Fenix scowled at her too.

"Oh fine," she huffed and dropped off Vail's lap, a pout to her lips as she went to her own chair. "You're such a spoilsport."

"Look, I had to put up with you two throwing off pheromones like crazy in that dungeon. I don't have to put up with it here. You want me to talk rather than walk, then keep it in your pants." Fenix gave them both a look he hoped conveyed that he meant every word he had said and he would carry out his threat if they didn't keep their hands off each other.

Rosalind really pouted now as she folded her arms across her chest and gave him a look. "You're no fun."

He didn't dispute that. He wasn't any fun right now, hadn't been since the day he had been cursed to lead a miserable existence pining for his mate and watching her fall in love with him, experiencing a few glorious days where things were back to normal for them, and then having her wrenched from him.

"When Frayne killed her, her partner was alive." Fenix hoped that would get the conversation back on track. Just the mention of Archer was enough to have his darker side prowling to the fore, hungry to find the bastard and take him out of the equation. He gritted his teeth instead, denying the need to hunt him down, one that would only lead to him going after Evelyn instead.

"Her partner?" Hartt flicked him a look. "The one you said had too tight a hold on her for you to get it through to her that she wasn't human?"

Fenix nodded and then shook his head slightly as he thought about Archer. "Here's the rub. I swear that *he* isn't human."

Rosalind leaped from her chair as if her arse was on fire. "He's the Crow! The bloody Crow is already inside Archangel!"

Her blue eyes darted between Vail and Hartt, as wide as saucers, as she bounced on the spot, more excited than he had ever seen her.

"Uh, Archer's a what now? Crow?" Fenix felt sure he was missing something when neither male looked confused about her outburst.

"Oh. Silly me. I forgot you weren't there for that part." Rosalind idly waved a hand at him. "A Crow is a witch… a male witch. Warlock. Whatever you want to call them. They're rare. Legend says that there's only a handful of them in existence. When one dies, another is born, and with the... blood? Soul? I'm not sure of the finer details... but one dies, another is born, and all the knowledge possessed by the previous Crow gets passed to the next. Of course, they're not born all Crow-ish... Crow-y? They're normal until they near their terrible tweens... speculation says it's on their ninth birthday. Ninth for the nine. But anyway, the magical birthday rolls around and then... boom... they're a Crow!"

Fenix still wasn't quite following. Rosalind was rambling so fast that he could barely keep up. He tried to run over what she had said and straighten out the facts in his head.

"So, let me get this straight. A group of nine warlocks exist called Crows, and when one dies, all the knowledge they've accumulated is passed on to another... host... who when they're old enough awaken as a Crow?" Fenix spoke each word slowly, feeling them out.

Rosalind nodded.

"And how long have these Crows existed?" Fenix hoped she was going to say it was a recent development, something that had occurred in the last few hundred years. Witches could live for a good two or three hundred years as far as he knew. Maybe Archer was only the second in his line of Crows.

"Um." Rosalind tapped her chin, her face screwing up as she pursed her lips and looked at the canopy of the parasol. Her blue eyes dropped to him as her hand fell away from her face. "Three... maybe four... might be five thousand years."

"Shit," Hartt muttered.

Fenix's thought exactly. He really didn't like the sound of Archer having the magic of the ages stuck in his head and at his disposal. It was no wonder Fenix always lost in a fight with him.

A thought popped into his head.

His eyes widened.

"While I like the thought of Archer possessing that much power as I do the idea of a hot poker shoved up my arse, it does explain one thing for me. Sometimes... he looks ready to really go off... like unhinged." Fenix glanced at Vail and held back the smile that wanted to curve his lips. "You'd know the look."

Vail scowled at him.

"Spells can sometimes be a little... rambunctious." Rosalind sidled over to Vail and stroked her fingers through his blue-black hair, tousling it as her expression shifted towards thoughtful. "They have a will of their own. It might be that he's having difficulty leashing some of them."

Her voice dropped to a murmur.

"I'd love to pick his brains."

Vail had been slowly relaxing as his mate fussed over him, but his features hardened in an instant and he glared up at her. "You are not going anywhere near this male."

The tips of his ears grew even pointier as they flared against the sides of his head and his violet eyes darkened.

Rosalind smiled sweetly at him as she teased those pointed tips, attempting to distract her mate. "I wasn't thinking of hunting him down or anything. I swear!"

She wasn't a good liar.

Vail didn't look convinced either. "First Atticus bloody Darcy and now this Crow."

Rosalind planted her hands on her hips. "Stop bringing up Atticus like I'm swooning over him. I'm not interested in anyone but you and you know it… however… Atticus… bloody git owes me, and he does have some good spells, ones that might help us."

"Help us how?" Fenix tried to ignore the black look that settled on Vail's face and the aggression he was throwing off as he continued to glare at his mate. He looked ready to lock her up and throw away the key to keep her away from other males.

Wasn't like Fenix had been there or done that with his own mate.

Not at all.

"If the Crow is Evelyn's partner, then she doesn't know what he is, right? Well, what if we can reveal that to her and convince her that Archer isn't as human as he seems? It might be a good way of turning her against him and severing the bond they have." Rosalind had hope building inside Fenix with every word that left her lips and by the time she finished, he was on the edge of his seat and eager to locate this Atticus she kept mentioning.

"And how do you propose we reveal what he is? He looks human. You look human. Unless you're planning to make him use magic, which I don't think will happen. I've fought him and he fights like a human would." Fenix didn't want to doubt her plan, but he needed to know how it was going to get the result he needed, and he had to keep his hopes down somehow. Sprinkling a little doubt around often helped achieve that.

She settled sideways on Vail's lap and the elf's expression immediately softened as she looped her arms around him. The little witch definitely had her mate wrapped around her finger and deep under her spell, and Fenix was glad something good had come of the time they had spent trapped in the dungeon together.

"I propose we get a spell from Atticus, one that will drive the spells inside the Crow's mind wild and reveal what he is." Rosalind smiled wickedly, the stars in her eyes fading as they darkened, and Vail stroked her side, concern flitting across his face as he gazed at her.

Fenix didn't like the look on her face either. It wasn't like Rosalind to look so dark. Even in the dungeon she had never looked like this, so close to letting the shadowy side of magic draw her away from the light.

"It sounds dangerous," Vail put in and her gaze snapped to him, the darkness leaving her eyes in an instant as they locked with her mate's violet ones. "If just one of those spells goes haywire... we do not know what will happen."

"We either risk it or we risk the Crow getting his hands on the power to cast a curse upon immortals that will strip us of our power and banish us to Hell." Rosalind sighed and leaned her side against his chest.

She snuggled up to Vail as she looked at Fenix, and casually placed all the weight on his shoulders as she put the decision in his hands.

"So what's it going to be?"

CHAPTER 20

It was a pleasant evening, warm and clear, with just enough moonlight for Evelyn to see into the deepest shadows in Hyde Park. It should have been relaxing, but the air between her and Archer was still tense.

Or maybe that was her.

She flicked a glance at him as he pushed his glasses up his nose and regarded the trees on his side of the path, trying to think of something to say to break the heavy silence that had settled over them from the moment he had suggested a patrol.

Part of her felt sure he wanted to clear the air too. He didn't want this tension between them to carry on. Maybe he was struggling for something to say just as she was.

Evelyn pushed aside the questions she really wanted to ask him, aware that if she probed into why he had gone off alone the other night and had ordered her to go home that he would grow angry with her again. She didn't want that. She wanted things to go back to how they had been, before they had gone to Hell on that initial mission to scout the Fifth Realm.

"Archer," she started and faltered, her words failing her.

His sigh said it all.

He knew she was trying to heal the breach between them and he wanted it too.

They both sucked at this.

"I went to look into something regarding Aryanna." His deep voice curled around her, soft and comforting, easing some of the tension from her soul. She glanced at him, her eyes meeting his. "I was worried it would be dangerous and I didn't want you coming along. I wanted to protect you. I didn't mean to—" He scrubbed a hand over his hair, tousling the dark lengths, and stopped as it reached his nape. On a long sigh, he tilted his head back, still clutching the back of his neck. "I think I spend most of my time apologising to you recently. I don't mean to be the way I am. I just have a lot on my mind."

She got that. His promotion to the position of commander must have doubled his workload. He hadn't been in the Central Archive much recently, and when he had been there, she had found him leaning over a roster of hunters, trying to figure out new team builds that would have a broader spread of skills that would make them more effective in the field.

"Want to ditch patrol and get a coffee and catch up?" She reached for his arm and brushed her fingers down the sleeve of his black Henley. His gaze fell to her, his brow furrowing as his eyes softened and he nodded, and she could see how much he appreciated her being on his side and not making a big deal of things. "All water under the bridge. If I was in your position, I'd be a ball of stress too."

He smiled and his hand dropped from the back of his neck, and then his look turned deadly serious. "Evelyn... there's something I've been wanting to tell you and I'm not sure I should, but I can't go on like this. It was wrong of me to—"

His shoulders tightened.

Evelyn tensed as she sensed it too.

They weren't alone.

She spun on her heel to face the intruders and barely bit back her gasp as her eyes collided with Fenix's swirling blue and gold ones. He was like a shadow in the dimly-lit park, his black shirt and jeans hugging his lean but muscular body in a way that had the whole of her focus shifting to him, the world falling away as his gaze held her immobile.

A shiver rolled down her spine, heat blooming in her veins as warmth spread through every inch of her. Her pulse quickened, blood rushing as she stared into his eyes, as awareness of him speared her soul and had her unable to tear her gaze away from him. The fierce reaction he always evoked in her felt so wrong, as if she was betraying her own kind and Archangel by feeling attracted to him.

But at the same time, it felt so very right.

As if they were meant to be together.

God, he was gorgeous.

His wild tawny hair made her fingers itch to brush through it, to feel the silken strands against them as he gazed at her with so much heat and need in his eyes. She could so easily imagine how he would react if she braved surrendering to that urge, how every muscle on his bewitching body would tense and his gaze would fall to her lips.

How he would bend his head towards her, tempting her into claiming his lips.

Placing them within her reach.

An ache bloomed deep inside her, the heat becoming an inferno that threatened to burn her will to resist to ashes as it whispered about how good it would feel if she captured his mouth in a kiss, how that simple action would steal command from him and place him firmly under her control. Didn't she want to know how good it would feel to have Fenix at her mercy? Didn't she want to fist his hair and hear him groan in response? To see the hunger and desperate need in his eyes and know she wasn't the only one feeling that way?

Didn't she want to wreck him with only a kiss?

To claim him with it.

Fire licked through her veins, blazing hotter still, making her head hazy and her body come alive.

She burned with a need to bring this male to his knees.

His lips parted, beckoning her.

Movement beyond him had the spell he had placed on her shattering in an instant, the world rushing back in like a cold tide to kill the heat in her veins.

Evelyn curled her fingers into tight fists at her side and reminded herself that Fenix wasn't just any breed of non-human. He was an incubus. For all she knew, this reaction she had to him was purely because he was using his powers on her. It wasn't real.

She took a step back, towards Archer.

And Fenix's expression shifted, the sculpted planes of his face hardening as his eyebrows drew down and his lips flattened.

"Confessing now?" Fenix's voice was a black snarl, the look he turned on Archer nothing short of murderous, and something deep inside Evelyn liked it.

There was possession in that look.

As if he wanted her for himself, despised the thought of another male taking her from him, and would fight to protect her and stop her from choosing another over him.

Evelyn fought to shut down her rogue thoughts and the feelings they stirred, battling to clear her mind and focus.

It wasn't hard when she took in the fact he wasn't alone this time.

There was a blonde female wearing a black dress to his left. A witch if she had to guess. Behind him were two men who looked like elves to her, both of them tall and lean, with dishevelled blue-black hair and noble features. The fact the tips of their ears were rounded and their eyes weren't violet didn't fool her. She knew elves could manipulate those parts of their appearance, allowing them to blend in with humans.

She reached for the dart gun holstered at her hip and froze when one of the elves looked at her, a hard look settling on his face that warned her that if she went for the weapon, she would regret it.

Instead, she waited for Archer to do something.

The moment he made a move, she would too. Together they could handle this threat.

Only he remained perfectly still beside her.

Her gaze slid to him and she found him staring at the group, but it wasn't the incubus on the receiving end of his glare.

It was the petite woman.

"Hello," she said breezily, as if they knew each other or she wanted to be friends.

Archer flexed his fingers.

She clucked her tongue.

"That's my move."

Evelyn's eyes widened as the woman raised her left arm and elegantly flipped her hand over and a bright red sphere surrounded by jagged black ribbons appeared above her palm.

And shot towards Archer.

"Archer!" Evelyn lunged for him.

He shoved her away from him, his palm hitting her hard in the centre of her chest to knock the wind from her as he pushed her out of the line of fire. The spell hit him dead on, detonating in tiny orbs of red that zoomed around him and sank into his skin wherever it was exposed. He cast her a stricken look as she landed on her backside on the grass a short distance from him, the pain in his eyes tearing at her, filling her with a need to go to him.

And then he clutched the sides of his head, threw it back and bellowed at the night sky.

The sound was more demonic than human, had a chill racing down her spine as she stared at him, unable to believe her eyes.

Flares of violet and cerulean burst from his shoulders to form a corona around him, laced with fingers of onyx shadows that lashed at the air.

His eyes flicked open.

They were jet black.

Blue flames engulfed his hands and rushed up his arms, burning away the black sleeves of his Henley.

Revealing bands of markings on his forearms that were just like the ones she had seen in her dreams.

He sneered at the blonde, flashing his teeth at her, and for a heartbeat it looked as if he might attack her, but then he cast another look filled with regret and hurt at Evelyn.

Bellowed like a beast.

And disappeared.

"Son of a bloody bitch!" the blonde witch yelled and hurried forwards, but the taller of the elf males, one who bore a striking resemblance to Prince Loren of the elves, seized hold of her and pulled her back against his chest, pinning her there.

"I did say he could probably teleport." Fenix levelled a look on her. "You didn't think to work some... anti-teleport... spell into the mix?"

"Oh, fuck off. I don't see you casting magic." She wriggled free of the elf's grip and turned on the incubus, her large blue eyes pricked with shining silver stars. "Anyway, the plan wasn't to capture him. We're not equipped to hold a Crow."

"Sounds like your plan was to capture him. You are rather upset he got away." The other elf weathered the black look she cast at him, shrugging it off.

"Little Wild Rose." The elf who had grabbed her murmured that with a strained, possibly pained, look on his face.

She huffed and softened as she turned to him, as she opened her arms to him and he bent and scooped her up, clutching her tightly to him with one arm around her back and the other under her bottom. She stroked her fingers through his blue-black hair as she whispered, "Just a little magic. You did good. I didn't want the stinky Crow, really."

Evelyn mentally checked herself over, realised that the initial wave of shock that had hit her had passed and she had no reason to be sitting on the damp grass with a group of non-humans.

Only she couldn't convince herself to move.

Or stop looking at the spot where Archer had been.

The incubus had been right.

Archer wasn't human.

And somehow, she had known it. She had dreamed of those black eyes and tattoos. Had she seen them before and forgotten them?

She forced her gaze to shift to Fenix, a weight settling on her chest as she remembered the other things he had said to her, things that had sounded like the ramblings of an insane or desperate man at the time.

But what if he had been telling her the truth?

What if she wasn't safe at Archangel?

He had wanted to set her free. What did that even mean? She was free. Wasn't she?

Her focus drifted back to where Archer had been. Archer, who had been hit by a spell and had transformed before her eyes, had become the man who haunted her dreams. She tried to convince herself that the spell the witch had used had caused those changes in him, but attempting to bury her head in the sand and make excuses wasn't going to cut it.

He had teleported.

And he had looked at her as if he was sorry, as if he was hurt that she had discovered that he wasn't human after all.

Evelyn wasn't sure what to make of that.

Fenix slowly approached her and she could sense his wariness. And wasn't that weird? Why could she sense things about him? Why did she feel... *comforted*... by his presence?

She looked up at him, aware that everything she was feeling was there on her face for him to see. There was no point in hiding it. She was confused. Hurt. Felt betrayed. Even used. Had she just been a part of Archer's plan? Or had she really been his friend?

What had he wanted to tell her?

Part of her, some desperate, hurt part of her, wanted to believe he had meant to tell her what he was and all about his plan, but she would never know.

Fenix extended his right hand to her and his gaze implored her to take it.

She looked at him and then the trio who had remained where they were, all of them watching her now.

Waiting to see what she would do.

Trust the non-humans who had done something terrible to Archer?

Or run?

CHAPTER 21

Fenix could see the war playing out in Evelyn's golden eyes, could feel how torn she was as she stared at the hand he offered, and was soul-deep aware of her hurt. It beat inside him too, had him regretting agreeing to Rosalind's plan. If he had known revealing what Archer was, and apparently wounding that male emotionally in the process, would hurt his mate this deeply, he wouldn't have agreed to it. He would have found a gentler way to convince her that Archer wasn't all that he seemed and would have stuck to his original plan to wait until he knew how to break the curse before approaching her again.

Even when he knew there wasn't time.

Whatever Archangel were planning to do with Aryanna, whatever Archer was planning to do with her, it was already in progress and as much as he hated the thought of losing his mate and beginning the curse cycle again, he couldn't ignore that.

The whole world was in danger.

Including his mate.

So stopping Archangel and Archer took priority.

Because he needed to protect his mate from their machinations.

When she looked as if she might run, he silently apologised to her and lunged for her, seized her arm in a tight grip and held his other one out behind him. Hartt was quick to grab it and Fenix willed the teleport, one that took a monumental effort with a powerful elf and an even more powerful phoenix shifter in tow. He landed on the long patio of his home in Scotland and released both of them, staggered to the grey stone wall beside the bay window and pressed his hands to it as he breathed hard, fighting to stop himself from collapsing.

"What the hell?" Evelyn barked, her panic hitting him hard.

He sensed Hartt disappear, twisted to face her and sagged into the wall, using it to keep himself upright.

Being alone with her was dangerous.

He felt that right down to his bones as he stared at her, as she twisted left and then right, taking in her surroundings and looking more and more like she was going to go for the gun and nail him with a tranquiliser dart.

It wasn't fear for his life that made him will Hartt to hurry back with Rosalind and Vail.

It was fear that he might surrender to the urge to charm his mate. Not in the traditional manner an incubus used, since his powers didn't work on her. He wanted to charm her in the manner a male who was interested, who wanted, a female would behave—being nice to her, schmoozing her a little, slowly breaking down her barriers.

Until she fell in love with him.

He couldn't let it happen. He needed her to dislike him. Not hate. He didn't want her to hate him, because then she would fear him, and he couldn't bear that. He wanted her to remain emotionally distant from him.

He wanted her to not love him.

A strange predicament for a male so madly in love with his female to be in, sure, but one he had to roll with. Keeping her distant from him, giving her no reason to fall for him, was a key part of his plan this time.

Given that she worked for Archangel and had been moulded to despise non-humans, and the fact he had just kidnapped her, it shouldn't be too difficult.

"Take me back." She turned on him, her golden eyes flashing brightly.

Her phoenix side was showing.

"I think I'll just keep propping up this wall." He couldn't risk another teleport even if he had been inclined to do as she wanted. He didn't have the strength, had just blasted through his reserves by teleporting her and Hartt, and hunger was going to hit him at any second.

He willed Hartt to hurry.

Stared at his mate.

Gods, she was beautiful.

Gods, he loved her so damned much. If she asked it of him, he would carve out his heart. If she said she would kiss him, he would do whatever she demanded in exchange, no feat too difficult for him to master if he could claim her lips as his prize.

"Why are you looking at me like that?" Her voice trembled, betraying the nerves he could feel in her.

Because he wanted to devour her.

He wanted to pleasure her for hours and feast on the bliss she experienced, on the love she would feel for him.

Because he craved her.

Was sure he would go insane if he went another second without feeling her in his arms, without savouring the warmth of her breath skating over his lips, without that sweet anticipation swirling inside him as he gazed down at her and wondered what she would do.

Kiss him?

Fight him?

He stared at her, sure she had to be aware of how much he needed her, how desperate he was for her, and how deeply he loved her. She had to feel the bond that connected them too, one that relayed her growing desire and that told him she wanted him too.

Dangerous.

Too dangerous.

Fenix shored up his resistance, clawed his strength together and fought the urge to cross the short span of flagstones to her and sweep her into his arms. He couldn't. If she fell for him, she would die. It might take minutes, it might take days, but in the end, she would be torn from him again. He would be forced to watch her die and know there was nothing he could do to stop it and stop the cycle from beginning again.

He vowed that he would make her love him again, but not yet.

As soon as the curse was broken, her heart belonged to him.

Until then, he had to go against his every instinct, had to shut down the softer part of himself that despised himself for what he was going to do, and had to live with her hating him too.

"Nothing personal," he drawled and casually jammed his hands in his pockets, his fingers closing over the pillbox in his left one.

He pulled it out, opened it, and popped two into his mouth. He swallowed them and the instant they hit his stomach, his hunger faded back to a manageable level. He ran his eyes over her, taking in how her black uniform hugged her figure, revealing it to him to keep his mind traversing a wicked route. He wanted those shapely thighs wrapped around his waist, crushing him as she rode him. He wanted those pert breasts rubbing against his bare chest to create a maddening friction that would add to his pleasure. He groaned, ran a hand down his mouth, and flashed a grin at her, aware he was about to sound like a monumental dick.

A good thing for once. It would push her away.

"Just been a while since I fed and I'm hungry. Don't fancy a quickie do you? Up against the wall would be fine, or I could just bend you over and take you from behind. Probably better that way. A functional fuck. No pesky emotions. Just scratching an itch and feeding. Or maybe that warlock stole your heart on top of brainwashing you?"

She took a sharp step backwards and scowled at him, her lip curling as her fair eyebrows knitted hard.

The thought that Archer might have claimed what was his had his markings churning obsidian and red, and his hunger transforming into a black need to find the male and kill him.

Evelyn spat, "You're disgusting."

That wasn't a no. He didn't like that it wasn't a no.

He pushed away from the wall and glared at her, the ruse to anger her and make her keep her distance falling away as his own rage got the better of him. "Did you fuck him?"

Her golden eyes widened and then narrowed. "It's none of your business if I did."

"Oh, it's my business, love. So answer the damned question. Did you sleep with the warlock?" His breaths came faster as the part of him he always struggled to deny, the insidious voice that breathed poison in his ear on a daily basis, began to win ground against the side of him that knew she had been faithful to him.

She always was.

Her cheeks flushed and her mouth flapped open and closed, and her words were jerky as she grew more and more flustered. "I... We weren't... It wasn't... We were partners."

"Partners sexually?" He moved a hard step closer to her.

Her gaze darted off to her right, and then it narrowed and she calmed, and her eyes snapped back to him. "It's really not your business."

"You, sweetheart, are my business and you have been for decades."

Those stunning golden eyes widened again and her mouth dropped open. "Decades? I haven't been alive decades!"

He chuckled at that. "Last count, you were a hundred and... sixty-one... no... sixty-three. If the age you told me you were when we met in a little tavern in Hell was true."

She swallowed hard. "I don't know what you're talking about. You've mistaken me for someone else. I'm barely thirty."

"Archer tell you that?" He shook his head and sneered as he saw something in her eyes that only stoked his anger. "And you believe him. You still believe him."

The depth of her trust when it came to Archer irritated the hell out of Fenix.

He wanted her to trust him like that, to need no other male.

To want no other male.

He curled his fingers into tight fists and shut down those dangerous thoughts, denying his needs.

Her gaze faltered, dropping to her boots again, and she frowned at the flagstones.

Fenix huffed. "He's a liar."

"And you're not?" she bit out and tossed him daggers. Her shoulders slumped a heartbeat later. "Just take me home, and I won't tell Archangel anything about your involvement in this. I won't bring them after you."

He shook his head again. "I can't do that. You're staying here."

She folded her arms across her chest and he noticed that she wasn't going for her weapon. Was he getting through to her?

"I've never lied to you." He backed off a step, changed his mind and closed the distance between them instead, because he didn't want her getting too comfortable around him. "Archer lied to you. He used you. You're a pawn to him."

"And what am I to you?" she whispered, and the look she gave him made him feel a lot hinged on his answer, and it was too much weight on his heart.

Everything. She was everything to him.

"Nothing," he spat. "Just a means to an end. Unless you're up for that quick bang against the wall? Then I guess you'd be dinner."

She backed off, hurt flaring in her eyes for a heartbeat before they hardened again. "You're such an arsehole. I don't get you. You act like you want to help me... or save me... You make out that we're old friends... but then you're a callous, cold bastard towards me. Why? Are you always like this?"

Fenix pivoted away from her on a frustrated sigh and ran his right hand through his tawny hair, still hating how short it was now, how a moment of weakness had made him cut it to look like the Crow's hair.

He glanced back at Evelyn, his gaze colliding with hers, and the hurt in her eyes, the confusion, hit him hard and had him heaving another sigh as the need to comfort her rolled through him.

This was dangerous, but perhaps it was better she knew what she was up against. She deserved to know what would happen if he stopped being cruel to her from time to time so she could guard her heart.

"I don't want you falling in love with me," he husked, all the pain he had felt over the decades rolling together in an agonising knot in his chest. All the brief moments of happiness. All the long, aching months of grieving her. All the fear of it happening again. The hopelessness. The cruel sense of it being unavoidable.

Inescapable.

Decades of feeling powerless.

Driven to find her.

Aware that when he did, it would only result in her death.

"No danger of that happening, incubus," she scoffed and glared at him, but then a flicker of curiosity lit her eyes. "But, I'll play along. Why can't I fall for you?"

He was really going to do this. It was something he hadn't tried before, and maybe it was the one thing he had been missing and would lead to success.

"If you fall for me, the curse that affects both of us will become active and you'll end up being killed again, transported elsewhere for your rebirth, and you'll forget everything."

Her brow furrowed. "Killed *again*?"

He held his hands up, his palms facing her, when she looked ready to run or possibly laugh in his face. He wasn't sure which it would be. There was a high probability she was going to call him a liar again.

Fenix sucked down a deep breath, held it and then sighed it out.

"You're not human, Evelyn. You're a phoenix shifter."

CHAPTER 22

"You're not human, Evelyn. You're a phoenix shifter."

Evelyn stared at Fenix, reeling as those words hit her, the desire to laugh in his face and tell him to pull the other one because it had bells on it falling away as she fell into his green eyes and saw in them that he was telling the truth.

Or what he believed to be the truth.

She wasn't sure what to believe.

Archer had turned out to be a warlock, a non-human, just as Fenix had warned her. That alone had part of her wanting to believe the incubus, while the rest of her wanted to run for the heather-covered hills that surrounded the bleak grey mansion.

Because the thought that Fenix was telling her the truth and she wasn't human had her feeling more off-balance than ever, even as it had some things making far too much sense—like the fact she had started to feel she was different.

That something was wrong with her.

Her dreams came back to her. Fire. Always fire. It never hurt her. It warmed her. Comforted her.

Just as the sight of Fenix had whenever he had appeared in her dreams.

And Archer had always left her feeling afraid.

And lost.

Lost.

That single word seemed to sum up how she felt a lot of the time. When she was alone on the roof of Archangel HQ watching the sunset. When she was in her apartment and found her thoughts drifting. When she woke from one of those dreams.

She felt lost.

And as if she had forgotten something vital.

It was always there, just beyond her reach, impossible to grasp and bring into focus.

Was this what she had forgotten?

That she was a phoenix shifter?

"Impossible," she muttered, unwilling to believe it. Her life had been taking strange enough turns as it was. Believing she was a phoenix shifter was one step too close to crazy for her liking.

She tensed and whirled when she swore someone was behind her.

Her eyes widened when the two elves and the blonde witch appeared a split-second later.

"You sensed them. It's a phoenix thing. You have incredibly acute senses for things like this." Fenix's deep voice rolled over her like a warm wave, had her heating right down to her bones as her tension faded.

Another strange thing. She should be afraid of these people, fearing for her life.

But she wasn't.

Some insane part of her didn't view them as a threat.

Because she was a mystical shifter? One so powerful that they *weren't* a threat to her?

She barked out a laugh at that, caught the look in the shorter elf's eyes that said she was losing it, and shook her head as she turned in a slow circle, taking in her surroundings.

A mansion in the middle of nowhere.

Scottish if she had to guess based on the colour of the stone and the design. Pitched roofs placed side by side that formed a jagged line and decorative pointed finials that gave it a gothic look, together with bay windows and an entrance set into the building beyond a stone arch. Definitely Scottish. The mountains made her think Highlands.

Incubi couldn't teleport to Hell without the use of the portals, which meant there was either one nearby or this place was close to the underground fae town in Fort William.

"I don't like that look." The blonde witch raised her hand and light burst from it, shot into the air and fell in the shape of a dome as it flickered and died. "There, now she can't go for a run beyond the walls. The grounds are plenty big enough for you to get your cardio."

The witch slid a look at Fenix.

"You didn't tell me this place had spells on it."

He gave her an unimpressed look in return. "You didn't ask. Your little spell better not have messed with the ones already in place."

She shook her head, causing her ash-blonde waves to brush the black shoulders of her dress. "Not at all. Merely supplemental. Nice work though. Someone local do it?"

He nodded.

Increasing that feeling Evelyn had that said he lived near to the fae town. Witches lived there in droves, together with demons and shifters, and fae like incubi and succubi. It was a hotspot for immortals.

She settled her gaze back on Fenix, the warmth his voice had stirred in her growing stronger as their eyes locked and she fell into his, losing track of her surroundings as the world narrowed down to only him. That warmth became a flicker of heat, flames that licked through her veins and had her heart beating faster. An ache rolled through her, rousing a fierce need to lower her gaze to his lips as she imagined what it would be like to kiss him.

Would he be soft with her?

Hard?

Demanding?

She shivered at the thought of him gripping her tightly, clutching her arms to pin her in place as he took her mouth, saw it all play out in her head so clearly it felt as if she had done it before and it was a memory rather than a fantasy. The heat blazed hotter still, had her head growing hazy as her entire body came alive, yearning for the feel of his hands on her. She could almost feel them. Squeezing her backside. Palming her breasts. His lips on her throat as he murmured how much he loved her.

How crazy he was for her.

Cold chased down her spine as she shoved the fantasy out of her head, the warm haziness evaporating to leave her mind clear and focused.

"Stop charming me," she snarled, anger curling through her veins to replace the heat of desire.

The incubus held his hands up, revealing the markings that tracked up the underside of his forearms. "I'm not. I can't. I can't charm you, Evelyn. My powers don't work on you."

She refused to believe that. Her gaze fell to the swirls, dots and slashes that formed the line of markings. They shimmered in hues of blue and gold, a sign that he was hungry, but amongst those colours shone deepest pink.

"What does that mean?" She pointed to his markings, needing the answer to that question this time, because her gut was screaming one at her and she didn't like it.

He had told her he couldn't let her fall for him.

She hadn't stopped to wonder whether he was already in love with her.

She almost jumped out of her skin when a sandy-haired man dressed in jeans and a navy cable-knit sweater appeared beside Fenix.

"Hella's pet escaped and she went after him. I tried to stop her… but she didn't take it well, and now she's probably chasing him over the moors—" The blond's head slowly swivelled towards her, his hazel eyes gaining spots of gold and cerulean that rapidly spread to fill them. "Hello, who's this beauty? Got a name for me, gorgeous?"

Her spine stiffened as heat rolled through her. Not the pleasant sort that she felt whenever Fenix looked at her. This heat felt like an invasion, had her wanting to step away from him even as she found herself taking a step towards him instead.

Powerless to deny him.

She opened her mouth to give him her name, to satisfy his desire to hear it and him in the process.

Fenix grabbed him by the front of his sweater, twisted with him and slammed him into the granite wall of the house. The back of the blond's head cracked off the stone as Fenix pulled him towards him and shoved him back again, harder this time.

"Get out of her head or I'll rip yours off," Fenix snarled, sending a shiver bolting down her spine.

Her blood heated again, a pleasant warmth that chased the strange sensation from her body, ridding her of it.

"You're the mate." The blond made the mistake of looking at her.

Fenix cocked his left fist and smashed it into the man's mouth, snapping his head to his left and splitting his lip. Before the other incubus could recover, Fenix had struck him again, following it with a hard knee to the kidney.

"Get the fuck back inside, Mort, and stay away from her," Fenix growled as he twisted and shoved the one called Mort, sending him to the ground. He stalked towards the man, shoved his booted foot into his side and flipped him onto his back. His eyes shone gold and blue as he glared down at the younger man. "You so much as look at her again and I'll gouge your fucking eyes out. Understood?"

Mort was quick to nod as he clutched Fenix's ankle, fear dancing across his face as he stared up at him. "It was a mistake. I'm sorry."

Fenix breathed hard, his chest heaving with each one he sucked down, and his fingers curled into fists at his sides. For a moment, Evelyn felt sure he would strike the other incubus while he was down, but then he unleashed a frustrated sound and shoved with his foot, rolling Mort away from him.

"Get out of my sight, and tell the others what I just told you. Evelyn is off-limits."

She stiffened as Mort disappeared and Fenix pivoted to face her, shoving his fingers through his tawny hair as he huffed. He froze as his eyes locked with hers, his expression gaining an awkward edge. She wasn't sure how to interpret what he had just done, how savagely he had reacted when Mort had attempted to charm her, or the fact they weren't the only incubi in the mansion.

Her mind got stuck on that small fact, using it to distract her from the bigger problem—the fact she had liked how vicious Fenix had been in dealing with the younger incubus.

"How many other incubi live here?" she said, her voice lacking strength as she flicked a glance at the imposing granite building.

Fenix bit out, "You'd better not be thinking about telling Archangel about this place."

Apparently, his protective streak wasn't limited to her. He was protective of the people who lived here too. Because they were his family, and he cared for them despite the fact one had just tried to come on to her?

"I'm not." She froze, feeling as surprised as Fenix looked by that. "It... it never even crossed my mind. I just wanted to know how many other men I have to be on my guard against."

Which shocked her too.

Because it made her realise she wasn't planning on running and escaping this place. She was planning to stay.

What was wrong with her?

"Four," he grunted and then his tone softened, turning reassuring. "None of them will hurt you, Evelyn."

She believed that.

He folded his arms across his chest and huffed as he looked away from her, glancing over his shoulder at the mansion. She stared at the markings on his forearms, watching the gold, blue and pink churning.

Was he in love with her? Mort had implied she was Fenix's mate.

Her gaze lifted back to meet his again and there was no mistaking that softness in his eyes as he looked at her. She had never had a man look at her as if he loved her before, but she felt sure that was the emotion she could read in his eyes, and in his markings.

Evelyn corrected that thought.

She couldn't *remember* a man ever looking at her the way Fenix did anyway.

For all she knew, he might have looked at her like that for the decades he swore they had been together. She might have been wildly in love with him too.

"Is there a way to unlock her memories at least?" Fenix cast a hopeful-but-worried look at the witch. "Maybe it'll help."

"You want to risk that? If she falls for you, she'll die and forget you." Those words were said in a bright tone, but they hit Evelyn hard, drawing her gaze to the witch. The blonde gave her a sympathetic look. "He's telling you the truth, you know? You're not human. A little spell would prove it."

Evelyn backed off and lowered her hand to her gun as an urge to lash out flooded her. "No one is casting spells on me!"

Fenix held his hands out again, his palms facing her, and his tone was soft as he murmured, "No one is going to cast a spell on you, Evelyn. I swear. No one will use any magic on you. No witch, warlock or mage will ever hurt you again."

He slid the witch a black look.

The blonde shrugged. "Fine. No magic. There has to be a way to make her see what she is though."

Evelyn had gotten stuck on the word *mage*. Just thinking that word roused a powerful anger inside her, one that struck her out of nowhere and had her restless, wanting to pace and lash out at anyone who stood in her way. Why? What was wrong with her?

The shorter of the elves stepped forwards. "I have an idea."

And then he was gone.

The witch looked at the other elf. "How about we take a turn around the garden and poke around a bit while the two love birds argue it out? Maybe we could find the witch the barrier spell is meant to keep out?"

The elf was quick to dip his head and hold his hand out to her, and Evelyn didn't miss that his armour was in place beneath his clothing, transforming his fingers into sharp black talons. Despite the danger, the witch slipped her hand into his, lacing their fingers together, and began walking with him, tugging him away from Evelyn.

As they drifted into the distance, she caught the witch saying, "I was only suggesting a little spell. I knew he wouldn't go for it... given their history. I thought it might prompt her to remember."

Evelyn studied her feelings, frowning as she thought about how she had reacted to the mention of a spell. It hadn't been fear that had gripped her in that moment. It had been anger, a rage so deep it had startled her, and she wasn't sure where it had come from, but some part of her felt as if she'd had a bad experience with magic in the past.

With a *mage*.

Because she was cursed?

CHAPTER 23

Evelyn looked across her shoulder at Fenix, seeking the answer to whether she was cursed or not in his eyes. He looked as if he wanted to come to her but was holding himself back, forcing himself to remain at a distance. Because he didn't want her falling for him.

"I'd like to go home now," she whispered as the mansion and the mountains seemed to close in on her. It was all too much. She felt as if she was being bombarded with information that didn't make any sense to her, but at the same time made perfect sense, and she couldn't handle it.

She had all the space in the world, so why did she feel as if she couldn't breathe? She pulled the collar of her T-shirt away from her chest and fanned herself, struggling to get air into her lungs as panic prickled down her spine and her temperature soared.

"Evelyn," Fenix husked and his tawny eyebrows furrowed.

He flexed his fingers at his sides and then sighed and looked at his feet. For a moment, she felt sure he might do as she wanted and take her back to Archangel.

And that panic she felt increased, closing her throat and causing a riot in her mind.

She couldn't go back there. She couldn't really stay here, not like part of her had been considering.

She had to go somewhere, but she wasn't sure where. She just needed to get away and clear her head. She needed a moment to think and process everything that had happened. Archer was a warlock and had been lying to her. And God, did that mean she had died in the Fifth Realm but he had brought her back? Was she dead?

Again?

According to Fenix, she had died multiple times. How many?

"You're panicking, sweetheart." He held his hands out to her again, his green gaze soft with a need she could name. He wanted to comfort her. He wanted it but he feared it at the same time.

Because he didn't want her falling in love with him. Because if she did, she would die.

Because she was cursed.

"No shit," she muttered and began walking in a circle, trying to shake off the panic that gripped her, desperate to clear her head and for everything to sink in and make sense.

It wasn't going to happen. Not while her mind was whirling with everything Fenix had told her and she was caught up in the maelstrom, unable to find her footing or something to hold on to.

She glanced at Fenix and her gaze lingered on him as that sense of solidness she badly needed filled her. She had no reason to trust him, but something deep inside her did, and she found herself just looking at him, narrowing the world back down to him in an effort to let everything else fall away.

Evelyn's gaze drifted over him, from his wild tawny hair threaded with gold, to his green eyes that held a hint of that colour too as he gazed at her, down over the black shirt that hugged his lean figure. Her eyes roamed over his left arm as everything dropped away, as calm flowed through her again and she felt at peace. What colour were his markings as he gazed at her?

Still incubus blue and gold, laced with that dash of dark pink? Colours he wouldn't tell her about, and she suspected it was because they were colours that betrayed his feelings for her. She couldn't see the markings on the rear of his left forearm, so she shifted her focus to his right.

And frowned.

Just below the rolled-up sleeve of his shirt, close to the inside of his elbow, was a circular black mark. She stared at it, trying to make out the design while resisting the urge to step closer to him so she could see it more clearly.

"Got new ink?" She kept her eyes on it, squinted a little and thought there was a dragon in the design within the circle, and possibly a deer or some other creature with antlers.

Fenix raised his right arm and twisted it, his head tilting towards it as he stole it from view, increasing that urge to move towards him.

"Not by choice." He ran his left thumb over the mark as he angled it towards her again, as if he had felt her need to see it. His features hardened as he stared at it and traced the outside of the circle. "It's a brand, I think. A promise... maybe. Like a pledge?"

He didn't sound sure.

"Where did you get it?" She tried to ignore how much she liked this easiness between them, how normal everything felt here in this moment, where they were talking about something other than her or Archer. Or a curse. Or her multiple deaths. Her throat closed a little and a weight settled on her chest again, so she focused more intently on the mark, picking out all the details she could. There was writing that followed the ring, marks that were in a language she didn't know.

His green gaze lifted to lock with hers, held her immobile and had that tight feeling falling away again as his soft voice swept over her. "Remember the bloke Archangel were holding in the cell opposite mine?"

A knot formed in her stomach at the reminder she had taken him captive and had been the one to subject him to the terrible things Archangel had done to him. An apology balanced on her lips. One part of her wanted to let tumble into the open while the rest of her held it back.

"Turns out he was an unseelie prince. Never seen one before." He glanced at the mark again and idly brushed the pad of his thumb over it. "Don't think I ever want to see one again either... but... apparently he owes me and now I have this... token? I think I can cash it in for a favour."

Again, he didn't sound sure.

When his gaze locked with hers, she shrugged.

"Don't look at me. I've never read anything on the unseelie. I don't think Archangel knew what they had." She pictured the male. Nothing about him had stood out. He had looked like just another fae—resembling a human. "If they had known, they wouldn't have been holding him in a regular cell."

And for some reason, her stomach squirmed as she said that and the knot in it became one made of snakes that writhed and made her feel sick.

She cast her gaze down at her boots and drew in an unsteady breath, trying to calm her mind again and ignore the guilt that wracked her as she thought about Fenix in the cells, about all the ones she had put there. Looking back, she couldn't find a good reason for detaining most of them. At least seventy percent of them had been like Fenix—reacting to the presence of Archangel. Was that a good enough reason to capture and contain them? To experiment on them? Torture them?

If she were an immortal, as Fenix insisted, and was in a fae town or a club or anywhere and Archangel showed up, how would she react? Deep in her heart, she knew she would feel threatened by the presence of hunters, would go on the defensive and jump to the conclusion that they were there to capture and harm her. How many of the immortals Archangel captured were only reacting to their presence like that, feeling threatened and as if they were in danger?

With good reason.

Archangel had been treading a darker path recently, one she had witnessed with her own eyes. She looked at Fenix. One he had witnessed too. He had been there in Hell. He had followed her to the forward operating base Archangel had set up there and that meant he had seen the things she had.

"Your feelings shifted course. What are you thinking?" Fenix's deep voice curled around her, soothing her, and she didn't fight it this time—she savoured it and the effect he had on her.

"Nothing." She glanced at him and the look he gave her called her a liar.

"If you're questioning your life choices—"

"I'm not." She was.

She was questioning them in a big way.

Archer had saved her from non-humans according to what he had told her and had convinced her to join the fight at Archangel, but now everything looked different, as if a cold light was shining upon it. She couldn't trust that Archer had been telling her the truth. According to Fenix, she was cursed. They both were. If she fell for him, she died and was reborn, and her memories were taken from her.

She forgot everything.

Which was exactly how she had been when Archer had found her and had told her he had saved her from non-humans who had stolen her memories.

The thought that he had lied to her hurt, cut her soul-deep and had her staring off into the distance again, swimming in the pain that filled her. The thought that he had done it to manipulate her into working for Archangel with him, that he'd had a plan for her that Fenix had stopped him from putting into action, made her want to just give up.

And at the same time made her burn with the fire of a thousand suns.

"Evelyn," Fenix murmured, his tone gentle, soothing. It reached out to her, wrapped her in a cocoon that had her rage falling away again. "You're hurting."

She nodded, because there was little point in denying it, not when he could apparently sense her emotions. An incubus trait? Or because they were bound? She was beginning to think it was the latter. She was beginning to believe him.

"Archangel are dangerous, Evelyn. You know it in your heart. You can't go back there."

She didn't want to go back. She didn't want to stay here either.

Another lie.

She looked at Fenix again, an ache forming in her breast, one she could name. She didn't want to leave him. Her mind didn't remember him, but her body did.

Or was it her soul?

Some part of her knew him, a deep and powerful part of her that urged her to trust him, to believe the things he told her and have faith in him.

She had trusted Archer and look where that had gotten her. So she wouldn't be trusting Fenix. She wouldn't trust anyone. Whatever was happening to her, she could only rely on herself to get her through it.

Fenix twisted the gold band on his left hand around his index finger, drawing her gaze to it as his expression shifted.

"Pretty soon, Rosalind and Vail, and Hartt, are going to come back, and they're going to want to know a few things. Archangel are up to something involving a sorceress called Aryanna and from what I saw in Hell... What Archangel are doing with the fae and mapping the portals... I need to know what's going on, Evelyn. I need answers." His handsome face was sober as he stared at her, no trace of gold or blue in his irises. His eyes were hard and flat, his lips an unyielding line as he waited for her to speak.

To betray Archangel.

The part of her that refused to trust him whispered that he was playing her again. Manipulating her just as Archer had been.

She shook her head.

She had no intention of returning to Archangel, but she also wouldn't betray them. She might have ended up there because Archer had manipulated her into joining them, but they had been good to her. They had given her a home. A purpose. She could turn her back on them, but she couldn't set them up for a potential fall, and her gut said Fenix was asking her to do just that.

"I need you to help me get into Archangel." Fenix took a step towards her, his tone as hard as his expression.

Demanding.

He wasn't asking her to help him—he was ordering her.

That got her back up and she glared at him again, the calm he had made her feel gone in an instant as she tried to see in his eyes what he was planning. Whatever it was, it involved using her. He was no better than Archer.

She shook her head again. "No. I won't help you."

"You have to help us. You can get me inside. I need to know what they're up to, Evelyn. I saw those crates in Hell and I know Archangel have been mapping that realm. They want to close the portals. That's the only reason I can think of for them needing to know where they all are." He took another hard step towards her, his face darkening as gold and cerulean danced in his eyes. "They have a sorceress capable of cursing entire species and they're learning all the portal locations. It doesn't take a genius to see they're planning something and it's something big... something that will affect us all. This is our world too. It doesn't only belong to the humans."

She stood her ground, even as part of her wavered, was swayed by his words. Her mind filled with the crates she had seen and the reports she had read, and the feeling that had been growing inside her over the last few months.

She struggled to put that feeling into words, fought to find her voice as Fenix stared her down.

He took her silence as a refusal.

Disappeared and reappeared right in her face, so close to her that his chest brushed hers as he breathed hard and glared down into her eyes, his gold and blue fire that captivated her.

"These are your people too!" he barked and she flinched. "If Archangel curses everyone and makes it so we'll die if we remain in this world, then you'll die too!"

Evelyn opened her mouth, unsure whether she was going to deny she was an immortal or admit that she felt Archangel were doing something bad too, something that would affect everyone.

Even her.

She didn't get a chance to see which one left her lips.

A shiver chased down her spine, a flare of heat that struck her to her soul, and she whirled on the spot to face the other direction.

And froze as her eyes collided with the golden ones of a beautiful redhead and a feeling hit her.

Home.

CHAPTER 24

Evelyn reeled as the sensation of being home swept through her, as heat chased in its wake and she stared at the redhead who had stepped away from the elf to move a step towards her, a lost look on her face that Evelyn felt sure was mirrored on hers.

She couldn't stop herself from moving a step towards the newcomer too, was powerless to resist the urge to be closer to her. An incredible sense of connection bloomed inside her, as if she shared a bond with this woman, and it was startling.

Unsettling.

Right.

The woman stared at her, her rosy lips parting as her scarlet eyebrows rose high on her forehead.

She murmured, "Phoenix. You're a phoenix."

Tears lined the woman's lashes.

Lined Evelyn's too as a sense of sorrow and pain engulfed her, swirling among the warmth and the feeling of being home, as if she bore a terrible grief she hadn't known about until this moment.

Fire flickered in the woman's golden eyes.

"Mackenzie, this is Evelyn." The elf stepped up behind the woman, his black clothing a contrast to her burgundy leather corset and trousers, and gently clasped her upper arms. His violet eyes were tender as he angled his head and gazed down at her face, and Mackenzie continued to stare at her. "Evelyn doesn't know she's like you."

Like you.

Evelyn swallowed hard.

Couldn't deny the need to close the distance between her and Mackenzie.

She was a slave to her instincts as they overruled the part of her that screamed at her not to trust them, that this was all another lie to trick her into doing what they wanted.

Mackenzie lifted her hands and held them out to her.

Evelyn ached to place hers into them.

Fenix stepped up beside her, his green gaze as soft as the elf's had been as he looked at her and she glanced at him. "Your phoenix is showing."

What did that mean?

She must have looked confused, because he took hold of her shoulders, spun her to face the mansion, and guided her towards the bay window. She gasped as she caught her reflection in the glass.

Her eyes were glowing gold just like Mackenzie's were.

Panic prickled down her spine and she shirked Fenix's grip with a shrug of her shoulders and shook her head as her brow furrowed. "This is a trick, a way to make me stay with you."

She cast a look at him, her eyes darting back to him again as he moved away from her, giving her the space she needed as she fought for air, as she was torn between looking at him and at her reflection. It had to be a spell. Magic. Some kind of deceit. They were playing her.

Fenix's handsome face softened and his voice lowered to a tender whisper, "You know in your heart that it isn't."

Evelyn looked at the window again.

At herself.

He was right. She did know that the reflection of her was real. She could feel the fire that shone in her eyes burning inside her, an inferno she had felt so many times over the last few weeks and had seen every night in her dreams.

Now, as she stared into her flickering golden eyes, she could no longer deny that she wasn't normal.

She was different.

A phoenix shifter?

Evelyn wanted off this rollercoaster, wasn't sure she could take much more.

Fenix inched closer to her and his presence was a comfort, the scent of him soothing and calming her, grounding her. "I met you decades ago... in a little tavern in Hell. You were causing a heck of a ruckus. Drew me to you straight away. Gods, you were beautiful... are beautiful."

He sighed, drawing her gaze to him.

Her brow furrowed again as she looked deep into his eyes and silently begged him to keep talking, to make the panic and the fear fall away, to make the ground beneath her feel solid and real again.

His lips quirked at the corners into a smile that was somewhere between apologetic or sad and relieved, and then his expression sobered again.

"Your name is Aderyn. When we met, you were beating the crap out of some wankers who had told you a fib about the location of a mage and phoenix shifters." He looked as if he wanted to lift his hand and touch her face, but instead backed off another step, placing more space between them. Space she didn't like. Instantly, an urge to close that distance swept through her, had her rocking towards him, and he noticed it. He cast a sorrowful glance at the gap between them and then looked into her eyes, his revealing pain.

He wanted to be close to her.

But he couldn't.

And it hurt him.

That feeling he was speaking the truth grew stronger in her heart, had sorrow washing through her too, because she knew why he couldn't let himself be near her—he feared she would fall for him and that she would die.

He drew down a deep breath and exhaled it on a shaky sigh as he scrubbed a hand over his short tawny hair, flashing the markings that tracked up the underside of his forearms. Markings that shone in hues of black, purple, blue and a dash of burnished gold.

"What are you feeling?" She shifted her gaze from his arm to his face and silently demanded an answer to that question this time.

He dropped his hand to his side and for a moment she thought he wouldn't answer, but then with a sober look at her, he said, "Sorrow... fear. I don't know how dangerous it is to tell you things about yourself. I want to leave, but I can't." He lowered his gaze to his boots and then lifted it to meet hers again. "I can't leave you. It's the curse."

Was that all it was?

One look into his eyes was enough to tell her that it wasn't the curse that made him want to stay near her even when he knew it was dangerous and might end with her death. He wanted to stay near her because he felt something for her, something deep and powerful, a love that had lasted despite the curse that apparently kept them apart.

Her gaze dropped to his left hand and the gold band that encircled his finger. A band that was worn and old.

"Did... Aderyn give you that?" She wasn't ready to say *I*, wasn't there yet by a long shot.

Fenix lowered his gaze to his hand and twisted the gold band around his finger with his thumb, his gaze growing distant and his expression turning lost. He subtly nodded, drew down another breath that tightened his black shirt across his chest, revealing muscles that stirred heat in her veins, and then lifted his gaze to her.

"You wanted one too, but gold can't survive a phoenix rebirth. So I said I would wear it for both of us... to show everyone we were bound." He toyed with the ring again, keeping his gaze on it as Evelyn let that sink in.

They hadn't just been lovers then.

The other incubus had been telling the truth.

They had been mates.

Were mates.

She looked across her shoulder at Mackenzie. The instant her eyes settled on the woman that feeling of home bloomed inside her again. Was Mackenzie mated to the elf? The two were clearly more than lovers. The way the male looked at the redhead was the same way Fenix looked at her, with a softness that could only be love.

"I'm not saying I'm buying this crazy shit, but..." Evelyn shifted her focus back to Fenix. "How did we come to be cursed?"

Maybe if she knew that, it might trigger a memory or something that would make her believe everything he was saying.

And she was beginning to want to believe him.

"A long time ago, blood mages forced a lot of phoenix shifters through a gateway linking your world to this one. They closed that gateway behind your ancestors, trapping them in Hell, and then proceeded to round them up." Fenix cast an uncomfortable look at Mackenzie and then Evelyn. "They use your blood in their spells. It makes them immortal. Your blood is powerful. The mages still capture phoenixes for their spells."

A low burn began in her blood, gradually heating it as she listened to him and thought about what the mages were doing. She curled her fingers into fists and frowned as her nails bit into her palms, opened her hands and stared at them. Her nails were longer than before. Sharp too.

Panic swept down her spine like a thousand needles pricking her skin.

Fenix took a step towards her, his tone gentle. "You're okay, sweetheart. It's normal."

"It isn't normal!" she barked and cast a glance at him, frowned and backed away as she shook her head. "It isn't normal for me. None of this is."

She was freaking out again and she hated that she had a bigger audience this time. She could feel the elf and the phoenix staring at her and she wanted to lash out at them and scream at them to leave her alone. Her temperature soared and she gripped the front of her T-shirt and furiously fanned herself.

"You need to calm down." Mackenzie's tone was hard as steel as she closed the distance between them. "You can't go nuclear here. You'll destroy this place and kill everyone. You have to calm your mind and the phoenix within you will calm too."

Evelyn stared at her hands, her eyes widening as the air around them shimmered like a heat haze and she could see all the veins beneath her skin. They were glowing. Her throat closed, her chest tightening, and she tossed a look at Fenix as panic morphed into fear. She didn't want to hurt anyone.

She didn't want to hurt him.

"It's okay, love. Just look at me. Listen to me. You just have to breathe. Don't be afraid. You're in control." He held his hands out to her and she shook her head, refusing to take them as he clearly wanted.

She would burn him if she did.

"Something is wrong with me." Her brow furrowed and she clutched the front of her T-shirt, gasped when smoke rose from the point where she gripped the black material and quickly released it. "Ever since I came back from the Fifth Realm... something has been wrong with me."

Fenix's handsome face darkened as his eyes brightened dangerously. "That fucking warlock. He interfered with your rebirth. Son of a bitch!"

"The gang's all here." Rosalind came to an abrupt halt and looked from Fenix to Evelyn. "And we're somehow not all happy. What's this about a warlock? You talking about that Crow?"

Fenix positively growled. "She did die. I wasn't wrong. She died and he brought her back."

"Wait." Evelyn's eyes widened. "So I'm like a zombie?"

"No one said the Z word." Rosalind bustled over to her and patted her on the shoulder in a way Evelyn supposed was meant to be comforting but came off as awkward. The witch slid a look at the others. "Did we?"

Fenix rolled his eyes. "She's not a zombie. Stop trying to make her think she's a zombie. I swear, you're nothing but trouble."

Vail growled and flashed fangs at him and Fenix held his hands up beside his head. Rosalind sashayed over to the elf and wrapped both of her arms around his left one. She fluttered her lashes at him and he growled for a different reason as he dipped his head and captured her lips.

"I told you to stop winding your mate up," Fenix snarled and paced away from Evelyn and her gaze tracked him as he ran his hands over his hair, frustration rolling off him in powerful waves that buffeted her. He muttered, "Gods, I'm starving."

His gaze slid to her, swirling cerulean and gold, and then he huffed and pivoted on his heel and paced away from her. He took something from his pocket, lifted his hand to his mouth and then swallowed.

Heat spread down her spine to suffuse every inch of her and this time it wasn't panic or fear making her temperature soar.

It was that look he had given her.

That wicked, heated look that made her toes curl and had an ache blooming inside her, a fierce need to have him cross the span of flagstones to her, sweep her into his arms and kiss her.

Which couldn't be good.

He had said he couldn't charm her, which meant this attraction she felt was real.

And intense.

"Those pills aren't going to help. You need to find a nice woman to snog," Rosalind said.

Everything was a blur as those words registered.

Suddenly Evelyn had the witch's throat in her hand and was squeezing it hard as she glared down at the blonde, the fire that blazed through her blood so intense that she couldn't breathe, couldn't think, could only feel one emotion.

Rage.

The elf seized her shoulder and she turned on him, reacting in an instant, her other hand snapping around his wrist to rip his hand from her. The scent of burning flesh filled her nostrils as that rage blazed hotter still, had her burning up.

"Evelyn," Fenix barked.

She came back to the world with a harsh bump, her eyes flying wide as she realised what she was doing. She released the elf and the witch and stumbled backwards, shaking her head as her brow furrowed.

"I—I didn't—" Evelyn threw a look at Fenix as guilt swamped her, colliding with the shock that had her reeling.

"It's okay." He kept saying that and the more he said it, the more she felt it wasn't okay.

"Something is wrong with me." She strode away from everyone, unable to trust herself around them as the world pitched beneath her feet again and she felt sure that at any moment she was going to lose her balance.

She was going to break down.

Evelyn cast a glance over her shoulder at Fenix, some part of her needing to hear him tell her again that there wasn't something wrong with her, that she was fine.

That she would be okay.

But it was the witch who spoke as she finished healing the wrist of her mate.

"I deserved that... but I guess now we know the mate instincts are alive and kicking inside her."

It wasn't a comfort.

Some unknown part of her recognised Fenix as her mate and had reacted violently when the witch had suggested he found another woman to kiss. That couldn't be good. Just the thought of him with someone else had her skirting the edge of lashing out again, filled her with a fire that blazed so hot she feared she wouldn't be able to control it and might go nuclear, just as Mackenzie had said.

"I need some air." She started to walk away from everyone.

Fenix appeared in front of her and she stiffened as she came to a dead stop, sure he was going to order her to remain where she was, was going to lay down the law and forbid her from leaving his side. Only his hard expression softened as she looked at him, waiting for that to happen.

On a long, weary sigh, he stepped aside and cast her a hopeful look, one laced with worry. "Promise you won't stray too far?"

She nodded.

And ended up standing there staring into his eyes.

In fact, she stood there for so long that he rubbed the back of his neck and canted his head slightly as he murmured, "Not going for a walk?"

She shook her head. "Apparently not. I don't know what I want anymore."

That was a lie. She was deeply aware of what she wanted.

It was standing right in front of her.

"Fenix," she whispered and he tensed. Because she had spoken his name? She sighed and tried to let the tension melt from her body, but it was hard with so much spinning around her head. "Will you finish telling me why we were cursed?"

His look softened again, that spark of hope she kept seeing in his eyes shining more brightly now. Because she had revealed she was beginning to believe him.

He heaved another sigh. "I was helping you locate mages. You wanted to open the gateway to the phoenix realm again and believed mages had the knowledge of how to make that happen. It was important to you. You'd lost all your family a long time ago and thought you were the last of your kind in Hell."

He looked beyond her towards the others and then his gaze slid to meet hers again.

"It's the reason I called myself Fenix. I gave myself that name because I didn't want you to feel alone in this world. I wanted you to feel there were others like you... and there are, Evelyn. Hundreds of them. In the years we've been cursed, I've freed dozens of phoenixes. The only one I haven't managed to free is you."

That look in his eyes touched her soul and warmed her heart. It told her how much he wanted to break this curse and she knew it wasn't because it affected him too. He wanted to save her and stop her from suffering.

He wanted to stop her from dying.

"You were close to finding a way to open the path between the phoenix realm and Hell. We found the mate of a mage and you befriended her. He knew how to open it. We were both sure of that. She... You discovered she wanted to lure you into a trap to capture you so she could give you to her husband, and there was a fight. You killed the female and he came after us. I was injured so we withdrew." He twisted the band around his finger, his gaze solemn but laced with darkness, with a hint of accusation. "You didn't want to wait."

Even though she didn't remember any of it, a feeling stirred in her gut and she pressed her hand to it, trying to calm the turbulent sea of acid that scoured her insides.

"What happened?" She searched his eyes for the answer to that question.

"I passed out when you were healing me and when I came around you were gone." Fenix ran a hand over his hair, mussing it, and let it fall to his nape. He rubbed the back of his neck. "I knew where you had gone. I got there too late. The mage had already won. He was taking your blood. He blamed us both for destroying the quiet life he had wanted to lead with his wife. Apparently, he'd planned to live as long as he would have naturally with her and then die, and he didn't believe me when I told him his wife had planned to gift him with your blood to make them both immortal. He was angry."

Evelyn could understand why. The whole thing sounded like a series of betrayals to her. The wife had betrayed the mage by planning to make him live forever, despite what he wanted. The wife had betrayed her by pretending to be her friend and help her. She had betrayed Fenix by going against his wishes and heading out to fight the mage alone.

"He cursed us to make us suffer for what we had done by taking his love from him. His words that day are seared on my soul and I can't forget them." Fenix looked at the ring on his finger and then into her eyes, his tone empty as he recited, "I condemn you both. Her to die and forget you if she ever recalls her love for you. You to forever chase her ghost, desperate to make her love you again."

His gaze grew bleak as he looked at her, his brow furrowing slightly, and she swore she could feel the pain that beat inside him, could feel how he had suffered since that moment, afraid of her falling for him but desperate to be with him as he had been before the curse, and driven to find her whenever she inevitably died and was reborn.

She wasn't sure what to say as sorrow swept through her, as his pain became hers, and she tried to remember something. Anything. Everything before the moment she had met Archer was blank though, like a void in her mind. No matter how hard she pushed, how desperately she tried to remember the Fenix she had known back then, she couldn't.

But while her memories of what had come before were gone, her mind scrubbed clean, some part of her did remember him.

She knew him.

Was it like the witch had said and her instincts as his mate still existed within her? Was this feeling her soul recognising his and the bond they shared?

"I know this is a lot for you to take in… that you need time… but Archer isn't going to wait. Archangel have Aryanna and it's only a matter of time before they find a way to use her or that warlock gets his hands on her. If he does, I'm not sure what will happen. None of us are." Fenix glanced past her again as the witch spoke.

"Whatever he plans to do with the sorceress, you can bet your balls it won't be good. That Crow wants her for a reason."

Rosalind kept calling Archer that term, one Evelyn had never heard before, and whenever she said it, she spat it like it was a curse. Was a Crow different to a regular magic user? More powerful?

More dangerous?

Evelyn couldn't scrub that image of Archer when he had been hit by the spell from her mind. It was seared there, kept replaying itself, and every time it did, she noticed something a little more.

That look he had given her.

Pained. Regretful. Wounded.

She wanted to believe he was sorry for the things he had done and that the thing he had wanted to say to her before Fenix had appeared had been an apology. She wanted to believe he wasn't evil like Fenix and the others made him out to be.

That however he had felt when they had met, it had changed over the years.

Bloomed into a real friendship.

"Aryanna has to be in the London HQ. It must be the reason he's there." Fenix shifted his focus back to Evelyn, his eyebrows knitting to narrow his eyes as she snapped herself out of thoughts of Archer.

That look he gave her said he wanted to ask what she had been thinking about and she braced herself for it, steeled her heart and shored up her defences because if he knew she had been thinking of Archer as a friend, he would be angry with her, but she couldn't help it.

Archer had been her friend.

He had saved her life.

More than once.

And he had brought her back from death.

She couldn't just cast aside the years of friendship they had shared and she wouldn't believe they had been a lie, not until she heard it from Archer himself.

Fenix huffed and she swore she could feel him shaking off his urge to demand to know what she was thinking.

"You have to help us." His gaze implored her to do just that. "We need to get to her first. It's the only way to stop both Archer and Archangel."

Evelyn held his gaze, unsure of what to do and who to trust now. She was sure of something though. She looked over her shoulder at Mackenzie, that familiar warmth filling her the moment their eyes met, together with something else. Anger. The reason she hadn't been able to let the fact Archangel was documenting so many portals go was that it angered her. She knew in her gut what Archangel were doing. Fenix was right about it. Archangel had Aryanna, a sorceress who could cast powerful curses, and they were seeking the locations of every portal in this world.

They meant to close them and then cast a curse upon the immortals.

And that made her want to rage, to burn the hunter organisation to the ground.

They were no better than the blood mages.

Hunting and trapping entire species. Using them against their will. Killing them.

She looked into Fenix's eyes as resolve flowed through her, as the need to fight rose within her, and this time she embraced it.

"What do you need me to do?"

CHAPTER 25

"No, you're not listening to me. You need to concentrate." Mackenzie's tone had an edge as sharp as a blade as the fiery redhead threw her hands up in the air and pivoted away from Evelyn to stalk a short distance across the lawn of Fenix's mansion.

"I am concentrating!" Evelyn snapped back at her.

She wasn't.

She had been finding it hard to focus since Fenix had spoken to Rosalind and Vail about something and had teleported away. Her mind was running amuck, hurling images of Fenix with another woman at her, their bare sweat-slicked bodies straining in unison. It was hard to shake that vision of him as it poisoned her mind and set her body aflame with rage that burned so hot she wished she could do what Mackenzie was trying to teach her.

Teleport.

If she could, she would teleport to the nearest fae town and bang on every damned door in the place until she found Fenix.

Her heart laboured, blood running hard in her veins as she struggled to tamp down the anger and convince herself that she didn't care what he did. He might be handsome, and some stupid part of her might want him, but he wasn't hers.

A rumbling sound echoed around her and she twisted and turned, seeking the source of that noise.

Mackenzie blinked at her. "Did you just growl?"

Evelyn's eyes widened as they leaped to meet Mackenzie's golden ones, her eyebrows shooting high on her forehead as her body locked up tight. "No."

She didn't think she had anyway.

But for a heartbeat, a split-second there, she had been so furious with herself and with Fenix that she had wanted to growl.

"She growled," Hartt put in.

Evelyn shot him a glare, her lips flattening and compressing hard as she resisted the urge to tell him to go to hell. She had done that once already and he had mocked her with a smile and casually mentioned he lived there, so going to Hell was hardly a punishment to him.

He rolled his wide shoulders, shifting his black tunic jacket with the action. "I just say it as I hear it. You growled. Sounded like you wanted to rip something apart with your talons. I would say you were close to screeching."

"Screeching?" A shiver traipsed down her spine and her gaze leaped to Mackenzie.

The pretty redhead shrugged. "I only screech when I'm *really* angry about something."

The thought of being able to screech like a raptor unsettled Evelyn so she pretended she hadn't heard that it was something phoenixes like her could do.

Like her?

Her shoulders slumped as it hit her that she was beyond starting to believe that she was a phoenix shifter. She was already there.

"What made you want to screech?" Mackenzie took a slow step towards her, a cautious edge to her expression as she studied her closely.

Evelyn clammed up, because she wasn't the sort to pour her heart out and share her feelings and fears with people she barely knew. The only person she had ever confided in was Archer.

Something inside her popped and deflated at the thought of him. Had he wanted to explain himself before Rosalind had hit him with that spell? Had he really been her friend? Part of her wanted to find him and ask, and the rest was bone-deep afraid of confronting him, fearing what he might say.

She wasn't sure she could handle him turning on her with a cold, mocking laugh and announcing that she had been nothing but a pawn to him.

It would be the cherry on a very crap cake someone was currently forcing her to swallow.

"Fenix is my guess." Hartt sighed in a way that said he knew exactly how she was feeling when it came to the incubus and he pitied her, so she glared at him again, daring him to continue. He clearly didn't see the threat in her eyes, or maybe he didn't care, because he said, "Her mate has run off somewhere while he's hungry. Idiot. There are probably a thousand scenarios spinning through her mind and you expect her to concentrate? I am not sure I could concentrate if you had gone off somewhere while you were aroused."

He glanced at his mate.

"That isn't helping," Evelyn bit out and paced away from him and Mackenzie, needing some space as the fire in her veins blazed hotter, stoked to an inferno by one word.

Aroused.

Fenix had been fired up and he had left her, had gone off somewhere alone.

The pressure building inside her became too much, made her feel that if she didn't unleash it all somehow that she might explode. She gritted her teeth, desperately trying to calm her mind and convince herself that she didn't care what Fenix was doing.

She didn't care who was satisfying his urges for him.

Dealing with his needs.

A shimmering red veil descended over her vision and before she knew what she was doing, she had thrown her head back and screamed.

Only it wasn't a scream that left her lips.

It was a high-pitched shriek that carried around the mountains.

A raptor's cry.

"What the bloody hell is happening here? What did you do to her?" Fenix's bass voice rolled over her, but it did nothing to calm her this time.

She turned on him, her eyes narrowing as she dragged in a great gulp of air and caught his scent.

Smelled a feminine trace of something like lilies.

On a keening cry, she launched at him, seized his throat and kicked off, hurling them both across the fifty-foot span of grass between where he had been and the grey granite wall of his house. He grunted as his back slammed into it, as she drove him against the ageing stones, and stared him in the eye. Her lungs felt too tight as she struggled for air, her chest heaving as her heart thundered, and heat rolled through her, an inferno so hot it felt as if it would burn her to ashes.

"Evelyn," he murmured.

She pulled him towards her and shoved him back again, fury rising inside her as he tried to calm her, to placate her. It wasn't going to happen.

"What's wrong?" His eyes leaped between hers, his brow furrowing as concern filled them. "Did they do something to upset you?"

His face fell.

"Did I?"

On a vicious growl, she slammed him into the wall once more for good measure, released him and pivoted on her heel. Panic joined the rage lighting up her veins as her mind caught up with everything and she realised what she had done, how she was acting.

"Evelyn." Fenix grabbed her right wrist.

She twisted towards him, her left fist coming up at the same time, and somehow managed to stop herself from hitting him. His stunned expression slowly faded as his green eyes danced between hers, the look in them making her feel as if he was trying to peel back the layers to understand why she was so upset.

Good luck with that.

She wasn't sure herself.

She wasn't sure of anything anymore.

Something surfaced in his eyes, making the flecks of gold and sapphire swirl among the emerald, and dread pooled in her stomach, a need to get away from him before he could wound her with the words she could feel coming flooding her.

"Evelyn—"

She didn't hear the rest of what he wanted to tell her.

All of a sudden she was standing in the middle of the lawn, closer to the perimeter stone wall.

Her eyes widened as she turned in a slow circle, shock rolling through her as she saw how far she was from the house.

"I can teleport," she muttered, hoping that if she said it aloud, she would believe it. She twisted this way and that, trying to make it sink in. Her gaze locked on Mackenzie. "I can teleport!"

She was still reeling when Fenix appeared in front of her, a big smile on his face, as if he was proud of her.

Evelyn punched him on the jaw.

Her eyes flew wide as he went down, surprise and guilt rushing through her as he landed on his backside.

"Oh my God. I'm sorry. I just..." She dropped to her knees beside him and checked him over as he rubbed his jaw. She wasn't sure what to say when he gave her a stunned and confused look. Her shoulders sagged and she shifted so she was sitting on her backside on the grass. She picked at the blades, her focus on them as she lined up the words. She owed him an explanation, even though she wasn't sure what she was going to say would explain anything. "You smell like... perfume."

And it had a white-hot inferno coursing through her veins.

An urge to strike him and make him hurt running through her.

His eyes widened as he pushed himself up, and she hated how he sat there staring at her, saying nothing, all but confirming her suspicions that he had been with another woman.

"I guess your memories really are gone then," he muttered, a trace of softness in his tone as he lowered his gaze to the grass she was furiously picking at. "If you remembered me, you'd know I would never do that to you. I feel terrible if I have to kiss another woman to—"

She punched him again.

"Oh God!" She winced and reached for him, drew her hand back when he scowled at her. "I'm sorry. I can't... I don't seem to be able to stop myself. It's like an instinct."

He rubbed the red spot on his jaw, still frowning at her. "It's fine."

It wasn't. None of this was fine.

She breathed deeply, fighting to calm herself and clear the red haze from her mind. As the urge to lash out at him fell away and she thought about what he had been saying before she had punched him, something dawned on her.

He was telling the truth.

She had seen in the CCTV footage she had watched that he resisted other women. He had fought so hard against what Archangel had wanted him to do, and had only kissed a few of them. She figured he had only done it to keep his energy up, because he had looked disgusted and ashamed whenever he had broken away from the woman's lips. As if he was angry with himself.

Fenix shifted, drawing her focus back to him, and he pulled his hand from his pocket. He uncurled his fingers, revealing a small box.

"What is it?" She took it from him when he offered it to her, eased it open and stared at the pills it contained. She glanced up into Fenix's eyes. "What are they?"

"A witch... Hella... makes them for me. They take the edge off my hunger. It means I can go longer between needing to find a hit of sexual energy. It's not a great solution, but it's the best one I have."

Evelyn studied the pills and remembered something else. Fenix had taken them in front of her soon after he had brought her here. He had taken quite a few of them in fact. How many pills did he have to take each day in order to stop himself from having to find a host? She nudged one of the pills, moving it around in the box as she considered how desperately he didn't want to feed on a woman other than his mate, how he was denying his instincts as an incubus—his very nature—to remain faithful to her.

A feeling built inside her.

It was really rather noble of him.

Beautiful even.

His expression sobered as she lifted her head and her gaze locked with his, all of the light leaving his eyes.

"You can't fall for me, Evelyn. Remember that."

"I'm not," she snapped, the need to defend herself swiftly rising to the fore to tear those words from her as she closed the doors to her heart, protecting it from the hurt that wanted to well inside her. She snapped the pillbox closed and tossed it at him as she shoved to her feet. Held his gaze. Steeled her heart. "I'm not."

She walked away from him.

Breath trembling.

Heart racing.

Limbs shaking.

Because she was.

She was foolishly falling for him.

And some part of her felt it wasn't the first time this feeling had blossomed inside her.

She cast a glance back at Fenix as he picked himself up off the ground, warmth spreading through her to clash with the cold that trickled down her spine.

She felt sure she had already fallen for him once.

And she had died because of it.

And Archer had brought her back.

CHAPTER 26

It turned out that Fenix had returned smelling like a woman because he had gone to visit the owners of a nightclub in London, one where Evelyn had been several times in her years with Archangel—Underworld. He hadn't gone there to find a host. He had gone there to talk with a tiger shifter called Talon and his mate, a woman Evelyn had met in the past. Sherry had offered him some clothes she had used when she had broken into Archangel with a huntress.

Apparently, the rumours about Emelia had been true.

She had run off with an angel of all things.

An angel.

Evelyn was still having a difficult time processing that one.

Sherry had thought Fenix might need a change of clothes for Evelyn and had kindly offered them, and he had taken them, inadvertently rubbing her scent all over him.

Triggering a response in Evelyn that continued to shake her if she paused for a second to think about it. Thankfully, she was too busy trying to look inconspicuous to have a moment to breathe, let alone think.

Fenix strode beside her along the corridor in the lower ground floor of Archangel headquarters, as bold as brass with his head tipped up and his shoulders squared. She still wasn't sure about this. His plan was solid and he believed the information the tiger shifter had given him was good, but Evelyn still felt on edge as she walked with him, acting as if they were just a pair of hunters heading towards the pens.

The first part of his plan had worked without a hitch.

Evelyn had entered the building alone, had gone to the department responsible for outfitting the hunters and had made up some lie about needing to get a new set of clothes for Archer. She had been nervous as hell as she had stood there waiting, sure that the woman behind the counter was going to phone for confirmation or call her on her lie. Only the brunette had merely looked up Archer's sizes, gone into the backroom and returned with a plastic-wrapped black Henley and combat trousers and a fresh pair of boots.

Evelyn had signed for them, grabbed her haul and resisted the urge to run with it. It had been difficult to vanquish that compelling need to flee the scene when her mind had locked onto Archer and the fact the woman had found his information on the system.

Meaning he was still working for Archangel.

The thought of running into him had set her on edge and she had hurried to the nearest supply closet, shut herself inside and pictured the roof. Surprisingly, it had worked and she had teleported there, landing in the middle of it close to where she had enjoyed sitting once, with Archer.

Fenix had found her standing there, staring at the spot where they had sat so many times, talking about the view and the weather and mundane things.

Like friends did.

"You okay?" Fenix murmured, dragging her back to him, and she knew she had to look as bleak as she felt when she glanced at him and his gaze softened.

She wanted to talk to him about Archer, but held her tongue because he would grow snappish with her if she so much as mentioned his name. He had made it clear several times during their meeting with the others to plan tonight's mission that he didn't like anyone bringing up the warlock. Why? She saw a flash of how violently he had reacted when he had seen her with Archer, how he had accused her of sleeping with him, and it hit her that she wasn't the only one who hated the thought of the other being with someone else.

Evelyn shrugged it off and returned her gaze to the corridor in front of her, following the route that the tiger had given them, one that was leading them dangerously close to the cellblocks.

She tensed when she spotted how busy the path ahead of them was and her gaze strayed to Fenix again. The black Henley covered him from neck to wrist, concealing his fae markings, and he looked like every other male hunter in his fatigues and boots, but it only took a look into his eyes to see he wasn't like the men who were coming and going along the corridor.

He might be able to hide his markings, but he couldn't hide the spots of blue and gold that coloured his irises.

A passing hunter looked at him and Fenix smiled, flashing straight white teeth, and winked. The man's cheeks flushed and he averted his gaze, dipped his head and hurried away from them.

She had learned something new about incubi tonight.

It wasn't only women who were susceptible to their power to charm and manipulate feelings.

Fenix had been disarming women *and* men left, right and centre, throwing them all off his scent if they looked his way. One of the men had even paused to hit on him, and Fenix had slung his arm around Evelyn's shoulder and asked if he wanted a threesome. That had sent the man running and Fenix had assured her that it was his loss. It had struck her then that she was the reason the man had left. He hadn't wanted to be with a woman too.

Two female hunters rounded a corner, their gazes instantly straying to Fenix. A blush bloomed on their cheeks, their eyes growing dark with hunger, hooded as the distance between them narrowed.

Fire burned up Evelyn's blood when she glanced at Fenix and found him smiling at them, the gold and blue in his eyes swirling faster now. Charming them.

When the women were level with them, she scowled at both of them and then grabbed Fenix's arm and shoved him down a corridor to his right, away from the hunters.

"You know, you'll undo my hard work if you keep looking like you want to murder the females," Fenix grumbled and the terrible urge to punch him again ran through her.

Because it sounded like he was enjoying charming the females.

"Oh, what a shame. You'll have to make do with my company." She rolled her eyes. "This way."

Fenix caught her arm, spun her to face him and pinned her back against the pale wall, his eyebrows knitting hard as he looked down at her. Whatever he had wanted to say to her, it faded away in time with that look as his expression softened, and she glanced down as he lightly stroked his thumb up and down her arm.

He sighed.

"We don't have time for a lecture," she muttered and wrenched her arm free. "And stop looking at me like that. You don't want me falling for you? Keep hitting on those women."

"I am not hitting on them." He huffed and strode after her, easily catching up with her as she scanned the corridor, looking for the service lift.

It had to be here somewhere.

"I'm just trying to throw them off my scent," Fenix said and then mumbled, "Maybe steal a little juice for the tank too."

"So you are hitting on them?" She spied the dull grey panel of the lift ahead of her at a branch in the corridor and hurried for it, her pulse picking up pace as her nerves kicked into high gear.

"The pills only take the edge off. I've been using up a lot of energy recently, teleporting everywhere," he hissed as he followed her, and she felt those words like a dagger in her back.

Because she had tried teleporting them to London and had failed dismally. He had been forced to do it for her, bringing them to the park near Archangel HQ, and had looked tired afterwards. When she had asked him what was wrong, he had snapped that teleporting with a powerful phoenix shifter was taxing, and had reached for another pill.

She had felt so guilty that she had fought harder than ever to teleport when he had told her to take them to the roof, a short hop that he had declared would be easy for her since she could see the building now.

He had been right, and it had been easier. Teleporting the vast distance between Fort William and London had sounded impossible. Teleporting a few hundred metres to the top of a building she could see had looked like something she could probably do.

Apparently, belief was ninety-nine percent of successfully using a power like teleporting.

She was still working on it. She failed to teleport more times than she succeeded.

The second part of Fenix's plan had been for her to steal the access card from Archer's apartment, something which had made her so nervous that she hadn't been able to teleport inside and had stood there staring at the door like an idiot, aware of all the people who passed her in the corridor and glanced her way. Fenix had been the lookout, telling her whenever the corridor was clear and she could go. She had locked up every time.

In the end, Fenix had made her play lookout while he had gotten inside via the more traditional method of breaking and entering. Waiting outside in the corridor with everyone looking at her as they passed had only made her more nervous, and she had been a wreck by the time Fenix had reappeared and waggled the card at her.

"Besides... the top-up is just a perk of making them turn a blind eye to me." His voice dropped to a whisper as he closed the distance between them. "If you had teleported us here instead, I wouldn't have to be charming everyone who looked my way."

Evelyn turned on him and hissed, "I can barely teleport and I don't know this area well. You can't honestly expect me to suddenly pick this up and land where I mean to be, or take someone with me. I landed fifty feet from where I meant to appear on the roof."

His eyebrows rose. "I didn't know that. You need to work on your focus."

She clenched her jaw and her fists, bit her tongue and refused to say what was on the tip of it. This was new to her. He might not view it that way because in his eyes she was the same woman he had known for decades, but as far as she was concerned, she had so far only managed a handful of teleports and was still honing her skills. Rather than getting into an argument with him, something he looked as if he wanted, probably to keep her guarding her heart against him, she turned her back on him and pressed the button to call the lift.

Evelyn shifted foot to foot as she waited, her nerves off the scale as she expected everyone who passed them in the corridor to ask her what she was doing. This was madness. They were going to get caught and thrown in the cells.

Or worse.

The lift door opened and she hurried inside. She waited for Fenix to join her and the doors to slide shut again before she waved the card over the reader.

Nothing happened.

She swallowed her racing heart and tried again, but the light on the small black device remained red.

"Shit," she muttered and Fenix inched closer to her and looked at what she was doing as she swiped the card again and again, willing it to work.

"Something wrong?" He frowned at her and then at the card.

"Archer doesn't have the clearance we need. Whatever is in this secret basement you told me about, it requires a rank higher than commander to access it… or only a few are allowed down there." She tightened her grip on the card and her eyes widened as the plastic began to bend.

She was quick to loosen her hold on it. Apparently, she was stronger than she had thought.

The sound of metal hitting metal drew her gaze to Fenix. He settled back on his heels and turned to her, stooped and formed a cradle with his hands in front of his knees.

"Up you go," he said and she glanced at the hole in the ceiling where he had pushed the access panel open.

"Can't you just teleport us to the bottom of the shaft?" She wasn't a fan of dark, cramped spaces, or of getting squashed by a lift when someone else called it.

He shook his head. "I can only teleport where I can see. You could probably manage it."

Crawling into a dark, dangerous place it was then. She wasn't going to risk her life, and his, by attempting to teleport somewhere she had never seen. She had read enough research papers on species that could teleport to know that it was possible to teleport into a solid space and suffocate before escaping.

No, thank you.

She placed her right foot onto Fenix's hand, gripped his shoulders and drew down a steadying breath as he lifted her, quickly sending her towards the hole that was already looking too small. It was panic talking. The square hole was plenty big enough for someone twice her size.

It didn't stop her arms from trembling so much that she found it hard to pull herself up as she gripped the edges of the hole. Maybe she wasn't as strong as she had thought. Or the idea of getting on top of a lift frightened her more than she had realised. She hung there, breathing through a wave of panic as images of a black space filled her mind together with a long drop to the bottom of the elevator shaft.

She gasped as Fenix planted his hands against her backside and shoved, heat rolling through her to have her cheeks burning and heart racing for another reason as his fingers dug into her bottom.

And he lingered.

"Are you going to help me here or what?" he snapped.

It hit her that he wasn't lingering, taking advantage and enjoying holding her backside—he was waiting for her to pull herself onto the top of the lift. Only she had frozen the second his warm hands had pressed into her flesh, stirring wicked needs in her that were startling in their intensity.

She shook off those needs and grabbed the first two things that looked solid enough to bear her weight, and hauled herself up, tilting forwards onto her belly at the same time.

Fenix grunted as her boot hit him in the face.

She pushed up off her stomach and scrambled to face the hole, peered into it and whispered, "Sorry."

He rubbed a spot on his chin and scowled at her.

Evelyn offered her hand, feeling like she was extending an olive branch to him as he huffed and reluctantly took it. She expected to struggle to lift his weight, but it was impossibly easy to pull him up towards the hole. Incredible. She scratched her previous thought. She was strong. It just disappeared whenever she let fear get the better of her.

She sat back to give him room as he grabbed the sides of the hole and hauled himself up, her eyebrows pinned high on her forehead as she marvelled at how strong she was.

"How come I'm suddenly like Supergirl? Surely I should have noticed how strong I was before?" She kept her voice low, not wanting to rouse suspicion.

Fenix quietly closed the access panel and everything went dark.

For a few seconds.

Her eyes adjusted, revealing him again.

Another perk? She could see in the dark. At least enough to make out details. It made the thought of being in an elevator shaft far less terrifying.

"Not sure," Fenix grunted as he stood and gripped the mass of thick metal cables attached to the centre of the lift car. "Might be that Archer was feeding you something laced with a potion to suppress your abilities. Might be a spell he needed to periodically renew."

Either way, Fenix thought Archer had something to do with it and he didn't sound happy about it, had that growl to his voice again, the one that made her feel he wanted to kill Archer.

Evelyn still wasn't sure how she felt about him. Archer had done terrible things, but he had been good to her too. He had brought her back from death, and in the last few minutes she had seen him, he had looked as if he genuinely regretted how things had turned out.

"You're awfully quiet. Thinking about your lover?" Fenix snarled those words.

She ignored him, because in her heart she knew he was only saying it to rile her and make her hate him a little, which was pointless. She was starting to feel more and more certain that she had already fallen for him, and her death in the Fifth Realm had been thanks to the curse.

Which meant she was responsible for the death of her teammates. She had fallen for Fenix and fate had set her on the path to being captured just so it could kill her as the curse dictated. She had gotten everyone killed with her. Not quite everyone. Archer had survived, and he had saved her. But still, there was so much blood on her hands. Many in her team had been her friends. Not as close to her as Archer, but she had cared about them. She rubbed her stomach through her T-shirt as she felt queasy and her heart felt heavy.

"Hey now, love," Fenix murmured and brushed his hand down her arm, the light caress soothing her. "What's with the shift in mood?"

The soft look he gave her made her feel he was worried he had caused it.

She wasn't sure whether she liked or hated the fact he could feel it whenever her mood changed course. In a way, it made her feel as if she wasn't alone, and it always revealed that for all his bark and bite, Fenix cared deeply about her.

Loved her.

She stared at him, warmed by his soft look, by the way he continued to stroke her arm, attempting to soothe her. She didn't bother stopping him or pointing out he was breaking his own rules. She savoured his caress, clung to the warmth he made her feel, and the feelings he stirred in her.

There was no point in her trying to hate Fenix or guarding her heart against him. It wouldn't change anything.

She had already fallen for him.

She had died.

Only she hadn't been reborn.

And that gave her hope.

Maybe the curse would never bother her again. If she died and was reborn, she might remember Fenix. She might not be whisked away from him and her memories stolen from her. She clung to that, because the thought of dying was frightening enough, but the thought of not remembering anything terrified her. Coming around and not knowing who she was, where she was, had been incredibly hard on her and had taken her a long time, and years of counselling, to get over.

She didn't want to go through that again.

She didn't want to forget.

"Come on. Down we go." Fenix's hand slipped from her arm and he moved towards the wall, causing the lift to sway beneath her.

Her stomach swayed with it.

"Can you move a little more… I don't know… gently?" she hissed and clung to the roof of the lift, had to breathe deeply to stop herself from vomiting all over it.

"No." He made it to the wall and she wanted to call him on the fact he was back to being an arsehole again.

Trying to make her hate him.

She lined up the words to tell him her theory, sure he would laugh his backside off, but the lift began to rise upwards.

"Fuck." Fenix lunged for her and hauled her to him, leaped the small gap to a ladder she feared wouldn't hold both of their weights, and pinned her against it.

He forced her to grip the rung in front of her, curling her hands around it, and covered them with his as his front pressed to her back. She squeezed her eyes shut and told herself that she was going to be fine, that he was going to be fine, as mechanical whirrs and clunks filled the heavy silence. Fenix pressed closer to her, shielding her with his body as the carriage moved past them.

"You okay, sweetheart?" he murmured into her ear, back to being gentle and tender again, and she swore she could feel the concern in him.

Maybe this connection they shared worked both ways and in time she would be able to use it as he did, detecting shifts in his mood.

Her breath leaked from her as she sank into the ladder, the tension draining from her as the lift rumbled into the distance and it hit her that they hadn't been killed by it.

"No," she whispered and wrapped her arms around the ladder, clinging to it even though Fenix had a tight hold on her and she knew he wouldn't let her fall. "I can't move. Please don't make me move."

His left hand dropped to her waist, sending an electric thrill over her skin, and he eased his arm around her stomach.

"You never did have a head for heights. Not going to make you climb down, love." His breath tickled her neck as his cheek brushed her nape. "I can teleport us from here."

Darkness whirled around her before she could say anything to stop him from using up more of his strength and she almost crumpled as her boots hit solid ground. Fenix's grip on her kept her upright and she was thankful as he held her, as she looked at him and found a soft edge to his eyes, no trace of judgement in them. She had always hated looking weak, and she had never felt as weak as she did right that moment. Her legs were noodles beneath her, barely able to hold her weight.

When Fenix looked up the height of the shaft, she glanced there too, peered into the darkness and tried to make out where the lift was. The thought that it might come down again had her legs steadying beneath her and a desire to get moving rolling through her.

Fenix seemed to sense it because he loosened his grip on her and eased back. "You good?"

She nodded and he released her, went to the lift doors and prised them open with his bare hands. He jerked his chin towards them as he held them open and she hurried through, pulling herself up onto the floor that was at waist height to her. She turned and pressed her hands to the doors, holding them for Fenix. He glanced at her and she nodded to let him know that she had them, and he crawled through.

Evelyn eased them towards each other, until they were a few inches apart, and then released them.

Fenix had already moved, was standing with his back to her, facing a gloomy corridor. The dark grey-blue walls were lit at intervals, but the few lights weren't enough to brighten the place. She pushed to her feet and moved to stand beside Fenix, her pulse racing again as she considered what he had told her.

The tiger had mentioned there was a door near to what he had called *the cage*, one that the shifter suspected they were hiding something behind. Fenix believed it was as good a place as any to look for a secret holding cell. They had to be holding the sorceress in this facility, one few in Archangel knew about. She agreed with him on that.

She couldn't believe it was actually here. An entire area she had never known about. An area she doubted Archer knew about, or most of the people who worked in the building. It was quiet, as if only a few people were down here. A selected few who had probably been sworn to secrecy.

When Fenix had asked the tiger how he would recognise the door, Talon had told him it was the only one with three security locks and two guards stationed outside it at all times.

Which, Evelyn had to admit, did sound terribly suspicious.

Fenix motioned for her to follow. She fell into step beside him, on high alert as she listened hard, straining to hear anything. The area opened up into an enormous room at the end of the corridor, with six doors coming off it, and she baulked as the disgusting scent of dried urine, vomit and blood hit her.

She covered her mouth with her hand and Fenix glanced at her, a trace of worry in his green eyes.

"I'm fine," she mumbled into her palm and waved him away. "You're up."

He looked in the direction she was and she knew when he had spotted the guard standing outside of one of the doors, because he made a beeline for the male. She kept her distance as Fenix charmed him, disarming him, and looked away when he snapped the man's neck, caught his body and dragged him towards one of the doors. He opened it and peered inside, must have been satisfied that it wasn't somewhere someone might check because he returned for the body and pulled it inside. He eased the door closed and casually walked back to her, as if he hadn't just committed murder.

Fenix jerked his chin, silently motioning for her to keep moving.

Ahead of her, light streamed from the left side of the room. She peered down that corridor as she passed it, glimpsing a row of empty white cells. The place where Talon and his friends had been held? The tiger had told Fenix that the cage was to the left of the cellblock. She looked towards the doors in that direction and seized Fenix's wrist when she spotted it.

A door with two guards.

Fenix's eyes narrowed and he disappeared, reappearing behind one of the men. He snapped his neck too, but let the body fall this time, his attention immediately leaping to the second male. She hurried towards him as he charmed that one, using his powers to manipulate the man's feelings.

"I forgot the codes for the door. Be a darling and open it for me?" Fenix stroked his fingers down the man's neck and the guard's dark eyes grew hazy, losing focus as his eyelids drooped.

Evelyn turned her back and kept watch as the man did exactly as Fenix wanted, punching a code into one of the locks.

"I don't have the other one."

She looked back over her shoulder at the guard and frowned at Fenix as it hit her. "Two guards. Two codes. You killed one of them before you got his code. Now what are we supposed to do?"

"I can't charm two people," he bit out and glared at her. "Don't act like you knew both would have a different code either."

She wasn't. Much.

He snapped the guard's neck before she could stop him and she scowled at him.

"You're up." He grabbed her arm and yanked her to him, seized her wrist and pressed it to the cold steel door. "Just think about wanting to be on the other side. Think of teleporting a few feet. That's all you have to do."

He made it sound easy.

It wasn't.

She stared at the door, afraid that there might be a wall on the other side of it and the few feet she teleported might put them both inside it.

"Come on, sweetheart. You can do this," he murmured close to her ear.

She wished she had his confidence.

She glanced around, seeking another way in. It wasn't going to happen. Fenix had killed the only guards they had seen, and the door didn't have a peephole or anything he could use to see the other side.

So it was down to her.

She grabbed Fenix's arm and sucked down a breath, held it and blew it out as she built up her courage and focused on making a tiny hop that would transport her to just the other side of the door. That was where she wanted to be. Just three feet north of where she was now.

There wouldn't be a wall there. Nothing that would hurt her or Fenix. She just had to make a tiny hop. Easy-peasy.

"Come on," Fenix whispered.

She scowled at him. "Stop rushing me!"

She settled her gaze back on the door and focused again, breathing through the spike in her panic, letting it all fall away. Just a few feet. A little leap. That was all she had to do.

As she exhaled, emptying her lungs, the world around her went black.

And then she was standing an inch from a crumbling dark stone pillar.

Her heart shot into her throat.

"Oh God." She reeled backwards into Fenix, and he caught her, his arm snaking around her waist. "I messed up. Maybe I teleported us to Hell?"

Because the column resembled one she had seen in the castle in the Fifth Realm.

Fenix rumbled, "You can't teleport to Hell without a portal. Not the right breed for popping in and out of that realm. No... this isn't Hell."

He released her and eased away from her, and she trailed after him.

Her eyes widened as she saw what was on the other side of the column and she looked at Fenix.

"What is this place?"

CHAPTER 27

"What is this place?" Evelyn breathed as her gaze seared him.

Fenix wasn't sure of the answer to that question as he tried to take everything in.

"A church?" It was the best he could come up with as his gaze drifted over the towering thick stone columns that supported a vaulted ceiling and were linked by arches. Several of them had fallen down, the heavy stones strewn across the flagstone floor, replaced by modern constructions of steel beams.

Only there weren't any stained-glass windows or windows of any sort in the plain stone walls that had been patched in places with concrete to stop them from falling down too.

"A crypt." It felt like the better word for the enormous room they were in, one that stretched a good two hundred feet in all directions.

"Why would they be keeping the sorceress here?" Evelyn's voice echoed around him, but he didn't bother telling her to keep her voice down.

As far as his senses could tell, they were the only two here.

"Not sure." He moved forwards. Slowly. His gaze scanned everything, charting every shadow as his senses stretched around him, and he noticed something. "The lights."

He nodded towards the floodlamps someone had set up, ones that followed the line of the columns, as if they were illuminating a path.

"I don't like this," Evelyn murmured but she followed him anyway, sticking close to his side as her gaze leaped around. Her nerves trickled into him through their bond, filling him with a need to comfort her.

It was hard to deny that need, but he had to stop giving in to his desires. He had done that far too many times already on this mission, comforting and calming her whenever the need had become too great to deny.

"I think there's something over there," she hissed and he tracked the path of her gaze.

More lights. A cluster of them all pointed towards something.

Silver and black ducting snaked across the uneven floor, heading towards that point. Power for the lights? The flexible silver pipe looked as if it might carry air and he could hear mechanical whirring ahead of them, and the closer he came to the circle of lights, the fresher the air in the crypt became.

But he still couldn't sense anyone other than him and Evelyn.

"How long do you think this place has been here?" Evelyn whispered.

Fenix didn't take his eyes off the area ahead of them. "Millennia maybe. This place is old."

"How do you know?" She looked around them. "It looks like it could be any old cathedral."

He shook his head now. "Think about how deep we are. This place might have been closer to the surface when it was built. Makes me think of some of the places in Rome or Greece. I'm getting serious old-world vibes from it."

And he didn't like it.

"Why did they build it?" Evelyn moved a step closer to him as the air chilled.

"To worship something." That was his best guess. "Why else would you build a place that looks so much like a temple?"

"Worship what? God?"

A wall to his right that formed a line that cut across several of the columns ended, revealing that the room expanded further in that direction than he had first thought, and he moved between a set of columns into what had to be the centre of the room.

And locked up tight.

"That," he muttered and Evelyn was swift to join him, her eyes widening again as she saw what he had. "They were worshipping that."

He drifted forwards, towards the huge sphere that stood ahead of him on a raised dais in the centre of the room. The modern lights positioned around it reflected off the smooth glass surface, and Archangel had constructed a round base beneath it, making it look like the world's biggest snow globe.

Only it wasn't a winter scene or a tourist attraction inside the ball.

It was a woman.

She floated in a foetal position with her side to him, her toes pointed towards the ground and her body curled over. Long lilac hair streamed behind her, drifting slightly while her bare body was perfectly still, and as Fenix moved, the liquid around her shimmered and glittered.

"Do you think it's her?" Evelyn whispered, sounding as awed as he felt, and he wanted to look at her as she drifted away from him but couldn't tear his eyes away from the woman.

"Maybe." He wasn't sure though.

"What kind of cell is this?" She moved further from him, wrenching his gaze from the female as the need to tell her to remain close to him blasted through him.

It turned to relief when he saw she was only a few feet away, within lunging distance if anything happened. She pored over a trolley that had equipment on it, tools he had never seen before, and inspected a machine that was beeping. He tracked the leads that emerged from the back of it to the point where they had been affixed to the glass ball.

"Some kind of cryogenics?" he offered and shrugged when she looked at him. "Your guess is as good as mine. What's all the machinery for if not to monitor her vitals and keep her on ice?"

"Makes sense, but…" Evelyn glanced at the woman, a frown knitting her fair eyebrows. "It doesn't feel quite right."

He silently admitted that it didn't. If Archangel wanted to use her, why keep her on ice?

The great silver canisters that clustered together to the left of the ball, beyond the beeping machine, and were attached to the base of the snow globe by silver ducting made him feel this was a cryogenic chamber of some kind though.

Evelyn moved to one of the computers on another trolley and began scrolling through documents that flashed up on the screen.

Fenix looked at the globe and frowned as something caught his eye. He drifted towards it, his eyes narrowing on the plaque mounted on the base.

"Subject Zero," he murmured and glanced at Evelyn. "Try looking that up."

She nodded.

He stared at the inscription again and figured out the roman numerals.

"Seventeen-twenty-eight." He looked at the woman in the sphere. "The year you were found?"

It certainly didn't feel like the date this place was built. It looked as if it had been here for long centuries before Archangel had discovered it and stabilised the building to preserve it.

He moved around her, watching the liquid shimmering with flecks of turquoise, violet and crimson as the angle of the light changed, and then frowned, backtracked a few steps to confirm his suspicions and peered closer.

"It's two spheres."

"What?" Evelyn said, lifting her gaze from the screen. When he pointed to the glass ball, she came to him and looked at it, angling her head and causing her fall of golden hair to drop away from the shoulder of her black T-shirt. "You're right. There's another sphere inside the glass one."

"Not cryogenics then." He peered closer at the woman, easily seeing the other sphere now he knew it was there. The surface of it rippled at times, reflecting him and the light as he moved around it, heading to the right, away from all the machinery.

He lowered his gaze to the bottom of the sphere as he crouched and frowned. It was floating. The sphere containing the woman was floating a good twelve inches away from the bottom of the glass ball. Archangel must have constructed the glass around her, sealing her inside it, and they were using the gas to do something. He wasn't sure what.

Evelyn remained where she was. "Do you think it's Aryanna?"

He nodded, rose to his feet and stared at the sorceress, a weight settling in his chest as he gazed at her. She was beautiful, and seemed... sad... as she floated in the liquid, holding her knees to her chest.

He couldn't stop looking at her as Evelyn went back to the computer.

"Um... someone digitised records dating back to the year you gave me. Subject Zero was the first non-human Archangel discovered and the reason they founded the organisation. They did it to study her... Named it after her." She glanced at the woman and then at him, something in her eyes. "They thought she was an angel. Something about her having wings."

Fenix couldn't see any wings.

He moved around her to her back at the same time as Evelyn, meeting her there, and couldn't believe his eyes.

There were silvery scars on the woman's back that did resemble wings. Only they didn't look like they belonged to an angel.

Evelyn hurried away from him to the computer. "Ah... there's several mentions of the wings over the next two centuries of reports. They're growing apparently... transforming from what they had believed to be angel wings into something more demonic."

"They look like dragon wings to me." Fenix had to put it out there, because that feeling that this was Aryanna had grown more concrete the moment he had seen the scars that stretched from her shoulders to her hips. "The mate of a dragon."

He held his hand out towards the sphere.

The air vibrated, sending a tremor through him that had his blood humming in his veins.

He snatched his hand back.

"Don't do that again," Evelyn snapped.

He glanced at her and wanted to apologise when he saw how pale she was and felt the fear in her.

He shook his head instead. "Believe me, I don't want it to happen again either."

He moved back a step, distancing himself, but while the air stilled, awareness continued to vibrate within him. He could feel her power lacing the air, swore she was agitated as the liquid around her shifted, and a bad feeling settled in his gut.

One that said that if she ever woke, all the realms would be in danger.

"Archangel want to use her, but they have her in this cell." He looked across his shoulder at Evelyn.

She lifted her head, the light from the screen washing over her face, and looked from him to the sphere.

"I don't think it's a cell. Not like you're thinking. They're not holding her captive right now. As far as I can tell… the feeling I had back in Hell when I saw that cave… it's right." She pushed away from the trolley and came to him, gazing up at the woman. "Archangel are looking for a way to break her out of the sphere surrounding her. They're looking for a way to wake her. I think the glass is there to keep her protected and hidden until they can achieve that."

Which made sense in a way.

"I can't sense her. I can sense you, but not her. If she's alive, I should be able to feel her, but I can't." He wanted to press his hand to the glass as he mulled that over, but resisted the temptation. "Maybe the glass sphere is also there so Archangel can safely study her. It's not just protecting her. It's protecting their researchers from her."

Evelyn went to the computer and scrolled through another document. "I think you're right. There's a few records of deaths in the early days of studying her. It sounds like people were drawn to her and when they touched the liquid surrounding her, they… well, let's just say they died."

Despite him keeping his distance, the humming in the air was growing stronger, and what had been calm rippling liquid around her now shifted restlessly. He glanced at Evelyn.

"Is there anything in the database about the sphere reacting to its environment or people?" He had the feeling the sphere was reacting, but that it was reacting to the feelings of the one inside it.

Was Aryanna aware of them?

He stared at her, at her closed eyes and serene expression. There was no trace of the agitation he felt sure she was feeling. She looked as calm and still as she had when he had first seen her.

Evelyn's fingers danced across the keyboard and he waited as tense minutes ticked past.

She glanced up at him. "Nothing. Not even when the scientists were drawn to her and killed. Do you think she's reacting to us? Because we're immortals like her?"

He would have smiled at the fact she had called herself an immortal if the ground hadn't shaken beneath his boots at that very moment. The air vibrated again, so fiercely this time that it made his bones ache and Evelyn gasped and covered her ears.

"What's wrong with her?" she barked.

Fenix really hoped she wasn't waking up. "I don't know! We know she's here now. We can bring backup to this place... so maybe we should just get out of here."

Because the instinct to protect his mate was going haywire, had him on the verge of teleporting to her and gathering her into his arms to shield her from whatever was happening.

A male voice echoed through the room.

"Oh, you're not going anywhere."

CHAPTER 28

Evelyn locked up tight as Archer's bass voice rolled over her, every muscle in her body clamping down onto her aching bones. She twisted away from the computer and Fenix, her breath lodging in her throat as her eyes landed on Archer.

He strode towards them down the middle of the rows of columns in the centre of the cavernous room, the loose tails of the long form-fitting black coat he wore swirling around the ankles of his black knee-high boots with each hard step.

His brown eyes settled on her, the darkness etched on his face lifting for a heartbeat, but then his gaze shifted to the sphere beyond her.

And his eyes went all-black.

His lips peeled back off his teeth as he snarled, "Shut up! I'm here, aren't I?"

The vibrations in the air grew stronger in response.

Archer's face crumpled, twisting hard, and he jerkily brought his right hand up and shoved his stiff fingers into his dark hair as he muttered in a strained voice, "Shut up."

Evelyn sensed Fenix edging closer to her.

Archer's gaze darted to him, his eyes brown again, and a cruel smile twisted his lips as he shifted his focus back to the woman in the sphere.

He positively growled at her.

"I'll get you out," he barked and took swift strides towards her, ones that had Fenix seizing hold of Evelyn and pulling her to one side, away from him. Archer didn't seem to notice they were there as he stopped before the sphere, his expression blackening and voice echoing around the room. "You're not helping though! You need to tell me the spell I need to get you out. How am I supposed to get you out without it? Hmm?"

Fenix took a few more sidesteps away from him and pulled Evelyn with him when she didn't move. The need to reach out to Archer and calm him, to soothe him somehow was strong, had her wanting to remain close to him, even when part of her felt it was dangerous.

That he was a threat to her.

The ground trembled beneath her boots and she swallowed hard as the sense of power in the air grew thicker, pressing down on her, and every instinct she possessed said it wasn't coming from the woman in the sphere now.

It was coming from Archer.

His gaze snapped to Evelyn.

She tensed.

"Siding with the enemy now?" he drawled and slowly turned to face her, scowled over his shoulder at the sphere, and then faced Evelyn again. "How ungrateful of you. Reviving you and bringing you back wasn't easy. I can still taste your death... Can't shake the things that followed me back from the shadowy place between life and rebirth... It tastes like ashes."

Fenix's hands tensed against Evelyn's arms and she sensed the shift in his emotions, the shock that swept through him.

He whispered, "You did die."

She looked back at him, and the way he slowly frowned at her told her that he had seen in her eyes that she was already aware of what had happened to her and that this wasn't a surprise to her.

"You could show a little gratitude," Archer growled and then glared at the sphere. "Shut up! I wasn't talking to you." His gaze slid back to Evelyn, his voice loud in the cavernous room, echoing around it with each hard word he flung at her. "Do you have any idea how draining and dangerous it is to use the concoction I drank to cross into that dark place and bring you back?"

Before she could answer him and tell him that she was sorry, that she hadn't asked him to do that for her but that she appreciated the pain he had put himself through for her sake, and that she wanted to help him now, he levelled a black look on Fenix.

"And you," he snarled, flashing his teeth as he sneered at the incubus. "You could thank me too. That little curse on her didn't trigger because of me."

She gasped as it hit her that she had been right. She had fallen for Fenix and that was why she had been killed in the Fifth Realm. Only Archer had moved heaven and hell to bring her back, stopping her from being reborn.

He turned on the woman in the sphere again and barked, "Some good you are too. You couldn't even tell me where you were! *Years.* Years I've spent with you in my damned head and I want you out of it. Do you understand? I want you to leave me the fuck alone, so just tell me how the hell to get you out of this prison of your own damned construction!"

With every harsh word he tossed at the sphere, the ground beneath her shook a little harder, the air growing a little thicker and harder to breathe, and the vibrations grew stronger, until she felt as if they were going to rattle something loose inside her.

Or kill her.

"Archer," she whispered, as calmly as she could manage, trying to lure him back from whatever dark place he was heading as she struggled to make sense of what was happening.

His gaze whipped to her and his shoulders instantly sagged, his breath leaving him on a long and weary sigh. He pushed his glasses up his nose and his fingers tensed as his jaw flexed and he glared at the sphere again.

"Is she talking to you?" she murmured softly.

He slid her another black look. "Always. Telling me to help her. Wanting me to find her. Plaguing me... Yes, plaguing. It's what you do. Constantly pushing into my fucking head!"

He hurled those last words at the sphere with so much contempt that she felt as if she was looking at an entirely different person. She couldn't imagine what he had been through, what it would be like to have someone sharing your head all hours of the day, pestering you to do something but not helping you do it.

"Archer... there's something wrong with you. We were friends... are friends... let me help you." She held a hand out to him and tried to ignore the way it was shaking as his gaze slowly slid back to her and darkness bled from his irises into the white of his eyes.

Behind her Fenix muttered, "Friends?"

He huffed and she wanted to glare at him, because she knew it sounded strange to him, and part of her felt she should view Archer as the enemy, but she couldn't just throw away all the years they had worked together and how close they had been. They had been friends. The best of friends, she had thought.

But he had been using her.

She was deeply aware that he'd had a plan for her, a reason for helping her and doing everything he had done, but she still foolishly clung to the thought that he had changed and that he had wanted to confess everything to her the night Rosalind had hit him with the spell and revealed what he was.

"You're sick, Archer." She stretched her hand towards him and willed him to show her that she wasn't wrong about him.

He regretted the things he had done. He thought of her as a friend too. She needed him to show her both of those things. She needed him to show her that the only reason he had kept things secret from her, had manipulated her, was because he thought she could help him with his problem but had feared telling her about it.

She had embraced life as a hunter after all.

There was a chance that if he had revealed what he was to her, that she might have thrown him in the cells.

Not only that, but he hadn't known where to find the sorceress. Maybe he had been holding on until the day he knew where Aryanna was before turning to Evelyn for help. She wasn't sure how she could help him, but she wanted to do it. She wanted to free him of the sorceress.

"I don't know what's happening to you, but I want to help you." She didn't like how the swirling black that had been seeping back into his irises gained ground against the white again as she said that or how the air seemed to chill around her as the flagstones trembled beneath her boots.

"You can't help him," Fenix hissed, voicing the feeling growing deep inside her.

Her brow furrowed as she stared at Archer. She couldn't just give up on him. He needed help. The sorceress was somehow communicating with him, which made a lot of things over the years make sense at last. All the times Archer had looked crazed, as if he was about to go off the rails, or had abruptly excused himself and forced her to leave him alone. He had been struggling against this witch as she tormented him.

"We can help you, Archer." Her heart went out to him when the darkness in his eyes disappeared and he cast her a pained look, the same wounded one he had given her before he had teleported away from her in the park. "Just tell me what's wrong. Talk to me. Let me help you. I want to help you."

His eyes suddenly narrowed on her, darkness washing across his features as they twisted into a vicious smile and his eyes went all-black. "You can help me."

She swallowed hard as he advanced on her, his fingers flexing at his sides, his expression pure malevolence that had her instincts screaming at her to teleport before it was too late.

"I'm sorry, Evelyn. If it could be any other way…" He lifted his hands and tiny globes of black and crimson light chased around them.

He hurled his hands forwards and the orbs shot towards her.

No, not towards her.

She realised that too late to move.

Could only watch as the spell shot past her.

And hit Fenix.

CHAPTER 29

Rage burned through Evelyn's blood, sending her temperature soaring, but before she could unleash it on Archer, Fenix grabbed her and pulled her into the darkness of a teleport. She turned on him as they landed on the moonlit grass of the mansion, the urge to lash out at him verbally falling away in an instant as he sank to his knees and curled over, breathing hard.

"Fenix." She dropped to her knees beside him and pressed her left hand to his shoulder as she leaned forwards, trying to see his face.

"You're back. Did the mission go well?" Rosalind's bright voice swept around her, but the light in it faded as she came to a halt a short distance away. "It didn't go well."

The witch hurried to Fenix and eased to her knees on the other side of him to Evelyn, her blue eyes bright with silver stars that swirled as she looked from him to Evelyn, silently demanding an explanation.

"We found her... but Archer found us. Something is wrong with him. I tried reaching out to him, but he grew... agitated doesn't seem like a strong enough word. He cast a spell. I thought it was for me, but—" Evelyn looked back at Fenix as he struggled for air and his shoulder trembled beneath her palm, and then looked at Rosalind as rage became fear. "The spell hit him."

Rosalind moved around in front of Fenix, nudging her aside. "Let me take a look."

Evelyn tried to convince herself to release Fenix, but her hand wouldn't move from his back. The need to be close to him had her remaining where she was, her focus locked on him. Rosalind gently cupped his face and lifted his head, and stared deep into his eyes.

"Hmm. Doesn't look too bad. Let's take a closer look." The witch closed her eyes and her shoulders relaxed as her spine straightened.

Tense seconds ticked past and Evelyn kept her eyes fixed on Fenix, even as Vail approached them. He stopped at a distance and Evelyn swore she could sense the conflict in him. Because Rosalind was using magic? It hadn't taken Evelyn long to figure out that Vail didn't like being around magic.

Rosalind finally opened her eyes, shifting them to Evelyn. "A draining spell."

That didn't sound so bad.

"Can you undo it… or reverse it… or whatever it is you do?" She cast Rosalind a hopeful look.

"Maybe. You say Archer aimed this at him?" Rosalind frowned at Fenix and continued before Evelyn could answer. "Odd that the Crow hit you with such a weak and silly spell."

Fenix's eyes swirled gold and cerulean and his jaw tensed as he gripped his knees, his fingers digging into them through his jeans. Sweat dotted his brow and his arms shook as they flexed.

Rosalind shrugged. "Or maybe not."

Evelyn didn't like the sound of that.

"What do you mean by that?" she snapped, fear getting the better of her, driving her to grab the blonde witch and shake the answer out of her even when she knew it would be a mistake.

Worry emerged in Rosalind's blue eyes. "A double-edged sword. The Crow knew what he was doing. If Fenix had remained, the spell would have drained him enough that he couldn't fight to protect you. You would have been open to whatever assault Archer wanted to launch on you, or plan he had for you. Did he give any indication why he attacked?"

She shook her head. "No, not really. He apologised and said something about… if it could be any other way. I had the feeling—"

"He wants to kill you," Fenix gritted and grunted as he pushed himself up, causing his skin to pale further, until he looked as white as a ghost. "Phoenix fire. Aryanna… in a sphere. Magic."

Evelyn stroked his shoulder, worry lancing her heart, cleaving a great hole in it as her brow furrowed and she willed him to be all right. "I'll tell her. Conserve your strength."

She looked at Rosalind again.

"The sorceress we found. She was in a glass ball of Archangel's construction, but within it was another sphere. It rippled, reflected light, and the surface grew unstable at times…" She paused as something hit her. "When Archer was coming. The air hummed and the sphere trembled, as if the witch inside it was restless or excited maybe?"

"Aryanna knew he was close." Fenix wheezed in a breath.

She cast him another worried look. "He said he's been searching for her for years. Called the sphere she was in a prison of her own construction. If she cursed the dragons... those scars on her back looked like dragon wings. You were right about that."

"Might be the dragon magic she stole with the curse she cast. Sometimes curses backfire. Sometimes even a sorceress can take on too much and can't handle it. She would have been the conduit for the magic she was taking from them." Rosalind rubbed her lower lip with her thumb and looked over her shoulder at Vail. "What do you think?"

Evelyn looked at him. He wasn't alone now. Hartt and Mackenzie had joined him, both of them looking at Fenix with the same worried expression she was sure she wore.

"It is possible. Drawing something from someone requires a connection to them. The magic must have passed through her and rather than leaving her as intended, it remained." Vail came to Rosalind, concern in his violet eyes as he looked down at her. "The sorceress cursed herself by cursing the dragons. I do not want you going near her. If she escapes the prison the dragon magic caused, she will be dangerous. Too strong for you, Little Wild Rose."

Rosalind looked as if she wanted to protest, but then her delicate features softened. "I understand... but if we all need to fight... I will have to be there."

His eyes darkened, the corners of his lips turning downwards as his black eyebrows met in a hard frown. "Rosalind—"

Evelyn had the feeling he didn't often use her proper name when speaking to her, because the witch tensed and reached for his leg, her fingers curling around it to grip the black material of his jeans.

That action was enough to silence him, to have his handsome face shifting towards an unimpressed or perhaps displeased look, but one that had a reluctant edge to it that said he was going to let this fight go.

He eased into a crouch before her and murmured, "Wherever you go, I go too. I will not let danger befall you though. If I feel the witch has the upper hand or is a threat to you, I am taking you away to safety."

She sighed and leaned into his touch as he cupped her cheek, her eyes slipping shut as she whispered, "Deal."

Fenix clenched his jaw and gritted, "She's in that sphere. Safe for now. Archer—"

"I think he'll be coming for you," Rosalind cut him off and tossed a worried glance at Evelyn. "I think the reason he helped you, why he befriended you, was because you're a phoenix. Phoenix fire is devastating during a rebirth. We proved that in Norway."

The witch looked over her shoulder at Hartt and Mackenzie.

"Norway?" Evelyn bit out, the images she had seen springing to mind. She looked at Mackenzie. "You were reborn in Norway? In a valley… near a fortress of some kind?"

The look dawning on everyone's faces said that had happened and she could only stare at Mackenzie, shock rolling through her as she remembered how the entire area had been scorched, reduced to ashes. Not a small area either. Most of the valley had been affected. "My God. Archer thinks that fire can break the prison she's in. If he does that… everyone… not just the HQ building… The crypt is underground. Would that contain the fire?"

She hated that she was thinking in terms of it happening, as if it was inevitable, but she couldn't stop herself.

If she was reborn in that cathedral-like room, her fire would destroy the foundations beneath Archangel. Even if her fire didn't roll up the lift shaft to the floors above, it would bring the entire building down on top of her and Archer and the sorceress.

"What the hell is he thinking?" she snapped, not waiting for someone to answer her. "Is he that desperate to free Aryanna?"

She looked at Fenix. His blue and gold eyes were sombre as he gazed at her, his eyelids heavy. He looked tired and she didn't like it.

"Take one of your pills. It might help." She rubbed his back, feeling useless. She wanted to help him, and she could, but he wouldn't allow it. She knew that deep in her heart. He would dig his heels in and reject her.

Fenix's arm shook as he shifted his hand and made several attempts to get it into his pocket. When he withdrew it, he grunted and his entire body spasmed and he dropped the pillbox. Evelyn quickly picked it up for him and opened it.

She removed one pill.

He shook his head. She took a second pill from the box and brought them to his lips, helping him. He opened his mouth for her. She popped the pills into it and waited as he swallowed them. The last time he had taken a pill in front of her, the effect had been instantaneous. She held her breath, desperately hoping that it would be the same this time.

Fenix's face crumpled. "Not working."

She looked from him to Rosalind, imploring her to help.

Rosalind took one of the pills, placed it in the centre of her upturned palm and studied it closely. After a minute that felt like an eternity to Evelyn, the witch shifted her gaze to her.

And solemnly shook her head.

"I think it's because they're magic... a spell of sorts. Something about Archer's spell is counteracting them and stopping them from working. I'm sorry." Rosalind placed the pill back in the box.

Fenix loosed a frustrated growl and snatched the box, spilling his pills on the grass. He shook as he desperately picked them up one by one, taking several attempts to pluck each of them from the grass. Evelyn tried to take them from him when he lifted them to his lips and she realised he was going to take all of them. He flashed his teeth at her and angled himself away from her, and hurt arrowed through her.

She was only trying to help.

She frowned at him as he swallowed the pills, refusing to let him push her away.

"You need to undo this spell." She turned on Rosalind. "Now."

"I don't normally take orders, but I've been working on it. There's a little spell just doing its thing inside him." She waggled a finger up and down Fenix.

He grimaced and looked at himself, shock mingled with disgust rolling across his handsome features. "There is?"

"Uh-huh." She nodded. "I've undone most of it, but some of the magic he used to forge the spell is old... ancient. I'm having trouble with it. Mother earth, he's powerful though. This is a top-notch spell. I thought it was silly and low-level before, but it's intricate."

That didn't sound good.

"But you can undo it?" Evelyn gazed at Fenix again, her worry building to new heights as she realised Rosalind had never told her the other reason why Archer had chosen a draining spell.

As his swirling cerulean and gold eyes shifted to her, growing even more hooded, she knew why.

It was continuing to weaken him, stealing his strength.

Making him need to feed.

Archer had done it to force him to face a choice.

She drew down a deep breath and pushed her hurt aside, focusing on Fenix's wellbeing instead—on how he felt. Fear shone in his gold and cerulean eyes. Fear and hunger. He was afraid of what was happening to him.

Because he knew his options were slim.

He needed to feed, and soon, otherwise he would end up losing control of himself. She had read about incubi. Archangel had starved several of his breed to record the effect it had on them. All of them had lost their minds and savagely attacked the first female presented to them, forcing them against their will to surrender to them, brutal in their pursuit of pleasure.

More than one of them had killed their host.

Fenix was scared of turning into a monster who would do that, but he was also afraid of feeding now before it was too late, because he only had two choices—find a female host and betray his mate by sleeping with her or turn to his mate—to Evelyn—for help and risk the curse triggering.

He still believed it could take her from him.

Only she knew something Fenix didn't.

When he drew away from her, a pained edge to his gaze as he cast it down at his knees, the need to reassure him and make him see that everything was going to be all right became too powerful to deny.

"I'm already in love with you," she blurted.

Everyone turned surprised looks on her.

She held Fenix's gaze, shutting them all out as the need to comfort him and steal his pain away coursed through her. When she reached for his hand, he withdrew it slightly, and then relented, shifting it back to within her reach. His eyes searched hers, a trace of disbelief in them that she could understand.

"Archer said it himself. Confirmed my theory for me. I fell for you before I died in the Fifth Realm, and heading into the dark place where Archer went to bring me back... my death... messed with my memories a little and made me forget... but I know now. I know I was already in love with you... I am in love with you." She stroked her fingers over the back of his hand and willed him to believe her, and she lifted her other hand to her chest and pressed her palm to it over her heart. "I'm not just saying this, Fenix. Remember what Archer said—the curse didn't trigger because he brought me back. Meaning... the curse was active and he knew it. Only I don't think he knows it begins when I fall for you. I think he believes that when I die, I'm cursed to forget everything, and that's all... that it's always active inside me. What if it always is?"

She was rambling now, but something else had just dawned on her.

She stared into Fenix's eyes.

"You're always in love with me," she whispered and he nodded, didn't hesitate for even a second, and his eyes warmed with affection, stirring that same warmth in her heart. "What if I'm always in love with you? I just forget I am... but the feeling is always there. The curse is always active."

A bleak look entered his eyes as his dark eyebrows furrowed as he croaked, "But if that's the case... all the times I stayed away..."

They would have meant nothing.

She would have died regardless, because she still loved him. She just wasn't aware of it until she saw him and those feelings surged to the surface again, making her feel as if she was falling for him when she had already fallen.

A long time ago judging by what he had told her.

Her heart went out to him as he stared at her and she felt a sliver of what he was, was sure it was his feelings treading a dark and sombre path, one that felt like hopelessness to her. It struck her that he thought it was over again, or over forever—that he was constantly going to lose her because of the curse and there was nothing he could do about it.

She squeezed his hand and held his gaze. "Archer interfered with the curse. I'm not dead. I might never die because of the curse now. As long as we're careful, we have a chance to break this and free ourselves from it."

She held on to the belief that they could, because the thought of dying and forgetting Fenix was too painful to bear. He needed her.

She needed him just as fiercely.

"Holy crap on a cracker... what if the Crow can break it? If he recognised the curse on you and intervened before it could fully play out... Well, there's a chance he can break it." Rosalind gripped Fenix's left shoulder and he looked at her. "The gods know none of us like him, but if he can break this curse, we have to try to find him."

Fenix looked as if he wanted to reject that proposal and Evelyn wanted to call the witch on the fact she believed no one in their group liked Archer. For all his faults, for all the bad things he had done, and the fact he wanted to use the flames of Evelyn's rebirth to break Aryanna out of her prison, she still couldn't hate him. If she had a sorceress constantly tormenting her, she would probably do terrible things to make it stop too.

In fact, she probably would have lost her mind long ago.

Losing her memories had been hard enough for her to bear. She couldn't imagine what Archer was going through.

Her gaze slid to Fenix again, heat swift to bloom in her veins as she thought about what she was going to propose, rousing a fierce need to bend him to her will and make him surrender to her.

"First things first," she murmured, her voice thick and low, drenched with the desire running rampant through her veins. Her cheeks burned at the sound of it, heat rising to make the whole of her face feel hot as she blushed, awareness of the other people surrounding them making her want to shy away and pretend she wasn't crazy horny for the incubus in front of her. "You need to tell me where your bedroom is."

Mackenzie whistled low. "You go, girl."

Hartt opened his mouth to say something as he scowled at his mate, but she slid him a heated look. Rather than chastising her, the elf snaked his arm around her waist and disappeared, leaving only a faint silvery outline where they had been.

"Oh, I know when I'm no longer needed." Rosalind held her hand out to Vail. "Let's split. We'll reconvene tomorrow. That gives you lovebirds plenty of sack time."

She disappeared too.

Leaving her alone with Fenix.

"I want this, Fenix. I want you. You need to feed, and either you do that with me, or… with…" She couldn't bring herself to mention another woman. Just the thought of him touching someone else turned the flames of desire in her veins into rage.

She swallowed and met his gaze again, the heat of need swift to blaze back into an inferno in her veins as their eyes locked, causing the spark of rage to fall away again.

She shivered as she stared into his swirling irises, as anticipation built inside her to have warmth pooling low in her belly, and waited for him to say something as she watched the war playing out in his eyes.

When he didn't move, Evelyn leaned towards him, placing her hands on his knees and bringing their faces level as she whispered.

"So what's it going to be?"

CHAPTER 30

Fenix answered her by setting her world aflame. His fingers tightly grasped her nape as his lips claimed hers and he mastered her body with only a kiss. Heat bloomed, fire that was swift to consume every part of her, turning her blood molten. She moaned into his mouth as his tongue stroked hers, as their breaths mingled and desire devoured her. She surrendered to it, on fire for this male, a slave to the primal needs he awoke inside her.

Needs only he could satisfy.

Darkness swept around her and her breath burst from her lips as she landed on her back, wonder at where she was now forgotten as Fenix landed on top of her. She groaned in time with him as his weight pressed down on her, as his left thigh slid between hers to brush the apex of them and the hard steel of his shaft pressed against her hip.

"Evelyn," he murmured, his voice thick with need.

Pleasure rippled through her at the sound of it, with the thought that he ached for her as fiercely as she ached for him, needed this moment and this connection as badly as she did. He moaned as he seized her mouth again, his kiss stoking the fire inside her, making her burn hotter still. It shouldn't be possible to make her temperature soar any higher or make the wild need that was stealing control of her grow any stronger, but somehow he managed it.

Fenix eased off her, dropping to his feet at the end of what she now realised was an old four-poster bed, and gripped the hem of his black Henley, tormenting her with a slow reveal of his body. Her breaths grew shorter with each tantalising inch of hard, honed muscles he revealed to her, her body going molten at the thought of touching and feeling all that powerful flesh. The ridges of muscle that arched over his hips kept trying to draw her gaze downwards to the bulge in his fatigues, but she couldn't get enough of the ropes of his stomach and the smaller clusters of muscles on either side of his ribs just below his pectorals.

She wanted to start there. Wanted to lick that tempting lattice of muscles that stretched as he raised his arms. She swallowed and bit back a moan as he revealed the square slabs of his pecs, the primal response to the sight of him swift to steal control of her, pushing her to the edge and goading her into surrendering to the urge to have him.

God, she had never felt so on fire, so close to burning up.

It felt as if she might explode if she didn't touch him soon, didn't get him sprawled on the bed beneath her for her to feast on and savour. She needed to lick every inch of his body, putting it to memory.

He cast his Henley aside and she noticed his markings. They shone in hues of gold and cerulean, laced with that deep pink that told her what he wouldn't.

He loved her.

She loved him too.

It wasn't just the glorious sight of him making her feel that. She soul-deep loved this man, feared that something might happen to her to rip her from him, and wanted to do all in her power to make sure it didn't.

But right now, that need to be with him, that fear of losing him and forgetting these feelings she had for him, culminated in a powerful urge to have him, to lose herself in the moment and lay claim to all of him.

She raked her gaze down his body, soaking up the sight of him, how his muscles shifted with each hard breath he pulled down as he gazed at her. There was no trace of green in his irises now. They were lit with pure hunger as he stared at her, that look scorching her and making her bold.

Evelyn sat up and pulled her T-shirt off, tossed it aside and didn't care where it landed as Fenix's glowing gaze fell to her body. She bit her lip as hunger surged, pooling in her belly, heating her to a thousand degrees, and couldn't resist the temptation to tease him too. She brushed her right index finger over her lower lip, luring his gaze there. His eyes grew hooded as he stared at her mouth and the gold and blue in his irises shone more brightly as she slowly lowered her finger, tugging at her kiss-swollen lips before she traced it down the line of her throat.

Fenix's gaze followed it, the enraptured look in his eyes a powerful drug that had her feeling hazy all over as she let her finger drift downwards. His throat worked on a hard swallow as she stroked the swell of her right breast with her fingertips and her arousal soared as her nipples beaded and she thought about touching them, swirling her fingers around them to see what he would do.

It was tempting.

But attempting to stroke them through the lightly padded cups of her modest bra was hardly going to hurl him over the edge. She ached at the thought of revealing her breasts to him and seeing how he would react, the heat curling through her growing hotter as she imagined his pupils dilating and his hunger getting the better of him. Swept up in a fantasy of him mounting the bed and then her, she reached around behind herself and unhooked her bra.

Let the black material fall away from her breasts.

Fenix bared his teeth as his eyes narrowed on them, his entire body flexing, hips surging forwards as if he had no control over himself. Maybe he didn't. She was so swept up in the moment she felt as if she had little control. Desire dictated her actions, had her wrapped up in the heat of her need and feeling drunk on it.

Evelyn skimmed her hands beneath the curves of her breasts and cupped them.

On a wicked groan, Fenix launched at her.

She gasped as he swept her up in his arms, as his lips descended on her breasts and he sucked her left nipple into his mouth. She came close to screaming his name as he rolled the sensitive bead between his teeth, was teetering on the edge of begging him for more and pleading him to be gentle with her. She wasn't sure how much of this she could take, was new to it in this life.

A thrill bolted through her as he pressed her back into the mattress and kissed and suckled her breast, as he tortured her with the divine feel of his mouth on her flesh. She groaned and arched to meet him, unable to hold back the reaction as she sank into her lust, was swept up in it and the need to climax building within her.

She didn't realise what Fenix's hands had been doing until he yanked her trousers down and cool air kissed her hips. He eased to one side and shoved them down as he kissed over the plane of her stomach, nipping at it whenever he groaned, his rumbling moans music to her ears that kept her passion at boiling point.

Together with the thought of what he might do next.

Oh God, she needed his mouth on her there.

Throbbed at the thought of his skilled tongue teasing her sensitive bead as it had teased her nipple.

He broke away from her on a strained groan, as if he knew the wicked path of her thoughts, and made fast work of removing her boots and the rest of her clothes, slowed as he peeled away her panties to leave her naked. She had never been more aware of a man's gaze on her as she was in that moment. She gazed down the length of her bare body to him, shivered as she caught him staring at her like a man starved.

He slowly moved between her legs, the way he gently eased her thighs apart making her hyper-aware of him and what came next, making her breath lodge in her throat as she waited. Every inch of her stilled as he kneeled between her legs, his palms skimming upwards over her trembling flesh. His hungry gaze seared her, had her aching with a fierce need of him and willing him to take her.

She needed to feel his mouth on her flesh. She needed to feel him filling and stretching her.

Claiming her.

He swooped on her sensitive flesh, tearing a scream from her throat as pleasure blasted through her. He groaned, as if he had felt that pleasure. It struck her that he had. Her pleasure was giving him strength, and the thought that she was making him stronger drew back the bolt on the floodgates.

Rather than holding back, she let herself go.

With each skilled flick of his tongue, she moaned, loud enough that anyone in the house would hear, but she didn't care. She wouldn't hold back. She would show Fenix everything he made her feel, would let it all flow through her. He eased her legs further apart, opening her to him and she cried out as he lowered his head and speared her with his tongue, probing her. Warmth rushed from her, a flood of desire that had him groaning and lapping at her, and she couldn't stop herself from tunnelling her fingers into his tawny hair to grip it hard as she worked herself against his mouth, seeking that one push that would send her tumbling over the edge.

When it hit her, she didn't tumble.

She soared.

Stars winked across her vision as pleasure detonated inside her, every inch of her shaking as release wracked her, had her crying his name over and over again, on every panted breath that burst from her lips.

Fenix didn't give her a chance to come down.

He impaled her in one slow, impossibly deep thrust, stretching her quivering body around his thick, hard shaft, and set a pace that had her soaring through the haze of one climax towards the next.

She moaned as she wrapped her arms around his neck and clung to him, as she kissed him and tasted herself on him. His answering groan was pure male as he drove into her, one hand gripping her hip to pin her in place while the other was anchored over her shoulder.

Holding her at his mercy.

As if she wanted to be anywhere else.

Heat built inside her again, stoked by every press and withdraw of his cock, with every brush of his pelvis against her bead, and she couldn't hold back the moans that burst from her lips between kisses.

Couldn't stop herself from dropping her hand to his bare backside and gripping it tightly. He moaned and jerked forwards as she dug her fingertips into his bottom, spurring him on, and then he was taking her harder, driving her towards release with each fierce plunge of his length.

It hit her in another blinding wave of bliss as Fenix drove deep into her and his rigid shaft kicked hard and throbbed, the feel of his hot seed pumping into her pushing her over the edge with him. She moaned as he held her to him, keeping her in place, making her take all he had to give. Her body greedily accepted it, flexed around his shaft to milk every drop from him.

After a few long minutes, he sank against her, his breath leaving him on a contented sigh as his head drooped to hit her shoulder. His body trembled against hers, his softening cock twitching occasionally, sending aftershocks of pleasure through her.

Fenix shifted his head and kissed her, softly this time, slowly bringing her down and rekindling her desire at the same time.

He drew back, his gaze soft as he looked down at her, his eyes searching hers as he stroked his fingers over her damp brow. "What are you thinking?"

There was a flicker of worry deep in his eyes and she knew what he was thinking. He feared something terrible would happen to her now. She didn't. Nothing could touch her in this moment and she wouldn't let anything spoil it.

Tomorrow, she would face reality again.

Right now, she wanted to live this dream a little longer.

She smiled wickedly and rolled him onto his back, mounting him at the same time.

"I'm thinking… encore."

CHAPTER 31

Fenix couldn't remember the last time he felt this sated, or this powerful. He slid a glance at Evelyn as she stepped away from him, the early morning sunlight casting highlights in her fair hair and warming her skin, making it glow in contrast to her black T-shirt and fatigues. She was radiant today, fitted into the country garden of Rosalind's cottage, rousing a vision of her drifting among the colourful blooms that bordered the sloping lawn at the back of the house and how she would pause to look at him, and how her backdrop would bring out her beauty. He wanted to capture an image of her like that.

Her golden gaze slid to meet his, the heat in it as her pupils slowly dilated telling him that she was far from done with him.

Gods, his little phoenix was insatiable.

Even more so than she had been when they had been together before the mage had cursed them.

She had ridden him to another two powerful climaxes before finally succumbing to a need to sleep, and then she had curled up in his arms as if it was the most natural thing in the world for her to do, cementing that feeling that she was right.

She always loved him.

She only forgot that she did whenever she was reborn. The memory of her love for him was stolen from her by the curse, but her feelings came back into focus whenever they met.

He didn't want to believe the other theory she'd had though. The thought that all the times he had fought his need to see her and had tried to let her live a peaceful life had been for nothing sat heavily in his stomach, weighing him down. He had tried to do the right thing for her and it hadn't changed a thing if her theory was correct and she loved him whether she remembered that feeling or not.

How many times had she died?

He had counted eight based on the times he had caved and surrendered to his need to see her and try to be with her, but the true number could be twice that or more. All those deaths he hadn't known about. He hated the thought of her suffering like that, having to go through death and then being left with no memories of who she was.

His fingers curled into tight fists and she noticed, her steady gaze falling to his hands before it lifted to his face again and she stepped towards him, closing the distance between them down to nothing. Her fingers brushed his, her caress sending a thousand volts shooting up his arm and jolting his heart into action. It thundered against his ribs as his gaze dropped to her mouth.

Fenix eased towards her, intending to claim her lips again, not to steal energy this time but to steal a drop of comfort and reassure himself that last night hadn't been a hunger-induced hallucination.

And that she wasn't going anywhere.

Someone cleared their throat.

He slid a black look at Rosalind where she stood next to her mate on the dewy grass of her cottage garden, the old thatched building standing behind her up the slope. The petite blonde witch merely smiled at him in return, her blue eyes bright with mischief.

"Someone got laid," she said in a sing-song voice that had him clenching his jaw and on the verge of telling her to behave because he wasn't in the mood to be teased.

Archer was still out there. The male was a threat to his mate, one that needed to be eradicated.

The thought of the warlock coming after Evelyn was enough to have his mood souring and he couldn't stop himself from firing off a retort aimed at Rosalind. "I'm not the only one. You two reek of sex."

Rosalind pressed a finger to her chest, prodding the black material of her knee-length dress, and cast him a look of wide-eyed innocence. "Me? Never. I didn't just ride my husband *all night long*."

She sang the last three words, shimmying a little at the same time.

Opened her mouth to keep singing.

But Vail sighed.

Rosalind whispered, "All night."

And cast her mate a sheepish look.

Vail rolled his violet eyes, the reaction a marked difference to how the elf prince would have responded only a few months ago, back when the two had met. Rosalind really had been working her magic on the male, smoothing off his rough and somewhat razor-sharp edges. Fenix could hardly believe the change in him and how relaxed he was now compared to how he had been. A good thing. Vail had been strung so tightly that he had been in danger of snapping.

Fenix put his new easier-going personality down to copious amounts of sex.

And a lot of love.

Rosalind bustled over to Vail and the male stooped, swept her into his arms and kissed her. Softly. Reverently. With so much love that Fenix couldn't stop himself from glancing at Evelyn. She blushed when their gazes collided and looked away at the same time as he did.

What was it about her that had him feeling like a boy all over again, new to love and a little afraid?

Gods, his mate had a way of unravelling his strength.

He wasn't the only one with the affliction either.

Vail cast Rosalind a soft look of longing laced with hope and a side order of fear as he eased her away from him.

The reason for the sliver of fear in his eyes became apparent when Rosalind broke away from him, coming to face Fenix and Evelyn.

"Let's take a look at you." She held her right hand out to Evelyn, who only stared at it.

Fenix gently placed his hand on her shoulder and gave her a look he hoped conveyed that it was all right and she could trust Rosalind. The witch wouldn't hurt her. Evelyn glanced at him, her golden eyes lingering on his for a moment, and then she looked back at Rosalind and took her hand.

Rosalind turned towards the sandstone cottage, walked a few steps and paused near a washing line that had been strung between two apple trees that were heavy with fruit. She looked back at Vail.

"Did you want to maybe check on the orchard to see how the peaches are doing?" Her tone was soft, each word carefully spoken as she locked gazes with her mate.

Because she intended to use magic.

Fenix had witnessed how badly Vail reacted to the use of magic around him and the thought of him losing it and attacking Rosalind, or Evelyn, or even himself, had him willing the male to accept her suggestion.

Vail looked from her to the bottom of the sloping garden, where trees stood in uniform lines, luring Fenix's gaze to the rolling fields beyond. The elf glanced back at his mate and then at the orchard again, repeated the process five times, each one completed more quickly than the last as his brow furrowed.

His violet gaze settled on his mate again and this time he shook his head.

She held her free hand out to him, her soft expression filled with love and warmth that put a sparkle in her blue eyes as her mate went to her. "Just a little magic. Maybe we could do it out here. It's a nice morning. I could make us all some coffee and we could sit on the patio."

Vail's shoulders sagged as all the tension bled from him, his deep voice a rumble as he said, "I would like that."

Rosalind released Evelyn, turned to her mate and pressed her palms to his chest. Her fingertips curled into the soft material of his black cable-knit sweater as she tiptoed, her fair eyebrows furrowing as she lifted one hand to his face and cupped his cheek.

"Perhaps you'd like to make the coffee today?" Her tone remained as soft as the breeze that played through the garden, causing the blooms that bordered the lawn to sway.

Vail swallowed and nodded, and lingered a moment as his gaze dropped to her lips. A war played out in his eyes, the tension that had drained from him swift to return as he stared at Rosalind's mouth, his throat working on another hard swallow.

She curled her hands over his shoulders and he bent for her, his concerned look going nowhere, gaining a trace of disbelief as she eased towards him and gently claimed his lips in a tender kiss.

Something was up.

Vail had been mercurial in the Fifth Realm, his mood dangerously unpredictable. Fenix had foolishly believed that he had changed, but he could see now that Vail was still troubled and was still treading a dark path that looked as if it might swallow him whole. He brightened as his mate kissed him though, as if her affection banished the shadows from his mind and filled him with light. His pointed ears flared back against his wild blue-black hair as he lowered his hands and hesitated for only a second before claiming her waist and tugging her closer.

Fenix slid another look at Evelyn and found her watching Vail and Rosalind, not with concern but with a soft, almost yearning expression on her beautiful face. Did she want him to hold her and kiss her like that? Gods, he wanted it.

Her golden gaze drifted to him, the heat and need in it hitting him hard as it trickled into him through their bond, igniting his instincts—both his ones as her mate and his ones as an incubus. His tank was full, but just the thought of finding a quiet place to be alone with her had his engine revving again.

Rosalind stepped back from Vail and gave him another soft look as he twisted away from her and headed for the house. Her gaze tracked him and when he disappeared inside, she turned to Fenix.

"Bit of a rough morning. Had a visitor while Vail was sleeping and I should have known better." She shook her head, frowned at the grass and then over her shoulder at the cottage. A sigh escaped her. "I think he's getting better and then I mess up… and it's days of him struggling to live with himself again and losing hope."

That didn't sound good.

"What happened?" Evelyn beat him to asking that.

Rosalind heaved another sigh. "He teleported into the living room and beat the absolute hell out of Atticus. I knew I should have gone upstairs straight away to wake him. Vail hates Atticus as it is and I told that idiot to stay away… but he needed a potion I knew how to make so of course he just pops by like he always does… and sometimes I think he's trying to antagonise Vail. Sometimes I swear he's flirting with me."

If Fenix had been in Vail's boots and someone had been flirting with his mate, Fenix wouldn't have sent him away with a bloody nose. He would have killed him. Just the thought of someone coming on to Evelyn had white-hot jealousy surging through his veins.

Fenix remembered being on the receiving end of Vail's jealousy in the Fifth Realm and couldn't help thinking that Rosalind was playing with fire. Vail was extremely possessive and fiercely protective of his mate, and she needed to lay down the law with Atticus before Vail ended up killing him.

"I'm so stupid." Her slender shoulders sagged and then she rallied. "Well, if he shows up unannounced again, I'm not going to intervene this time. Lesson learned. It's better I let Vail get it out of his system and Atticus learns a lesson about boundaries than I have to coax Vail back from that dark place he goes to whenever he messes up with me."

"With you?" Fenix frowned at her, feeling a little lost. "I thought he messed up by beating up this Atticus fella."

Her eyebrows rose and then she waved him away. "Oh no. Mother earth, no. I don't care if Vail and Atticus get into a fight. Atticus deserves a good spanking for still coming here after I've told him repeatedly to use the bloody phone if he wants something. No. I… well they were causing a ruckus and things were getting broken, and there was a high danger of my entire ingredients collection getting trashed... and you don't know how long it took me to get my hands on some of those herbs and mushrooms... and I kinda... might've... tried to intervene and paid the price."

She hooked her fingers over the sweeping collar of her black dress and tugged it down a little, revealing two long pink streaks that darted from her left shoulder towards her breasts.

Claw marks.

Vail was upset because he had hurt his mate.

"They're fine." She angled her head so she could see them. "I took some blood from Vail and of course he went overboard and stole the injuries from me through our bond too."

"Wait. What?" Evelyn piped up, confusion washing across her face as she frowned at Rosalind. "You took his blood and he stole your injuries?"

"It's the perk of mating with an elf." Rosalind tried to smile but it faltered as she stroked the marks. Her blue gaze shifted from them to Evelyn. "Vail's blood heals me, and he can also use our connection to take on my injuries, meaning they appear on him instead. It's something we've discussed in the past and he agreed not to do it unless it was absolutely necessary... mostly because it's dangerous. If he loses blood or is hurt... well... things can get a little dicey... for everyone else in the world."

"I've seen it happen." Fenix looked at Evelyn. "Back in the Fifth Realm where I met Vail and Rosalind. I saw it happen. There's another side to Vail, one born of the darkness. Tainted elves are dangerous, and Vail is about as—"

"He's getting better," Rosalind interjected, a sharp edge to her tone, and the sense of power in the air rose as she planted her hands on her hips.

Fenix held his hands up in an act of surrender.

"It was just a hiccup this morning." The witch pouted and looked as if she wanted to argue more about how sane or not her husband was, but the male in question exited the wooden kitchen door and stilled on the patio, a tray of drinks clutched in both hands before him.

Fenix felt it when Vail's gaze shifted from Rosalind to him. A shiver bolted down his spine and he mentally zipped his lips and kept his hands in the air, hoping Vail wouldn't rip him a new one.

Deeply aware that the elf knew Fenix was responsible for his mate being upset.

Rosalind's mood changed in the blink of an eye, a bright smile curving her rosy lips. "Coffee! Vail has been working hard to master the art. We bought a nice new machine and so far there's only been a few incidents of milk covering every inch of the kitchen and exploding espresso grounds."

Fenix didn't want to ask how someone managed to make espresso grounds explode.

He followed her as she bounded towards her mate, falling into step beside Evelyn, who cast him a look he could read.

One that silently asked him who the hell these people were.

Friends.

He smiled.

They were his friends.

He had never really been one for making friends, few incubi were, especially outside of their own species, but he could honestly say that Rosalind and Vail were the best friends he had together with Tiny and Des, and the three witches—Hella, Abigail and Agatha. Far better than the pains in his arse Mort and Rane.

Vail set the tray down on the wooden table just as Rosalind reached him.

And tackled him from behind.

He lurched forwards and cast her a black look as he came dangerously close to knocking the drinks, but there was no malice in it. There was only love. The elf shook his head as she wrapped her arms around him and pressed against his back, and he lifted his right arm and looked under it at her. She grinned up at him and swept around him, and he gathered her into his arms.

"No explosions?" she said.

Vail shook his head and she glanced over her shoulder at the coffees.

Fenix looked there too as he reached the patio. There weren't just four coffees. There were nine in total. Three espressos in small white cups. Three cappuccinos complete with a dusting of chocolate on the frothy milk. And three tall glasses of latte.

"I was not sure what coffee you preferred." Vail's violet eyes landed on Fenix.

"Latte! Oh God, I need some caffeine." Evelyn drew a smile from Fenix as she lunged for one of the tall glasses and it only widened as she lifted and sipped it, and sighed, a look of pure bliss washing across her face. She murmured dreamily, "Oh… vanilla. Heavenly. Just the right amount of syrup too."

Vail puffed his chest out.

Rosalind beamed up at him, pride shining in her eyes.

"I told you females love vanilla coffee." She grabbed one of the lattes for herself. "Your brother is going to be so jealous when he discovers you can make coffee. Loren needs to step up his game."

"Wait. Loren?" Evelyn lowered her drink from her lips and flicked a surprised look at Vail. "Your brother is Prince Loren?"

Rosalind curled her arm around her mate's right one. "Duh. He is Prince Vail. Who else would his brother be?"

Evelyn looked as if she had a thousand questions she wanted to ask. Rosalind tugged her mate to a chair and pushed him down onto it, and then seated herself on his lap. She wriggled to get comfortable as Vail wrapped his arms around her waist, pinning her to him.

The witch sipped her coffee and then said, "So we need to take a look at your curse. Not that I have any hope of being able to figure out how it works. The bloody Crow is better equipped to do that. And we really need to take a look at this sorceress. At the very least, we need to track down her mate and find out what he knows about her."

Fenix shook his head. "Neither of those things are going to help us. Archangel will be on high alert right now so we won't be able to get close to Aryanna and Brink is afflicted by a curse that makes him forget."

He winced as Evelyn tensed and her golden gaze swung his way.

"They're very popular apparently." Rosalind's tone remained bright as she leaned back against Vail's chest. The male responded by clearing her golden hair from her throat and pressing kisses to it, and Fenix didn't miss the fact his fangs were down. "But let's rewind to the part where you said Archangel are on high alert. Why are they on high alert?"

"Ah." Fenix scrubbed the back of his neck and grimaced, and then scowled as Vail nicked Rosalind's throat with his fangs and closed his lips around the small cut and the pair of them threw off enough pheromones to make an entire incubus frat-house horny. "Could you not?"

Vail's eyes opened and he looked up at Fenix, but didn't take his mouth away from his mate's throat.

"He's hungry. Let him feed." Rosalind waved Fenix away again and he was getting tired of her doing that. "Back to this problem we have."

"I might have—" Fenix averted his gaze.

"He left a trail of dead bodies in our wake." Evelyn's blunt words had him scowling at her and had the witch scowling at him.

"Subtlety is not your forte." She sighed dramatically, and he wanted to point out that it wasn't hers either as she wriggled on her mate's lap but held his tongue. She must have noticed his look because she rolled her eyes and patted Vail on the back of his head. "Fine. We'll behave."

Vail growled and tightened his grip on her and didn't release her neck.

"Or not," she muttered and tossed an apologetic look at Fenix. "Just give him a little longer."

Fenix paced away from them, stopping at a point where the desire they were both feeling didn't bombard him or fill him with a need to sweep Evelyn into his arms and kiss her until she submitted to him. He was trying to focus on the mission, but gods it was hard, felt as if the entire universe was challenging him and it was only a matter of time before his resolve crumbled.

"I think we should find the mage who cursed me and Evelyn." He started pacing, trying to work off some energy, hoping the motion would help him remain focused. "I don't want her to die again and I don't trust that whatever Archer did to her has changed anything. If she dies, she'll forget everything. The curse will activate."

His gaze collided with Evelyn's and he could see in it, and feel in her, that she wanted the curse broken too. It wasn't only important to him. It was important to both of them.

"Shouldn't we be focused on getting Aryanna away from Archangel?" She looked as if she hadn't wanted to ask that question and he had the feeling she had only said it because it seemed like the right thing to do—focusing on the greater good rather than just the two of them.

He had been living a life of hell since they had been cursed and while he was worried about the world just as much as she was, he was more worried about letting this chance they had slip through their fingers. If Archer's intervention did mean that the curse wouldn't kill her, as it already had, then they had time to find the mage and fix their problem.

They might never get another opportunity like this one.

So he was taking it.

"I don't think that's going to happen without waking her and we don't know how to wake her." He looked from her to Rosalind and Vail, and thankfully the elf was done sucking on his mate's throat and arousing her. "You saw her. She's in some kind of sphere of magic or something and Archangel can't break it, and I don't think we can just teleport into it and whisk her out of there. Archangel would have tried that."

"True." Rosalind slipped from her mate's lap and set her empty drink down. She tapped her chin, her expression growing pensive as she stared at the endless blue sky. "A sphere of magic."

239

She wandered a few steps from her mate and then back to him, and idly stroked his hair as he gazed up at her.

"Would another spell free her of it?" Vail settled his arm around her waist and she shrugged.

"Maybe. But what spell?" She broke away from him again, moving towards Fenix, and then stopped dead. "We could ask Archer."

"Hell no," Fenix barked. "Team up with the warlock who wants her for himself?"

"I don't think Archer wants her," Evelyn murmured and he sensed her nerves. Because she was defending Archer? Fenix knew that despite what Archer had done Evelyn still didn't consider him the enemy and he only hoped that didn't bite her on her arse. He didn't like the male, wanted him dead, but he wouldn't view her with scorn because she could see the good in him. She placed her mug down on the tray and shook her head as her brow furrowed slightly. "I think Archer wants to free her because she's asking it of him. They're connected and she's speaking to him."

Rosalind arched an eyebrow at that. "Speaking to him? That doesn't sound good. A powerful sorceress trapped for millennia in a big ball is speaking to a Crow. This can only go badly."

"Very badly indeed." A deep male voice rolled around them like thunder.

Fenix swung left and then right, his senses reaching out as he tried to locate the owner of that voice. The chair Vail had been sitting on toppled as he stood sharply and growled, and Rosalind muttered something beneath her breath in a strange language as she came to stand between Fenix and Evelyn.

Evelyn locked up tight.

Fenix looked at her and then in the direction of her gaze.

The air there rippled and Archer lunged out of it, appearing in a swirl of violet sparks on a collision course with Evelyn.

And then his dark eyes landed on Rosalind.

And he grabbed her instead.

CHAPTER 32

It took Evelyn a moment to catch up as Archer shot past her, but the second she did, she sprang into action. On the other side of Rosalind, Fenix twisted and lunged for Archer.

He disappeared in a swirl of violet sparks.

Together with Rosalind.

Vail roared and shoved Evelyn aside, his eyes wild as black spots coloured his amethyst irises, his head swinging left and right as he scoured the garden. Evelyn's heart thundered, her blood rushing in her ears as guilt swallowed her, and she exchanged a look with Fenix, sharing his worry as the elf growled and snarled and prowled forwards.

Evelyn couldn't believe Archer had snatched Rosalind.

This was all her fault.

She lifted her right hand and swallowed hard, an apology balanced on her lips as she edged her fingers towards Vail, unsure whether touching him would be a good idea or a very bad one.

Fenix beat her to it.

He gripped Vail's arm just as the elf's sweater and jeans disappeared, revealing the skin-tight black armour that hugged his tall frame.

"Vail, we'll find—" Fenix cut off as a masculine grunt sounded, sharply followed by a feminine chuckle that was laced with amusement and pure victory.

Evelyn's gaze shot towards the source of the sound just as Vail kicked off, wrenching free of Fenix's grip with such force that the incubus fell forwards and landed hard on his knees with a grunt of his own.

Relief poured through her as she spotted Rosalind struggling against Archer's grip, wriggling to get her arm free as she kicked at his shins. Archer's eyes went all-black and he disappeared with Rosalind again just as Vail reached them. Vail bared his fangs as he spun in a circle, his eyes narrowing as they darted over everything, and it hit Evelyn.

He had known Archer wouldn't get far with his mate.

And he knew the warlock would fail this time too, was waiting for him to reappear so he could attack him.

Her heart lurched for a different reason, even when she told herself that Archer wasn't the man she had thought he was. Everything between them had been a lie. Hadn't it? He meant her and these people—this world—harm. Didn't he?

It was hard to convince herself of that.

The look Fenix gave her as he picked himself up said he could feel the conflict raging inside her and he wanted to comfort her, so she stepped away from him, not because she didn't want him to comfort her but because she didn't want to feel weak. Not right now. Relying on him like that would only shred whatever strength she had managed to gather over the last twenty-four hours. She needed to face this alone.

Didn't she?

She glanced at him, her brow furrowing slightly.

Tempted to take the comfort he was offering to her.

But then Archer reappeared near the washing line with Rosalind, his face a black mask as he scowled at her and breathed hard, his chest straining against the tight breast of his long black coat.

Rosalind managed to break free of him this time, planted her hands on her hips and laughed right in his face. "You big dumb Crow. My home is well protected. I say who gets to come and go and I knew you'd make a play for the one solid part of your plan."

She looked right at Evelyn.

Archer flashed his teeth at her and flexed his fingers. Tiny flickers of light chased around them but Rosalind didn't seem at all bothered by the threat. She kept staring Archer down.

Vail slammed into him from behind, tackling him to the ground, and both men grunted as they hit the grass. Before Archer could even react, Vail had flipped him onto his back and was hitting him hard in the face. Blood burst from his nose and splattered over one side of his glasses and the light leaping around his fingers shone brighter, casting a violet, green and orange glow across the grass.

Archer brought both hands up towards Vail's head.

The elf disappeared, leaving only a faint shimmering outline of him behind, and reappeared near his mate. Archer flipped onto his feet and turned on Rosalind, his eyes flashing dangerously. Vail grabbed her and teleported again, landing next to Fenix this time.

The air chilled and thickened as Archer pivoted to face them, his chest straining as he curled his hands into fists and wiped the back of his left one across his bloodied nose. The darkness swallowed the white in his eyes again as he stalked towards them, the dark slashes of his eyebrows drawing down as his lips compressed.

And the air grew so cold Evelyn's breath fogged in front of her face.

Fenix held his arm out in front of her, placing himself between her and Archer, and she swore she could sense the tension in him and something else.

He was waiting for the right moment to strike.

"I have to say, I'm impressed with that tracking spell and I really want to know how you teleport like that." Rosalind sounded as if they were having a delightful conversation, as if Archer wasn't about to unleash hell upon them. She flicked her wavy ash-blonde hair over her shoulder. "Who did you track? Was it Evelyn? I'm thinking it was Evelyn. You've had plenty of time to cast the necessary spell on her since you're a big fat phoney of a friend."

Archer snarled and teleported, landed right in front of Rosalind and lunged for her.

Vail backhanded him, sending him flying across the grass.

Archer landed hard near one of the apple trees supporting the washing line, rolled at speed into the trunk and grunted as the impact shook the branches, causing a deluge of apples to hit him as he curled into a ball and covered his head with his arms.

Vail bared his fangs at that.

Rosalind cast him a pointed look. "You were the one who threw him at the tree. You can't really blame him for the damage."

Vail gave her a look in return, one that said he was blaming Archer for the damage and that was final, and then he teleported.

Archer disappeared in a swirl of violet sparks just as Vail appeared next to him, and the elf growled and flashed his fangs again as he twisted at the waist and his gaze swept the garden.

Evelyn gasped as Archer appeared close to her.

For a heartbeat, she was sure he was going to grab her, but Fenix launched at him, slamming into his chest and knocking him backwards. Archer bared his teeth and took a hard blow to the face, one that had blood trickling from his nose. Fenix didn't let up. He punched Archer again, knocking him off-balance, and when Archer tried to retaliate, he teleported.

Archer spun in a circle on the grass, twisting to face the other direction, breathing hard as he sought Fenix.

Her incubus appeared beside Vail and gave him a look. The elf nodded, a grim expression settling across his handsome features, and then they both teleported. They reappeared near Archer, one behind and one in front of him. Light burst from Archer's hands and he threw the orbs at Vail, who cast his hand through the air and sent them shooting towards the clouds gathering above them. Archer grunted as Fenix struck him in his back, landing a fierce blow on his right side, and staggered forwards. He twisted and hurled a black orb with twisting red lightning arcing around it at Fenix.

At point-blank range.

Fenix bellowed as it hit him in the chest and sent him flying backwards across the grass and she gasped and lunged towards him. He disappeared just as Vail attacked Archer, raking claws down his back while he was distracted. Archer cried out and her heart hitched, the part of her that couldn't reconcile the fact they weren't friends anymore making her take a hard step towards him and flooding her with a need to help him.

Archer ducked beneath Vail's right hook and shoved his hand against the elf's chest.

And sent him flying too.

Fenix reappeared, looking worse for wear and breathing hard as flickers of red lightning chased over his shoulders.

Archer pivoted to face him, a grin stretching his bloodied lips, and her heart lurched into her throat as she lunged for Fenix instead, cold fear blasting through her as she sensed the malevolence inside Archer.

He was going to kill Fenix if she didn't do something.

She froze, her entire body locking up tight as Fenix hurled himself at Archer, closing the distance down to nothing.

And kissed him.

Evelyn's eyes widened as he slanted his mouth over Archer's and she blinked, unable to believe what she was seeing even as the sight of it heated her blood in a wicked way.

Beside her, Rosalind muttered, "Mother earth... that's the sexiest thing I've seen in a long time."

Vail growled as he staggered to his feet and shook off Archer's blow, and then froze too as he saw what they were all staring at. She tried to tell herself that Fenix was only using his abilities as an incubus to weaken Archer, stealing his strength through a kiss so they could take him down and stop him, but it didn't make it any less sexy. She could feel Fenix growing stronger as he kissed Archer. She could sense Archer growing weaker.

Archer's wide, stunned eyes slowly slipped closed and he relaxed, sinking into the kiss, and Evelyn decided Rosalind was wrong and *that* was the sexiest thing she had ever seen. The way Archer melted into the kiss, his hands coming up, edging towards Fenix's hips as if he wanted to pull him into his arms.

Only Fenix broke away from him and wiped his mouth on the back of his hand as he flicked a look at Vail.

"Now!"

Archer blinked, confusion shimmering across his face as he stared at Fenix, his cheeks flushed and eyes filled with desire. It morphed to darkness a heartbeat later, his eyes blackening again as Vail launched at him, his claws poised to cut him down.

Vail slashed through the air, aiming at the back of Archer's neck.

Archer disappeared just as his claws would have connected.

And reappeared in front of Evelyn.

She gasped, fear bolting through her as she stumbled back a step, sure he would grab her, but then he dropped to his knees, dug his fingers into his dark hair to clutch his head and unleashed a pained bellow as his body bowed forwards.

Fear crashed over her, not fear that he was a danger to her, but fear for him. She reached for him and stopped herself, told herself that he was a danger to her and everyone here, that he wasn't her friend.

That he had been using her.

And maybe now he was getting what he deserved.

She hated herself for thinking that way as he cried out again, his face screwing up in obvious pain as he clawed at his head.

"Remind you of anyone?" Fenix whispered out of the corner of his mouth to Rosalind as he appeared between them and the witch levelled a black look on him, giving Evelyn the impression he had been comparing Archer to Vail.

Just how dangerous was the elf? His mood changed frequently, and whenever it darkened, his eyes did too, gaining splotches of black that made her think about all the reports she had read of what Prince Loren had called the *tainted.*

The same Prince Loren who was his brother.

Vail strode towards Archer, an elf on the warpath as his fingers flexed and the tiny black scales of his armour rippled over them and formed talons at their tips. He was going to rip Archer apart. She had to do something.

As much as he had hurt her, she couldn't let Vail kill him.

But getting between Vail and Archer felt like suicide to her.

He had hurt his own mate just this morning, proving how violent he could be and that in the midst of a fight he found it hard to distinguish friend from foe.

Archer teleported again before the elf could attack him, the world falling eerily quiet and the air growing thick with tension as everyone waited for him to reappear. Just as she thought he wouldn't, that he had found a way to escape Rosalind's spell, he dropped out of the air forty feet away, crashed into a wooden bench and rolled off it to hit the grass. His glasses ended up crooked, the right side of them halfway up his forehead, and his heavy breaths shifted the green blades as he lay motionless.

And then everything about him righted before her eyes. The blood on his face disappeared, his glasses repaired themselves, and even the dirt and slashes on his long black coat vanished.

He shoved himself up onto his feet and snarled at Rosalind.

"Let me go!" Archer shoved his hands into his hair again and clawed it back, his black eyes wild. "I cannot be here. She doesn't want me here."

"Where does she want you?" Rosalind said, her air casual. "You are talking about Aryanna, aren't you?"

Archer bared his teeth at her. "She must wake. She must rise."

Rosalind looked from Vail to Fenix and then Evelyn, her eyebrows high on her forehead and a look in her eyes that asked if they were seeing this too, and then her blue gaze settled back on Archer. "Did you forget to sip your anti-psychotic elixir this morning? Got a spell in there that will help with the madness? Maybe if you told me about it, I could help you."

His eyes narrowed on her.

She went flying, sailed backwards through the air like a rocket and slammed into the sandstone wall of the cottage.

And remained there, five feet off the ground and spreadeagled against the stones.

The petite witch struggled, her face twisting and contorting as she tried to move, but nothing she did helped.

"Put me down," Rosalind gritted.

"Let me go," Archer countered and staggered towards them, shaking his head from time to time.

Rosalind looked as if she was considering it.

"I don't think I weakened him at all," Fenix hissed and cast a worried look at Vail. "You up for this?"

"It's the spells," Rosalind bit out as she struggled against her invisible bonds. "You did weaken him and now they want to protect him. I'm not sure draining his strength was a good idea. We're playing Russian roulette with dangerous spells. The gods only know which ones will come out to defend their host."

Archer wasn't in control of the spells he knew? That didn't sound good.

Rosalind stared at the back of Vail's head when he eased his feet further apart, adopting a warrior's stance. "Vail... stay where you are."

Vail launched at Archer on a vicious growl. A strange turquoise light shimmered over Archer's eyes and Vail grunted as a hundred tiny lacerations suddenly appeared in his armour.

Blood burst from every one of them.

The elf stumbled a step and dropped to his left knee. He pressed his right hand to the grass as he bent over and breathed hard, his wild blue-black hair falling to caress his sweat-dotted brow.

"Oh, you... bloody wanker!" Rosalind hollered and fought harder, her eyes fixed on her mate's back. "It's okay, gorgeous. Just hold it together. Breathe."

Archer blinked, his expression laced with surprise as he stared at Vail as the elf fought to recover from the blow Archer had dealt him, as if he was as stunned by what had happened to the elf as everyone else was. He eased back a few steps and pressed his right palm to his forehead as he muttered something beneath his breath.

"Vail, honey, come to me." Rosalind kept fighting her invisible bonds, her voice soft and laced with affection as she coaxed her mate. "Come here. Come away from that big mean Crow."

Archer slid her a look and twisted away from everyone, his muttering growing more intense. What was wrong with him? Evelyn wanted to ask him that, but she feared the looks everyone would give her and the fact they might misinterpret her words, mistaking them for concern.

Which they totally wouldn't be.

God, she was lying to herself now.

"I... *Crow* this... *Crow* that," Archer snarled and looked over his shoulder at Rosalind, his face a black mask and a dangerous light in his eyes. "Call me *Crow* one more time..."

He didn't need to finish that threat.

Archer looked from Rosalind to Vail as he continued to struggle against whatever spell Archer had hit him with and then his black eyes shifted to Fenix.

Her heart lunged into her throat as sparks of white lightning chased around his fingers, growing stronger by the second, and he narrowed his eyes on the incubus. Fear seized her and she couldn't stop herself from reacting as he raised his hands to strike.

She leaped between him and Fenix.

CHAPTER 33

Evelyn's blood rushed in her ears and she squeezed her eyes shut as she braced herself, waiting for the spell to hit her instead, willing to take the blow to protect Fenix. She would be reborn if she died. He wouldn't.

Only the expected pain didn't come.

Evelyn cracked one eye open.

Archer stood where he had been, his hands by his sides now, no magical light chasing around them as he stared at her.

His eyes were brown again.

Something deep inside her said this was her chance, the moment a secret part of her had been waiting for, and she couldn't waste it.

"I know you're not a bad man," she whispered and swallowed to wet her dry throat as she gathered her courage. She shut out Vail and Rosalind as their eyes landed on her, and tried to shut out Fenix too as he stared at her back, his disbelief a tangible thing inside her. She knew she looked crazy, or perhaps foolish, but she had to go with her gut, and her gut said Archer wasn't as evil as everyone was making him out to be. "You saved my life."

Archer's face softened.

And then hardened again when Fenix barked, "He did it to further his own agenda."

She ignored that and kept her eyes on Archer, willed him to focus on her and shut everyone out just like she was.

"All those times you protected me," she said as her mind filled with countless patrols where he had stepped in to shield her, taking blows meant for her, and the fact he had saved her life in the Fifth Realm. "Were you really going to kill me when the time was right for your plan?"

A flicker of regret lit his dark eyes and he shook his head, then nodded, and then his face screwed up and his jaw clenched.

And all the tension flooded out of him and he looked right into her eyes.

"I always intended to lift the curse first."

Those words would have wounded a weaker soul, but Evelyn could see in his eyes that he meant well, that he had wanted to make sure that she would come back from death with her memories this time, able to continue her life, and that it had been the best he could offer her.

And she saw something else too.

He hated himself for it.

"You really do know about the curse then." She knew he had mentioned it before, but the thought that such a powerful warlock knew about her affliction nourished the tiny seed of hope in her heart, making her believe there was a chance she could be free of the curse.

She glanced over her shoulder at Fenix.

That both of them could be free of it.

He didn't look happy about her holding a conversation with Archer rather than attacking him. She had seen enough to know that attacking Archer wasn't going to solve anything. He was too powerful.

"I've been researching mages... trying to find the one who cursed you," Archer said and Fenix stared at him now, his green eyes widening slightly.

She caught the flare of hope in them before she turned back to Archer, her own hope growing stronger as his words sank in and something dawned on her.

"Is this why you're always looking for information on magic and magic users in the Central Archive?" She searched his eyes, wanting to know the answer to that question, because it would go a long way towards restoring her faith in him, and strengthening the hope she had that she could convince him to help them. "You're trying to break my curse."

He nodded, tunnelled his fingers into his dark hair and snarled, "Shut up!"

He flicked her an apologetic look and she wasn't sure whether it was because he had meant to kill her, had been using her, or because of his outburst. What was Aryanna saying to him?

"I do care about you, Evelyn." His gaze implored her to believe him.

Fenix was by her side in an instant, scowling at Archer.

Archer sighed.

"Not like that." He went to the bench he had hit, sank onto it and looked beyond her to the cottage and sighed as he removed his glasses.

Rosalind squeaked and Evelyn glanced over her shoulder in time to see the witch's boots hitting the flagstones of the patio, and then Vail growled, drawing her gaze to him. The cuts she could see through the slashes in his black armour healed before her eyes, and then the tiny scales knitted back together, so his armour was perfect again. She looked at Archer as he casually cleaned his glasses on a small black cloth.

A little awed by his power.

Not that she wanted to swap places with him.

She would take being a cursed phoenix shifter over being a warlock with a sorceress in his head.

He scrubbed a hand down his face, an air of weariness about him now, and heaved a sigh as he sagged forwards to rest his elbows on his knees and put his glasses back on. "I want to help break this curse… but I can't think straight. I wanted to make sure you didn't forget who you were when you died. I'm sorry I wanted to kill you. When I came up with the plan, I didn't know you, and I thought I would find Aryanna quickly… but years passed and I got to know you… and I came to care about you."

"But you still wanted to kill her," Fenix put in, his voice a dark snarl.

"Everything was moving so quickly and Aryanna was right there, shouting at me to do it, and I just wanted to be free… I'm not sure I would have gone through with it."

He wasn't sure? That didn't fill Evelyn with confidence. There was a chance he would have gone ahead and killed her.

She muttered, "How sweet of you."

Rosalind walked over to Vail, dusting off her black dress as she went, and grumbled, "Believe me, that's more than I expected from a Crow."

Archer glared at her.

"I warned you. I'm sick of the way witches treat me as if I'm filth on the bottom of your shoes… as if you all believe I'm a stain on the name of magic users and I never should have been born. I didn't ask for this life! I didn't ask to be what I am!" The air chilled and trembled, becoming harder to breathe as his eyes narrowed on Rosalind. "And you know what? What I am doesn't change a damned thing about me."

He pushed to his feet and Evelyn's breath fogged in front of her face as he stared Rosalind down, contempt flashing in his dark eyes as he curled his fingers into fists.

"You witches…" he spat and Evelyn had half a mind to turn on Rosalind too and remind her about what she had said about playing Russian roulette with the spells in Archer's mind. Antagonising him would only get them all killed. "You're all just scared of us. No. You're all just *jealous*. When it comes down to it, you're jealous of the power at my disposal, and it's easier for you all to cover it with scorn and name-calling than face the fact you hate that I have this power and you don't. I'm not a bad person, dammit."

His handsome features hardened, and Evelyn hated the pain that laced his voice, the hurt she could see in his eyes—the desperate need to be accepted. How long had he lived with his own kind hurling insults at him and hating him? Long enough that it had done some serious damage to his heart, that was for sure.

"There are mitigating circumstances at play here." His fists shook beside his hips as he growled those words, tiny sparks of violet electricity coursing over them. "I need to get Aryanna out of there. I need to free her... before I lose my mind. There's a piece missing. A way of freeing her. Something I need. Always a piece missing and I can't find it, no matter what I do."

He was rambling again, the darkness slowly encroaching to devour the whites of his eyes as they grew wild and lowered to the grass.

"Like a key?" Evelyn offered, hoping to regain his attention.

His head snapped up and his eyes cleared as they locked with hers and he whispered, "Like a key."

Evelyn took a step towards him when a thought struck her, but Fenix gripped her wrist, holding her back. She looked over her shoulder at him, catching the worry in his green eyes, and eased back a step. She could understand his caution and knew she needed to be cautious too. Trusting Archer could be a recipe for disaster, but in her heart she believed what he had told her. He had come to view her as a friend and the thought of having to kill her had upset him. Still upset him.

Maybe if she could suggest another way to free the sorceress, if they could find this key he was missing, then she would spare them both pain and they could return to being friends.

"What about Brink?" she offered.

"Brink?" His dark eyebrows met hard, forming a crease between them.

She nodded. "That's the name of the dragon mate of Aryanna."

His frown melted away. "The one from the note?"

"Maybe he's the key. If they're mated and she's held in a prison of dragon magic, maybe he can help her. I know dragons can't be in this world, but maybe..." She shook her head slightly as her brow furrowed. "Is there any spell you could do that would stop the curse from affecting him?"

Archer's eyebrows pinched again and he cast his dark gaze at the ground, and then sighed as he sank back onto the bench. "I don't know."

He pushed his glasses up his nose and massaged the bridge with his thumb and index finger as he closed his eyes.

"It's not that easy. It's like standing at the entrance of a vast library you're unfamiliar with and just asking the stacks whether they have some obscure book in it. I can't tell you." He let his glasses fall back onto his nose and scrubbed his forehead instead, as if he was getting a bad headache and was trying to ease it away before it fully hit.

"I don't get it. Surely you should remember what spells you've learned?" She had the feeling he didn't though and that feeling only grew as he looked up at her, his hand dropping to his thigh, and he heaved another sigh.

"It's not that simple," Rosalind said, her voice soft, not a trace of the disgust that had been in it before lacing it as she drew Evelyn's focus to her. The witch kept her blue gaze trained on Archer. "He didn't learn most of the spells at his disposal."

"That doesn't make any sense. How do you know spells if you didn't learn them?" She shifted her gaze back to Archer.

He sat a little straighter, squaring his shoulders, giving her the impression he was bracing himself. "They were passed to me."

"Stolen," Rosalind muttered.

He narrowed his eyes on her and Evelyn realised this was the reaction he had been bracing himself for. He had known Rosalind would twist whatever he said to make it sound as if he had done something terrible.

And in turn make him feel as if he was something terrible.

"I stole nothing. I didn't ask for this." That wasn't the first time he had said that.

When Rosalind opened her mouth to say something, Evelyn shot her a look that told her to back off, because tormenting Archer wasn't getting them anywhere.

"I was only going to say he's got several thousand years' worth of accumulated knowledge in his head," the witch muttered and pouted.

Vail patted her on her shoulder and looked ready to murder Archer, as if he had been the one to upset his mate.

"How is that even possible?" Evelyn's gaze darted back to Archer and she braced herself as an answer hit her. "How old are you?"

He reached into his pocket, causing both men behind her to tense, as if he was reaching for a weapon. As if he needed one. He had attacked both Rosalind and Vail without even moving a muscle. When he pulled out his pack of cigarettes, took one out and lit it, neither man relaxed.

Archer sighed, blowing smoke into the still air, and then waved the cigarette slightly as he rolled his wrist. "I don't know. Two hundred and eleven... no... two hundred and twelve... I think. You sort of lose track."

She stared at him, her eyebrows rising. "I can imagine."

It was better than him being thousands of years old, but still, the thought that Archer was one hundred and eighty years older than she had thought was quite the shock. But then, who was she to speak? According to Fenix, she was far older than she had imagined.

Which still messed with her head.

"And you came to have thousands of years' worth of spells in your head." That messed with her head too.

"I inherited them." He took a long pull on his cigarette and she noticed his hand was shaking. "It wasn't pretty. I didn't ask for it. I didn't ask for any of it. Do you have any idea what it's like to watch your family being murdered... hearing your sister screaming and crying as men—and thinking you're going to die and then suddenly everyone else is dead and you don't know what happened and there's a hundred spells clamouring in your head and—I was a child. I was a *child*."

His voice broke on that last word and he swiped his glasses off his face and palmed his eyes as he dropped his head, and Evelyn's heart went out to him. She could only imagine how terrifying it must have been for him to see his family killed and his sister abused like that, let alone what had come afterwards.

"I didn't know," Rosalind muttered in a low voice and looked up at her mate. "Normally they just transform... awake... on their ninth birthday or some crap like it."

The heart that had been going out to him hurt a little more for him upon hearing that. The trauma of witnessing what he had and the fear it would happen to him must have triggered the awakening. Not only that, but he had become something other witches seemed to fear. Had he been alone in this world? A mere child left to face it and the hatred of his own kind by himself.

She took a step towards him and Fenix tried to hold her back, but she scowled at him and twisted her arm free, because she wasn't going to stand by and let Archer hurt and do nothing about it. She went to him and placed her hand on his shoulder, and he tensed beneath her palm, his head jerking up.

Tears lined his lashes, but he was quick to wipe them away before anyone but Evelyn saw them. The pain remained though. Fathomless. Cutting. She smiled for him, hoping to alleviate some of it, even when she couldn't lift the burden from his heart or his shoulders. All she could do was let him know he wasn't alone in this world. Not anymore.

"I tracked the mages I could find," he murmured huskily, swallowed and coughed to clear his throat, and then added, "One of them might have the key to your curse. It's better we focus on you first. I can hold on and everyone is right. Archangel don't know how to get Aryanna out of there either and they've been working at it for centuries. I want to help you. We don't have much time to break your curse."

Evelyn didn't like the sound of that.

She nodded and then hesitated as a need rose within her, as she gazed down at Archer and felt as if she couldn't breathe, not unless she asked him what was on the tip of her tongue.

"How..." She pulled down a breath and exhaled it slowly. "How did we meet?"

His gaze grew distant and a smile wound its way onto his lips, as if he was recalling a fond memory, and in that moment she knew with perfect clarity that she wasn't the only one who had come to view the other as a friend. He had come to care for her too.

"I found you in Hell. Close to a place I call home. No one knows of it and nothing ventures near it. I came back from a shift at Archangel to mull over what to do next and then I sensed movement in the air, and you were there. I tried to help you remember who you were at first, but no spell I used worked and that was when I discovered you were cursed." He lifted his hand and placed it over hers on his shoulder. "Aryanna was screaming at me that you were a phoenix. She filled my head with the notion of using your fire to free her. I had already infiltrated Archangel but couldn't find her, and I still had no way of freeing her if I did discover where they were keeping her. I latched onto that plan of hers, desperate to be rid of her. Only I didn't bargain on coming to care for you. When I realised that if you died, you would forget everything again, I focused on finding a way to break your curse. You had been so terrified when I had met you, and there had been so much despair in you whenever you struggled to remember anything and couldn't. It caused you so much pain and suffering. I couldn't let that happen to you again, so I ignored Aryanna as much as I could."

She couldn't imagine how terrible that had been for him. The sorceress was tormenting him and he had put up with it for her sake, delaying his plans until he knew she was free of her curse and would remember who she was when she was reborn. As twisted as it still sounded to her, it touched her. He had altered his plans for her, making himself miserable in order to help her, prolonging his own suffering.

"I used spells to mask what you were so Archangel didn't find out, and those spells became more intricate as we grew closer. I wanted to keep you safe." His hand slipped from hers and his gaze grew conflicted and she knew why.

Because he had intended to kill her.

She stared at him, wondering what she would have done if she had been in his position. What lengths would she go to in order to free him of his curse of having Aryanna constantly in his head, pushing and tormenting him?

The answer to that question surprised her.

She would do whatever it took, even dying in order to use the flames of her rebirth to free the sorceress and him in the process.

She kept that to herself, sure that everyone would think her crazy for considering such a thing when the sorceress was dangerous, liable to be captured and used to hurt all immortals.

Archer's gaze drifted to her side and she placed her hand over the spot where her scar was as another question plagued her, one that had been bothering her for months.

"Why did it take me so long to heal the wound from the Fifth Realm?" She couldn't bring herself to call it the wound that had killed her.

Archer took a long pull on his cigarette and exhaled, and she noticed it smelled like herbs. Was there something in that cigarette that was helping him retain control and calm down? Did it contain magic like Fenix's pills?

"When you were—when I... brought you back, I wove a little magic into the wound to ensure it would be slow to heal. I needed you safe." His dark eyes told her how much he meant that. The same look he had given her so many times, one that had always revealed the depth of his feelings for her. She believed that look. He truly wanted to keep her safe. He sighed. "I needed you away from Hell and the immortals. I had almost lost you. I knew the doctors would sign you off for months if the wound was having trouble healing. I was buying myself time to find a way to break the curse, but damned Archangel kept sending me on missions to Hell."

Regret shone in his eyes and for a moment he looked as if he wanted to ask her something, and then he looked away from her and took another drag on his cigarette.

"I know I should hate you." She paused when his shoulders went rigid, battling the urge to comfort him or take back those words. "You meant to hurt me. You saved my life so you could choose when to end it. A friend wouldn't do that."

His head jerked up. "Evelyn—"

"So I want to know, Archer," she cut him off, unwilling to let him stop her now she had found her flow. She needed to put it all out there. She needed to know the truth. "Are you my friend or my enemy?"

Was he still planning to kill her?

That was the question she had wanted to ask, but one she had been too afraid to voice, so she had veiled it within another.

He swallowed hard and his brow furrowed as he gazed up at her, his voice scraping low with the pain that glittered in his eyes. "I... I want to be your friend."

She had the feeling he had never had one before her, that he had been alone for two centuries, spurned by others, living in a place where no one ventured in order to protect himself.

"Then we're still friends." She ignored the muttered remarks from Rosalind and Fenix, because she wasn't being reckless by trusting Archer. They didn't know him like she did.

And she did know him.

She knew how to make him smile. She knew what made him laugh. She knew what really irritated him. She knew which brand of beer he liked and the foods he hated. She had spent years with him, slowly growing closer to him, piercing the barrier that had been around him when they had first met to reveal the man behind it.

"Are we really doing this?" Rosalind muttered. "Trusting him might backfire on us."

Evelyn waited to see what the others would say, sure they would side with the witch.

"We should start in Norway," Fenix said and all the tension drained from her as she sensed the shift in his mood, the darkness that had laced it falling away as he took a step towards her.

Archer's eyes widened. "Norway. The valley from the images we saw?"

She nodded and eased to one side so he could see the others. "They fought mages there. One of their friends is a phoenix shifter too and her resurrection caused the damage we saw in the satellite images."

"Some of the mages got away." Rosalind looked between Archer and Evelyn. "We didn't check the stronghold for information either. There's a chance a way of breaking this curse could be in there, or the mage himself might be holed up there."

"There's also a chance that the way of breaking Aryanna out might be in there too. Archangel have it on their list of places to check out. They're hunting for mages too." Archer put his glasses back on and crushed his cigarette with the heel of his boot, earning a black look from Vail before his violet eyes lowered to the grass. "There was another location too, one in New Hampshire. Archangel went to investigate it, but it had been ransacked."

Fenix cleared his throat. "I might have been the one responsible for that. I have all the documents at my house, but I didn't see any mention of Aryanna in them."

"I'd still like to take a look at them. They might be written in a language you don't know." Archer cast Fenix a wary look. "Although walking into an incubi den might be the biggest mistake of my life. Even a cigarette can't rid my mouth of the taste of you."

"I did the only thing I could in order to weaken you." Fenix tossed him a disgusted look. "Believe me. I didn't enjoy it."

"I did," Rosalind murmured, earning a black look from her mate.

"What is it with females and two men acting in such a manner? That fiendish little succubus wanted me to wrestle her demon king naked and oiled up, and I distinctly recall you wishing for it to happen." Vail's expression darkened, his violet eyes brightening as his fangs flashed between his lips with each word he snarled.

Rosalind sidled closer to her mate, wrapped both arms around one of his and beamed up at him. "I would never make you do it. No one gets to see my mate naked but me. I'd claw their bloody eyes out."

Vail growled and swooped on her lips.

Fenix groaned.

Archer rolled his eyes.

"I think we should follow up the one remaining lead we do have, and then you can talk nicely to Fenix about getting access to those documents." Evelyn ignored how Vail swept Rosalind into his arms, pinning her to his chest, and bent her over backwards as he kissed her. Heat swept through her regardless, drawing her gaze to Fenix as she thought about him kissing her like that.

Archer huffed. "So, we're going to Norway?"

Rosalind loosed a long, weary sigh as Vail righted her and released her.

She grumbled, "This time, I'm wearing thirty layers and packing more heat spells."

Evelyn looked at Fenix, catching the spark of hope in his eyes, a spark that caught inside her too, spreading warmth through her that had her wanting to cross the short span of grass between them and step into his arms.

She glanced at Archer, and then Rosalind and Vail, and finally stared into Fenix's eyes again as resolve filled her.

He nodded.

Evelyn looked back at Archer and gave him his answer.

"We're going to Norway."

CHAPTER 34

Rosalind had mentioned inviting Hartt and Mackenzie to join what she had termed their 'raiding party' and the elf and phoenix had wanted in on it the moment Fenix had told them about their plan to head to Norway and track down more mages. Mackenzie was as intent on taking out as many mages as possible as Evelyn had been before they had been hit with the curse.

Fenix braced himself as a frigid wind scoured the valley, churning the snow up into the air to reduce visibility. That same snow had covered the evidence of the fight that had taken place here not long ago, leaving only the scorched fringes of the pine forest behind to signal something had gone down. The trees further back from the valley floor were untouched, their branches heavy with snow, making them blend into the foothills of the mountain they covered.

Beside him, Evelyn huddled down into her thick black jacket that matched the one he wore, folding her arms across her chest, and worry arrowed through him as he saw how pale she was. He reached across and tugged her black scarf up so it covered the back of her neck and the lower half of her face, and she glanced at him, her golden eyes soft with surprise and a lot of affection. He could drown in those eyes and he would be happy.

"Get a room," Rosalind muttered and he wanted to call her on the fact she was using her mate as a mobile radiator, her back plastered to Vail's front as he stood with his arms wrapped around her and his back to the wind that blasted through the trees surrounding them.

Trees Fenix had expected to give them some shelter but offered zero protection from the bitter cold as night had slowly fallen and the temperatures had plummeted.

Vail gently rubbed Rosalind's arms through her long thick coat that reached her knees, covering equally as hardy trousers. Even the elf had donned protective clothing too, although Fenix guessed that beneath the layers of waterproof material and fluffy goose down, the male was probably wearing his armour.

Hartt lowered the binoculars from his eyes and looked across at his mate, wearing the same look of concern as Fenix had been for the last thirty minutes they had been standing in the valley. He liked the thought of his mate going anywhere near a blood mage about as much as Hartt did, but like Hartt, he also knew that telling Evelyn to remain behind while they all went off to fight would end in an argument.

And possible castration.

He reassured himself by taking in their side, focusing on the two powerful elves and the two even more powerful magic users they had. He hated to admit it, but the fact Archer had come along was a comfort in a way. For all his faults, and the things he had wanted to do, Archer obviously cared about Evelyn. If the male wanted to make up for everything by sacrificing himself to protect her if things got dicey, Fenix wouldn't complain. Not that he was hoping the warlock would meet his end.

Much.

"So, now that it's nice and dark so they won't see us coming," Rosalind started, her voice loud in the heavy silence, and everyone looked at her, "I have a cunning plan."

She hit everyone with an expectant smile.

It fell off her face when Archer said, "Why are you quoting Black Adder?"

She pouted at him, her fair eyebrows knitting hard as a disgruntled look entered her eyes. "How do you know—never mind. You're no fun."

Because Archer had understood her cultural reference and she had expected the whole group to be confused and miss her joke.

"I'm going to put him in the comfy chair one of these days," she muttered to her mate and slid Archer a black look.

Vail's brow crinkled as his violet gaze shifted down to her. "But the armchair is your seat, Little Wild Rose. Why surrender it to such a vile male?"

She beamed up at him and it hit Fenix that this was the sort of response she had wanted to receive. She liked it when her jokes went unnoticed, her references slipping past people.

Archer opened his mouth, but Fenix shook his head, silently telling the male that he knew that she was quoting Monty Python now but to let her have her way. They needed Rosalind on their side.

The warlock huffed and reached into the pocket of his long black coat to pull out his smokes. The same long black coat he had been wearing back in Rosalind's garden.

"Aren't you cold?" Evelyn's teeth chattered as she asked that and Fenix inched closer to her, moving to shield her from the wind as another blast swept up the slope to them.

"No." Archer lit the cigarette and took a hard pull. "Basic shielding spell."

"You didn't think to share with the group?" Rosalind huffed and frowned at Vail. "See what we have to deal with. He could have made us all nice and warm, but nope... only thinks of himself."

Archer's dark eyes narrowed on her. "If you think you can harness the seventh plane of the eidolon to bend their matter around you and constantly keep it in check so it doesn't flay the flesh from your bones and devour your soul, then I will be more than happy to tell you the incantation."

Rosalind merely muttered something about him being a 'show off' in response to that.

"Let's go. Before my balls fall off," Hartt growled. "Someone is home at that stronghold. We should move closer to get the lay of the land and figure out what we are up against."

The binoculars in his hand disappeared and he started down the slope with Mackenzie. Her flame-red hair fluttered from beneath her black woollen hat as she carefully navigated the trees, using their thick trunks to stop her from sliding all the way to the valley floor. Everyone had agreed to conserve their strength, reserving teleports and spellcasting for when they became absolutely necessary.

Like, in the thick of the upcoming fight.

Fenix took hold of Evelyn's hand, their gloves making it impossible for him to thread their fingers together and denying him the comfort he needed as he thought about what lay ahead of them. They would make it through this. He told himself that on repeat as he helped her down the snowy incline.

Archer trailed behind them.

Rosalind and Vail brought up the rear, the petite witch still muttering about the warlock.

They crossed the deep moonlit snow that covered the basin of the valley in silence, heading for the trees that hugged the mountain range that spanned from the end where they were to the one where the stronghold loomed. Fenix kept his eyes on the distant glow of the fortress, on high alert even though there had to be at least a mile or more of silent snowfield separating them.

They were nearing the trees when Rosalind's leash on her tongue failed her.

"I still don't know why we're expected to trust someone who has been working for Archangel." She slid an apologetic look at Evelyn when everyone looked over their shoulder at her.

Archer was the only one who didn't look back at Rosalind.

He heaved a long sigh and flicked his cigarette onto the snow, and for a moment, Fenix was sure he wasn't going to rise to the bait, but then his jaw flexed and his face twisted, and Fenix saw it in his eyes as he lost the fight against saying something.

"I only worked with Archangel because I sensed the presence of strong power there and Aryanna's voice was louder. She led me to that facility. Only I couldn't find her. She cannot see where she is." Archer didn't look back at Rosalind. He looked at Evelyn instead, his gaze steady on the back of her head as she walked, navigating the deep snow. "Now I have seen her, I know why she couldn't guide me better. I have no allegiance to Archangel. My ties with them have been severed now I know where Aryanna is... Yes... yes, I will free you. I swore to do so, didn't I? You know, I could live without you doubting my every move. I found you. Now you could be of more help and tell me how to free you. No, I'm not going to kill Evelyn to achieve it."

He huffed and scrubbed a hand over his tousled dark hair, rubbing the flecks of snow into it, and Fenix didn't like the darkness that began to bleed from his irises into the whites of his eyes.

"I know you don't know. You don't know anything. You're never helpful. You sit there in my head, barking orders night and day, stealing sleep from me with your incessant noise." Archer's voice was a deep growl as his expression blackened and flickers of violet and crimson light sparked from his fingers as he curled and flexed them.

Rosalind eased away from Archer, tugging Vail back so the distance between them and the warlock grew, and Fenix considered doing the same thing with Evelyn. Archer was throwing off aggression now, his aura tainted with fury and frustration and tinged with desperation. Fenix had seen enough desperate men in his life to know what they were capable of and he wouldn't put it past Archer to be the sort who exploded and caused mass destruction and death when that emotion got the better of him.

Archer noticed everyone distancing themselves and began muttering things beneath his breath, fogging the air in front of his face as it chilled further. The hairs on Fenix's nape rose as the air didn't only chill. It crackled with energy that lit up his senses and had his instincts firing, telling him to move Evelyn away from Archer now before it was too late and the male took her out when he went nuclear.

"I can whip up a nice potion if you need one?" Rosalind offered, her voice calm and light despite the fear Fenix could sense in her. "Might help with the voices."

Archer glared over his shoulder at her and the light leaping from his fingers grew brighter, illuminating his face and casting deep shadows around his eyes.

Or at least Fenix hoped it was the light making the area around them black.

"You know what might help with this voice in my head?" Archer snapped. "A spell that would transfer this problem to you. I think I know one."

Rosalind stuck her tongue out at him.

Vail growled low and his fangs flashed between his lips as he spoke. "Try anything, and I will hunt you down and savour ripping you apart."

Archer shrugged that off. "You can try. You might end up being the one ripped apart."

Vail's eyes only darkened further, the black slashes of his eyebrows drawing down to form a deep crease between them as he glared at the warlock. "Are you threatening me?"

"Russian roulette, gorgeous." Rosalind patted her mate's arm. "Crows have a lot of spells and some of them can be a touch protective of their host. I really don't want to lose you, so you have to play at least a little nice with the Crow. Promise?"

Before Vail could swear not to antagonise Archer, the warlock began muttering again.

"I have a name. I'm sick of being called Crow. Sick of your kind thinking I'm some kind of cursed being... a murderer and a psychopath without any shred of feeling." His eyes went all-black and the light flickering around his fingers became jagged scarlet bolts that illuminated the trees as they entered the fringe of the forest. His voice lowered further, a feral snarl. "No, I will not return. I have important business. My friend needs help. No, you are not my friend. I do not think you are anyone's friend... and that is why you are in that prison. Cursing an entire species... there is something seriously wrong with you."

Rosalind slid a look at everyone that blatantly said she thought there was something wrong with him and that he was psychotic, but didn't risk saying it aloud.

"That's it!" Evelyn snapped and rounded on Rosalind, startling everyone, even Archer. "His name is Archer. It's not Crow or any other horrible thing you want to call him. It's Archer! I'm sick and tired of you treating him like he's some sort of unfeeling monster when you can see it hurts him. If you have a problem with him, then you have a problem with me."

The air around Evelyn shimmered and the snow by her feet began to melt as she curled her hands into trembling fists and stared Rosalind down. Rosalind stared at her, her blue eyes wide and a stunned look on her face. Beside the witch, Vail growled low.

Evelyn shifted her glare to him. "Try it, elf."

"Evelyn," Mackenzie whispered softly and approached her, slowly raising her hands. "Calm down."

"No, I won't calm down." Evelyn scowled over her shoulder at the other phoenix shifter. "I've had enough of this shit. I'm tired of her hurting Archer just because she can. Maybe I should find something offensive to call her and see how she likes it. Hag? How about that? How would you like it if I called you a hag all the time? I really don't like your *friends*."

She turned on Fenix as she said that, hurt and anger flaring inside her, warming the air around her.

Fenix eased towards her, aching to comfort and calm her, to make her see that Rosalind wasn't all bad and that he didn't want this coming between them. "I swear, love, she'll be on her best behaviour from now on… so you just need to calm down and rein it in. Okay?"

"Not good enough," she barked. "I want to hear it from her."

She levelled a dark look on Rosalind.

Fenix did too.

Rosalind's lips thinned and for a moment he thought she would tell them all to go to hell, but then she huffed and the tension melted from her. She muttered, "Fine. I'll call him Archer."

There was a definite pout to those words.

The air around Evelyn cooled again and she turned away from Rosalind and began walking. Archer followed close on her heels. Fenix cast one last warning look at Rosalind and then followed. Evelyn glanced at Archer, worry in her eyes, and Fenix could feel the shift in her mood and knew the source of it. Archer had been referring to her when he had mentioned helping a friend. Fenix didn't want his mate trusting the warlock and falling foul of his plan to use her to free Aryanna, didn't trust him when he said he wouldn't kill her, and he hated the male with a passion, but he couldn't fault her for feeling as if the warlock was her friend.

Because he had been.

Fenix had seen it himself.

When he had first discovered her location over a year ago and had begun watching her from afar, he had seen how close she was to Archer, and had seen the male protect her more than once. Archer had taken care of her, and deep in Fenix's heart, he knew the warlock had done it because he cared about her and not because he had been protecting a valuable asset and keeping his plan in motion. The two of them had gone out for drinks or coffee at least once a week, had laughed and teased, and had taken care of each other, cheering the other up whenever they were down or helping them through a crisis.

The two of them had appeared so close that watching them at times had been unbearable, the white-hot jealousy he had felt driving him to part them, to make sure Evelyn didn't fall for Archer.

Only she never had.

She had never looked at the male in the way she looked at Fenix. From the moment she had set eyes on him, there had been a spark of warmth and interest in them that hadn't existed when she had been looking at Archer.

Love.

Maybe her theory was right and she always loved him. She just didn't remember that she felt that way about him until she saw him again.

They trudged along the treeline, sticking to cover beneath the pines as they headed in silence towards the stronghold at the far end of the valley. When they were close, Hartt halted and his binoculars appeared in his hand again. A neat trick that all elves possessed. They could call anything they owned to them no matter where they were or where it was. Fenix was a little jealous of that talent. It meant the elves could travel light, didn't need to bring any necessities with them—like swords.

Hartt and Vail had offered to arm everyone with the weapon of their choice before the battle began.

It hadn't stopped Evelyn from packing her guns, strapping them over her thick black woollen sweater she wore beneath her coat.

He hoped they didn't have tranquiliser darts in them. They weren't here to make friends. Although, if Drystan was here, then knocking him out sounded like a good plan. It would give them time to build a cage for him so they could ensure he didn't escape while they were questioning him and forcing him to lift the curse.

"I can do a spell to see what we're dealing with," Rosalind said.

Just as Archer released several cerulean orbs of magic that shot through the trees, whizzing between the trunks as their light faded and then disappeared.

Rosalind huffed.

Archer slid her a wicked look. "What? Are you upset that you're not the only magic user in the group now? No longer feeling special?"

"Not really." Her slight shoulders lifted in an easy shrug and then her gaze grew sincere as she pressed her right palm to her chest and smiled fondly at Archer. "I just want you to know it's been swell and it was so nice knowing you."

His brow crinkled and confusion lit his eyes.

And then Vail snarled and launched past her, barrelled into Archer and took him down, landing hard on top of him.

CHAPTER 35

Archer took several blows to his face as he struggled to catch up with what was happening.

Rosalind mock-gasped, her eyes wide. "Shoot! I forgot to mention my husband hates magic being used around him unannounced."

Vail gripped Archer by his forehead and began bashing the back of his skull into the snowy dirt, his lips twisting in a vicious sneer as the pointed tips of his ears flared back against the sides of his head.

When Archer's eyes went fully black, Rosalind was swift to lunge for her mate, her hands coming down on his shoulders as he growled at the warlock, flashing his fangs.

"That's enough now, gorgeous. I think he got the point. Your mate needs cuddle time." Rosalind squeaked as Vail shoved Archer's head against the uneven ground, twisted to stand in one fluid move and swept her up into his arms.

He prowled away from the warlock with her, fussing over her as she petted him, her fingers brushing through his hair to make the blue-black lengths of it even wilder and then teasing the pointed tips of his ears.

Archer remained flat on his back, his eyes wide and lips parting as he stared at the canopy of the trees. Fenix went to him and offered his hand, and the male eyed it with suspicion before he took it. Fenix didn't hold it against him. There had been a time he would have gladly re-enacted Vail's attack on him to bloody his face a little more after all.

He pulled the warlock up onto his feet and released him as Evelyn came to him, and did his best to dial back the urge to pull her away from him as she took a look at his split lip with a worried edge to her golden eyes. Those eyes widened a little when the cuts on his face healed and the blood disappeared.

Archer slid a black look at Vail, who was busy petting Rosalind's hair now, smoothing the golden lengths with his fingers as he held her to him. "There's something seriously wrong with him."

Rosalind scowled over Vail's shoulder at Archer. "Pot, kettle."

Archer huffed and dusted down his coat. He gave Evelyn a look that told her not to fuss, and strode away from them, stopping a few feet down the incline. He gazed in the direction of the stronghold.

"I count several servants and three mages. Three mages means—"

"We could be facing sixty enemies if they're at full strength and can make enough clones." Rosalind cut him off as Vail set her back on her feet.

Archer clenched his fists. Evelyn went to him and ran her hand down his arm. His dark eyes slid to her and something passed between them, the look she gave him enough to have the tension bracketing his mouth fading and his shoulders easing lower. A weaker male than Fenix might have been irritated by how close they were.

Fenix wasn't.

He really wasn't.

He did his best to let the familiarity between his mate and the warlock not bother him as he joined them and stared at the high walls of the stronghold, focusing on mentally preparing himself for the coming fight.

"Sixty sounds like a lot." Evelyn looked from him to the others and he knew what she was thinking.

He didn't like the odds either, but he had fought mages in the past and knew their tricks, and their side was strong.

"We can do this," Rosalind said as she came up beside him, forming a line with him, Evelyn and Archer. Vail joined her, and Hartt and Mackenzie did too. She looked along the line. "We can handle sixty. We handled more and a lot worse odds last time. I'll put together a spell that will protect us from the worst of the mages abilities."

"I already have one in place. Hella did it for me." Fenix had learned quickly that mages liked to freeze their opponents in place, making it easier for the clones to kill them, and had taken precautions against it.

"I'll put something together for everyone else then. Shouldn't take long." Rosalind looked at everyone. "Just take a moment to prepare while I work on it."

Fenix nodded at the same time as Vail, and took hold of Evelyn's hand, squeezing it lightly. He tugged Evelyn with him, needing more than just a moment to ready himself for a fight. He needed a moment alone with her.

She followed him up the incline, deeper into the trees, and gasped when he twisted with her and pinned her to the broad trunk of a pine. He swallowed that gasp as he claimed her mouth, savoured the way it turned into a moan as she looped her arms around his neck and opened for him. Her tongue brushed his, sending a thrill down his spine, and he groaned as he deepened the kiss.

He told himself that everything would be fine, that nothing bad would happen to either of them, but it was hard to convince himself of it and drown out the voice of his fears as he clung to Evelyn.

She pulled back and smiled up at him, her golden gaze a little dazed. "What was that for? Needed a top-up?"

He shook his head, because he hadn't taken a single drop of energy from her, would never risk her like that. She needed all the strength she had.

"I... I just needed to kiss you." As those words left his lips, her look softened and understanding dawned in her eyes followed by a look that told him that he wasn't alone.

She lured him down for another kiss, this one softer and slower, a kiss that warmed him right down to his soul and gave him comfort, because it told him how deeply she loved him and offered the reassurance he badly needed.

"Um. Guys." Rosalind's voice rang out in the darkness. "Archer's gone rogue."

"Shit," Evelyn muttered, seized his hand and pulled him with her back to the group. Her fear ran into him through their bond as she reached Rosalind and looked out into the snowfield and saw the witch hadn't been lying.

Archer was *flying* across the snow.

The damned warlock's boots hovered a good foot above the surface of the powder, as if he was standing on thin air, but he was moving at the same time.

And he was moving at speed.

Evelyn broke away from him and began running.

"Spell. Now!" Fenix barked at Rosalind, who immediately muttered words beneath her breath and sent a glowing golden orb after Evelyn. She teleported before it could strike her and Fenix growled. He held his hand out to Hartt. "Sword. Now."

A black katana appeared in Hartt's hand and he pressed it into Fenix's, and then two shorter silver swords appeared in his grip. He tossed them to Mackenzie and she caught them as another golden orb struck her and Hartt to have light shimmering over their bodies. She shot after Evelyn at the same time as Fenix began sprinting through the trees.

Fenix teleported and landed behind Evelyn. "What the hell are you doing?"

She jumped out of her skin and scowled at him before facing forwards again, her focus locking back on Archer. "I can't let him fight alone. He's doing this because he feels bad about his plan to hurt me."

If the warlock wanted to make things up to Evelyn by dealing with the mages and their clones alone, Fenix wasn't going to stop him. He huffed at himself for thinking that. Archer didn't know what the mage they were seeking looked like, so he couldn't let the male fight alone, and he knew his mate would be devastated if something happened to him too.

So he grabbed her and teleported, landing just in front of Archer.

Right in the middle of a group of males who all wore a similar coat to Archer's long black one and who all looked the same, right down to their milky blue eyes.

Clones.

Archer shot Fenix daggers and then cast his right hand out and a shimmering violet bubble appeared around Fenix and Evelyn.

Evelyn broke free of Fenix's grip as Archer turned his sights on the clones and lunged for him.

And bounced backwards as she hit the wall of the bubble.

Fenix caught her before she fell onto her backside, righted her and kept hold of her left arm. He tried to teleport with her and growled when he found he couldn't. Her eyes widened and she turned back to face Archer, and banged her free hand against the violet wall, making it shimmer every time she struck it.

"Let me out!" She bashed her fist against the bubble in time with each word and Archer cast her a look that said it wasn't going to happen.

Behind him, several clones exploded.

Fenix shuddered.

Another reason he didn't want to get on the warlock's bad side by holding on to his grudge with the male. Archer could probably pop him like a zit with only a thought.

The explosion he had started swept outwards in a wave, causing a grotesque sight as one after the other, the clones' heads blew up, showering the snow with bone, flesh and blood.

Some of which hit the violet dome protecting him and Evelyn and made her rear back against his chest. She pulled a disgusted face as blood and entrails rolled down the bubble in front of her.

"Ew." The female voice that appeared close to him sounded as disgusted as his mate looked and he shifted his gaze to Rosalind in time to see her grimacing at the carnage that covered the snow. "He has some serious issues."

Fenix wasn't going to argue with her about that. "He's also made it inside and we need to stop him from killing all the mages."

Rosalind waded through the snow to him and pressed her hands to the violet bubble, closed her eyes and frowned. She remained still for long seconds in which screams and agonised bellows filled the tense air, and then she muttered something and the bubble popped.

"He was nice enough to make it a low-level spell. I think he wanted me to free you." Rosalind rubbed her bloodied hands on her coat.

Another howl of pain rent the air and Fenix grabbed Evelyn's hand and started running with her, heading for the arch in the thick grey stone wall. The urge to teleport was strong, but he couldn't, not without being able to see where he was going.

His lips pulled taut as he rounded the entrance of the stronghold and came to an abrupt halt before a wall of bodies. Their limbs were bent at unnatural angles, their forms twisted into horrific shapes.

"I told you he was a few beers short of a six pack," Rosalind muttered as she stopped beside him.

Vail stepped past her, his violet gaze scanning the courtyard and the half dozen buildings that encircled it. Long streaks of blood splattered their grey walls and inside one a fire was raging, black smoke billowing from the broken windows to rise high into the still night air.

Fenix looked around, taking in the carnage. It was a war zone and the fact such destruction and so much death had been wrought by the hands of one male in only a matter of minutes had him wanting to grab Evelyn and teleport her far away from Archer.

But then a male bellowed.

Evelyn shot forwards, leaping over the wall of bodies, landing in a slick patch of blood on the snowy flagstones. She kicked off and Fenix followed her, staying close to her heels as his senses stretched around him. He felt Hartt and Mackenzie running in another direction, towards the buildings to his right where he could sense more people, and wasn't surprised when Rosalind and Vail remained where they were.

The tinny scent of magic and the heavy sensation of Rosalind's power swept around him and he felt it as the spell she was casting was completed. A bright orange dome of light covered the area and warmth curled around him, the temperature rising sharply to that of a pleasant spring day.

Evelyn stripped off her coat, leaving it at the entrance of the largest building as she rushed into it. Fenix cast his off too, together with his gloves, using his teeth to remove first his left and then his right as he swapped his sword to his other hand.

"Speak," Archer barked, his deep voice echoing down a stone staircase.

Evelyn was swift to change course and head up it, her blonde hair bouncing against her shoulders with each step. She stopped at the top and looked left and then right along the corridor there, and he lunged for her and seized her hand as he sensed the warlock off to his right.

Fenix tugged her in that direction, his heart pounding as the scent of blood filled his nostrils and the air chilled again. His breath fogged in front of his face as he ran for the open door at the end of the corridor, his fingers flexing around the hilt of the sword as he readied himself.

Archer swung his way when he burst into the room, a scrawny dark-haired male hanging from his right hand by the front of his coat. The young male's fearful grey eyes shifted to Fenix and then back to Archer, his eyebrows pinned high on his forehead as the scent of urine joined the coppery tang of blood in the air.

Evelyn gasped and Fenix knew why.

There was a gaping hole in Archer's shoulder, one that was slowly healing before Fenix's eyes, knitting back together at the same pace as the holes in the front and back of Archer's coat.

Fenix slowly edged towards Archer, his pace measured as he calmed his racing heart and eased around the remains of what he suspected had been another mage. Suspected because pieces of the body were littered across the entire library and Fenix couldn't find the head. He sent a prayer up to whatever gods were listening, hoping that the male Archer had literally ripped apart hadn't been the one they were looking for.

"Archer," Evelyn murmured and his black eyes shifted to her, some of the darkness lifting from his face as they landed on her.

He moved his left hand behind his back. Attempting to hide the black claws that tipped his ashy fingers? He didn't want Evelyn to see them. He could hide them from her all he wanted, but it wouldn't change the fact his hands weren't the only things different about him. His facial features were sharper, more angular, and his ears had grown pointed. Not just one point like an elf either. The tips of his ears had split into two points, the top one longer than the bottom.

And the male had fangs.

Teeth as sharp as Prince Oberon's had been.

The bastard looked like he would be right at home in the Unseelie Court.

273

"I-I'll t-tell you what-whatever you want. Just d-don't d-d-do that to me." The wiry lad still hanging from Archer's other hand paled as the warlock's black eyes edged back to him.

"Put him down, Archer." Evelyn took slow steps towards him, lifting her hands so her palms were facing him.

Everything in Fenix roared at him to get her away from the warlock but he tamped it down, put a leash on it and reined it in. Evelyn had reached Archer more than once and he had every faith she could do it this time.

He really needed her to do it this time.

Because this male was now the only living thing he could sense in the area other than his own friends.

Archer grunted and released the male with a shove, sending him slamming into the wooden floorboards with enough force to shake the timbers beneath Fenix's boots. The warlock paced away from her, muttering things beneath his breath again as he headed towards a window that looked out onto the mountains beyond the wall.

The male picked himself up, rubbing his hands up and down his arms as if he was freezing, and Fenix closed the gap between them at the same time as Evelyn. Fenix clutched the male's shoulder as he hunkered down beside him, keeping him in place and hoping it would be enough to stop him from teleporting if he possessed that ability.

"I-I'm just a servant," he mumbled.

"I know." Fenix couldn't sense a shred of magic in the male now he was close to him and he doubted that Archer had either, but the male had looked ready to go to town on him regardless of the fact he was just a human.

Archer slid him a look, his lip curling as if he had sensed Fenix's opinion of him shifting back towards how it had been before they had teamed up, and then paced away. When Evelyn went to him, it was hard to stop himself from telling her to keep away from him, but he somehow managed it, choosing to keep tabs on her as he questioned the male instead of barking orders at her.

Fenix reached into his pocket and pulled out the silver frame, opened it and showed it to the traumatised male, not daring to hope he was going to get anything useful out of him. He was babbling to himself now, his dull eyes flickering between Fenix and the body parts just a few feet behind him.

"Have you seen this mage?" Fenix didn't take his eyes away from the male as he sensed Rosalind and the others entering the room, shut them out as they exchanged whispered comments about the mess Archer had made.

Evelyn murmured to Archer, soothing him by degrees, making the chill in the air and the heavy sensation of his power gradually fade away.

The scrawny lad in front of Fenix nodded.

Fenix blinked. "Wait. You have seen him?"

He couldn't believe it, not even when the male nodded again.

"Where have you seen him?" Fenix's heart raced in his throat as he searched the male's eyes, some part of him still refusing to believe the kid was telling him the truth.

Until he spoke.

"Drystan is here."

"Drystan," Fenix murmured, a name he had never thought he would hear someone involved with the mages say, not without him prompting them. He looked over his shoulder at Hartt and the elf's violet eyes shifted to meet his. "Did you see a male who looked like this?"

He flashed the portrait at Hartt and the male shook his head. "We found only servants and clones, and none of them looked like him. I was worried he got away, but the clones had dark blond hair. Not white like your mage."

Fenix turned the picture towards Archer. "What about you? Slaughter anyone who looked like this?"

Gods, he hoped the male hadn't.

Archer scowled at him. "No. I sensed the same energy as what is in your curse. I was following it and it led me here."

Fenix didn't like the sound of that.

His gaze leaped back to the kid. "Where is he?"

Something caught his attention and he glanced there, frowned as the shadows seemed to shift and blur behind Evelyn as she turned away from Archer to look at Fenix. He realised too late what was happening.

The shadows parted and Drystan seized hold of her arm.

His words echoed in the air as he disappeared with her.

"Right here, and now I am gone."

CHAPTER 36

Rage burned up Fenix's blood as Evelyn disappeared, fear sinking icy claws into his heart to squeeze the breath from his lungs. Archer's wild, dark eyes fixed on the spot where she had been and his features twisted with the fury that Fenix could sense in him, anger that told him that he wasn't the only one blaming himself for her abduction.

Fenix seized the servant by his coat and leaned over him, shook him hard as he growled, "Where would he have taken her?"

It had to be far away, because Fenix couldn't sense them in the vicinity and he figured that if they had moved to another location within the stronghold, Archer would have been there in a flash.

Archer.

He looked at the male. "You tracked her to Rosalind's house. Can you track her now?"

Before the warlock could answer, the scrawny lad trembling in Fenix's grip muttered a word.

"England."

Fenix's gaze shot down to him as shock swept through him.

"England." He stared at the male, reeling as one possible location hit him, and didn't dare to hope he was right. He glanced at the others as he thought about the country house he had scouted and how many mages and servants he had sensed inside it, and then looked at Archer. They could do this. He shoved the servant away from him and straightened. "I think I know where Drystan took her. There was an estate. I went there to find him, but I sensed too many mages, far more than I could handle alone. Mages weren't the only people there either."

His focus edged towards Mackenzie and she stiffened as their eyes locked, revealing that Hartt hadn't told her about the country house yet. Fire lit her irises, making them glow, and her expression hardened as she took a step towards him.

"Phoenixes. They have phoenixes there, don't they?" She looked ready to seize hold of him and shake an answer out of him as he had with the servant, so he nodded. She pivoted to face Hartt, her voice gaining pitch. "We have to go there."

"We will. But you need to be calm, Mackenzie. You have to keep your head." Hartt reached for her, his handsome face soft and violet eyes laced with concern, and she wrenched her arms away from him before he could touch her to calm her.

The air around her shimmered and the temperature in the room rose.

"Now. We have to go there now," she barked.

"I'm staying," Archer said and Fenix glared at him, because he had been counting on having the warlock at his side during the fight. They needed him. The male swept his arm around, drawing Fenix's gaze to the rows of bookshelves crammed with rolled parchments and ancient tomes. "There's information here for the taking and I need to gather it before anyone else can get their hands on it. Archangel are on the verge of dispatching a team here."

"It can wait." Fenix turned on him, pressure building inside him as he considered saying what was in his head. The part of him that wanted to keep the warlock at a distance and continue hating him warred with the part that kept pointing out what a valuable asset the warlock was and that they needed him in this fight. In the end, that side won. "We can't do this without you, Archer. I think you proved that here. We're strong, but you... we need you."

Archer's eyes widened, the surprise the male felt rippling across his face as his jaw slackened and washing over Fenix's senses. What kind of life had this warlock led to be so shocked by the fact someone was asking him for help? When he had ranted about his past and the things that had happened to him, Fenix had thought he was embellishing everything. The look in his eyes as he stared at Fenix said he hadn't been. He really had lived a hellish existence, cast out and spurned by his own kind.

"Please, Archer. Evelyn needs you." Fenix held his gaze, hoping the male would see in it that he needed him too. They all did. If they were going to survive the coming fight and save Evelyn, they needed his strength and his power.

"I will tell my brother." Vail stepped forwards. "Loren will dispatch an army here to gather this knowledge for you and prevent Archangel from getting their hands on it."

Archer's eyes widened a little further. "Loren. Prince Loren of the elves?"

Vail nodded, causing a rogue strand of blue-black hair to fall and caress his forehead. He swept it back.

"I will go to the elf—" Vail grimaced and pain surfaced in his eyes. "I cannot."

Rosalind stroked his arm, her fair eyebrows furrowing as she gazed up at her mate. "They won't turn you away. Loren wants you there. What if I went with you?"

"No," he barked as he looked at her, his face blackening for a heartbeat before it softened and he reached for her, smoothed his palm over her cheek and sighed. "What if they hurt you too?"

Rosalind looked as if she doubted the elves would attack her, but wisely held her tongue as her mate fussed over her, showering her with affection as he stroked her cheek and bent to kiss her. Fenix could understand Vail's reluctance to go to the elf kingdom. Having been manipulated for four thousand years by a dark witch claiming to be his mate, he had been forced to attack his own kingdom and his people, including his brother, turning him into the number one enemy of the elves.

Now he was free of the witch and was regaining his sanity, clawing his way back towards the light, but many in the elf kingdom still didn't trust him. Rosalind had told him that Loren was working hard to change their minds about Vail so he could visit at the very least, but it was slow going and his council were still against him.

Hartt approached Vail, a steely look in his purple eyes. "I will go. I will tell your brother everything and make sure you get the credit."

Vail broke away from his mate, cast a grateful look at Hartt and placed his hand on Hartt's left shoulder as he nodded.

Hartt disappeared, leaving only a shimmering outline of himself behind.

Mackenzie began to pace.

Seconds ticked by, turning into minutes that each felt like an hour as they waited, and Fenix grew restless, began striding back and forth across the library to work off some energy as his mind trod a dark path, conjuring images of Evelyn in the hands of Drystan.

The gods only knew what he was doing to her.

He feared he would be too late again, that he would fail to save her this time too.

The urge to teleport was strong, but he denied it. If he teleported, the others wouldn't know where to go, and if he sensed that Drystan was at the country house, he wouldn't be able to convince himself to return for them. He would fight, and he would undoubtedly get himself killed.

But waiting for the elf to return was hell, sheer agony that ripped at his soul with every breath he took, scoured his insides and made him feel hollow.

Finally, Hartt returned.

With a split lip and black eye, and another elf.

This one had a regal bearing and fine bone structure that reeked of nobility and his appearance was immaculate, from his neatly clipped short blue-black hair to his crisp thigh-length black jacket embroidered at the hem and cuffs with a flowing pattern of silver leaves, and the pressed tight black trousers and riding boots that were so highly polished Fenix could see the library reflected in them.

Mackenzie rushed to Hartt, knocking the other elf out of the way and not noticing his sneer as worry creased her brow. "What happened?"

"I ran into Bleu," he grumbled and released the elf he had brought with him. "As always, he was not pleased to see me, but thankfully Loren intervened. This is Leif. He pulled the short straw."

And he looked unhappy about it as he took in the musty library, his lip curling in disgust.

"It's been nice, but the clock is ticking." Rosalind pulled the sleeve of her coat back and tapped her naked wrist. "Time to go. Have fun."

Leif looked as if he wanted to say something as his amethyst gaze landed on Vail.

Fenix didn't get to hear what it was, because he grabbed Rosalind and Vail and teleported to the spot in the forest where he had landed the last time he had come to scout the mansion.

Only this time, it was pitch-black and eerily still, as if the night was waiting for something to happen.

Archer appeared behind him with Hartt and Mackenzie, shocking the life out of Fenix.

"How did you do that? Do you know this place?" he hissed at the warlock, keeping his voice down so no one would hear him, even though the forest where he had landed was a good distance from the elegant sandstone mansion.

Archer shook his head. "No. I followed you through the teleport trail. There is always a teleport trail."

Mackenzie wrenched free of the warlock's grip.

"Shit," Hartt growled as she disappeared.

He disappeared too.

Fenix didn't have to guess to know where she had gone.

He fixed his gaze on the illuminated patio that stretched along the back of the mansion—a sprawling building that had more lights glowing in the windows now—and teleported there.

Right into the middle of a group of clones who must have appeared during his teleport.

He cursed as the dozen carbon copies of a black-haired male closed in on him, their milky eyes glowing faintly as swords appeared in their hands. Cursed again when he realised he had forgotten his blade in the rush to reach this place.

Fenix teleported to the roof of the house and scoured the fray below him, seeking Hartt. The second he located the elf, he teleported again, landing beside him on unsteady legs. Hartt swept towards him, his black sword cutting through the air, and stopped just short of removing Fenix's head.

"Are you insane?" Hartt snarled and pivoted away from him to cut down a blond clone and then thrust the blade of his sword through the chest of another.

"I need a weapon." Fenix ducked beneath the silver sword of a clone, swept his leg out and took out his ankles. He lunged at the male, grabbing his arm and wrestling with him, trying to get the weapon from him. It disappeared. Damn it. He glared at Hartt's back as the elf slashed and hacked at more clones. "Sword. Now."

"You are so demanding." Hartt waved his hand through the air and several clones went flying as the blast of telekinesis hit them, and when his hand was closest to Fenix, the steel blade the male had given him in Norway appeared in it. "Don't leave it behind this time."

Hartt dropped the blade.

Fenix caught it, spun on his heel and brought it up in time to block the blow a clone aimed at him. He thrust forward with the blade, knocking the male off-balance, and skewered him through his side. The clone grunted as Fenix swept his sword at an angle, slicing clean through his flesh to free the blade, and dropped to the flagstones.

He turned to thank Hartt, but the male was gone.

A bright blue blast of light off to his left almost blinded him as it drove the night back and he looked there.

Vail lunged for Rosalind, but she hurled an orb of violet light before he made contact and it struck the blue one that was whizzing towards her. They detonated on impact, the light stinging Fenix's eyes and causing several of the clones around him to grunt and cover their eyes. He took advantage of their temporary blindness, cutting them down before they could recover, chipping away at their numbers.

He paused for breath when the area around him was clear, hope building inside him, a sense that they could do this rising to buoy him up.

He dropped like he was on a rollercoaster the height of Mount Everest when a dozen more clones appeared before him, replacing the ones who had fallen.

Fenix looked left towards Vail and Rosalind, and then right towards Archer, watching the clones as they appeared there too. He fixed his gaze on the mansion beyond the wall of milky-eyed blond males in front of him. Whoever was making these clones was inside there and they wouldn't stop coming until Fenix dealt with him. The mages here were at full strength thanks to their phoenix captives, were probably using potions made with their blood to keep them strong, able to continuously make more clones.

He braced himself as the dozen males lunged at him as one and burst into action again, dodging their attacks and landing as many blows as he could as his senses stretched outwards. He located Mackenzie and Hartt and a trickle of hope flowed into him as he realised they were inside the mansion, somewhere below him.

She was going for the phoenixes.

If Mackenzie could free them and convince them to fight on their side against the mages rather than flee, there was a chance they could do this.

He sensed someone else inside the building too.

Evelyn.

His gaze fixed unerringly on her location as he cut down another clone, cleaving its head from its body. He redoubled his effort, slowly inching forwards through the endless sea of enemies, heading for the house. If he could just get a clear view of it, he could teleport inside. It would be risky, and would drain him, but he needed to reach Evelyn.

Hope soared as he caught a glimpse of the inside of what looked like a ballroom.

And then a harrowing feminine scream rent the air.

A chill skated down his spine.

"Evelyn!"

CHAPTER 37

Thoughts blurred together, tangled and twisted into knots she couldn't unravel as she bobbed and swayed, feeling as if she was floating on the surface of a turbulent sea. Images flickered across the dim corners of her mind, things that were both familiar and unfamiliar to her at the same time.

Evelyn groaned as her head ached, tried to lift her hand to rub her brow and soothe the pain, but her arm felt too heavy to move.

She tried to open her eyes and look at her hand to see what was stopping her from moving it, sure it couldn't just be the hazy fatigue rolling through her. She grimaced as light stung them and made them water. The fuzzy blur of colours she could see told her nothing. Black. Peach. Gold. Crimson. Everything mashed together and no matter how much she blinked, her vision didn't get clearer.

She let her eyes fall shut again and sank into the rocking motion that lulled her, drawing her towards sleep. A quiet voice screamed at her from within a void, telling her not to succumb to it.

Roaring that she was in danger.

In danger?

She tried to piece together the images fluttering past her, snatched a few that fitted together and frowned as she remembered something.

A stronghold in Norway.

Fenix.

A young man who had mentioned someone called Drystan.

"Yes?" A deep male voice echoed in her ears like thunder, increasing that sensation that she was in danger. "I am surprised you remembered my name."

Remembered his name? Her head ached more fiercely. No. She didn't remember that name, not from her past at least. She remembered the man saying it as Fenix had tried to get the location of the mage from him.

Shock rolled through her, clearing the haze in an instant, and her eyes snapped open to lock on the smear of peach and white above her. She blinked rapidly, willing her vision to clear this time, and gasped as a man with long white hair came into focus. His crimson eyes lowered to her and she tried to get away from him, meant to shuffle backwards, only she wasn't on the ground.

She was in his arms.

"Calm now, Aderyn. There is no point in struggling." He smiled a predator's smile at her and she felt there was every point in struggling.

She was damned if she was going to remain in his arms.

She curled her left hand into a fist and punched him.

Only she didn't.

Evelyn looked at her hands where they rested in her lap, limp against her black sweater. Fear rolled through her when she tried to move them and they didn't obey her. They remained lax and useless.

"What have you done to me?" she breathed, panic closing her throat as her gaze darted from her hands to meet his crimson eyes.

His smile widened a little further, chilling her. "You have grown more powerful than I imagined possible. I found it necessary to take steps to ensure you did not make another attempt to kill me."

Another attempt to kill him?

It hit her in a rush of images and a blur of noise. She had attacked him when he had snatched her, had lashed out at him when they had been drifting through a pitch-black world, and had managed to injure him. Her gaze zeroed in on the two long streaks of red that cut down his left cheek.

Claw marks she had left on him.

It also hit her that her own haste was the reason he was able to incapacitate her. She had rushed after Archer before Rosalind had placed the protection spell on her, leaving herself vulnerable to the mage's magic.

He carried her from the crimson corridor into a dark, windowless room and a strange pressure pressed down on her, making her feel as if she couldn't breathe. She struggled for air and to calm herself as she looked around her, unable to make anything out in the gloom.

And then the man muttered something beneath his breath and colourful light shimmered over the walls, tracing the elegant lines of interlocking circles and the glyphs and runes within them.

Was that a spell?

It had to be one, because she suddenly felt as if she was in a void. She couldn't sense anything. The flickers of life she had been slowly starting to feel all disappeared and her head felt heavier, the ache in it worsening as her panic mounted.

That panic stole control of her when the man set her down on an angled board and strapped her left leg down.

She summoned all her strength, put it into one burst of action and somehow managed to get her sluggish body to obey her. Her right boot hit the mage in his chest, knocking him away from her. His back hit the wall near the open door and her eyes leaped to it.

Before she could reach for the strap around her left ankle, the door slammed shut and the mage was on her. She desperately wrestled against him, her strength swiftly failing her as he caught hold of her left arm and shoved it down against the board. Evelyn cried out when he tightened a strap around it, causing the thick leather to bite into her skin and her bones to ache.

The haze returned, rolling through her mind like dense fog, stealing her strength and leaving her at his mercy.

He strapped her right leg down followed by her wrist and then paused to loom over her, the green and blue light from the spell that covered the walls shining across the harsh planes of his face.

"I have been looking for you for so long." He reached a hand down and smoothed it over her hair, and she spat in his face. He sighed and wiped it away, his crimson gaze never leaving hers. "I realised soon after I completed the curse that I should not have done it."

The curse.

Her eyes widened and she stared up at him.

This was the mage who had cursed her and Fenix all those years ago.

Her heart called for Fenix now, sure that he would be coming for her, that he would find her and get her out of this mess. Both he and Archer would be out for blood. God, she hoped they found her soon, before this mage had time to carry out whatever his plan was for her.

A plan she feared would result in a fate worse than death.

He confirmed it for her as he canted his head and raked a gaze over her, his crimson eyes growing heated. A shudder wracked her, the vile feel of his eyes on her making her want to spit in his face again, to yell at him to take his filthy gaze off her while at the same time it made her want to shrink away and beg him not to hurt her.

"I could have used your blood to resurrect my beloved Cyra... but I was blinded by rage," he murmured and stroked a lone fingertip down from her collar bone to between her breasts. He paused there with it pressing against her sweater, right over her heart. "I have been working tirelessly since we were parted, constructing a fitting use for you. I found a spell. Ancient. A little unstable. One that will make use of the tie that links my wife's death to you... that tiny black thread of fate you formed when you killed her. I am going to use that to bring her back... and you will be the vessel for her soul."

He grinned.

"The ultimate in necromancy."

Fire swept through her, a thousand prickles dancing down her spine, and she bucked up off the table as he shoved the top end of it down to lay her flat. No. She wouldn't let him do that to her. Tears burned her eyes as she struggled against the bonds that held her and the spell that had her head growing hazy again and her limbs feeling heavy, refusing to give up and accept what he was going to do to her.

She had to break free and escape.

Only she wasn't strong enough.

As she was.

That hit her hard, knocking the wind from her and making her go still against the board.

She thought about what she was. She wasn't human. She was a phoenix shifter.

Shifter.

Meaning there was another form within her.

She just had to figure out how to transform into it.

Evelyn closed her eyes and calmed her mind as best she could, focused on the thought of becoming something else. The mage murmured words in a language she didn't recognise and the air hummed, making the hairs on her arms stand on end. She pushed harder, willing herself to transform, only nothing happened.

And then it hit her.

The fire she kept seeing in her dreams.

Kept feeling coursing through her body.

That was her other form.

She focused on the fire instead, conjuring images of flames racing over her body, sinking into the heat that seemed to run through her veins as her mind filled with a flickering orange and red glow.

"I would not do that." The mage placed his right palm to her forehead, his voice a black snarl that relayed his anger to her and only made her try harder to shift, because he didn't want her to do it. He tossed a bucket of ice on her when he added, "If you transform into a phoenix, your physical body will be destroyed and the only way to return to your current form would be by dying."

Evelyn couldn't do that.

Her heart screamed that the curse would trigger if she died.

But the only other option she had was letting this man turn her into someone else.

Both would destroy her.

But one would give her a chance to come back.

She trembled as she thought about what she was going to do, her heart aching at the thought of not only dying but of forgetting Fenix, and the pain she would put him through. She had to do this though. It was the only way to save herself. Sorrow swept through her, muting the fire in her mind, and she reached for the connection that linked them.

Felt only a void where it should have been.

She cursed the spell that surrounded her and stopped her from reaching him when she needed to feel him, needed to reassure herself that everything would be all right. Fenix would find her again and he would break this curse.

They would be together.

Just not in this lifetime.

Evelyn gritted her teeth and steeled her heart.

And surrendered to the fire.

CHAPTER 38

Fenix slammed into the door and grunted when it didn't give as he had expected. His shoulder burned from the force of the impact, but that didn't stop him from barrelling into it again. Evelyn was on the other side. He needed to get to her.

His second attempt to break the wooden door down ended in the same way as his first, with pain ricocheting along his bones.

On his third attempt, the door flew open before he could hit it and he stumbled through it and into the dimly-lit room. Archer. The male thundered along the corridor behind him, closing in fast.

A tremendous sense of power pressed down on Fenix as the glyphs and circles scrawled on the walls shone brighter, rainbow colours shimmering across them. The spell had his senses going haywire as he swung left and then right, seeking the mage. No sign of him.

His gaze snagged on Evelyn where she lay strapped to a table, and his heart clenched as he saw the fire rippling over her hands and blazing brightly around the leather bonds that held her down.

Fenix shook his head and dropped his sword, fear gripping his heart in a tighter fist as not only the flames around the straps grew brighter.

"Stop this," he barked and was by her side in an instant, his eyes wild as he looked between her face and her hands. Her fear hit him hard, there in her shining gold eyes for him to see as well as feel it in their bond.

"I can't." Her fair eyebrows furrowed, her face stricken as the fear he could feel in her grew, mingling with his as he looked at her hands again.

"You have to." The desperate need to help her had him reaching for her hands and he hissed in a breath as the fire heated his flesh, snatched his hand back and looked at her face again. All of the strength left his voice as he saw in her eyes that she couldn't stop the shift from happening, a hollow opening inside him as he whispered, "You have to."

Because he couldn't lose her.

Not again.

Not this time.

It would destroy him.

He had fallen harder than ever for his mate, hadn't thought it possible to love her more than he already did but somehow this incarnation of her had managed it. She was brave, strong, and warm. Far warmer than she had ever been. There was a deep and powerful love in her, one that shone in her eyes as she looked at him and then Archer as he came to loom over her.

"Both of you need to get out of here." She tossed a pleading look at Archer and then her gaze shifted to Fenix and lingered. "Please. Go."

"No," he barked and moved to her feet, attacked the straps that pinned her and made fast work of freeing her legs. "I'm not leaving you."

He wasn't going to give up.

He glared at Archer.

"Do something!"

The male glanced at him, his dark eyes widening slightly, as if Fenix had shaken him back to the room with those barked words and he was surprised to see him.

The flames began to spread, crawling up her arms, and Evelyn's breath hitched, her fear tainting the air and choking Fenix as she tossed a wild and desperate look at him. One that told him she didn't want to die. She didn't want to leave him.

"Fight it." He hurried back to her head. "You have to fight it... for me. For us."

Tears burned his eyes as Archer drew down a breath and held his hands out over her chest and stomach. The warlock closed his eyes and exhaled, his shoulders relaxing as he tilted his chin up. Fenix willed him to do something. He had countless spells at his disposal. One of them had to be able to contain Evelyn's shift and reverse it.

Fenix looked back at her.

Grunted as he was thrown clear across the room and hit the wall.

The marks on it seared him, burning clean through his sweater to singe his left biceps, filling the air with the vile scent of charred flesh.

He rolled away from the wall and onto his feet, his muddled senses stretching around him as he checked every corner of the room, his heart pounding in his ears. Drystan. The bastard was here somewhere.

Archer opened his eyes and looked as if he wanted to help Fenix find the male, but Fenix shook his head. It was more important that he helped Evelyn. Fenix would take care of Drystan.

The shadows in the far corner of the room shifted slightly.

Fenix lunged into a roll, swept his sword up off the wooden floorboards and came onto his feet near the corner, sweeping the blade out at the same time. Hitting nothing. He gritted his teeth and pivoted as his senses said someone was behind him. No one. Archer gave him another look. Fenix shook his head again. He had this.

"You know what kind of male hides in the shadows? Starts with a P," Fenix hollered and scoured the shadows, searching them for even the smallest sign of movement, "and it's another name for a cat."

Fire seared a line down his back and he arched forwards, crying out as pain licked over his muscles and felt as if it was burning his bones to ashes.

He wasn't the only one who cried out.

The male behind him bellowed too.

Fenix staggered forwards and scowled at Archer as he caught his breath. "I had that."

Archer's left eyebrow rose but he said nothing, merely returned his focus to doing whatever the hell he was doing to Evelyn. It was working, whatever it was. The fire engulfing her hands and forearms was growing dimmer. He glanced at Archer again to tell him to keep going and stilled as he saw the sweat rolling down the male's face and the tight lines that bracketed his mouth as his lips compressed.

That didn't look good.

The flames grew brighter again, bathing the room in golden light.

Fenix glared at Drystan as he twisted and contorted, his boots hovering a foot off the floorboards. "What did you do to her?"

"Nothing," Drystan gritted between clenched teeth and unleashed an agonised bellow as his right arm snapped backwards with enough force that Fenix heard the bone break.

"Dial it back, Archer. We need him alive." Fenix tossed a black look at Archer and froze again.

Archer's ears were pointed and his hands were ash-black tipped with sharp claws. The male bared razor-sharp teeth at him.

"Archer." Fenix shifted his focus to the warlock, aware that the male needed him. He flicked a look at Evelyn, meeting her wild, fearful gaze, and then gave Archer the whole of his attention. "Come on, mate. Hold it together."

Violet light shimmered across Archer's all-black eyes.

The mage screamed.

Fenix held his hands up, hoping to calm Archer, and not only because he needed the mage alive. He was standing between Archer and the mage, and he had a bad feeling that if Archer lost it, he would gladly go through him to reach Drystan.

"He did this," Archer snarled, his voice gaining a strange echo as he bared fangs at the mage. "Pushed her to this. The pain. The fear. She doesn't want to die. Not again. Never again."

"I know." He flicked a look at Evelyn, tears misting his eyes as hers locked with his and he saw her feelings in them as well as felt them in their bond.

"He was going to... use her... as... a vessel... for his... wife." Archer pushed those words out, each one taking effort.

Rage burned up Fenix's blood again, obliterating his fear as he swung towards the mage. The urge to kill him for trying to use Evelyn like that, turning her into someone else after all the pain he had put her through already, was strong and he fought it as he stalked towards the male. The mage's crimson eyes edged towards him as he screamed again, his body arching forwards, bending at a painful angle. He deserved to suffer.

But gods, Fenix couldn't let Archer kill him.

Not yet, anyway.

"We need him alive, Archer." Fenix looked over his shoulder at him. "He'll pay for what he's done once this curse is broken and Evelyn is free."

His gaze dropped to her again and his heart ached as she stared at him, as he saw the hurt in her eyes together with something else. Regret. Acceptance.

"No." He turned back to her. "You can't give up."

"I can't stop this," Archer bit out as the flames spread up her arms and flickered around her legs now, growing brighter by the second. His black gaze landed on Fenix. "I'm sorry."

Fenix lunged for Evelyn.

Archer teleported and grabbed him and the mage, and Fenix felt the heat of Evelyn against his fingertips before the void swallowed him. He staggered forwards across the grass as Archer released him and turned on a pained growl, a demand that he take him back to Evelyn rising to the tip of his tongue.

Heat surged over him, knocking him to his right, and he grunted as something sharp cut across his left cheek.

"Brace!" Rosalind yelled as she appeared close to him and bright blue light burst from her palms.

She leaned towards the mansion, drawing his gaze there as she grunted, and his eyes widened as huge chunks of the sandstone walls came flying at him and hit the barrier she had constructed. The clear blue shield sparked brightly wherever the stones hit, ripples chasing outwards from each point of impact.

Archer hurled the mage to the grass and shoved his boot into his back to pin him down as he twisted towards the building and swept his right hand out, his black claw-tipped fingers cutting through the air.

Rosalind's barrier gave out and Vail lunged for her, tucking her to his chest and turning with her so his back was to the blast as one of the flying blocks rocketed towards her.

A deep violet dome shimmered across the air between them and the chunk of sandstone before it could strike them, repelled the block with such force that it shot back towards the burning mansion and took out one of the remaining windows on the lower level.

Vail uncurled to reveal Rosalind, his head twisting to his left, towards Archer.

"I guess you're not so bad," Rosalind muttered, as close to a thank you as the warlock was going to get. Her shoulders sagged as she looked beyond her mate to the building. The entire right side of it was on fire, the flames leaping high into the air. "Mother earth. Mac and Hartt! They're still in there."

She winced as a huge section of wall crumbled and fell, sending flames and sparks high into the air.

"We have to help them." Rosalind lunged forwards but Vail caught her wrist, holding her back. She cast a glance at her mate and lingered as their eyes met, a look of despair laced with resignation crossing her face.

"Hartt will teleport Mackenzie out. If they do not appear soon, I will go inside to find them." Vail flexed his fingers around her wrist, his gaze softening as he stared down into her eyes.

She looked as if she wanted to argue with him, and then she sighed and eased back a step, falling into line with him again, and stared at the building.

Fenix crouched beside Drystan, grabbed his white hair and yanked his head from the dirt as Archer stepped off him. "Tell me how to break the curse."

Before it was too late.

Drystan's crimson eyes narrowed as he smiled at Fenix, a look that said he wasn't going to talk. So Fenix reintroduced his face to the ground, smashing it against it, breaking his nose, and then lifted the mage's head again. This time when he smiled, his teeth were bloodied.

Fenix's senses sparked another warning and he tensed as his head snapped towards Rosalind. Relief swept through him when he saw it was only Hartt and Mackenzie.

And a male who looked strikingly similar to the redhead.

He hung limply from Mackenzie and Hartt's hands, his bare knees on the grass and his head bent forwards. His glassy golden eyes remained fixed on the ground as Mackenzie released him and eased to her knees beside him. She smoothed her hand over his bare back, whispering something to him. Trying to bring him back from wherever he was? He wasn't here, that was for sure. Someone had really put him through the wringer. Was it blood loss that had him unaware of the world or the trauma of what the mages had done to him?

Another fireball exploded into the air and Mackenzie looked over her shoulder at the burning end of the mansion.

"That isn't good. The rate she's burning, she's going to die and resurrect in only a few minutes." Mackenzie's golden eyes shifted to him, the concern in them genuine.

"I can't let that happen." He took a step towards the mansion, unsure what to do to stop it. If Archer hadn't been able to halt her shift, what hope did he have of bringing her back from it? He had to do something though.

Because he had seen in her eyes that she didn't want to forget him.

A low chuckle had his gaze edging towards Drystan.

Archer grabbed him by the back of his neck and hauled him onto his knees, and the mage spat blood on the ground near the warlock's boots, earning himself a black look. Drystan was pushing his luck.

Fenix gave Archer a look that ordered him not to kill the mage and squared up to Drystan, coming to stand over him. "Tell me how to break the curse."

He might not be able to stop Evelyn from dying and resurrecting, but he could make sure that when she came back, she still remembered him and she was still the Evelyn he loved with all of his heart.

Drystan flashed bloodstained teeth in a sly grin and then laughed in his face. "I will tell you… if you swear not to kill me."

Fenix wasn't sure that he could make that promise. "You have to swear in return that you'll leave her alone."

The mage didn't look inclined to agree to that. Neither of them trusted the other. Fenix needed to know how to break the curse though, before Evelyn died and was reborn, so he would be the bigger male.

And if the mage came after them, he would kill the bastard.

"Very well," Drystan muttered.

"You've got my word." Those words tasted bitter on Fenix's tongue, made him want to choke as the thought of letting the mage go after everything he had put them through scoured his insides raw and made him want to immediately take them back and kill him. He pushed out, "Tell me how to break the curse."

"I would have told you without the promise." Drystan smiled slowly again, a vicious edge to his crimson eyes that Fenix didn't like. The male was up to something. "I have waited so long to capture Aderyn and use her to resurrect my wife, but that is no longer possible. I know when I am outmatched." He tipped his head back as far as he could manage and cast a black look at Archer. Archer returned it, sneering at him and flashing his fangs for good measure. Drystan grimaced as Archer tightened his grip on his nape and shifted his focus back to Fenix. "I am forced to concede and yet I will also take great pleasure in this, because I have also waited so long to see your face when you learn the only way to break this curse is to do the one thing I know you could never do."

Fenix didn't like the sound of that.

Drystan's grin widened.

"You have to kill her yourself."

"You're lying," Fenix barked and glared down at him, sensing no trace of a lie in his aura, but gods, the mage had to be lying. It had to be a trick.

"He's probably telling the truth." Archer pressed his claws into the mage's neck. "I can take a look, do a deep dive into his mind to make sure, but it's dangerous."

Archer held his free hand out and a slender black glass vial appeared in his fingertips.

The phoenix Mackenzie was fussing over suddenly jerked his head up.

Snarled and launched at the mage, ripping him away from Archer and killing him with a vicious twist of his head that popped it clean off.

Archer's eyebrows rose. "Or maybe not."

Fenix shot to his feet. "What the fuck, Mackenzie?"

She was on hers too, her face twisting in harsh lines as she stared him down, her eyes glowing brightly. "My brother isn't well! The mage got what he deserved."

Archer huffed and disappeared, and Fenix thought it would be the last he saw of the male.

But then a masculine bellow tore through the night.

Fenix teleported in a heartbeat, aware of where Archer had gone and what he was trying to do. He coughed as rather than landing in the room where

Evelyn was, he landed on a heap of rubble in a huge opening in the building. Smoke billowed around him, invading his lungs, and he lifted his arm to shield his face from the heat of the flames.

"Archer!" He squinted, trying to spot the warlock.

Fire licked at his ankles, forcing him to move, and as he skidded down the rubble, a shape formed inside the flames before him. Two shapes. Archer grunted as he was hurled backwards, sailing past Fenix to land on the top of the pile of rubble.

"Idiot. Get out of here! You'll be burned alive." The warlock picked himself up, wiped the back of his hand across his face, smearing ash across it, and kicked off, leaping back through the wall of flames. "I can get her out of the building and save her."

Evelyn shrieked.

Archer bellowed again.

Fenix rushed through the flames, grunting as they scorched him, searing his feet and his legs. He staggered to a halt on the other side, his eyes widening as he found Archer desperately trying to get hold of Evelyn. She fought him, lashing out at him with her talons, raking lines of fire down his chest that had the warlock unleashing another agonised cry, but didn't deter him.

And didn't burn him.

Maybe Fenix should have thought this through more, should have considered Archer would use a spell to protect himself from the flames, but the warlock had sounded so pained and he had reacted on instinct.

An instinct that had told him to protect the warlock his mate cared deeply about.

And he would do just that.

Fenix teleported between them just as Evelyn went to strike Archer again and she stilled, her glowing golden eyes enormous as they met his. She never had been able to hurt him. He grabbed both of them and teleported again.

Landed hard on the patio of the mansion and collapsed to his knees as his head turned.

"Fenix!" Rosalind sprinted over to him, Vail hot on her heels.

Vail grabbed him and hauled him away from Evelyn as she writhed on the flagstones, her heat making the stone bubble. Archer staggered to his feet and stumbled after them. When the air was cooler, Vail lowered Fenix to the grass and Rosalind sank to her knees beside him. She cast a worried look over him, one that lingered on his legs.

"You're going to be fine," she murmured and Fenix wasn't sure that he would be. His legs were still burning, the scent of his own charred flesh thick in the air, and the pain was building inside him, pushing him towards oblivion. She glanced at Vail. "Help me."

Vail nodded and held his hands out over Fenix, hovering them a few inches above his body as he closed his eyes and sighed out his breath. Rosalind went to work too, placing her hands on Fenix's shoulder and hip, and warmth ran through him, chased by an eerie cold.

"Idiot," Archer muttered, clutching his left arm to his side. Blood glistened on the sleeve of his black coat and Fenix stared at it and realised something. Archer wasn't healing. Had the warlock tapped himself out trying to save Evelyn?

He went up in Fenix's estimation, cementing the feeling that he really was her friend.

And Fenix's too now.

"Idiot yourself," Fenix croaked and a wry smile curled Archer's lips.

Fenix tilted his head back and yelled to the heavens as pain shot through him, his mind emptying and darkness swirling around him, followed by a warm light that was strangely comforting. For a moment, he feared this was it, the light everyone said not to go towards, but then it took on a shape.

A decidedly feminine shape.

He couldn't make out any details of her face or her figure, but he could see the violet flowers threaded in her hair like a crown as clear as day.

And then she was gone.

And so was his pain.

"What the fuck?" he muttered and cracked his eyes open.

Rosalind leaned over him, her blue eyes bright. "Did you see her?"

"Her?" he husked, recalling the female he had seen and how comforted he had felt, as if she had been embracing him. As if she was home. "Who?"

Rosalind lifted her head and beamed at Vail. "He saw her too! This is wonderful, Vail. Your connection really is back to full strength."

Fenix edged his gaze towards Vail and wasn't sure what to do or say as the usually grim elf dashed tears from his lashes only for them to be instantly replaced by more.

"Nothing like having a goddess on your side, huh?" Rosalind nudged Fenix and he grunted, still sore from whatever they had done to him.

"Goddess?" He pieced it together. "Nature."

Elves all had a connection to nature, one that varied in strength. As a member of the royal bloodline, Vail's connection to her was far beyond that of any elf other than his brother, and Vail had told him how his bond with her was weak because he was tainted. Being with Rosalind hadn't only allowed

Vail to claw back his sanity and step away from the darkness. It had allowed him to reforge his bond with nature.

Fenix had never thought of her as an actual goddess before though, a power that was shaping this world and all in it.

Vail and Rosalind helped him up into a sitting position.

His heart wrenched as he stared at Evelyn where she now lay on the patio, writhing as flames flickered over her, bursting from her bare back as she moved onto her hands and knees and then guttering as she rolled onto her back. She screamed, flinging her legs and arms out, and another wave of fire surged towards them.

It hit the barrier still in place around them.

"I'm sorry." Archer came to stand beside him and offered a delicate round red bottle that had gold filigree decorating the surface. "It will protect you from the worst of her fire while you—"

He looked from the bottle to Archer. "You're not seriously suggesting I kill her?"

"She's going to die either way," Mackenzie put in.

"Yeah... but killing her?" Fenix swallowed hard at the thought. He wasn't sure he could do it, but as he looked at Evelyn as she battled the shift and fiery wings blazed from her back, he knew deep in his heart that it was his only option.

He had to kill her and hope the mage hadn't been lying.

He took the vial from Archer.

Archer's expression grew grim as he looked from Fenix to Evelyn. "I'll monitor her once she's—and if it feels like something is wrong, I'll take a concoction and go into the dark realm between life and death to bring her back."

Rosalind rounded on him. "No. You can't do that. You need to let that moment of rebirth happen. We'll build a cage of magic for her so she won't be transported elsewhere upon death. That way, if the curse activates, we'll still have her."

The small seed of hope inside Fenix grew, spreading tendrils through him to give him the strength he needed. If killing her with his own hand failed to break the curse, and Rosalind and Archer could stop Evelyn from being transported away for her rebirth, then he wouldn't have to search for her. He could have Rosalind or Mackenzie take care of her until he found the real way to break the curse.

Archer nodded, seemingly satisfied with that suggestion too, and moved past him. He paused and looked back at him. His throat worked on a hard swallow, his dark eyes glittering with regret and pain, and he held his hand out before Fenix.

A jagged obsidian dagger appeared on his palm.

"It will grant a swift and painless death."

Fenix swallowed thickly as he looked at it, as he fought to find the strength to take it and do this.

Evelyn screamed.

Fenix snatched the blade, popped the lid off the vial and swallowed the contents. Frigid cold rushed down his throat and spread through his limbs, making him shudder as he flexed his fingers around the hilt of the dagger. He could do this.

Mackenzie was right. Either way she would die, but also either way she would come back, and if there was a chance the mage hadn't been lying, he had to take it. He thought about how Evelyn had looked at him as he approached her, filled his mind with how afraid she had been but also how much love had shone in her eyes.

Her next scream became a keening shriek as fire exploded around her, great plumes of it twisting and swirling to engulf her body.

His heart lodged in his throat, his breath hitching as she shed her mortal form, shifting into a great raptor made of flames.

It was now or never.

He reached the edge of the fire and steeled his heart as he forced himself to keep moving, to ignore the instincts screaming at him to keep away from the blazing flames. The heat of them wrapped around him, their brightness stinging his eyes, but they didn't scorch his flesh or burn his clothes.

Archer's potion was working.

Now all he had to do was convince the phoenix hovering in the air before him, a great beast that was three or possibly four times taller than Evelyn was in her human form, to come down to him.

Fenix stopped beneath her and held his free hand out, concealing the one that clutched the dagger behind his back as his heart raced, his pulse pounding quickly in his ears as nerves rushed through him. He wasn't sure what she would do if she realised he was going to kill her.

Her great head twisted towards him, blazing golden eyes blinking at him as she opened her sharp beak and loosed a delicate 'kek' sound.

She recognised him then.

She had always called to him in that way when she had been in this form, all those years ago before they had been cursed.

Things could be that way again. All he had to do was kill her and they could be free of the pain, could have the forever they had always wanted together.

He held his palm out to her. "Come to me, love."

She called again, only this time it was laced with pain as she beat her wings, remaining aloft in the air. She was close now, on the brink of succumbing to her fire.

"Come, my love." He moved closer to her, recapturing her attention, and this time when she looked at him, he saw the hurt in her eyes.

The misery.

"I'll take it away for you," he whispered, his voice hoarse as tears filled his eyes. They shone in hers too, molten tears that blazed as bright as the sun as she drifted down to him. The flagstones sizzled and hissed as she set down, her talons sinking into them as the stone melted, and the heat she was throwing off grew stronger, finally piercing the shield of the spell to caress his flesh. Fenix sucked down a breath and stared into her eyes, all the love he felt for her beating in his heart, roaring in his soul. "Come to me."

She bent her great head and pressed the curve of her beak to his palm, and glowing orbs of fire tumbled from her eyes as she closed them.

Her sorrow cut at him and he knew.

She was aware of what he was going to do.

Fenix closed his eyes and turned his head, bringing his lips close to her beak as she narrowed the distance between them.

"I love you," he whispered. "Come back to me."

He pressed a kiss to her beak.

And plunged the dagger into her heart.

Tears burned a trail down his cheeks as she sank against him, her heat scalding him at first as her heavy weight settled on his shoulder and he tried to hold on to her. He pulled the dagger from her chest and hurled it away from him, and caught hold of her with both arms as she rapidly chilled, the feel of her fire fading making him cold and hollow inside too, and her body swiftly transformed into her human form. He held her to him, clinging to her as a gulf opened inside him, and silently begged her for forgiveness and to come back to him.

He carried her to the softer grass and sank to his knees.

Cradled her to his chest as she drew her final breaths, tears cutting down his cheeks and his throat closing, making it impossible to breathe as he kissed her forehead and willed her to remember him.

A great shimmering violet dome cascaded down to cover them and the six other people he was deeply aware of as they approached him, but he didn't take his eyes off her face as he anxiously waited.

"How long does it usually take?" Archer whispered, sounding as worried as Fenix felt as the minutes ticked past and Evelyn didn't stir.

"Shh," Rosalind hissed.

"Shh, yourself," Archer muttered back at her. "It was a legitimate question."

"She might need help," Hartt said and shifted on Fenix's senses, moving closer to his mate. "Do you think she can find her way?"

"Yes." There was absolute faith in that word as it fell from Mackenzie's lips. "She knows the way home."

Home.

To him.

Fenix gazed at Evelyn's slack, dirty face, clinging to their bond, hoping she could feel it and knew how deeply he loved her and how much he needed her to come back to him. She belonged with him. He was her home. She had told him that once, decades ago, had admitted that she had never truly felt as if she had a home but that she had found it in him.

He listened hard to her, straining to hear that first weak beat of her heart, willing the gods to make it happen for him.

Her chest bowed upwards, as if someone had attached an invisible string to the point between her bare breasts and was pulling her into the air.

Fenix released her and rose to his feet as she lifted into the air before him. He moved back a few steps to give her space as heat rolled off her, aware of what would come next.

He glanced at his friends and they moved back too, Mackenzie ushering them to a safe distance.

Evelyn continued to rise into the smoky air, her arms and legs hanging limp at her sides, and then she stopped. Light glowed from within her, highlighting the veins beneath her skin, and then cracks formed in her skin and broke open to release blinding light and boiling heat that buffeted Fenix as he took a step back from her.

Fenix shielded his eyes with his right arm, squinting through the shimmering heat haze as her feet dropped, shifting her upright, and her golden hair turned to flames, fluttering and streaming from the back of her head.

Fierce light exploded from her, a wave of heat that swept him off his feet and dropped him on his backside further from her, throwing dust and pebbles at him as he landed. Fire licked over him and the air grew hotter still, scorching him despite the potion.

And then it stopped.

Cold air swept past him from behind, as if she was sucking it all towards her.

Fenix lowered his arm and stared at her where she hovered in the air, wings of fire wrapped around her bare body and flames dancing over her, fluttering brightest around her ankles and wrists.

He got to his feet and drifted towards her, relieved to see no trace of the wound he had delivered her. There was only perfect, unmarked skin. Light pulsed beneath that skin as she spread her wings and lifted her head to take in her surroundings.

"Evelyn," Fenix murmured and reached a hand up to her.

She angled her head towards him.

Stared blankly at him.

It hadn't worked.

The hope that had been building inside him shattered in an instant.

And then her lips parted and a single word fell from them.

"Fenix?"

CHAPTER 39

Fenix caught Evelyn as she drifted down to him, gathered her into his arms and sank to his knees with her, relief beating in every inch of him. She shook as he held her, curled up against him in a way that relayed her fear to him as clearly as their bond did, and he rubbed her arms, trying to soothe her.

And himself at the same time.

What if this was just a fluke caused by Archer stopping her rebirth in the Fifth Realm? What if the curse wasn't broken?

"I'm sorry I killed you," he murmured, voice thick and low, and didn't take his eyes off her even when Rosalind and the others came to them.

He appreciated it when the blonde witch removed her black coat and held it out to him. He took it and wrapped it around Evelyn, covering her bare curves, and rubbed her arm through it. Her shaking subsided and she leaned back, her gaze searing his face as her golden eyes glowed. The light in them slowly dimmed, returning them to their normal colour, and he smiled for her as he stroked her cheek.

"I'm sorry," he repeated, unsure whether he was ever going to stop apologising to her for what he had done. "Drystan said it was the way to break the curse. I had to be the one to kill you."

Something he never would have done, not in a million lifetimes, if the mage hadn't told him it was the only way.

The bastard had picked the only method of breaking the curse well.

If it had been the way to break it.

He looked at Archer as he eased into a crouch on the other side of her.

"Just going to take a look at you," Archer whispered, his dark gaze sincere, overflowing with worry.

Fenix didn't miss the tears that laced his dark lashes as he looked Evelyn over and then held his left hand out to hover his palm above her forehead. His eyes closed and he breathed slowly, deeply as his eyebrows knitted hard.

The wait was agonising. Every breath Fenix drew rasped in his ears as he looked at his mate, not daring to hope the curse had been lifted.

Archer finally opened his eyes, a smile tugging at the corners of his lips as he looked into Evelyn's eyes. "All gone. You're free."

"Gods," Fenix muttered and sagged a little as all the tension flowed out of him, as the breath he had been holding from the moment Archer had opened his eyes leaked from him and he struggled to make himself believe the warlock.

The relief that glittered in Archer's eyes told him that he wasn't lying.

They were free.

Archer gave Evelyn a tight smile and clutched her shoulder, his eyes betraying everything he was feeling as he looked at her. Fenix was starting to like the mad bastard. It probably helped that Archer had proven he was a noble male and a good friend, had somehow managed to shake off the taint of the things he had done.

When the warlock stood, Evelyn gripped the leg of his trousers, keeping him in place as she looked up at him.

"You're leaving," she said, and Fenix's heart warmed to hear her voice.

Archer nodded. "I have to. Aryanna has another lead for me. I doubt it will turn into anything, but I must follow it up. A potential key."

Evelyn didn't release him. She held him in place, earning a soft look from the male, one that might have made Fenix beat him to a bloody pulp in the past, but now he had seen the two together for longer than a minute or two at a time, he knew that Evelyn's love for him didn't extend beyond friendship.

Her worry trickled into him through their bond as she gazed up at the warlock and he knew what she couldn't bring herself to say.

So he said it for her.

"Make sure you swing by my house in Scotland to take a look at the documents we retrieved in New Hampshire. I'm sure you'll still be keeping tabs on Evelyn so you'll know where to find us. And… if you ever need help with Aryanna, you have it." Fenix held Archer's dark gaze as it shifted to him and ignored the spark of surprise in it. "I mean it. We owe you. Just say the word and we'll help. Whatever you need."

Archer swallowed and nodded, and glanced to his left as Rosalind moved up beside him.

"Whatever you need," she parroted, gaining a shocked look from the warlock. She huffed. "We might not have gotten off to a good start, but... I don't hate you... and when the world is in danger, we'll always be there... or some superhero sounding shit like that. We can't let Archangel wake your sorceress and use her power."

Archer looked at everyone, the disbelief in his eyes not going anywhere, and Fenix felt bad for the male. What kind of horrible life had he led that he couldn't believe there were people in this world who were willing to have his back and help him?

It almost made Fenix feel like a dick for the way he had treated him at first. Almost.

But back then he had viewed the warlock as a threat to his mate and also a threat to his relationship with his mate.

"We will free you of the sorceress, Archer, and we will ensure she is not a threat to the world." Vail's deep voice held a commanding note, one that Fenix was familiar with. The elf prince had made up his mind that they were going to succeed and Archer would be an idiot not to believe him. Once Vail devoted himself to something, the elf was nothing short of a dog with a bone until he succeeded. "We should return to Norway and see what documents the little elf noble Hartt brought with him has gathered for transportation and take them to our home for now. He will not be pleased we are not going to take the documents to the elf kingdom, but it is best we secure them all somewhere any species who is willing to help can access them."

Fenix doubted Leif would enjoy being called the 'little elf noble' but he didn't mention it.

"I need to get my brother home to rest." Mackenzie looked from the redheaded male who was sitting on the grass a short distance away, a lost expression on his face, to Vail and Rosalind. "I want to know what knowledge the mages were storing in Norway, but... he needs me."

Hartt came up to stand beside her and brushed the back of his fingers across her cheek in a tender caress, one that backed up the love that shone in his violet eyes. "Once your brother is settled, we can visit everyone in Scotland."

Fenix wasn't sure when his home had become their headquarters, but he wasn't going to complain. It was going to be nice having company other than his family.

Mackenzie nodded and then her soft look gained a wicked edge and she murmured, "We should probably give these two some privacy anyway."

Evelyn frowned at her. "What do you mean by that?"

Hartt went to Mackenzie's brother and disappeared with him, and Mackenzie smiled mischievously.

"Only that rebirth makes phoenixes one of two things. Either they get crazy restless or they get crazy horny, and I think you'll find out which you are soon. My money is on horny." She winked as she teleported.

A blush scalded Evelyn's cheeks as she stiffened against him.

Archer cleared his throat. "I'll be on my way then."

He tugged his trouser leg free of her hand.

"Wait," she barked and her gaze darted up to him. "I'll help you too. I can work from the inside of Archangel and keep an eye on things there. I can cover for you."

Archer looked as if he didn't want to agree to that, and neither did Fenix, but he knew better than to argue with his mate. Apparently, Archer knew better too. He nodded, stooped and pressed a kiss to her brow, one that had Fenix wanting to punch him.

He didn't get the chance.

Violet sparks swirled around Archer and he was gone.

"Have fun now. We'll give you a couple of days before we drop everything from Norway off and start to work on it. Enjoy your post-curse honeymoon!" Rosalind grinned salaciously and disappeared with her mate.

Fenix scowled at the spot where they had been, wishing everyone would stop talking about him and Evelyn getting physical because he was hungry as hell after all the teleporting and fighting. He didn't need them stoking his hunger by making him think of laying his mate down and making love with her.

He glanced at her, got caught in her soft look and stared into her eyes.

The guilt returned, a replay of what he had done to her tormenting him. He had been furious with Archer for wanting to kill her and in the end, he had been the one to plunge a blade into her heart.

He opened his mouth, but she pressed her finger to his lip, silencing him.

"No more apologising." Her soft look bewitched him, had him melting a little as she gazed at him with so much love that he felt as if he was drowning in it. She smiled slightly. "You did what you needed to do... and part of me... I wanted to die."

"Don't say things like that," he croaked, his heart aching even when he knew what she was trying to say. It wasn't that she had a death wish, it was that she hadn't been able to stop the shift and she had been afraid of what would happen, had that image of Norway in her head and had imagined she would destroy the entire area and everyone in it.

She snuggled closer to him, chasing away his hurt and his fears, the feel of her pressing against him like heaven to him as he wrapped his arms around her.

"Do you remember anything about your past lives?" he murmured as he pressed a kiss to her brow.

"No," she whispered and angled her head back so she could look up at his face. "Does that bother you?"

He shook his head and feathered his fingers across her cheek, warming from head to toe as he looked at her. "I love you as you are now. I don't want the old you back."

She smiled and leaned towards him, bringing her mouth closer to his.

A small gasp left her lips and she tensed.

"What's wrong?" He eased back and looked down at her face.

Her very flushed face.

Her wide eyes locked with his.

"Nothing." She was quick to say that.

He slowly smiled as her needs ran into him through their bond, and knew the moment his eyes had changed, swirling gold and blue with a need to satisfy his mate, because her gaze grew hooded and dropped to his lips.

"I just realised which type of phoenix I am," she murmured and claimed his mouth, capturing his lips in a fierce, wild kiss that tore a groan from him.

He had always hated it whenever he had watched his mate die, even in the years before they had been cursed, but he had always loved her resurrection.

His incubus side purred in approval as she gripped his nape and bent him to her will.

He swept them into a teleport that landed them in his bedroom in Scotland. She didn't miss a beat, shirked the coat from her shoulders and pressed against him, pushing him down onto the wooden floor at the foot of the bed.

He groaned as she tore at his clothes, short claws making fast work of ripping them away, and arched to meet her lips as she dropped her head and brushed them across his bare chest. Gods. He tangled his fingers in her tousled blonde hair, fisting it to hold her mouth to him and not missing how the markings that tracked up the underside of his forearm and snaked over his shoulder shone in hues of passion and love.

And need.

He had never needed his mate as badly as he needed her right that moment.

He couldn't breathe as she swept her lips over his flesh, the caress teasing and maddening, driving him to the edge. Every instinct inside him was at war, his need to feed and draw energy from her fighting the urge to make this about his love for her instead by holding that part of himself back. Another moan leaked from him as she trailed her lips downwards, following the valley between his abdominals, and her palms pressed to his pectorals.

She raked blunt nails over them, scoring his skin, eliciting another groan from him as he arched into her touch again, a thrill bolting down his spine. His cock kicked in response, so hard it hurt, his body primed and ready for her as the heavy scent of her desire swirled around him, filling his lungs and tugging his incubus side to the fore.

He needed to be inside her.

His eyes shot up and he gasped, every inch of him tensing as she wrapped her lips around his shaft, taking him into her wet heat. He shuddered and groaned, rocked his hips to meet her as she swallowed him, couldn't keep still as she tormented him with the pleasure of her touch. Her left hand wrapped around him to grip him fiercely as she lightly feathered the fingers of her right over his stomach, the twin sensation of hard and soft addling his mind as she sucked him. Oh gods.

He swallowed hard as every inch of him lit up, as her pleasure flowed into him with each moan that vibrated along his cock, with every swift stroke of her mouth and hand over his flesh.

"Evelyn!" Fenix bellowed and his hips jacked up, his lungs emptying and legs shaking as release boiled up his shaft and he spilled into her mouth.

Her little groans of bliss as she swallowed around him had him shuddering and aching for more, pushed him straight through one release towards the next, and he struggled to breathe and catch up as she released his length. She prowled up his body, the heated look in her eyes setting him on fire, rousing his incubus side into a frenzy.

On a low snarl, he seized her wrists and yanked her up to him, meant to flip her onto her back and bury himself in her, but she gripped him under his knees and pushed them up towards his chest and shoved his legs apart.

Pinning him in place as she manoeuvred over his still-throbbing cock, pulled it up like a flagpole and sank onto it.

His hands flew to his own knees instead and he spread his legs further apart as she kneeled over him, riding him hard, her breathless moans delighting his ears as she bounced on him. This was new, and gods, it was incredible, made his incubus side wild as she gripped the backs of his thighs to keep them bent towards his arms and took him.

Her breasts swayed with each powerful downwards thrust, her face screwing up as she moved faster, taking him harder, and he couldn't stop himself from soaking up some of her pleasure, devouring it as she dominated him. He groaned as he looked between his own legs to watch himself sliding into her, filling her as she claimed him.

Her rhythm faltered and she cried out, her entire body quaking as she sank onto him, taking every inch of him into her quivering core before she slowly rose up again, and then down, her pace leisurely. Fenix groaned as she flexed around him, tugging at him, the feel of her release enough to tip him towards another. He reached for her and she eased off him to sink to the floor beside him.

He rolled towards her and gathered her to him, lifted her left leg and fed his cock into her still shaking sheath, and slowly thrust into her as he kissed her. She moaned and he sensed her rising desire, focused on stoking it back to a rolling boil as he savoured the feel of her around him and couldn't stop thinking about the position she had taken him in.

His balls tightened, another release gathering at the base of his length, and he quickened his pace, a slave to his need to spill inside her. She moaned and lifted her leg higher, opening to him, and he grunted as he plunged into her, managing only three strokes before seed boiled up his shaft and stars burst across his closed eyes. She groaned and rocked against him as she quivered again, her body milking him, demanding more.

He would give it to her.

Later.

Right now, he needed to ask her a question.

He drew back when he had caught his breath and her eyes slowly opened, her golden irises hazy with pleasure that flowed from her into him.

"How did you learn to do that?" He searched her eyes, fearing the answer would be another man.

She smiled lazily and breathed, "Cosmo."

"Is that a bloke?" he growled.

She shook her head and shuffled closer to him, flexed around his length, sending a bolt of bliss through him.

"A magazine," she sighed. "It was *way* better than I thought it was going to be."

He couldn't agree more. It had been mind-blowing. As an incubus, he knew a lot of positions, had always been into the more adventurous ones, but he had never seen or done the one she had used on him, and it left him with another question.

One that felt oddly vital to him, something which he blamed on his incubus side since it was hungry for more, eager to try something else that was new.

"Was it the only position they showed?" He tried not to blush as he asked that.

Her golden eyes grew heated, sending a shiver down his spine, and a sultry smile tugged at her lips.

"No."

That single word made him swallow hard.

"There were others." She feathered her fingers down his damp chest, rousing his passion as fire chased in the wake of her touch.

Fenix groaned and tugged her to him, plastering her front against his. "Others?"

She nodded, her gaze growing hooded as she inched her mouth towards his, and whispered.

"I'm going to rock your world, incubus."

She already did.

He dropped his head and kissed her.

And for the first time in a long time, he wasn't afraid of tomorrow and what might come.

Instead, he was looking forward to seeing what the future held for them.

Because his mate was finally where she belonged—in his arms.

Home.

And nothing would ever take her from him again.

The End

ABOUT THE AUTHOR

Felicity Heaton is a New York Times and USA Today best-selling author who writes passionate paranormal romance books. In her books she creates detailed worlds, twisting plots, mind-blowing action, intense emotion and heart-stopping romances with leading men that vary from dark deadly vampires to sexy shape-shifters and wicked werewolves, to sinful angels and hot demons!

If you're a fan of paranormal romance authors Lara Adrian, J R Ward, Sherrilyn Kenyon, Kresley Cole, Gena Showalter, Larissa Ione and Christine Feehan then you will enjoy her books too.

If you love your angels a little dark and wicked, her best-selling Her Angel romance series is for you. If you like strong, powerful, and dark vampires then try the Vampires Realm romance series or any of her stand alone vampire romance books. If you're looking for vampire romances that are sinful, passionate and erotic then try her London Vampires romance series. Or if you like hot-blooded alpha heroes who will let nothing stand in the way of them claiming their destined woman then try her Eternal Mates series. It's packed with sexy heroes in a world populated by elves, vampires, fae, demons, shifters, and more. If sexy Greek gods with incredible powers battling to save our world and their home in the Underworld are more your thing, then be sure to step into the world of Guardians of Hades.

If you have enjoyed this story, please take a moment to contact the author at **author@felicityheaton.com** or to post a review of the book online

Connect with Felicity:
Website – http://www.felicityheaton.com
Blog – http://www.felicityheaton.com/blog/
Twitter – http://twitter.com/felicityheaton
Facebook – http://www.facebook.com/felicityheaton
Goodreads – http://www.goodreads.com/felicityheaton
Mailing List – http://www.felicityheaton.com/newsletter.php

FIND OUT MORE ABOUT HER BOOKS AT:
http://www.felicityheaton.com

Milton Keynes UK
Ingram Content Group UK Ltd.
UKHW011318020524
442122UK00027B/349